P9-CDH-657

A MURDER *in* TIME

A MURDER in TIME

A Novel

JULIE McELWAIN

PEGASUS CRIME
NEW YORK LONDON

A MURDER IN TIME

Pegasus Books LLC
80 Broad Street, 5th Floor
New York, NY 10004

First Pegasus Books edition April 2016

Interior design by Maria Fernandez

Library of Congress Cataloging-in-Publication Data is available.

ISBN: 978-1-60598-974-7

10 9 8 7 6 5 4 3 2 1

Printed in the United States of America
Distributed by W. W. Norton & Company

For my mom,
the best woman I know

And in memory of my dad,
who is still the wind beneath my wings

PROLOGUE

August 1815

He was in hell.

The fire from the torches lent a satanic flicker to the cavern's rough-hewn walls, molten gold and orange playing over the profane carvings and frescoes. The oily smoke from the sconces undulated, curled, and climbed like thick black serpents toward the ceiling.

The effect pleased him.

The environment was similar to the West Wycombe Caves favored by Sir Francis Dashwood and his notorious Hell Fire Club. Like those caverns, these chambers, thirty-five feet in the bowels of the earth, had been carved out by earlier man, desperate for the flint within the chalky walls, needing the rock to fashion their archaic weapons and tools. Later, someone had transformed the rocky environment into two rooms. He suspected it had been the Papists during Good Queen Bess's rule. After she'd made Catholicism an act of treason, families who wanted to practice their faith had been driven underground—sometimes, like this chamber, literally—fearing the priest-hunters and scandal, which could cost both their fortune and their lives.

Of course, he could not prove that these caves had been used for such a purpose—no stray religious relic had been left behind—but it amused him to imagine that the pious had once prayed here.

It amused him to take the holy and make it unholy.

He smiled, just a small movement of his mouth, as he thought of the stonemasons and carpenters that he'd hired five years ago from London for this venture. They'd thought him mad. He'd seen how their eyes were drawn to some of his more inspired details in the specially commissioned friezes. He'd seen the shock. And something else . . .

Excitement.

They could not deceive him, even if they deceived themselves. *Fools.* He refused to lie to himself. He knew who he was. He knew *what* he was.

Still, he had something in common with the Papists. He couldn't risk exposure any more than they could. He knew that if he revealed his dark appetites, which twisted his guts to dagger points of both pleasure and pain, society would call him a monster.

Hypocrites.

It enraged him. He could feel the anger heating his blood, but he hid that, too.

Abruptly, he rose to his feet, the swift motion causing the dark velvet cape he wore to swirl around his calves like black mist. He would have enjoyed that effect, too, had he been aware of it. Yet he'd chosen the silk-lined cape not for its appearance, but for its warmth. No matter how many fire pits and torches were lit, it was impossible to dispel the chilly dampness in the underground catacombs.

The wine, of course, helped.

The men before him had been drinking steadily since the evening began, their faces flushed with claret as much as cold, and the anticipation of what he'd promised them. As he stood, they turned their gazes in his direction. In their dilated pupils, he saw the tiny flames from the candles and torches around them.

Almost carelessly, he lifted the jeweled chalice, surveying the twelve apostles he had selected for his secret club.

So young. So eager. So deliciously depraved.

"Patience, my brothers," he ordered, and fleetingly wondered if he were addressing them, or himself.

The men laughed as though in agreement, and mimicked his gesture by lifting their own chalices, gold and silver, the metal a dull glint in the room's mottled light, and then drinking greedily. The wine had already robbed two of the young pups of their usual elegance. With a thin, cold smile, he watched them guzzle red wine, heedless when it ran in thin rivulets down their chins, staining their cravats like blood.

Even as he wondered how long they'd last, a sound, the scrape and soft slap of soles against hard stone, alerted him. The apostles heard the noise, too, and, one by one, the men fell silent. For a second, the dank air, heavy with the smell of wax and smoke, earth and brine, seemed to thrum with their expectations and peculiar excitement.

The shadows came first, bouncing off the walls in macabre distortions. Then the women rounded the corner, following the loyal servant who led them into the abyss, their dark hooded capes matching the style, if not the more expensive velvet fabric, of his apostles.

Initially, he'd considered ordering the women to dress as nuns, just as Dashwood had insisted for his Hell Fire Club more than sixty years before. As with the caves, he'd been inspired by Sir Francis's secret society, which had rocked England to its faithless core. But whereas the Hell Fire Club had been the ruination of many, he desired a more cautious path.

The men here thought it was a game, a bit of harmless debauchery against the rigid rules imposed upon them, against a lineage that was both a blessing and a curse. They were oblivious to the wild hunger inside him, the desperate need to satisfy his craving.

The women's awe at the cavernous hall was fast dissolving into nervous, ingratiating giggles. Several of them were trying to strike poses in the firelight to best show off their attributes despite the concealing cloaks they'd been asked to wear.

His mouth tightened with annoyance. That's what came from hiring whores. He'd instructed them to act innocent, but he supposed the concept was foreign to them.

Except for the little one.

Satisfaction eased aside some of his irritation as he observed her. He'd spent weeks hunting London's brothels for this particular venture. Through his emissary, he had picked thirteen of the soiled doves. Lydia was the only one he'd selected for himself.

She was young, probably not much older than fifteen. And, unlike the others, she was fresh. With her dark curls and apple-cheeked complexion, she exuded youth and innocence.

It was a sham, of course. But her eyes weren't quite as jaded as the other whores, and that appealed to him.

He set the chalice down on the long, pine serving table in the center of the room, and walked toward her, her smaller stature making her easy to identify among the relative anonymity of the cloaked figures. Her face was nearly hidden in the shadows of her hood, but he caught the nervous darting of her eyes as she glanced around. When she saw him, recognition flashed across her face and a smile trembled on her Cupid's bow mouth. Her cheeks flushed with pleasure as he reached out to grasp her slender wrist.

Her welcoming smile transformed into a surprised O when he yanked her across the cavern, to the jagged opening that formed a narrow passageway. Stopping abruptly, so abruptly that the girl stumbled into him, he turned back to the room and raised an arm.

"'Do As Thou Wilt,'" he quoted, borrowing once again from Sir Francis. His mouth curved with cold satisfaction as his apostles swooped on the harlots, and the chamber echoed with delighted laughter and thrilled screams. Distorted shadows danced against the cavern's walls. The game had begun.

Turning back into the passageway, his fingers tightening around the doxy's thin wrist, he yanked her behind him with little regard as he hurried down the tunnel. She had to run or be dragged.

"M-me Lord . . ." she gasped breathlessly. He didn't seem to hear her, as she was forced to race to keep up with his longer strides, the hood of her cloak falling to her shoulders, the dark curls tumbling around her pretty face.

A rustic oak door was at the end of the corridor. He stopped, releasing her to withdraw a key from his pocket. He tugged open the door, stepping aside in a courtly gesture that was sure to have her heart fluttering. With a flirtatious smile and a toss of her head, Lydia crossed the threshold, but he watched her coy sophistication crumble as her eyes drifted over the elaborate four-poster bed with its gleaming red satin sheets. Across the room was an enormous table and cupboard, the table scattered with at least twenty beeswax candles. Beneath that scent, one could detect other smells . . . sex, and something else . . . something not quite identifiable.

"Oh, la. 'Tis amazing, this," she whispered, as her fingers worked on the knot at her throat, and the wool cape she'd been given for the night's pleasure slid off her thin shoulders to pool on the hard stone floor. He locked the door and began methodically stripping off his own cape and clothes, leaving them in a crumpled pile behind him as he walked, naked, toward her. He was already aroused.

Lydia smiled in a way that never failed to attract the rogues who visited Madame's establishment. Her smile slipped, though, when he reached her and, taking the muslin gown in his hands, shredded it in two in a swift, violent motion. Before she could cry out over its destruction, he was tearing her cotton chemise and short stays from her body, lifting her toward the bed.

"Lovely . . . so lovely." His breath was hot against her flesh as he bore her down on the feather mattress. Shackling her delicate wrists above her head with one hand, he kissed his way down the slim white column of her throat to one small breast. Dress forgotten, she relaxed under the sensual onslaught, delighted to feel his mouth and tongue laving her. A soft sigh escaped her lips as she began to dream about a future that had nothing to do with Madame Duprey. A future far away from the fat, sweaty old men who came to see her at the academy.

To leave the house on Bacon Street, to have a place all her own . . .

'Twould be heaven . . .

The searing pain was so unexpected, she couldn't quite comprehend it even as her body jerked in reaction. Crying out, her eyes flew open in shock and met the man's as he lifted his head. Dread rippled through her as she saw the bright flecks of blood on his lips.

Even then it took her a moment to connect that to the hot, painful throbbing on her left breast.

Her eyes slewed downward. She felt a jolt of fear and horror as she caught sight of the wound.

She screamed.

His eyes glinted, his face suddenly a demonic shadow as he hovered above her. His free hand flashed toward her throat, wrapping around the slim column, choking off the shrill sound. The pressure increased. The sharp pain in her breast faded abruptly, swamped by the more pressing need to breathe. Frantically, she struggled to free herself from the punishing grip. As she bucked and writhed, her lungs began to burn, her vision dimmed. Her tongue seemed to swell in her mouth, further choking her.

Just when she thought her throat would be crushed, the pressure eased. Coughing and gasping, she sucked in great gulps of the scented air. And now she recognized that other smell in the room. It came to her in one horrifying flash.

Blood.

The devil's lips brushed her ear.

"It's not going to be that easy, my sweet," he murmured silkily, sliding over her. Skin against skin. His sweat mingling with her blood. "I am not through with you yet."

He reached for something above her, and though her heart pounded in her ears, Lydia heard the unmistakable clink of metal. Then, the cold bite of steel against her flesh.

Her eyes widened and the bone-shaking terror that flooded her made her yearn for the unconsciousness denied her a moment ago. Because now she knew that this was no sensual lair with the flickering candles and beautiful bed.

A choked sob escaped her.

This wasn't heaven, after all.

1

Present Day

"You're sure about this? *Absolutely sure*? We finally got the son of a bitch?"

Unease, as dark and slick as an oil spill, slid inside Kendra's belly. She ignored the sensation, putting it down to the dozen pairs of eyes locked on her at the moment.

And not just any eyes. Three sets of those eyes belonged to assistant directors or associate deputy directors from a veritable alphabet soup of agencies—the CIA, NSA, and her own FBI, including a senior official from the National Security Branch, which had been formed post-9/11 to coordinate counterterrorism, counterintelligence, and intelligence resources. The other members of the special task force were agents like her, although she was the only woman in the room. Depending on one's perspective, that made her either very special or a freak. She shied away from choosing a side on that one.

"It's Balakirev." Kendra kept her voice cool and steady with an effort, though she felt those eyes pressing against her like a physical weight. "We managed to get a lock on his IP address after we covertly piggybacked onto one of his client's wired accounts—"

"It wasn't easy," Special Agent Daniel Sheppard jumped in, excitement animating his usually taciturn features. "The sneaky bastard bounced the signal around the globe."

Daniel was, at heart, a computer geek, and used his skills brilliantly within the FBI's Cyber Action Teams. Normally, he was responsible for chasing malicious computer hackers throughout the world. This was the first time he'd been asked to track down a known terrorist.

"But Kendra—Special Agent Donovan—created a program that was absolutely genius," Daniel continued, shooting the woman beside him a look of admiration. "It tracked his previous patterns, allowing us to leap *forward*, rather than catching up with his signal—"

"I understand." Peter Carson, the FBI's assistant director of the New York field office, raised his hand in an impatient, preemptive gesture to ward off what would undoubtedly be a long-winded session of techno-speak. Carson wasn't a computer geek. He had no interest in the Internet, except to use it to nail the ass of one Vlad Balakirev, former KGB agent turned merchant of death.

The Russian had been Carson's mission for more than a year, ever since the NSA had picked up chatter linking him to an al-Qaeda terrorist group rumored to be on the verge of setting up a cell in New York City. They'd formed an elite, multi-agency task force to track Balakirev around the world. And they'd come damn close to capturing him twice: once in Jordan and then, two months later, in Spain. But he'd eluded them. In the process, he'd taken out five of their Special Ops agents.

That had been a bitter pill to swallow, but nothing compared to the gut-clenching fear that Carson felt after receiving intel a month ago that Balakirev had slipped into the United States with a cache of chemical weapons to sell. Specifically, ricin, the deadly compound favored by Balakirev's former KGB. Carson had been chewing Tums like they were candy after *that* news.

"I want to be sure—absolutely goddamn *sure*—that it's Balakirev," he said now, remembering the botched mission in Spain. How the hell had the Russian slipped through that net? He pushed that question aside to focus on Kendra Donovan.

If he felt a little squeamish about dealing with her, he was careful to keep that hidden. It had been his decision eight months ago to pull her out of the FBI's Behavioral Analysis Unit, where she'd been using her profiling and computer skills to work on the country's most vicious serial killer cases. It had given him a jolt to meet her in person, though. He put his reaction down to her age—only twenty-six, for Christ's sake. But he'd read her file; he knew who she was. Hell, he knew *what* she was. The offspring of two scientists who advocated eugenics, she'd been a child prodigy, landing at Princeton when she was only fourteen. By the time she was eighteen, she'd gotten degrees in advanced computer science, psychology, and criminology. No wonder the Bureau had wanted her badly enough to circumvent their age requirement of twenty-three to get her in. Kendra Donovan was a capable agent, Carson knew.

Even so, it was damn distracting, discussing tactical operations with someone who wore their hair in a jaunty ponytail. Feminists could kiss his ass, but Carson was old enough and, yes, old-fashioned enough to still believe that to bring a woman—especially a woman who looked like Kendra—into an all-male environment was to invite disaster. But if Kendra had found Balakirev, he'd kiss the foot of every feminist he met. Damned if he wouldn't.

"It's Balakirev." Kendra was pleased her voice was steady, revealing none of her inner tension. "We've tracked his signal to a warehouse in Brooklyn." She hesitated briefly, her eyes, as dark as onyx, unreadable. She kept her gaze trained on Carson, even though she wanted to glance at the man on the other side of the room. "The warehouse is owned by Berkshire, Ltd. That's a shell company for E.V. Inc., which is a subsidiary of Greenway International."

She held her breath. She'd just dropped a bombshell.

"Greenway International?" That came from Bradley Thompson, the CIA's associate deputy director. He surged forward in his chair. "Are you talking about Sir Jeremy Greene?"

"Yes, sir."

Thompson shot Carson a look. "You do know who he is, don't you?"

Carson found himself bristling for no other reason than Thompson having been a major pain in the ass since they'd been forced to work together—in the spirit of interagency cooperation, of course. While Washington had given him the leadership position, the decision hadn't stopped Thompson from trying to assert his authority every chance he could, the cocky bastard.

"I read newspapers," Carson responded testily.

"You should read the reports we've had on him," Thompson retorted. "The cleanest thing about him is his Savile Row suits."

While Balakirev was a shadowy figure in the underworld of gun-running and smuggling, Kendra knew that Greene was another matter entirely. The Brit graced the business and society pages. He'd had been born into money and had amassed even more. Twenty years ago, he'd been knighted. He'd dined at the White House; slept in the Lincoln bedroom. The public probably believed that sort of prestige made him a good guy. In reality, it just meant he was politically savvy and smart. And his connections hadn't prevented him from being scrutinized by the CIA, Israeli intelligence, Interpol, and Britain's own MI5.

"He's been suspected of money laundering, drugs, human trafficking, and," Thompson added significantly, "weapons smuggling."

Carson's mouth tightened. "Our mission is Balakirev."

"Don't be stupid," snapped Thompson. "Greene changes everything. He's the *big* fish. Washington will want to hook him."

There'd never been anything resembling friendliness between the two men, but Thompson's implied threat stripped away the pretense of professional courtesy. The very air in the conference room seemed to shimmer, a desert heat of hostility.

Kendra watched the men shift their positions. Those still seated now pushed themselves to their feet. The FBI agents joined Carson, while the CIA agents flanked Thompson, like two packs of dogs sizing up each other, ready to fight for their territory. The representatives from the NSA and NSB took a step back, separating themselves from the upcoming confrontation.

They were Switzerland.

And I'm a fool, Kendra thought wryly, stepping between these two powerful foes. "We may be able to hook both Balakirev and Greene." Dangling that carrot made her, once again, the focal point. This time was worse, though, because at least one of the pairs of eyes on her was furious, and they belonged to her current boss.

"What are you talking about, Agent Donovan?" Carson demanded. The snap in his voice made her flinch.

"When I realized that Sir Jeremy owned the warehouse Balakirev was using, I took the liberty of tracing his whereabouts. He—"

"Why?" Carson interrupted, his eyes bright with irritation and suspicion.

The question threw her for a second. Recovering, she said, "I recognized his name from an agency report I'd read." In fact, she'd read the report eleven months ago, but her memory had never been an issue. While it wasn't quite eidetic, it came pretty damn close. "Greene filed a flight plan from Heathrow yesterday. His private jet touched down at JFK this morning at three A.M. He was picked up by a limousine and taken to his penthouse on Park Avenue."

Thompson stared at her. "Greene's in New York?"

Carson scowled. "He has nothing to do with our mission, which remains *Balakirev.*"

Kendra didn't need him to emphasize the Russian's name to know that Carson was warning her. Jesus H. Christ, this was probably how it felt to find yourself in the middle of a minefield. Her stomach churned. One wrong step . . . "Greene is scheduled to be at the Brooklyn warehouse today at four P.M."

Thompson sucked in a breath. He looked like a man who'd just found God. "How'd you know that?"

"He uses a smartphone."

Carson didn't look like he'd found God—he looked coldly furious. But at that bit of information, he snorted. "For a smart man, that's pretty stupid." Even he knew that wireless technology, no matter how many layers of security measures one stacked on, could be infiltrated. Especially by somebody like Kendra Donovan.

"Not stupid—arrogant," corrected Kendra.

There was a short, heavily charged silence. Thompson threw her a speculative glance—it wasn't the first one he'd given her in the past eight months—before turning his attention back to Carson. "If we can get Greene on record consorting with a known terrorist, that's a fucking big deal. If we can hook him, we could blow apart not only Balakirev's operation, but a hundred more like it. We'll need him alive."

He didn't wait for an answer before pulling out his cell phone. As he moved off to the far end of the conference room, the stony-faced CIA agents broke away to stand near their leader.

Carson gritted his teeth. Diplomacy may be the watchword in Washington these days, but he knew Thompson was just salivating to take over the operation. *His* operation.

He turned back to his own agents. "If we're going to take them both down, we need to work fast. Sheppard, get me the blueprints for that warehouse. I want the layout, security. Two teams, plus FBI SWAT. Donovan, coordinate with HAZMAT." He swung away, striding toward the door, and slid a fiery glance at Thompson. "I'll call Langley."

No, Kendra thought. There was no way they were going to keep her from the front lines when this operation went down. She raced after Carson. "Sir. *Sir?*"

Carson gave her an impatient look. "In case it's escaped your attention, Special Agent Donovan, we don't have a lot of time here."

"Yes, sir. I want to be in on the final phase of the operation." Kendra fixed her gaze on his. "I'm not a computer geek," she reminded him, and again had to fight to keep her voice steady. But she was tired, so damned tired of having to prove herself. When she'd first joined the FBI, they'd taken one look at her and stuck her behind a desk. She'd fought hard for a chance in the field. To prove herself. The chance to be treated like everybody else.

Yeah, as if.

Her stomach knotted, but she refused to look away from the assistant director as he scowled. "I've been trained for the field—I've been in the field," she pointed out. "You know that. You know I can handle myself."

"I don't have time for this," Carson growled.

"She got Greene . . . and Balakirev." Thompson, who'd been standing near the window, pocketed his cell phone and now strode toward them. Something in his demeanor suggested that he didn't give a damn whether the woman went on the mission or not—he just liked pissing off Carson. "We're wasting time. You may have been put in charge—" Despite his best effort, irritation sizzled to the surface. Bureaucratic bullshit, to give jurisdiction to the fucking FBI. "—but we need to lock this down. *Today.* If you can't, the FBI can kiss my ass, because I won't have you screwing this up."

He shouldered his way past them, disappearing out the door. The three CIA agents followed. They were too well-trained to smirk, but by the gleam in their eyes, Kendra got the impression they were smirking all the same.

Carson glared at the departing men. *Fucking spooks.* Then his gaze shifted back to Kendra. Thompson was right—and he'd eat nails before admitting it—but they were wasting time.

"Fine," he spit out. If there was one thing he'd learned in the last eight months, it was that Kendra could take care of herself. She'd been born to win. Literally.

"Sir?"

Carson gave Sheppard a narrow-eyed look as he approached. "What is it, Agent?"

"Well, I *am* a computer geek . . . but I'd also like to be part of the final phase of the operation. I've had field experience."

"I don't have fucking *time* for this!" Carson snapped. "Fine—we're *all* in on the final phase. Happy? Now I want those goddamn blueprints! We've got five hours to finish this mission. We need eyes and ears in the warehouse so we can hook Greene and fucking nail Balakirev. No one leaves this building. No one takes a *piss* without my permission. I want Balakirev by nightfall or *all* your asses are on the line."

Kendra was careful not to smile, but she felt triumphant. She'd won.

She couldn't have been more wrong.

2

At somewhere north of 2.6 million residents, Brooklyn was the most densely populated borough in New York City. Even so, there were isolated pockets within the big, bustling city that made it feel eerily deserted. The warehouse in which Balakirev had made his base and that Sir Jeremy owned was in one of those pockets, too far from prime waterfront real estate to entice developers to tidy up the area and create upscale condos and lofts, cute little boutiques, and quaint restaurants.

Here, it was still gray and grimy. Beneath the swath of overcast sky, bunker-like structures and Quonsets lined the dingy streets. A scattering of semitrucks were parked next to warehouse loading docks, but it was Sunday, so the normally frenetic hustle was reduced to those tired souls anxious to clock out and get home to maybe crack open a beer and veg out in front of whatever game was playing on television. Thanks to Team One, the perimeter around the target was clear.

Kendra surveyed the scene from inside the Batmobile—the military van with souped-up technology that only the U.S. government could afford. Less than a mile away from where they sat, Kendra imagined the city pulsing with life, vibrant and wonderfully chaotic: people strolling, chatting, having a late afternoon coffee or early dinner at the small restaurants that dotted the streets.

Being normal.

Just for a second, wistfulness welled up inside Kendra. It shook her. Or more aptly, the *wanting* of it shook her. Normal was something she'd never had, never been. Didn't know how to be. And because she didn't know how to be normal, she chose to be good—very, very good.

"Nervous?"

She glanced up at Sheppard, who was squished next to her. He looked different, tricked out as they all were in a black military flak jacket, helmet, and tactical gloves, and carrying the standard-issue SIG Sauer. Prior to that moment, the deadliest object she'd ever seen in Sheppard's right hand was a computer mouse. Though after eight months of working side-by-side with him, watching as he hunted in cyberspace, Kendra knew that Sheppard with a computer mouse in his hand could be pretty damn deadly.

She smiled slightly. "No. You?"

"Shit, yeah. I haven't been out in the field in six years."

"Why'd you come then?"

He grinned, blue eyes twinkling. "Maybe I wanted to see *you* in action. See what everyone's talking about."

It's a joke. She knew that. Yet her stomach clenched.

"Just keep your ass out of my way, Sheppard," smirked Allan O'Brien, the youngest man on the task force. He gave Kendra a wink. "I don't want some newbie screwing this up. Balakirev's *mine.*"

"Your fat ass, he is," Terry Landon shot back. "I'm team leader. Twenty that I'll be the first to put a bullet in him?"

Sheppard grimaced and shook his head. "You guys are such assholes, betting on a man's life."

"He's not a man—he's a fucking terrorist," Bill Noone growled.

"Make that a fifty and you're on," grinned O'Brien.

"Just remember, we want Greene alive," Kendra reminded them.

"*Thompson* wants him alive," O'Brien smirked.

"Fuck Thompson," Noone said, and several of the men snickered. "This isn't a CIA operation."

"Fifty that I'll be the first to put *nonlethal* bullets into both bastards," Landon revised.

"Make that fifty *and* a date with Kendra." Noone shot her a lopsided, lascivious grin. It didn't matter that he was, at forty-nine, old enough to be her father, and married, to boot.

She shot him a cool look. "Funny. I don't remember putting myself on the auction block, Noone."

"Ah, come on, sweetheart. Everybody needs an incentive."

Deliberately, Kendra lifted the hand that held the SIG Sauer, weighed it with silky ease. "Just how much incentive do you need?"

Noone laughed, throwing up his hands. "My mama told me never to argue with a woman packing a pistol—or a fucking machine gun."

"Wise woman."

"You realize when this op goes down, we're done," Sheppard said suddenly, looking around the circle of faces. "The task force will be disbanded."

"No more fucking takeout on Saturday night," O'Brien said. "No offense—but the only mug I'm gonna miss seeing is Kendra's."

"Bet your wife will be glad when this is over then," said Noone.

Landon stretched and grinned. "After this is over, I'm gonna celebrate on a beach somewhere in the Caribbean. Flirting with hot island babes and drinking rum out of a fucking coconut."

"Yeah, what about *your* wife, Terry?" O'Brien laughed.

"She can stay home."

The van's side door rolled open, and Carson heaved himself up into the tight quarters. Like the rest of the team, he wore the military uniform, though he was only supervising the operation from inside the van with the five-member tech team.

"We've got Greene talking about the ricin with Balakirev," he informed them, keeping his voice neutral even though he wanted to rub his hands together. "Twenty-one body signatures have been identified in the warehouse. We've ascertained that Balakirev and Greene are two of the four in the room at the top of the stairs. The other two are probably Greene's bodyguards. SWAT will take the lead, but Washington wants the bastard alive."

"Which bastard?"

"Greene, dammit. D.C. seems to think the guy with the money is the most dangerous," he said.

"Washington wants to flip him," Kendra commented, and then wished she'd kept her mouth shut when Carson scowled at her.

"If I want your expertise on Washington politics, I'll ask for it, Special Agent Donovan," he snapped.

"Yes, sir."

"Ah . . . is there any indication if the ricin is in the warehouse?" asked O'Brien.

Carson shook his head. "No. But you'll be given self-contained breathing masks, which will protect you if it's released as a mist. We've also got HAZMAT and medical units standing by."

"They want to sell the ricin," Kendra said, "which means it's most likely in pellet or powder form. As long as you don't put anything strange into your mouths, you'll be fine."

She'd meant to be reassuring, but O'Brien frowned. "And if you're wrong?"

"If I'm wrong . . . then get to the HAZMAT team as quickly as possible. Get out of your clothes, wash down . . ." Her voice trailed away. She didn't have to remind them that there was no antidote to ricin poisoning. If they were unlucky enough to get a dose of the toxin—even an amount so small that it could fit on the head of a pin—they were as good as dead. They'd have four to eight hours before they came down with flu-like symptoms—congestion, respiratory distress before collapsing in muscle pain, fever, nausea—finally ending with a one-way trip to the city morgue.

It wouldn't be pleasant, but there were worse ways to go, Kendra thought. Like the Ebola virus. Now *that* was a truly ghastly death. But she didn't think anyone wanted to hear that, so she kept quiet.

"Shit. My one chance at seeing you naked, Kendra, and I'm not even looking forward to it." Landon shot her a wicked grin.

She ignored him. "I'm not wrong. Balakirev and Greene aren't in this for ideological reasons. They are, for wont of a better word, businessmen."

"Well, fuck me! Here I'm thinking we're taking down a couple of terrorists." Noone gave a derisive snort. "Is he gonna have his Palm Pilot out? Maybe Balakirev's giving Greene a fucking PowerPoint presentation in there. Shit, maybe we can all learn something before we blow the fucker's kneecaps off."

Kendra's mouth tightened at the sarcasm, but she said evenly, "Balakirev's a cold-blooded bastard. He doesn't give a shit about the innocent victims who are harmed by what he's doing. But neither do some corporate CEOs who are aware their products are killing people and yet choose to look the other way because of the bottom line—"

"If you're gonna go all bleeding heart liberal on us, Kendra, and actually defend a *terrorist*—"

"I'm not defending him," Kendra responded sharply, temper rising. She pulled it back with an effort. "I'm simply stating a fact. Balakirev and Greene are in this for money. *For greed.* They're not going to want to die."

"Yeah, I read your profile," Noone muttered. "Maybe you can do a *Wall Street Journal* article after this is over. Greed is good, right?"

Kendra narrowed her eyes. "It's good for us. If either Balakirev or Greene think they're finished, they'll want to deal. They're narcissistic personalities—Greene especially. There's no way he's going to risk his precious skin in a potentially toxic environment. This is essentially a business meeting."

"Let's hope you're right, Agent Donovan," said Carson. He glanced down at his watch and felt the zing of adrenaline. It was time. "I don't want any itchy trigger fingers." He looked at each agent. "You've been briefed on how Washington wants this to go down. C'mon."

He reached over, rolled the door open, and jumped down. His boots crunched on the gritty pavement. "I'll introduce you to the SWAT team commander. Then you're on your own. Don't screw up."

Jonathon Vale, the head of the FBI SWAT team, looked like he'd stepped out of a cyborg movie, his tough, muscular body clad in a dark uniform and loaded down with bulky equipment. It weighed at least forty pounds, but he moved easily back and forth as he instructed the special task force on what exactly he expected of them—namely, to stay the fuck out of his team's way.

Putting on the military goggles and breathing apparatus, Kendra clamped down on her resentment when Vale put her in the flank position, all her team members, including Sheppard—*Sheppard*, who hadn't been out in the field for six fucking years—ahead of her.

Still, there was no time to argue. She fell into formation as they jogged as quietly as possible to take up positions of concealment along the walls and corners of the neighboring buildings, facing the warehouse. The warehouse had no windows, so this was only a precaution in case one of Balakirev's men decided to step outside.

The day's light was beginning to fade. A soft breeze carried the scent of diesel fuel, strong enough to infiltrate the mask Kendra was wearing. She wished for a stronger wind to cool the sweat popping up on her brow. Her face beneath the heavy helmet, goggles, and breathing mask felt greasy, perspiration sliding beneath the black uniform she wore.

When Vale raised his hand for the signal, everyone's eyes fastened on his fingers. His voice crackled in their earpieces, counting down.

Five . . . Four . . . Three . . .

Kendra's nerves tightened in anticipation.

Two . . . One!

Vale's hand fisted and in the distance they heard the screech of tires, followed within seconds by a tremendous crash; the high-pitched, almost feminine shriek of twisting metal. A thunderous explosion, courtesy of the explosives packed into the decoy car, shook the ground. Vale's voice reverberated in her ear.

"Go. Go. GO!"

Kendra sprinted toward the front of the warehouse. Already, two men were in position with a battering ram. One quick thrust and the door went flying inward, the SWAT team pouring across the threshold like a dozen black beetles. Kendra followed, taking in the interior in one sweeping glance. It was an enormous, shadowy cavern, filled with row upon row of crates and containers, stacked twelve and fifteen feet high, some almost to the catwalk.

"It's a fucking maze," somebody observed in her earpiece.

The initial shock of the ambush was already over, swiftly replaced by gunfire as Balakirev's men engaged in battle. Heart pumping, her breath sounding too loud inside the breathing apparatus, Kendra jogged into one of the corridors formed by the stacks of boxes. Fleetingly, she wondered if the ricin was packed within any of these containers.

The sound of gunfire was deafening. Her earpiece cracked with a steady stream of orders, invectives, and curses.

"Fucking Russians!"

"How many? How many d'ya see?"

"—took two of the fuckers out!"

"Got one of the sons of bitches!"

Kendra rounded a corner, and a heavyset man darted into her path. Spotting her, he swung up his rifle, but Kendra was already firing the SIG Sauer. He crumpled to the ground. She keyed in her voice piece and shouted, "Got one. Four down—"

"Five! I—" A burst of gunfire was followed by a shriek that sent a shiver through Kendra.

"O'Brien?" Silence.

"Son of a bitch! Son of a bitch!" Noone was panting like a dog. *"My leg. The fuckers got my leg!"*

"Give me your position!"

"—to your left, Noone! Goddamn it, to the left!"

More gunfire.

"Fuck! I see a man to the left. Take him down! Take the fucker down!" Vale's voice boomed in Kendra's earpiece.

She flipped around a protective barrier of crates, and saw a man crouched on top of a container, firing a semi-automatic assault weapon. Her own weapon leapt in her hands as she squeezed the trigger. The man pivoted in her direction, fired off several shots, and jumped down, disappearing behind a tower of crates.

Breath hitching in her chest, Kendra dove for cover, after one shuddering heartbeat, rolled out into the aisle. She caught movement out of the corner of her eye, and she swung her gun around. It took less than half a second for her brain to register that the man leaping across the narrow aisle was an enemy before she squeezed the trigger. He gave a startled cry and fell to his knees. As though in slow motion, he brought his weapon up. Kendra got off several more shots. The man fell back and lay unmoving.

"Another down." She kept going, working her way toward the stairs that she remembered from the blueprints. "I think—" She broke off as an explosion filled the room, white light followed by brilliant orange, blinding her. *"Fuck!"* She whipped off the goggles and mask, blinking.

"Goddamn it to hell!" Vale's voice sizzled in her ear. *"Flash bomb. They've got a goddamn flash bomb!"*

"Take cover! They'll cut us down!"

The steady stream of pops shifted to her right. *Dammit!* Kendra tossed aside the goggles and mask, slithering on her stomach around another wall of crates. Blinking the sweat out of her eyes, she spotted Vale and Sheppard. Like her, both had discarded their masks and goggles. From somewhere in front of them, someone was shooting.

"Where the fuck is Greene?" someone yelled in her ear.

"Balakirev is on the stairs . . . !"

"Take him down!" That came from Vale. He sprinted forward, but his body suddenly jerked, spinning around like a top, a dark plume of blood squirting out from his neck. Sheppard, who'd been running behind him, fired his weapon into the dark shadows ahead and then crouched down beside the fallen SWAT leader.

"Fuck! Fuck!" Kendra heard Sheppard's ragged voice in her earpiece. *"Vale's been hit! He needs medical attention!"*

Kendra saw the man as he stepped around the corner, hoisting his rifle to his shoulder.

"Sheppard, get down!" Kendra screamed. She sprinted forward, lifting her own weapon and squeezing the trigger. The man fell behind the wall of crates. She prayed her shot had taken him out.

She skidded on a patch of oil—*no, not oil; Vale's blood,* she realized with a sick jolt—and dropped to her knees. Sheppard had discarded his gloves and was desperately trying to plug up the hole in Vale's neck with his hands. In the dim light, his fingers gleamed black with blood.

"I'm trying . . . I'm trying to stop the bleeding. I have to stop the bleeding . . ." he panted.

Kendra grabbed his arm. "He's dead," she said brutally. "There's nothing you can do for him."

Sheppard hesitated, staring at her with horror-filled eyes. "God . . . I'd forgotten . . ."

"This isn't the fucking time to talk about it," she snapped, making another effort to drag him to his feet, to yank him into a more protected area. "Move!"

"God—I've been hit!" someone else screeched in her earpiece. *"I've been hit!"*

"Got Balakirev and Greene pinned down."

Sheppard staggered to his feet. "Okay. Okay. We need—" Suddenly, he stiffened, and a ragged cry burst from his lips. Kendra's heart lurched in her chest as she saw Sheppard's features twist in agony.

"Sheppard? Oh, my God!" Mouth dry with fear, she tried to grab him, but he toppled on her, his heavier weight driving her to the floor. She hurriedly shoved him aside and fired her weapon into the shadows, even as she darted a quick glance at Sheppard. His eyes were open and glazed with pain, she noted with a surge of relief. Not dead.

Her breath came out in pants as she rolled to her feet. She clamped her fingers around Sheppard's arms, tugging frantically. "C'mon, Sheppard! *Daniel!*"

The horrible artillery fire still echoed; her eardrums felt numb. She'd lost her earpiece when she'd fallen and could no longer hear anything but the volley of gunshots echoing off the warehouse walls.

Out of the corner of her eye, she saw a shadow take shape. Biting back a cry, she let go of Sheppard and brought up her gun, checking the movement when she recognized Terry Landon.

"Son of a bitch! Sheppard's hit?" He ran lightly toward them. "C'mon. The door's just around that section of crates. Goddamn maze." He shifted, grabbing the wounded man, hoisting him up. "I'll get you to safety." He paused, glancing at Kendra. "Move your ass, Donovan!"

"Sheppard's the one wounded. Get him out. I'm going back for Balakirev and Greene."

"No! We've gotta go—"

"I can do this, Terry. You know I can." She pivoted toward the staircase.

"Dammit, stop! That's a fucking order! I'm team leader!"

"I'm going to finish the goddamn mission!"

"No. No, you're not."

Kendra stared in astonishment as he brought up his gun, and pointed it at her. "You're ordering me back at *gunpoint*?"

"I'm sorry, Kendra." He shifted his hand so the gun was pointed away from her. Despite the craziness around them, she almost wanted to laugh at his sheer chutzpah. Pulling a gun on her to get her to safety, for Christ's sake! Then everything seemed to freeze when Landon pointed the muzzle at Sheppard, still propped in his other arm.

"Oh, for God's sake, now you're going to threaten Dan—"

Abruptly Landon let the other man go. Before he hit the ground, Landon was pulling the trigger. In disbelief Kendra watched the horrific burst of blood, bone and brain matter, and Sheppard's face was gone. Then Landon was snapping his gun around again to point it at her.

"What . . . Oh, my God! *What the fuck have you done?*" She stumbled back in shock. Instinctively, she raised her weapon, but Landon was already pulling the trigger. The shot seared across her upper arm, like the hot lash of a whip. Her right hand went numb and her SIG Sauer clattered to the concrete floor.

"You're too fucking smart for your own good, Kendra," he said, advancing on her. He'd also abandoned his mask and goggles. His eyes glittered. Around them, the stink of gunpowder and death seemed to rise up like mist from a graveyard. "You found Balakirev."

"My God . . . the last mission . . ." She couldn't seem to catch her breath. "You're a fucking *traitor!*"

"Sticks and stones. You didn't think Balakirev got away those other times because he was *good*, did you?"

"You son of a bitch!" Her arm felt like it was on fire. Useless.

"When I said I wanna be drinking somewhere on a beach, I meant it. Uncle Sam is a penny-pinching bastard. Balakirev is a businessman. He understands the value of money. And Greene is the moneyman."

Kendra launched herself at Landon, kicking her foot up to knock his weapon to the side. He grunted, staggered back, but didn't release his grip on the gun.

"Fucking bitch!"

With her good hand, she aimed for his throat even as she brought her leg up for another kick. She connected with Landon's stomach, propelling him backward, but he managed to lift his gun and pull the trigger.

The blast caught her square in her chest, like an invisible punch, knocking her off her feet and down to the ground. The pain was excruciating, oxygen evaporating from her lungs. The world teetered dizzily around her. She fought off the whirlpool of blackness. The Kevlar vest may have saved her life, but it still hurt like a bitch to be shot.

Pushing herself to her knees, she crawled crablike around a crate, down one of the maze-like aisles. She blinked as sweat burned her eyes. From behind her, she heard Landon drag himself to his feet, cursing as he did so.

"I'm gonna tear you apart, you cunt!"

Through the dingy light, she could see Vale's prone body ahead of her. Her good hand felt the stickiness of the SWAT team leader's blood congealing like Jell-O on the concrete floor. Biting down on her lip to keep from gagging, she scuttled toward his body.

"You're *dead!*" Landon came around the corner just as her fingertips grazed Vale's weapon. She grabbed it by the muzzle, flipping it around in her good hand, even as Landon shot. Kendra's body jerked, and her leg burned like acid had been thrown on it. She screamed, rolled to the side. Another shot sliced into her abdomen, below the vest. Dizzy with pain, she lifted the SIG Sauer, and fired. In front of her, Landon's gun flashed in almost the same instant, and she was tossed back, the fiery pain so intense that she thought her head was going to split right in two. The bright, coppery smell of her own blood mingled with Vale's, filling her nostrils, making her choke. Her vision grew blurry. Then she realized it was the blood dripping into her eyes.

Weakly, she closed them.

And let go.

3

"How is she?"

"She's a fighter, I'll give her that. She took several hits—right arm and leg, lower abdomen, right temple. We had to remove a section from her large intestine and right fallopian tube. Whether she'll be able to have children . . ."

"But she'll live?"

"The head wound is the most severe. She's lucky. A centimeter over and you'd be talking to the medical examiner now."

The voices came in gentle waves, rising and falling as Kendra hovered somewhere . . . where the hell was she? She felt . . . *nothing.* No pain. No emotion. Just a detached fuzziness. The only things anchoring her to reality were those voices. Both male. One soft-spoken and calm. The other a little louder, the timbre of his voice more gravelly.

"Will she live?" The gravelly voice repeated the question, more insistent.

A small sound. A sigh, maybe. "I wish I knew."

"You're the doctor, dammit. If you don't know, who does?"

"If you would've asked me that when she was brought in, I'd have said no—she wouldn't live the night. But that was a week ago and she's still alive. And getting stronger. This morning we removed the ventilator, so she's breathing on her own. But will she live? I don't know."

"Goddamnit. The Director wants to know her prognosis."

"Then I hope the Director has a telephone line to God, because He's the only one who can answer that."

"I can't believe she's an FBI agent. She looks *sixteen*, for heaven's sake. I've got a daughter who looks older than her!"

"Twenty-six."

"What?"

"She's twenty-six. And your daughter looks older because you let her wear all that makeup. Not to mention that horrible tattoo."

"It was supposed to be a butterfly tattoo on her ankle. A small one." There was a long-suffering sigh. "How was I supposed to know that she'd get a skull and crossbones that takes up most of her back? If her father were around—"

"You're too lenient on her."

The two new voices penetrated the lovely fuzziness cocooning Kendra. She'd been feeling buoyant, as though she were hovering somewhere outside her body. But the disapproval in the one voice grabbed at her with tiny hooks, pulling her down.

"You've let her run wild since the divorce," the disapproving voice continued. "I'm not criticizing. Well, maybe I am. But it's only because we're friends, Annie. Can you hand me that? Thanks." There was a moment of silence. Then, "She's playing you, you know."

"She's just . . . going through a rebellious stage."

"Well, she's lucky to have you. There're plenty of people in this world who don't have anybody. Like this poor girl."

"What'd'ya mean? I heard that the Director himself was asking about her." The voice dropped to an almost fearful whisper, as though the woman, Annie, thought the Director—whoever he was—was lurking nearby. "And there's always someone from the Bureau coming around, checking in on her. Dr. Campbell was given the order to oversee her case himself."

"Work people." The other woman sniffed. Disapproval again. "Doctors. *Us*. No family. Look at her. Even with her head wrapped up like a mummy, she's a pretty little thing, isn't she? I'd kill to have lashes like that. You'd think she'd have a boyfriend at least worried about her."

"Hmm."

"My nephew, Joey, just broke up with his girlfriend—"

"Oh, for heaven's sake, Pamela! The girl hasn't regained consciousness since she was brought in." There was a thread of laughter now in the other woman's voice. "And you're trying to set her up with your nephew!"

"Her vital signs are excellent. Now that we're weaning her off the sedatives . . . I just feel sad for her, that's all. No family—"

"Oh, my God! Kendra Donovan."

"What?"

"*Kendra Donovan*. This girl—the patient. I just realized . . . I've heard about her, you know." The voice dropped back to a whisper. Annie's voice. For some reason, floating as she was, it was important to Kendra to know who was talking, to be able to identify the voices. "It was on *20/20* or *60 Minutes*—one of those news programs. Her parents were part of some movement to bring superbabies into the world."

"*Super*babies? That's . . . wait a minute. I think I read about that! Designer babies." The disapproval was back in the other woman's—Pamela's—voice. "Genetically engineered, tinkering around with their genes to make them smarter than normal. *Frankenbabies*."

"I don't know if they went that far. Not back then. God only knows what they do *now.* But the scientist who founded . . . I guess you could call it a society—"

"Cult."

"Cult, then," Annie conceded. "The goal was to bring these superintelligent scientists together to have superintelligent offspring. Crazy, huh?"

"More like sick." Pamela's voice went from disapproving to appalled. "It's *breeding,* like cattle. Put the best livestock together to breed a better cow. It's not normal for people."

The fuzziness was dissipating, leaving a dull ache in its place. Kendra didn't want to listen anymore. She didn't want to hear the revulsion in the women's voices.

Special, or a freak. In the eyes of Pamela and Annie, definitely a freak.

"So . . . she's one of those Frankenbabies?"

"Yeah . . . I think she started college at fourteen or fifteen."

"Jeez, that's young."

"I can't believe she's here. That this girl is *her.* Small world, huh?"

"Crazy world. Where are her parents? Why aren't they here?"

"I think they had some sort of falling out—"

"What's wrong?"

"I don't know. Her blood pressure is spiking." Annie sounded worried. "Should we notify Dr. Campbell?"

"Maybe she's in pain."

"They told us to wean her off the morphine."

"I'll page Dr. Campbell, then. He can check her." There was a shuffling sound, and the voice was farther away.

"Are you going to call your nephew?" The other voice—Annie—was also moving away, but Kendra could hear the ripple of sly amusement. "Play matchmaker?"

The other woman seemed to hesitate. Then, "I don't think she's Joey's type."

"What? Too pretty for him?"

"Too weird. There's something off about a Frankenbaby, even if she's all grown-up and gorgeous."

It was pain, not voices, that woke Kendra the next time. Her skull felt like it was being cleaved in two. If she wasn't mistaken, she was going to have the mother of all headaches. No, correction. She *was* having the mother of all headaches. It throbbed from the right side of her head and radiated outward in jabs that shuddered all the way down to her toes.

"Miss Donovan?" The voice was a quiet hum of concern, hovering somewhere above her.

With considerable effort, Kendra opened her eyes, and met hazel ones behind horn-rimmed glasses. Round face. Sixtyish. The man was a little blurry around the edges, but she realized that could be her eyesight. She blinked a couple of times, and he sharpened in focus.

"God. My head." And her right arm ached unmercifully. That pain joined the throbbing of her head. She licked her lips. "Hurts. Water."

"Of course." He poured water into a plastic cup and brought it over, holding a straw to her parched lips. Greedily, she sucked, unable to get enough of the icy liquid as it slid down her sore throat.

"We'll see about getting something for your head. We don't want you to lose consciousness again. Gave us a scare—we expected you to come out of the coma a couple of days ago." He pulled the straw away from her, ignored her tiny mewl of distress as he set the plastic cup on a metal tray table. "I'm Dr. Campbell."

What happened? She didn't think she said that out loud. But he turned back to survey her, asking, "Do you remember anything?"

"No." Something wiggled in her consciousness, a slight parting of the wispy gray layers. "Yes. I-I don't know."

"Do you know your name?"

"Donovan . . . Kendra Donovan," she whispered.

"Who's the president of the United States?"

"What? I . . ." *Oh, God!* The memory, when it came, was like a flash flood, uprooting and destroying her peace of mind. "Sheppard. He's dead. Oh, God." Her breath caught on a dry sob. "They're dead. Terry . . . Terry Landon. *Traitor.* The bastard! Shot him. *Shot him!*"

"Calm down, Miss Donovan. Your memory appears intact—"

"Did I shoot him?"

"Who?"

"The bastard. Landon." Her throat was still so parched, it was like pushing words through a cheese grater.

The doctor reached for her wrist, holding it lightly as he timed her pulse against the ticking seconds of his wristwatch. "Yes. I believe you did."

"Dead?"

"I believe so."

"Good. Balakirev? Greene?" She shook off his touch, but by then the doctor had finished and was letting her go. She tried to push herself into a sitting position but was too weak, her arms as limp as wet noodles. She found herself sagging back against the hard pillows. "Get them?"

"Miss Donovan, please, lie still." He waited for a second, then leaned over her, flicking a penlight in her eyes. Appearing satisfied by what he saw, he slipped the penlight back into the front breast pocket of his white jacket and moved to the foot of the bed, where he unclipped the medical chart and began jotting down notes. "I'll need to call your superiors. They left explicit instructions that I call as soon as you regained consciousness." He touched her foot. "Can you feel this? Move your toes?"

"Yes." She wriggled her toes for good measure, although it took an astonishing amount of energy. "Balakirev? Greene?" she repeated hoarsely.

"We need to do some tests. And I need to call your superiors," he repeated. His expression softened as he stared down at her. "I can wait before making that call."

Kendra understood he was offering her more time. She shifted her gaze away from the doctor's to the bland white ceiling of the hospital room. She was in the Walter Reed National Military Medical Center, according to one of the nurses. Private room. Slightly upscale décor with cheerful floral curtains framing the window that revealed a dull gray sky. Paint the color of a not-quite-ripe cantaloupe splashed on the wall. Nice—for a hospital room. But it was still a hospital room: an EKG machine, green line silently bouncing on the darkened screen, to her left, next to the IV bag, its thin tube doing a slow drip into her left hand. Her nostrils felt slightly pinched. Belatedly, it occurred to her that she must have an oxygen cannula inserted in her nose.

Aware that the doctor was waiting for her answer, she shook her head and instantly regretted it. The movement sent a fresh avalanche of pain crashing through her, followed by a greasy roll of nausea.

"No," she whispered huskily, and licked her lips again. She wanted to close her eyes, to somehow find her way back to that fuzzy, floating world where she'd been before she woke to discomfort, both physical and mental. But she refused to give into the temptation.

"Call them. Now," she ordered. "I want answers."

"Kendra." This time, she recognized the gravelly voice even before her eyes popped open and she stared into the lined face of Philip Leeds, the associate director for the Behavioral Science Unit. Her boss.

Except he hadn't been her boss for almost a year, she remembered with a frown. Not since she'd been loaned out to the New York office's special task force.

"Sir."

"Welcome back." The smile he offered didn't erase the worry that shadowed his eyes. "How are you feeling?"

"Like I've been shot in the head."

The door swung open, and Dr. Campbell swept in. "Ah. I heard you've come to see our star patient, sir. I'll have to ask you to keep this initial visit brief. Miss Donovan has a way to go before she's up to answering any questions."

Kendra flicked the doctor a look. "I'm the one with questions."

"Or up to conducting an interrogation," he continued smoothly. He turned to the associate director of the BSU. "We need to bring Miss Donovan down to Diagnostics. I've scheduled her for an MRI."

Leeds nodded. "Give us five minutes, Dr. Campbell."

Aware that the associate director was asking—no, *demanding*—a few minutes alone with the patient, Dr. Campbell moved toward the door. "Five minutes," he agreed, but there was a stern note in his voice. While he was aware of Leeds's clout, Dr. Campbell was the one with authority in this room, in this hospital, and with this patient.

Leeds waited until the door swung shut before turning back to Kendra. "Peter Carson is flying down here. He wants to talk to you."

"I'm sure he does. Could you please pass me that water?" As Leeds glanced around, Kendra fiddled with the gadget on her bed, elevating the mattress so she was in a sitting position. There was something undignified about talking to your boss while flat on your back.

He took the plastic pitcher and filled the cup. "Are you all right?"

Kendra hated the weakness in her arms as she reached for the water. "I said I felt like I'd been shot in the head," she muttered irritably, sticking the straw in her mouth. "Sir."

Leeds smiled, a little more genuine this time. "Well, your attitude's the same."

"I feel like shit."

The smile disappeared. "I'm sorry, Kendra. Carson will be the one to debrief you, but what the hell happened?"

Kendra's hands trembled as she put the plastic water cup on the metal-arm tray that had been wheeled beside the bed. "Major clusterfuck—sorry. Terry Landon sold us out. Or would've, if he'd had time."

Briefly, she closed her eyes; saw Sheppard's head explode. She opened her eyes, and Leeds could see the torment swimming in the inky depths. "He killed Daniel Sheppard right in front of me. Fucking bastard."

"Are you certain?"

"Yeah. He's a fucking bastard."

"Kendra."

"He's the one who shot me. I wanted to go after Balakirev, Greene. That's when Landon . . . shot Daniel. Then me." Her gaze fell to her hands restlessly twisting the bed linen. She forced herself to stop. "If I hadn't tried to go after Balakirev, Daniel would be alive."

"You know better than that, Agent Donovan." Leeds waited until she lifted her eyes. "You didn't kill Sheppard."

"I sure as hell didn't help him." Her breath hitched. "I worked with Landon. I'm a profiler, for Christ's sake. I should've seen him . . . should've recognized—"

"You're not that powerful. Or that perfect."

She raised her hands, pressing her knuckles against her eyes. She shook her head. A mistake, since it once again sent the merciless knives slashing into her skull. They'd offered to increase her morphine intake, but she'd refused. She sighed, dropping her hands. "I took out Landon. The doctor . . . Dr. Campbell said he's dead."

"He is."

"What about Greene and Balakirev? The ricin?"

"Balakirev's dead. He was caught in the cross fire. The ricin was packaged in pellet form, just as you predicted. We confiscated it—and Balakirev's laptop. We've got CAT working on it. There's a lot of encrypted information. Once they crack it, we hope to infiltrate several terrorist cells the bastard was doing business with."

"So we didn't need Balakirev after all. We just needed his laptop."

"Well, I don't think Peter Carson sees it quite that way. But technology makes most of us obsolete, doesn't it?"

"God, I'd love to get my hands on it." Kendra's fingers curled in frustration, digging into the crisp sheets.

"I'll bet you would." He glanced at his watch. "My five minutes are up. I'm going to go before Dr. Campbell boots my ass out. I'll check on you tomorrow. The Director indicated that he may stop by." He walked to the door. Hesitated. "If you need to talk to anybody—"

"I don't."

He stared at her for a full minute, and decided not to remind her that she'd be required to do a full psych evaluation before returning to the Bureau. For now, he simply nodded. "You're a valuable member of our team, Special Agent Donovan."

"Thank you. Ah . . . sir? Have you informed . . . do my parents know that I'm . . . never mind." Her throat closed tightly, cutting off the remainder of her words. She was embarrassed to see her fingers, twisting in the bed linen again, tremble. She already regretted her impulsive question, could see pity in the associate director's eyes.

"As your nearest relatives, both your parents were informed," he said gently.

She nodded, and could no longer hold his gaze. "Thank you."

Leeds hesitated, and felt an unfamiliar anger burn inside him against the two scientists. Both, he knew, were brilliant in their fields—Dr. Eleanor Jahnke, in quantum physics, and Dr. Carl Donovan, in genome research and biogenetic engineering. But, as far as he was concerned, they were both miserable human beings.

Because there was nothing he could do to ease the desolation he'd glimpsed in Kendra's dark eyes before she'd looked away, he simply said, "Get some rest, Agent Donovan."

Kendra struggled against the humiliation and odd ache in her chest that had nothing to do with her injuries. When she finally lifted her gaze, she was surprised to see that she was once again alone in the room.

And she still didn't know what had happened to Sir Jeremy Greene.

The next four days passed in a haze of tests and physical therapy. Kendra hated her weakness, hated how her limbs felt sluggish and ungainly. *Unnatural.* Every movement she forced herself to make was like pushing a giant boulder up a mountain, leaving her shaky and disoriented afterward, and in desperate need of a hospital bed.

Luckily, she had one available.

Leeds did not return, although she did hear that he checked on her regularly. As promised, Carson arrived to debrief her, solemnly informing her of the body count, which included Allan O'Brien in addition to Sheppard and Vale, and Danny Cortez from Team One. Two men from Vale's SWAT team were also killed. Bill Noone had taken a bullet in the leg, but he was alive.

Terry Landon didn't count.

Kendra thought of O'Brien, and his young wife who was now a widow, and wanted to weep. And to shoot Terry Landon all over again. *Fucking bastard.*

Carson left before she could ask him about Greene, and in truth, by the time their session was over, she was too drained to formulate any coherent questions anyway. She wondered if some of that lassitude was her mood, or if they'd added morphine to her IV bag after all.

Certainly time seemed to stretch out and then snap together, blurring and bleeding from one moment to the next, from evening to morning to afternoon. She never seemed to be alone. The nurses she'd heard talking—Annie (a motherly figure with sunny blond curls bouncing around a surprisingly youthful face) and Pamela (far less motherly, more angular with short salt-and-pepper hair)—now buzzed in and out of her hospital room like busy bees, checking her vitals, giving her little paper cups of pills, and accompanying her on her journey two floors below for tests, and then dropping another floor to the physical therapy department.

"For someone who was in a coma a couple of weeks ago, you're doing amazingly well," Dr. Campbell remarked as he came into the room one morning. He picked up her chart from the foot of the bed and gave it a brisk assessing glance before smiling at her. "You've got a visitor."

"Oh?"

"Kendra."

Her heart gave a lurch as her eyes swung to the door.

The man standing in the threshold was tall and thin, and so much older than she remembered. His once black hair was now streaked lightly at the temples with silver, and there were lines carved on his handsome face that she couldn't seem to recall. *It's been more than a decade.*

Yet as he stepped into the room, the expression on his face, in his thickly lashed, dark, dark brown eyes—*her* eyes, she realized with a weird sort of clutch of her heart—was sharply familiar, cool detachment laced with dissatisfaction.

Some things never change.

Seemingly oblivious to the undercurrents swirling in the room, Dr. Campbell continued to smile. "It's good of you to visit Kendra, Dr. Donovan," he said. If he thought it odd that the man hadn't visited or called when his daughter's life was hanging by a thread, he gave no sign. "I'll give you some privacy." He strode to the door, paused. "Kendra is doing remarkably well, but please don't overtire her."

"I understand. Thank you, Dr. Campbell." Dr. Carl Donovan waited until the other man left the room, then said coolly, "So . . . this is why you gave up what could have been a brilliant future?"

Kendra didn't know whether to laugh or cry. Twelve years, and his first words to her were a criticism. *Typical.* "What're you doing here?" She sounded a little breathless, but otherwise steady. "I'm the one with the head injury, but apparently you forgot that you disowned me."

"Don't be impertinent, Kendra." Her father's mouth compressed into a thin line. "I received a phone call from Associate Director Leeds, who suggested that if I wanted to keep doing my research, I should visit you."

Kendra frowned. "I'm not following. What does your research have to do with me?"

"I'm working at the Fellowship Institute in Arizona—"

"On human genome research. I know."

"Then you should know that the government is our largest donor."

Kendra remembered the look of pity in the associate director's eyes. "Ah. I see. Leeds blackmailed you. That's why you're here." Not because her father wanted to see her. Heaven forbid that he actually cared. And odd how that hurt. She hadn't seen her father in a dozen years, but he still had that power.

In a fastidious move, Carl lifted his pant leg to keep its pressed line before taking a seat in the chair next to the bed. He cocked a brow. "Are you going to tell me how you ended up here . . . like that?"

"Oh, you know. Just saving the world."

"I could point out that there are easier and undoubtedly more productive ways to save the world. If you had continued—"

"How's Barbara?" she interrupted. "The children?"

He hesitated. He wasn't a man to be diverted, but since the previous subject was distasteful to him, and pointless, he allowed it. "Barbara has taken time off from the Institute to write a book. The children are showing remarkable cognitive abilities."

"Patricia and Stewart, right?" She recalled the names of her half siblings. "Or do you just refer to them as Test Subjects One and Two?"

"I see your sense of humor has not improved."

"No, I don't suppose it has. But then, when it comes right down to it, I was a failure, wasn't I? Didn't quite fulfill the genius potential that you and Mother had hoped for. How is Mother, by the way? Will she be coming?"

"I have no idea. I'm sure she's being kept apprised of your condition."

"Nothing says motherly love like a good text."

Carl gave her a reproving look. "Eleanor has tremendous responsibility at CERN. She's part of the research team conducting experiments at the Large Hadron Collider—"

"I know. Leave it to Mom to want to create a black hole right here on earth."

"Don't be absurd. That is typical media hyperbole, as you well know," he said stiffly.

"My lamentable sense of humor." She sighed, and suddenly felt bone-weary. Phillip Leeds had meant well, she knew. But it would take more than blackmail to mend a family that had shattered years ago. Hell, who was she kidding? She never had a family, not in its truest form. She'd been a lab rat. A Frankenbaby, as Annie had called her.

"It is unfortunate," her father agreed. It took her a moment to realize he was referring to her humor.

"Too bad you couldn't have bred that out of me."

"Sarcasm is the lowest form of wit, and it doesn't become you, Kendra."

"Apparently nothing becomes me."

Irritation flickered over his face, and Kendra admitted that a small, petty part of her still enjoyed being able to provoke him. It was the only reaction, besides disappointment, that she'd ever gotten out of him.

"You were such a promising—"

"Experiment?"

"Student," he snapped.

"A student. Like the children of *Lebensborn*?" she suggested sweetly. "Hitler thought his SS breeding program was promising, too. All those Aryan babies. Superbabies."

Carl glared at her. "I had hoped that you would have finally understood the purpose behind Dr. Kapoor's endeavor. I might point out that George Bernard Shaw, Charles Lindbergh, and countless brilliant minds were also advocates of eugenics."

"Yes. I know. You want to make the world a better place by producing smarter children. But you failed, didn't you? You and Mother didn't factor in the human equation. You know—wants, desires, personal ambition."

"Personal ambition?" Carl shifted in his chair, and his cold eyes scanned her bandaged head, the hospital room. "Personal ambition to play cop? Look where that got you."

"I'm a special agent in the Federal Bureau of Investigation." She'd been the youngest person to ever be accepted into the academy, she wanted to point out. Except she knew that would mean nothing to Dr. Carl Donovan.

"A *glorified* cop. You could have done anything, been anything."

"No, I couldn't," she said quietly. And her eyes, unconsciously pleading, clung to his. *Do you even know why I became an FBI agent?* she wanted to ask. But of course, he didn't. He'd never asked her about anything. He'd instructed and ordered, expecting her to fall in line. And she had, for fourteen years.

"You didn't try hard enough," he said.

Something inside her, something that had been clinging to hope, withered and died. Christ, she hadn't even realized she still had hope, thought that had died years ago. She dropped her eyes. "I'm human. You didn't count on that. And after all your tests and your trials, you gave up on me, gave up on your marriage—"

"You were the one who threatened to sue for emancipation," he reminded her, and rose to his feet in a lithe move. "Your mother was asked to participate in the research at CERN. It was a once-in-a-lifetime chance. I certainly could not stand in her way."

"Of course not. Especially since Barbara was waiting in the wings to take her place, provide you with more experiments."

"This argument has become tiresome, Kendra. Life goes on. I believe that is what you told your mother and me when you asked for your independence. I really don't understand this melodrama. You broke away from us. While we did not agree with your decision, we accepted it. And we never blocked your access to the trust fund that we had set up in your name."

"The trust fund came from money *I* earned by appearing like a lab rat on TV and in competitions."

"Nevertheless, your mother and I set up the trust fund for you, which paid for your college education. This discussion is pointless." He glanced at his watch. "I'm on a tight schedule. Unless, of course, you have something to say that relates to the present day . . . ?" He waited, staring at her. When she said nothing, he turned and walked toward the door.

Words trembled on the tip of her tongue. It took every ounce of her willpower to keep from lashing out at him.

He paused at the door, looking back. His eyes swept over her again, lingering on the white bandage swathing her head. He didn't look concerned, Kendra noticed; only confused. "Goodbye, Kendra."

"Goodbye, Dr. Donovan." She waited until he left before grabbing the remote for her bed. Her fingers shook as she pressed the button, lowering the mattress so that she could lay flat and stare at the ceiling. She tried to ignore the sting behind her eyes, the pounding in her head, the viselike tightness inside her chest.

Her father was right about one thing.

Life goes on.

4

One month later

"You're killing me!"

"Don't be a baby. Two more. Keep your legs up, abs tight. C'mon, Kendra."

"I. Hate. You," Kendra puffed. She would have glared at the six-foot son of a bitch who stood over her, but it would've taken too much energy. And she needed that to work the Pilates machine with the appropriately sadistic name the Reformer. Her muscles burned and trembled, and for a second, she honestly considered giving up. She wouldn't do it; she *couldn't* do it. She dug deep for her willpower, determinedly pulling her body forward, inch by sweaty inch, with the straps.

"You're the one who wanted to push yourself," Brian—a blond-haired, blue-eyed, amazing male specimen, otherwise known throughout the physical therapy department as the Terminator—reminded her cheerfully. "This is the big day, huh? Formal discharge."

"God!" Kendra groaned, releasing the straps with a rush of relief. For a second she lay there, limp and panting. Then Brian tossed a towel at her. It landed on her face. "I think I'm dead," she muttered, unmoving.

"You're remarkably healthy for a dead woman." He grinned.

Muscles aching, Kendra sat up and swept off the towel. As she used it to blot the sweat streaming down her face, she caught a glimpse of herself in one of the mirrored walls and grimaced. She didn't look healthy. She looked like a prisoner of war. Her dark eyes were too big in a face now gaunt and pale. The bandage that had swathed her head had been removed a week ago. Her scalp had been shaved for surgery, but a half inch of dark hair had grown in. Better, she supposed, than the bald look, but a far cry from the thick, straight mass that had been long enough to hit the small of her back.

She'd never considered herself a vain woman. But she discovered that she really, really liked having hair.

Turning away from her reflection, she stood on legs that were still wobbly from the aftereffects of the workout.

"How's our star pupil?" Annie asked as she pushed the wheelchair into the room.

"I'm getting discharged today. Do I really need that?" Kendra glanced at the wheelchair.

"Hospital policy." The nurse smiled brightly. "And after a session with the Terminator, I'd think you could use it."

"I hate that nickname," Brian grumbled good-naturedly, as he watched with sharp eyes as Kendra eased into the wheelchair, her movements slower and more careful than either one of them would've liked. Not in a million years would she have admitted it, but Kendra thought that Annie was probably right about the wheelchair.

"We'll get the kinks worked out with a good rubdown," he promised when he saw her wince.

"Not today, I'm afraid," Annie said. "She'll have to settle for a hot shower. Associate Director Leeds will be arriving shortly."

She wheeled Kendra toward the door. "I believe he's escorting you home, Agent Donovan."

"I'm looking forward to it."

"Don't think you're getting out of physical therapy so easily," Brian warned, as he walked with them down the hospital corridor. At the elevator, he leaned forward to push the button. "I'm scheduling you for three times a week on an outpatient basis."

Kendra smiled at him as the elevator doors opened and Annie efficiently swung the wheelchair around, backing into the empty car. "You really shouldn't worry about being called the Terminator, Brian. By the time we're finished with those physical therapy sessions, I'll have come up with a few more nicknames for you."

Kendra felt halfway human after the hot shower. And she felt nearly human by the time she dressed for the first time in more than two months in something other than hospital-issued cotton gowns or T-shirts and sweats. Since the clothes—black sweater, khaki trousers, serviceable cotton panties and bra, black socks, and brown loafers—were her own, somebody had obviously been to her apartment in Mount Pleasant, Virginia. The makeup case tucked into the overnight bag made her think that the anonymous someone had been a woman.

The feminine tricks inside the makeup case couldn't quite erase the time she'd spent in the hospital. Still, she felt better when she swiped her mouth with a raspberry lip gloss and dusted her high cheekbones, which jutted out too sharply, with a bronze powder that was supposed to make her look sun-kissed. It fell short of the mark, she thought ruefully.

Stepping out of the tiny bathroom, she gave a start when she saw Phillip Leeds standing beside the window, staring outside.

He swung around, his eyes running over her in quick appraisal. "You're looking much better, Agent Donovan."

Self-consciously she put a hand up to her severely short hair. "I . . . thank you, sir. I'll be glad to go home."

"You'll be on medical leave until Dr. Campbell signs off on you returning to active duty at the Bureau. But we'll be looking forward to getting you back. We've missed you."

She doubted that. Other than Leeds and the top brass, she hadn't had any visitors from the Bureau. They'd sent her a bouquet, wilting on the built-in dresser, and a card. For the first time, Kendra was struck by how solitary her life had become. She'd always been an outsider (*a freak*). But ambition to prove herself, to make a life beyond her parents' prepackaged, narrow expectations had left her with few friends.

She moved to the small bag that had come with her street clothes, and stuffed her few personal items into it. Five books. Three magazines. She left the newspapers.

"You know that you'll have to talk to someone."

She glanced up at Leeds, not pretending to misunderstand. "You mean a shrink."

"I don't think they like that term."

"Then we're even. I don't like shrinks."

"Agent Donovan . . ."

"I'm fine." She closed the bag and was grateful when Annie arrived, pushing the wheelchair through the door.

She gave Kendra a wink and patted the back of the wheelchair. "Hop on, Agent Donovan."

Gingerly, Kendra sat down in the wheelchair, putting her bag on her lap. She summoned a smile for Leeds. "I'm fine. And you didn't have to come all this way to escort me home. I could've managed."

"That I have no doubt about. But I think I already told you that you're a valuable member of our team, Special Agent Donovan." Deliberately, he kept his tone light. He was grateful when the nurse chimed in, either urging or ordering Kendra to keep on her diet and exercise program, and teasing her about somebody called the Terminator.

Dr. Campbell was waiting on the first floor and added his own encouragement, reminding Kendra about her physical therapy schedule as well as follow-up exams.

Kendra was relieved when she was finally able to get out of the wheelchair. Waving at the doctor and nurse, she walked over to Leeds's BMW. She still felt sore from that morning, but no longer shaky. And God, it felt good to be outside again. The sun lightened the sky to a brilliant blue, and the temperature, if she wasn't mistaken, was on the plus side of seventy. Not bad for early May.

She'd gone into the hospital in mid-March. More than two months of her life gone, vanished like a puff of smoke. That depressed her. But it could be worse, she supposed.

She could be dead.

Sighing, she slid into the passenger's seat. Her finger itched to buzz down the window. But that could wait. When she got back to her apartment, she'd sit out on her tiny balcony, with her face turned up to the sun. God knew she could use some color.

Right now, though, she had more important issues at hand. She waited until after Leeds had steered the car onto the I-495 before she turned to look at him. "So . . . what happened to Sir Jeremy Greene?"

Leeds's fingers tightened on the steering wheel. As far as tells went, it wasn't much—but then Leeds had always been good at Texas Hold 'em, Kendra thought.

"I don't think it would be appropriate to have this conversation now," he finally said, glancing over at her.

"I see. Then when?" She kept her tone cool and calm, but her heart began to accelerate. "When we get to my apartment? Tomorrow? Next week? Never?"

"Agent Donovan—"

But she was already shaking her head. "You know that you can't keep it a secret. You've done a good job keeping me isolated, but you know that as soon as I walk in my front door, I'll get on the Internet and I can find out any damn thing I want to about Jeremy Greene. It doesn't matter how deep it's buried, I'll find it."

Leeds sighed. She would, too. She was the reason the FBI—hell, the U.S. government, not to mention MI5—had finally managed to get their hooks into the bastard.

"It wouldn't require much digging. You're not going to like it," he warned.

"No shit." It was her turn to sigh. "Sorry. I'm a little . . . wound up."

Leeds only nodded, a frown settling on his face as he maneuvered the BMW through traffic. Kendra wondered if he was stalling, and again felt an uneasy sensation, like static electricity, pop along the surface of her skin. If she were more superstitious, she'd have called it a premonition.

"Sir Jeremy was shot . . . in the arm. Barely a scratch, really."

"How . . . unfortunate."

"They patched him up quickly, and brought him to Washington. Very few people know about it. Only top officials . . . and now you."

Kendra stared at him. "How's that possible? Everyone who was involved in the operation knows that he was there that day. They'd know we got him."

"Not necessarily. They know we picked him up. But Sir Jeremy immediately got word to his lawyers. The U.S. government didn't want the political firestorm. He's a British national. He's a billionaire. It's plausible."

"Plausible," Kendra said slowly. "But not true."

"No. We had him a little longer than anyone realizes. And he agreed to flip."

"Flip . . ." Her mouth tightened. She'd known that was their original intention. Hell, she'd argued for it. But that was before.

"I see. We're working with the goddamn bastard who's responsible for members of my team being killed?" Despite her best efforts, her voice rose. She wanted to strike out at something, but ended up curling her fingers into her palms.

"We're not working with him," Leeds disagreed. "He works for *us*."

"Where?"

Leeds frowned. "Where?"

"Where's he working for us?" she demanded sharply. "He's not behind bars, is he? Not feeding us information about his clients from a military fucking prison, is he?"

"No, of course not."

"We've let him go back to his life, haven't we?" This time she couldn't stop herself. She slapped the console. "Goddamn it! I was *there!* I *saw* Daniel's head blown off right in front of my eyes! Allan . . ." Her breath hitched, and she struggled against losing control. "God, Allan had a wife . . . they'd just gotten married," she whispered, anger draining away and leaving only an unsettling despair. "So many died . . . and we're letting that asshole go free."

"He's not free. Not technically." He shot her a frustrated look. "Shit, I don't like this any more than you do, Agent Donovan. But it's not like you didn't know this would happen. Sometimes we need to get involved with a few bad guys to take down someone even worse."

"Like when we helped Osama bin Laden fight against the Soviets in Afghanistan?"

Leeds's jaw tightened at the cutting tone, and he focused on his driving. Equally silent, Kendra folded her arms across her chest and stared out the window. For the next five minutes, the only sound was the traffic outside and the hum of wheels against asphalt. He let out a sigh when he let up on the accelerator, moving the BMW off the expressway into the Mount Pleasant area.

He snuck a glance at his silent passenger. "Look, I hate that it looks as though the bastard's life is the same," he finally said in a much quieter tone. "But he's been working with us to set up several undercover stings. His intel has been good. The brass is pleased."

"Oh, well. I guess that makes it all right, then."

"Kendra—"

"I understand." The heat that had blasted him only seconds before was gone. Her words could have been chipped out of ice. Oddly, Leeds preferred the hot anger. He shot her a wary look, met the onyx eyes. The expression in them wasn't cold, exactly. But he couldn't read it, either.

"I wasn't supposed to talk to you about Greene."

"You know I would've found out."

Leeds steered the car into the lot outside her apartment complex and parked. "That's why I told you. I thought it would be better coming from me."

"Thanks. And thanks for the ride." She opened the door and slid out. "I can manage from here."

Before she could slam the door, he leaned over. "Kendra, you're not going to do anything stupid?"

She gave him a look. "I've been accused of a lot of things, sir, but never of being stupid."

"Reckless, then. Sir Jeremy Greene is in the hands of U.S. and British intelligence. They wouldn't look kindly on any quest for revenge that would have a negative impact on their operation."

She smiled, but it didn't ease the tension rising inside Leeds. "I can promise you that I would never go after Greene for revenge," Kendra said. "There, does that satisfy you?"

He searched her face. When the tension inside him didn't dissipate, he could only sigh. He couldn't pinpoint his anxiety, but there was something in the very stillness of her expression. Or maybe it was the smile . . .

Whatever it was, he could hardly challenge her. Instead, he nodded. "Okay. I'll call you tomorrow."

Shutting the door, Kendra clutched her bag, and stepped back. She waited as the BMW drove down the lane, disappearing from sight. Only then did she drop her smile.

She would keep her promise. She wouldn't go after Greene for revenge.

But she hadn't said anything about going after him for justice.

5

Three months later

"You're a dead woman, Kendra."

"I . . . don't . . . think . . . so . . ." It wasn't easy to push the words out, since the man had his sinewy arm wrapped tightly around her throat. His breath puffed in her ear. She managed to turn her head so her windpipe wasn't crushed, and put all her power behind an elbow jab. The puff in her ear became a grunt. His hold loosened, only fractionally, but she pressed her advantage, grabbing the thick wrist, twisting. Within seconds, she'd reversed positions, pivoting and taking him down. She could've taken him out, with her knee hovering above a sensitive area.

He knew it, too. His eyes widened. "Have mercy!"

She grinned and released him, letting him flop back on the mat. "You're lucky I'm feeling generous, Nate."

His broad chest rose and fell. "Yeah. Generous."

Feeling winded herself, Kendra snatched the towel off a chair and swiped it against her sweaty face. It'd been a long process, but she was finally feeling like her old self. She'd regained the weight she'd lost in the hospital, and her body felt limber and strong. Her hair had even grown out long enough for her to have it styled with blunt cut bangs and a sleek bob that curved an inch below her jaw.

She was almost ready.

The errant thought brought her up short, chest tightening like she was having an asthma attack.

"Hey." Nate pushed himself to his feet, his eyes on her face. "What's wrong? You're looking pale, even for a white girl."

"I'm fine." She began stretching. "I took you down, didn't I?"

"That's only because you're tricky." Snatching another hand towel, he mopped up the sweat from his gleaming ebony skin. "When are you going back to the Bureau?"

Kendra's hesitation was so slight, he might not have noticed it if he hadn't been watching so closely. Her face went carefully blank. "Soon."

"You're ready."

She ignored him as she went through the stretching routine followed by some intricate yoga moves. After a moment, he joined her. "You know, several of my clients are in the Bureau. Sam White mentioned you the other day, said you've practically fallen off the grid."

"Please. Phillip Leeds was at my door just the other day." She didn't mention that he'd shown up at her door because she'd let six of his calls go straight to voice mail. She was tired of him urging her to see a psychiatrist.

"Asking you to come back?"

She straightened out of the warrior position. "He wants me back, yes. There's a case in Florida. Someone's been killing college girls."

"I saw that on the news." He followed her as she walked to the locker room. "They need you, Kendra."

"And I need time." She opened up the door to the locker room, hesitating on the threshold. "The FBI has other profilers, Nate. They can do the job without me."

He frowned. "You sound like you're never going back."

"Of course, I'm going back," she replied easily, tossing him a smile over her shoulder. "Where else would I go?"

It was a lie, but she told it convincingly. Maybe she was being paranoid, but she didn't trust Nate's sudden interest in her career or future with the FBI. She certainly had no intention of telling him that she'd never go back to the Bureau. Hell, if everything worked out as planned, they wouldn't want her, either—except in prison or dead.

After showering, Kendra changed back into her pale green T-shirt, stonewashed Levi's, and Nike cross-trainers. Declining the cup of coffee Nate suggested, she swung out of the gym. She kept her pace unhurried as she walked down the sidewalk, gym bag over her shoulder, maneuvering between pedestrians. Every once in a while, she pretended to window-shop, using the glass as a mirror to scan the crowds for a possible tail. Phillip Leeds, she knew, was becoming nervous that she was avoiding returning to active duty. He couldn't force her, of course. Being shot in the head and severely wounded had an upside, she decided wryly. It had given her time to plan.

The government had a shocking amount of eyes and ears everywhere, but she'd been careful. She'd paid cash for a new laptop and burn phone. It had taken her a long time to shuffle funds around. Most Americans didn't realize the IRS tracked deposits around or above ten thousand dollars. To prevent any IRS triggers, Kendra made sure to stagger the times and amounts of money she wired to the accounts in the Cayman Islands and Switzerland that she'd set up under bogus corporations.

She'd also set up several new identities. The first would be Marie Boulanger. Under that name, she'd rented a charming cottage in the Cote d'Azur for the next six months. Of course, she had no intention of staying there or continuing the identity of Marie Boulanger. Instead, she'd slip into the skin of Angelica Lombardi, and settle into life in Rome for a couple of months at least. She had an aptitude for languages: Spanish, Italian, French, Portuguese. That, she supposed, she had her parents to thank for, and those endless lessons they'd structured her life around. She'd be able to keep a low profile in Europe.

Unlike Sir Jeremy Greene.

The anger rose swiftly inside her, choking her. She'd looked him up, of course. It had taken her two seconds to find him, often photographed with some waif-thin model young enough to be his granddaughter. The latest report was that he'd be attending a fancy-dress ball at some English castle.

It enraged Kendra. He may be feeding Uncle Sam vital intelligence—or so they believed—but he deserved to be in hell.

She had every intention of putting him there.

Kendra left her cell phone in her gym locker, and her car in the parking lot. She took a bus to the other side of the city, getting off six blocks from her actual destination. The Mexican Cantina was crowded with afternoon diners and smelled of frying onions and something spicy. The hostess, a young woman wearing traditional-style dress, smiled at her. "Only one?" she asked as she reached for a plastic menu.

"What I want isn't on the menu. *¿Dónde está* Lupe?"

The woman shot her a startled look, and then glanced around nervously. "You want to meet my uncle?"

"I've already met him. I have an appointment. Tell him Kendra's waiting."

"Un momento, por favor," the woman said, and disappeared into the kitchen.

Kendra studied the garish paintings on the wall. The cheerful Mexican music blended with the noise of the diners who'd come in for happy hour. The air-conditioning felt good after her six-block walk.

The woman returned, and smiled, although it didn't quite reach her eyes, which remained uneasy. *"Por favor, me sigue."*

"Gracias." Kendra followed the woman through the kitchen, earning quick looks from the men standing around steaming kettles on the stove. They exited the kitchen, stepping outside onto a small cement area. Flies buzzed around trash bins that reeked of rotting food. The woman crossed to a corrugated metal shack, and motioned to the door. *"El tío Lupe le espera adentro."*

Kendra nodded and watched the woman hurry back into the restaurant. She gave the tin door a quick rap before opening it and stepping inside. The room was long and narrow, the walls filled with shelves of canned food. At the back of the room, a fat man sat behind a desk, smoking a cigar that left a pearly haze hanging in the already gloomy interior. He was talking on the phone in rapid-fire Spanish. Seeing her, he gestured her over. *"Muy bueno. Bueno. Usted ha hecho bien, Jesus. Adios."* He cradled the receiver and smiled. It was a crocodile smile that revealed crooked teeth. "Senorita, you look as beautiful as the last time we met. Sit. Sit."

She remained standing. "This isn't a social visit, Lupe. You have something for me."

"Ah. Always business. You are too young and too pretty to be always business."

Kendra said nothing. He met her stare for a few speculative moments, then sighed. Opening his desk drawer, he yanked out a dirty manila envelope and tossed it toward her. "This is what you want, *si?"*

Kendra undid the clasp, and dumped the contents on the desk. There were six passports in all. She carefully inspected each one. The only thing missing was her photograph and identification. She'd take care of that later. "You do good work, Lupe."

"*Gracias.*" He inclined his head, his second chin quivering. "But not free work, senorita."

"Of course not." Sliding her gym bag off her shoulder, Kendra reached inside and took out a rolled athletic sock. She handed it to him, and gathered the passports as he hurriedly peeled back the sock to reveal a thick roll of bills. He gave a little laugh, and began counting. Kendra shoved the manila envelope inside her gym bag. Her fingers grazed the gun inside. She decided to keep her hand exactly where it was until she was out on the street again. The transaction was going smoothly, but it was best not to get complacent. "*Gracias* and adios, señor." She backed toward the door, never taking her eyes off the man sitting behind the desk.

"*Un momento,* senorita." He shot her a quizzical look. "A question, *por favor.*"

"I was under the impression you didn't ask unnecessary questions."

"*Si.* But it is most unusual, senorita. Why didn't you want me to put in your photo? Your identification?"

"Simple, Lupe. You can't tell someone what you don't know."

"You are *muy* careful *mujer.*"

"I am a careful woman. And you, Señor Lupe, will thank me, if anyone comes seeking answers you can't give."

He looked amused. "Who do you expect to come after you, senorita? The mob?"

"No." She pushed open the door, letting the afternoon sunlight spill into the gloomy interior. "The United States government. FBI. Maybe CIA, NSA, or Homeland Security."

The smile vanished, and for the first time fear flashed in his small eyes. "*La madre santa de Dios,*" he whispered. "*Qué has hecho?*"

This time she was the one with the crocodile smile. "I haven't done anything, señor. Yet."

6

Two days later

Kendra took the train to New York City and a cab to JFK, and flew out as French citizen Marie Boulanger. As the Boeing 747 winged gracefully over the darkening blue of the Atlantic, she tried to relax, tried not to think about everything she was leaving—and what she was planning to do. The internal battle sent her stomach churning, and had her skin feeling alternatively hot and dry, then cold and clammy. She reached for her purse, pulling out a small plastic bottle of aspirin. Popping the lid, she swallowed two tablets, swigging them down with the bottled water she'd purchased after the security check.

"Headache?" the woman next to her inquired with a sympathetic nod.

Kendra looked at her, careful to keep her expression confused. *"Je suis désolé. Qu'avez-vous dit?"*

"Oh. Oh, I'm sorry. I don't speak French." The woman gave her an embarrassed smile, hurriedly retreating behind the *People* magazine she'd been reading.

Kendra felt a twinge of remorse, but had decided that the best way to discourage conversation would be to pretend not to understand English. In a plane full of Americans, she knew she had a better than decent chance of sitting next to someone who wouldn't be able to converse in French.

Of course, she had her second line of defense, the iPod, which she now pulled out of her purse. Inserting the earbuds, she closed her eyes and forced her body, if not her mind, to relax as she listened to Bonnie Raitt's bluesy voice sing slyly about giving someone something to talk about.

She'd planned well, she reminded herself. Yesterday, she'd called Leeds to tell him that she would be returning to the Bureau in a week. She'd even scheduled an appointment with the FBI shrink. And if that didn't take off the heat, she'd made damn sure that if they began looking for her too soon, the trail would lead to Mexico.

She'd bought herself a week, maybe two. But all she needed was forty-eight hours.

Her stomach, which had been settling, lurched up again.

Forty-eight hours, and her life would change forever.

Kendra had always considered herself sophisticated and well-traveled, but her breath caught in her throat at her first sighting of Aldridge Castle. Maybe it was the contrast of the velvety green lawn and the craggy gray rock of the ancient fortress beneath silky blue sky. Or maybe it was its shocking size. Hell, she'd been in towns smaller than the castle, with its raised central tower, uneven castellated chimneys, and turrets that stabbed into the heavens.

The original tower, she'd researched, dated back to the time of William the Conqueror. Throughout the centuries, a series of wings had been cobbled onto the original structure. The effect was moody and magnificent, pulsating with prestige and barely-leashed power.

A gravel road, pale as moon rock, cut across the huge park, which was shadowed with trees and topiary. The automobiles parked in a gleaming queue along the curb were a stark divider between past and present.

Carefully, Kendra wheeled the Volkswagen Golf she'd rented that morning onto the drive, hearing the crunch of pebbles as she found a parking space. If her fingers trembled a little when she shut off the ignition, she chose to ignore it. Just as she ignored the acrobatic butterflies that invaded her stomach.

Slinging her big purse over her shoulder, she made her way toward the crowd of people standing in front of the stone steps that led to the castle's entrance hall. Most were young. Many, she knew, were professional actors. A nomadic group, which suited her purpose very well.

A ruthlessly efficient-looking woman was pacing the stone steps. Holding a clipboard in one hand, she pointed her pen like a stiletto in the other, the object of her ire being a man standing in the front row.

"Mark, you bloody chav, I told you to shave that silly patch on your chin." Disapproval rang in her voice. "You're to play a fucking footman—not some gangster rapper." She dropped her hand, tucking the clipboard under her arm and clapping briskly. "Oy, everybody! We've got three hours to get dressed and into our roles before the toffs arrive. They want realism! Now, follow the signs to the servant's hall, and get dressed!"

Kendra waited until the throng dispersed. The woman glanced up as she approached, scowling. "Who are you?"

"Cassie Brown," Kendra lied. "I'm sorry I'm late—"

"Those gits! I *told* them not to send me anyone with short hair." Scowl deepening, the woman began tapping the clipboard with her pen. "We need Sherlock Holmes—not Katie Holmes!"

"I thought this was a costume party for the early 1800s."

"Yes. What of it?"

"Sherlock Holmes wasn't created until the late nineteenth century."

"Well, aren't you bloody clever. And a Yank, too." Disgust replaced anger. She stopped tapping and rolled her eyes. "What were they thinking? They say they want realism, then they send me an American who looks like a bloody flapper. Oh, fuck it!" She gave a disgruntled shrug, and flipped through several sheets attached to the clipboard. "We're still short on lady's maids." Briskly, she scribbled a note and tore off a slip of paper, handing it to Kendra. She pointed toward the departing crowd. "Follow that lot there to the servant's hall. Heaven knows what they're going to do about your hair. We're trying to create a *mood*. Stark Productions should *never* have given you the assignment."

Before the woman could change her mind, Kendra hurriedly joined the others trudging along the path. A young woman with long red hair tossed her a sympathetic look. "I couldn't help but overhear. Don't let that old cow bother you. You look fab. I've been wanting to get my hair styled like that for ages."

Kendra lifted a hand to her hair, which swung in a thick ebony sheet below her jawline. Her mouth tightened involuntarily as her mind flashed to the reason she had this particular style.

"I shouldn't worry about it, if I were you," the girl continued, misunderstanding her expression. "Mrs. Peters has been nattering on all morning about our roles. She's been positively batty about it. But these wankers aren't coming for realism. They want to spend the weekend playing dress-up and getting smashed. They'll not care whether your hair is short or long. The men certainly won't. They'll be more interested in shagging you." She grinned at Kendra. "I'm Sally, by the way."

"Cassie."

"Are you an actress?"

"You could say that."

Sally didn't hear the irony. "Me, too. I've done the Shakespeare festivals. You Yanks *love* the Bard. And I was a tavern wench last summer at Littlecote House."

That remark drew the attention of one of the young men walking ahead of them. Turning, he gave Sally a lascivious grin. "Ah, Sally me girl, you can *serve* me anytime!"

"Cheeky bloke!" Sally laughed, and did a couple of skips forward to punch him good-naturedly on the arm. "This idiot's Ian, Cassie. And don't believe a word he says. What's your role here anyway?" She looked at him. "Court jester?"

"You're a saucy wench!" Ian looked over at Kendra. "American, eh? Hollywood? You've got the bone structure for the big screen, to be sure."

"Watch out, Cassie. Ian thinks he's bloody James Bond." This time Ian was the one to give her a playful swat.

With half a smile, Kendra listened as they traded barbs. Others within earshot joined in, their banter so easygoing that Kendra suspected they'd known each other before this particular job. It was nice . . . and, just for a moment, envy speared through her. They were a team, she realized.

She understood what it was like to be part of a team, although never with this lighthearted sense of fun. The stakes had always been too high. Catching serial killers, pedophiles, or terrorists was simply not conducive to a carefree atmosphere. The humor she was familiar with tended to be of the gallows variety, cynical and sarcastic.

A din of at least a dozen voices reached them as they entered the castle, growing louder as they moved down the wide corridor and through arched doorways. Here was the source of the noise: an enormous room with high ceilings and a fireplace that was big enough to roast a full-size boar. That should've been the focal point, but today it was a mere afterthought in the whirling dervish of activity. Every surface, including the long pine table, was taken up by boxes and piles of clothing.

It was a little like being backstage at a Broadway production, Kendra supposed. Organized chaos. Personnel from Stark Productions had divvied up the space into designated sections: Lady's Maid, Valet, Housemaid, Footman, Scullery Maid, and something called a tweeny.

As Sally bounced over to the line for Scullery Maids, Kendra joined the one for Lady's Maids, handing the woman the slip of paper she'd been given. Once again she was subjected to a measuring stare.

"The hair ain't right."

"So I've been told."

The woman shrugged. "Size eight, right?"

Kendra did the size conversion in her head, and nodded. The woman shoved a bundle of clothes at her.

"Shoe?"

"Seven—ah, I mean, four-and-a-half."

The woman pulled out a pair of ugly black half boots from a box. "You can change in the room down the hall. Third door on the right."

At least a dozen women, in varying states of undress, were already in the room, which had been converted into a women's locker room. Scanning the high, white walls, Kendra wondered at its original purpose.

"Isn't this exciting?" said Sally as she came up behind Kendra. She put her bundled clothes down on the bench and began stripping. "When I played a tavern wench, I could at least wear my own knickers," she remarked conversationally, lifting a shapely leg to tug on black wool tights, followed by a sturdy garter. "These drawers don't even have a crotch. Might as well go starkers."

Kendra surveyed the undergarments she'd been given. "They weren't kidding about authenticity, were they?"

Sally giggled and pointed at the simple, shapeless white linen garment that bore a passing resemblance to a thin nightgown. "That's a shift. And that," she moved her finger to the rectangular scrap of fabric with a single string attached, "is called a short stay. It's worn over the shift. Sort of like a bra."

"Hmm. What's this?" Kendra picked up a long piece of fabric that resembled a belt for a robe, but it had two pouches sewn onto it.

"Pockets. You tie the belt around your waist. Under your gown. There's slits in the skirt so you can reach into the pocket . . . See?" Sally demonstrated. It looked like a feminine version of a workman's tool belt. "Did you know that back in the day, pockets were considered sexy? Any woman showing off her pockets would've been considered a slut."

"I guess I'll keep my pockets to myself."

Kendra stowed her purse beneath the bench, and stripped off her shirt. Sally was lacing up her half boots, but stilled. "Holy God. What happened?"

"What? Oh." Kendra realized that the other woman was staring at the puckered scars on her leg, arm, and torso. Self-conscious, she hurriedly slipped into the old-fashioned garments. "Nothing. I was in an accident." She concentrated on figuring out how to tie the stay. Then she dragged on the muslin dress the color of an eggplant.

"Turn around so I can button you," Sally ordered, and after Kendra obediently presented her back, she nimbly did up the buttons. "I didn't mean to embarrass you. They look like . . . well, never mind. There!" She forced a jovial note in her voice. "You look a lovely lady's maid, Cassie. I, on the other hand, am a lowly scullery maid." She tied on her apron.

"You'd rather be a lady's maid?"

"I'd rather be a *Lady*!" Sally laughed. "I wonder how many of the toffs will be sneaking into someone else's bedroom for a little slap and tickle tonight?"

"You're such a romantic," Kendra said dryly.

"This is a Regency house party, Cassie. That's what they *did*! Have you got your room assignment yet?"

"Room assignment?" Kendra tugged on her stockings and garters before picking up the half boots.

"Well, you won't have your own room. You may be an upper servant, but you're still a servant," she grinned. "I noticed you didn't bring any luggage with you. If you need any help collecting it from the boot of your car, I'm sure Ian will volunteer."

Kendra's fingers stilled briefly in tying her shoes. "Thanks, that's very thoughtful of Ian. But I can handle it." Of course, she had no intention of staying the night. Once she accomplished her mission, she would disappear. It was imperative that she be gone before the police arrived. "I want to look around first."

"Be careful that Mrs. Peters doesn't catch you in the private rooms. You missed it, but she lectured us nearly an hour on how bleeding old and priceless everything is."

Kendra stood up, forcing a smile. "I promise to be careful."

At least here she could tell the truth. She planned to be very careful.

And she wasn't talking about Mrs. Peters.

More than four hundred guests mingled beneath the blazing chandeliers in the grand ballroom. At another time, Kendra would have enjoyed the experience, watching the crowd that included some of the world's most famous faces, wearing fashions befitting the early nineteenth century. They almost looked like they could've stepped out of the pages of a history book. Almost. If you ignored the tattoos and body piercings—most of which were sported by women.

"Authentic, my ass," she muttered under her breath.

Her eyes focused on the man across the room.

Sir Jeremy Greene.

His hair gleamed like polished silver in the room's soft light. His patrician features looked at least a decade younger than his sixty-one years, thanks to a cosmetic surgeon's careful scalpel, the judicious use of Botox, and the latest collagen fillers. His body, beneath evening attire that vaguely resembled a tuxedo, albeit with knee breeches, was trim and still fairly toned, credit, no doubt, to his membership in one of the most exclusive fitness clubs in London.

As she watched, he lifted the delicate crystal flute to his lips, drinking champagne that probably cost a week's salary of one of the lowly employees at Greenway International. Once again, Kendra felt the molten rage rise within her. Damn him. He was chatting, smiling, *laughing*. This man, this monster, who was responsible for so much destruction.

The anger felt good. *Cathartic*. It rubbed away some of the gnawing anxiety that had been building all day in the pit of her stomach.

It was time.

Kendra drew out the note from her pocket and glanced around. A footman was standing off to the side, observing the guests much as she had been.

Summoning a smile, she walked over to him. "Excuse me," she began, and was astonished when he flicked her a cold look before turning on his heel and stalking off.

"Asshole," she muttered under her breath, staring after him. She shook her head and scanned the room again, relieved when she spotted Ian, decked out in a similar wig and royal blue footmen finery, weaving his way through the guests, clutching a tray filled with empty champagne glasses. She intercepted him at the Carrara marble columns near the double doors.

"Ian? Hey."

His eyes swiveled in her direction, and he grinned. "Cassie. What're you doing here? I thought lady's maids were confined upstairs."

"I'm on a mission." She called on every ounce of her latent acting ability to infuse her voice with a lightness she was far from feeling. "One of the . . . er, *ladies* has an interest in a certain gentleman." She managed a chuckle. "Sir Jeremy Greene. Do you know him?"

"Cassie, *everyone* in Great Britain knows Sir Jeremy Greene."

That was probably true. They just didn't know *what* he was.

"Well, she wants this note passed to him discreetly—*very* discreetly, since she happens to be married."

"Really?" Ian's eyes gleamed with masculine interest. "Who is she?"

"My lips are sealed, but you've probably seen her in the movies." That seemed ambiguous enough. Kendra didn't want to name names in case the actress in question happened to be standing next to Sir Jeremy when Ian delivered the note. Better to be vague. "She wants to meet him in the study."

Ian frowned. "The study? That's in the old part of the castle, isn't it? We're not supposed to go there. I don't think the toffs are even supposed to go there. It's been cordoned off."

"I think privacy is what she's looking for."

"Guess it's none of my business where this lot wants to shag," he shrugged, reaching for the note. "Let me get a fresh tray of drinks, and I'll deliver it."

"Discreetly," she warned.

He grinned, nodding, and moved away. Kendra waited a moment before making her own exit from the ballroom. She dodged playacting servants rushing up and down the servants' stairs, and retrieved her purse from the locker room.

Earlier, she'd done a quick reconnaissance of the castle's rooms, based on her Internet research. She'd selected the study in the oldest part of the castle for two reasons. One, like Ian had said, it was off-limits. Whoever owned or ran the castle (probably England's National Trust) had roped that section off to discourage guests from traipsing into the area.

And, second, the room boasted a secret passageway.

In truth, that wasn't uncommon in the older, historic households throughout Great Britain. The country had a long, bloody history filled with political intrigue and religious persecution. Priest holes and secret passageways had come in handy for many of England's aristocrats. And, if anything went wrong, it might come in handy for her.

Kendra approached the velvet rope that cordoned off the private area, shooting a furtive glance around before ducking under it. Despite her best efforts, her heart began to race as she moved down the corridor.

This far away from the party, the castle was silent. The only noise was the whisper of her skirt and muffled footsteps as she walked the length of the burgundy and brown hall runner. The rug looked old—but then again, so did everything else in the castle. Still, she knew this section was older by centuries. If a castle had a heart, this would be it. These cold stone walls had been silent witnesses to both birth and bloodshed. It was a moody thought for a moody atmosphere. Adding to it were wall sconces, carefully spaced and cleverly designed to look like flickering candles, making shadows leap and dance.

Kendra suppressed a shiver. Even though she told herself that she was being fanciful, she was still relieved when she arrived at the door of the study. It had been locked earlier, and she'd made sure that she'd locked it again when she left the room two hours ago. Better to be safe than sorry.

Her heart began to hammer in her chest, so loud that the uneasy staccato filled her eardrums, but her hands were steady as she reached into her purse and withdrew two thin wires. Lock-picking wasn't a skill one learned at Quantico, but she'd studied it when she'd tried to get into the head of a perp who'd been entering homes in the middle of the night.

She held her breath as she worked the wires, then let it out in a rush of satisfaction as the tumblers fell into place. It had taken less than a minute, much less time than when she'd first entered the room. She dropped the wires back into her bag and slipped through the door, switching on the lights—more cleverly designed wall sconces.

She looked around. Nothing had changed, she thought. No one had entered this room since she'd been there earlier. The claret, in its cut crystal decanter, was exactly where she'd placed it on the elegant sideboard.

It was an interesting room. Octagonal in shape, it had high walls paneled in mahogany and papered in green silk, the same dark hue as the velvet-upholstered furnishings around the room. There was a fireplace here, too, as big as the one in the servant's hall, but the mantelpiece was more ornate, carved in a neoclassical design. Above it was an elaborately framed oil painting depicting a woman and child dressed in what looked to be late eighteenth-century garb. On the opposite wall were Grecian fitted bookcases, flanked by two breast-high Chinese vases with a blue dragon motif against a pearly white background. The mahogany desk—Chippendale, if she wasn't mistaken—was positioned in front of an enormous medieval-looking tapestry embroidered with a hunting scene. Behind the material, cunningly hidden in the wall's paneling, was a door.

She'd studied it earlier, had found the mechanism that sprang the lock. Behind the door was a claustrophobic space and stone stairs that spiraled upward. The steps led to a large room with enormous mullion-paned windows on the north and east wall. She didn't know what the space had been used for, because it was empty now, but there was another door that opened to the hallway not far from the servant's stairs that could take her all the way down to the ground level.

She'd take those stairs before anyone noticed Sir Jeremy had disappeared. Of course, he might not even be discovered until morning, and she'd be on the plane to Rome by then.

Kendra pulled her thoughts back to the present, and went to work. Opening her purse, she slipped on latex gloves and withdrew a small jar of face cream. Briskly, she unscrewed the lid, and fished in the cream for the small plastic packet, which contained exactly one gram of white powder.

Her heart thumped now for an entirely different reason. Her palms, inside the latex gloves, began to sweat. She wanted to be calm, but there was something terrifying about handling one of the most deadly toxins known to mankind. Ricin. One fourth of a teaspoon, and it could wipe out a population of 36,000.

She didn't want to think what it would do to one man.

Cautiously, Kendra tapped out the white powder into the Waterford crystal wineglass she'd brought. Her hands trembled only slightly as she lifted the decanter and poured the claret into the glass. In the soft light, it gleamed like blood.

She put the glass and decanter on the silver tray, and stepped back. Only then did she realize she'd been holding her breath.

She let it out and took a few minutes to regulate her breathing before stripping off the latex gloves, putting them into her purse. She glanced at the marble and bronze clock on the mantel. In ten minutes, Sir Jeremy Greene would arrive, believing he'd be rendezvousing with a mysterious starlet.

There was no doubt in Kendra's mind that he would come. She'd studied him. *Profiled* him. Even though he already had a mistress—a beautiful young Italian model who'd accompanied him here—he wouldn't be able to resist the coy invitation of another. That was his pattern. And when he came, she'd serve him the claret. It would only take one sip before the effects of the poison would shut down his system and he'd collapse to the floor with multiple organ failure.

Imagining it, she felt a little sick, and wondered suddenly if she could go through with the plan. Then she heard approaching footsteps.

Too late to reconsider.

She drew in a steadying breath, and tried to reassure herself that what happened next was justice. And once it was meted out, there'd be no turning back.

The door, only partially closed, swung open. From her position, she could see Sir Jeremy's hand, slim and elegant, wrapped around the doorknob. Kendra straightened, forcing her expression into one of subservience.

Sir Jeremy paused, and Kendra knew a moment of confusion when he took a step back from the door. Then she heard it. More footsteps.

Kendra froze. Had Sir Jeremy's mistress followed him, suspecting his infidelity? Her eyes cut to the glass of wine. *Crap.* The idiot might have bad taste in men, but she didn't deserve to die. She'd have to abandon her plan after all.

"What are you doing here?" Sir Jeremy said, his voice sharp and too loud in the silence of the hallway.

"Our last shipment was confiscated by the DEA." The other voice was lower, masculine and faintly accented.

"I heard. You should be more careful." Sir Jeremy's tone was dismissive.

"We were careful. Our sources tell us that somebody talked."

"What? Who—What the bloody hell do you think you're doing?" Greene's voice rose. "Are you *mad*?"

There was a strange *ppfftt*ing sound, and Kendra nearly jumped out of her skin when the door suddenly flew inward, crashing against the wall. Shocked, she watched as Greene fell backward into the room, his features contorted into grooves of agony while his hands clutched at his chest. Blood seeped between his fingers. Even as her mind reeled at the implications, she looked at the man in the doorway, recognizing him instantly: the unfriendly footman from the ballroom.

Their eyes met; time stood still. Then Kendra's gaze dropped to the gun he held deftly in his hand, a silencer elongating the barrel, and instinct took over. She raced toward the hidden passageway just as he pulled the trigger. Another *ppfftt*. The bullet scored the fireplace mantel, spraying chips of marble. Kendra made it to the tapestry as the blue-and-white Chinese vase shattered into a million pieces.

She'd left the panel door open a fraction—a foresight that now may have saved her life. Wrestling with the tapestry, she yanked the panel open and dove through. She pulled the door shut behind her, and was plunged into instant darkness.

It would take the killer less than a minute to figure out how to open the secret passageway, she calculated.

Oh God, oh God, oh God . . .

Blind, she stumbled up the stairs, using her hands to feel the way.

Fuck! Why was it so dark? She'd left the door at the top of the stairs open . . . but of course, it was evening, and whatever moonlight penetrated the windows in the upstairs room would be too weak to reach the stairwell. How could she have been so utterly stupid? She should've left the light on in the room above. But she hadn't anticipated this. Who'd have thought that she wouldn't be the only one after Sir Jeremy? What were the odds?

Listening for any sound that would warn her that the assassin had found the hidden doorway, Kendra attempted to hurry up the stairwell. But as much as she wanted to, she couldn't climb the narrow, twisting stairs fast enough. The darkness was too absolute. She couldn't even see her hands as they reached out to slide against the stairwell's cold, damp walls. One wrong move, and she'd fall, probably breaking her neck.

Would that be better than a bullet in the head?

She could hear her breath, coming in and out in fast pants. Her skin was oily with her own sweat, and there was a sour taste filling her mouth. *Fear.*

Her heart raced as she climbed upward, spiraled around. She was beginning to feel claustrophobic, like there was an enormous pressure on her chest, crushing her. How many more steps?

The air around her seemed to crackle with static electricity, and then suddenly the temperature plunged about twenty degrees. Even as her teeth began to chatter, and she struggled to make sense of that oddity, a wave of dizziness hit her, knocking her down a step.

Panic clawed like a trapped beast inside her chest, and stunningly, she felt pain. Like she was on fire. Her flesh was burning, the epidermis peeling away, layer by layer, exposing the subcutaneous tissue, then the stringy cords of muscle beneath, until that, too, was stripped, leaving only bone.

Screaming—surely, she must be screaming, even though she couldn't hear anything beyond the deafening roar in her ears—she fought against the squeezing darkness that was suddenly more solid, more substantial than she.

Oh, God . . .

She was caught in a sickening vertigo, around and around. Her skin melted like wax, then re-formed, reshaped, before dissolving again in a terrible spike of pain that was all-consuming. She no longer knew if the air was cold or hot, but she had the sensation that it was whipping across her face, slicing her like razor blades.

Then as abruptly as the phenomenon began, it was over. The agonizing pain vanished. Awareness came flooding back. She could feel the cold stone steps beneath her. The wetness of tears on her face. She was, she realized, curled into a fetal position.

Choking back a sob, she straightened and staggered to her feet. The darkness was no longer absolute. She could see her hands out in front of her, like white moths in the darkness, and knew an almost giddy relief. She hadn't disappeared after all.

Still, she couldn't shake the panic. What if the crazy darkness came back? What if the pain came back? *What if, what if, what if . . . ?*

She had to move. Up the stairs, to safety. Except . . .

Deep in her primordial brain she *knew* that whatever the hell she'd just encountered was waiting for her at the top of the stairs.

It was crazy. Irrational. She knew that, too, but still, she couldn't bring herself to go up. She'd have rather dealt with a thousand assassins than plunge back into that icy darkness.

Shuddering, she threw herself forward . . . and downward. With a ragged gasp, she launched herself at the closed door, banging her hands hysterically against the panel.

It was mere seconds, but it felt like hours before the door opened. Off balance, Kendra caught the surprised looks of the two men standing on the other side of the door. Then she was falling. Pain—natural this time—lanced upward from her knees as they hit the floor.

"Help . . . me . . ." she managed, her voice a croak. Then she collapsed completely, falling flat on her face.

7

1815

"Good God! Is she dead?"

Kendra felt hands on her shoulders, lifting, shifting. Pain rolled through her, followed by greasy nausea. Christ, her head hurt. She had a momentary, dizzying sensation of déjà vu as her eyes fluttered open. Above her, a man's face scowled down at her. Forest green eyes, fierce between spiky black lashes, beneath slashing black brows. She got the impression of sculpted cheekbones, a straight nose, a sensual twist of mouth, and square jaw that had a shallow dent in the chin before he moved away.

"She's alive," she heard the man murmur wryly.

"Thank God." That was said with a sigh of relief. Another face popped into her line of vision, far different from the other one. This man was older, late fifties, give or take, with a longish face, a rather bold nose, graying blond hair, and concerned pale blue eyes. "How is she, Alec?"

"I'm not an apothecary. Why don't you ask her? She appears to be awake."

The older man frowned. "Who is she? What was she doing in the passageway? What's your name, miss?"

Kendra blinked, lifting a hand to her aching head. What the hell had happened?

"Kendra," she whispered. "Kendra Donovan."

"What did she say?" That was from the good-looking, younger man.

"She said her name is Kendra Donovan." Kendra found her hand captured, gently stroked. "What happened, my dear? Alec, bring her something to drink."

There was a pause. Then a sigh, more irritable than angry. "Bloody hell."

Again, Kendra felt hands sliding awkwardly around her shoulders, lifting her into more of a sitting position. She stifled a groan as the movement sent more rockets exploding inside her head. Her body shuddered violently. Had she been shot again . . . ?

"Here, my dear. Drink this."

It was an effort, but she reached for the glass. Her fingers actually brushed the heavy lead crystal before she focused on the ruby liquid. Memory rushed back and her whole body jerked in horror. Her hand hit the glass in a reflexive action that sent it teetering out of the older man's hands. Its contents splashed, blood red against his white cravat and shirt, before tumbling with a spray of droplets to the floor.

"Son of a bitch!" Kendra jackknifed into a sitting position, staring at the stain in shock. Her heart leapt into her throat, pounding.

"Good God, what's wrong with the girl?" the older man asked, bewildered.

"Mayhap a strong aversion to drink?"

"Do not be amusing, Alec. She's trembling. She's obviously been ill. Look at her hair."

God, were they Stark Productions people? Kendra wondered frantically. She scrambled to her feet, her gaze swinging wildly around the room. A part of her accepted and understood that the footman with the silencer had disappeared. If she'd fulfilled her mission and given Sir Jeremy the ricin-laced claret, she would've disappeared, too. But what of Greene? He was dead. She was sure of it.

So where was the body?

Even as her eyes locked on the spot where the body had fallen, it began to dawn on her that there was something different about the room. The furniture seemed different, not only in appearance, but placement. Hadn't the sofa been positioned opposite the fireplace? Her confusion deepened when she realized that someone had lit a cozy fire in the fireplace, orange-yellow flames licking with a greedy pop and crackle against thick logs. *Jesus Christ, how long have I been unconscious?*

Her chest tightened as a fresh wave of panic crashed through her. She didn't really remember losing consciousness at all. She remembered the excruciating pain that seemed to peel the skin away from her bones. She remembered the crazy darkness. The dizziness. But she hadn't actually passed out, had she?

"My dear . . . ?"

She swung around to face the older man. He was dressed in a style similar to Sir Jeremy, except his jacket was a dark brown velvet. His shirt and neck cloth now carried the stain of wine. Her eyes darkened as she stared at it, remembering how the blood had bloomed on Greene's shirt in much the same way. Where was he? A dead man couldn't just vanish!

"Alec, she looks like she's going to faint again!"

"What do you want me to do about it? I don't have any vinaigrette on hand." Like the older man, this one had an upper-class British accent, although Kendra thought he looked, with his olive complexion and dark hair, more Italian or Spanish than English. Unlike the other man, he sounded dismissive.

He'd taken up a position by the fireplace, leaning languidly against the mantel. Yet Kendra got the impression that his pose was deceptive. His eyes remained sharp as he watched her, and there was a certain tension in the lean six-foot frame that made her return his regard with an equal dose of wariness.

Kendra dragged her eyes away from the intensity of his. "I'm not going to faint." A moment later, however, she wondered if that was true when her gaze fell on the candles flickering on the wall sconces, and she suffered another serious case of vertigo.

"My dear, perhaps you should sit . . ." The older man was speaking again, but she barely heard him through the dull roar in her ears. *Candles . . .*

Her eyes darted around the room, taking in the myriad candles flickering throughout the room. "How . . . ?" she wondered, and stepped toward the candelabra adorning the desk, the long tapers lit with more than a dozen dancing flames. "Candles," she whispered, reaching out even as her mind rebelled at what she was seeing. *Impossible . . .*

"What is she about?" the older man said.

"The odd creature appears fascinated by your candles, Duke."

She ignored the dry voice, too caught up in the mystery before her. How could somebody have replaced the cleverly designed electric bulbs with candles within the space of a few minutes? More importantly, *why* would anyone do it? It made no sense.

But there they were. They were real. Christ, she could feel the *heat* against her fingertips.

Suddenly she whirled around, and either instinct or fear propelled her forward to the fireplace. The green-eyed man straightened as she approached, gaze narrowing when she lifted her hands to touch the pristine mantel. *It's not possible,* she thought again. Her fingers shook as she traced the grooves cut into the unblemished marble. Closing her eyes, she could see the spray of stone chips from when the bullet scored the surface. Goddamnit, she hadn't imagined that! So . . . was she imagining this *now*? she wondered wildly, opening her eyes to meet the younger man's suspicious gaze.

"Miss Donovan, pray, sit down," the older man—Duke—urged. "You're not quite steady on your feet. Alec, we ought to ring for Mrs. Danbury."

"I, on the other hand, think you ought to ring for Mr. Kimble to inquire after this girl's character."

"She's ill, Alec. Anyone can see it."

For the first time in her life, Kendra felt as though her wits had completely deserted her. She couldn't wrap her mind around what she was seeing in front of her and link it to the reality of what she knew. Her breath hitched and seemed to shudder to a stop when her eyes fell on the two large Chinese vases. Not one, but *two* . . .

"It isn't possible . . ." she whispered, and her voice sounded faint and tinny to her own ears. It was as though she was walking underwater as she moved toward the vases, toward the vase that should not have been there. It had been shattered by the assassin's bullet, she *knew* it. She'd *seen* it with her own goddamn eyes! And yet the vase was standing before her, whole and unmarred.

She reached out to the porcelain, wanting—no, *needing*—to touch the smooth, glazed surface, to ascertain that it was not some bizarre figment of her imagination, but a hand snaked out to close over her wrist, preventing her fingertips from connecting. Shocked by the unexpected contact, her eyes flew to the man called Alec. She hadn't heard him move, but he was beside her now, his fingers on her wrist. His grasp wasn't punishing, but neither would she easily be able to break it.

"That is a very expensive, very rare vase, Miss Donovan, which you are about to paw." His voice was a low warning. "It's from the Ming Dynasty, which I don't expect you to understand. However, I can assure you, His Grace, as benevolent as he may be, would take a very dim view of having one of his heirlooms broken by careless hands."

For a second, Kendra could only gape at him, trying to organize her jumbled thoughts. *Who didn't know the Ming Dynasty, asshole?* she wanted to say, but couldn't formulate the words, even as her thoughts zipped off in another direction. Had someone replaced the vase, just as they had the lightbulbs? Stolen the body? That didn't make any sense.

This couldn't be real. It was an illusion. A trick of some kind.

Yet those strong and elegant fingers wrapped around her wrist *felt* real. The man attached to those fingers *looked* real.

She struggled against the coils of slippery fear that threatened to drag her under. Instinctively, she jerked against the man's viselike grip, but he only tightened his fingers. Suddenly both frightened and furious, she glared at him. "Let go, you son of a bitch. I don't know what you're trying to pull here, but I can still break your arm if I have to."

It was surprise—she saw it flash in the green eyes—as much as anything that loosened his grip, allowing her to snatch back her hand. Before he could retaliate, the older man was beside her, taking her arm and gently steering her to the sofa. "Here, now, you poor child. Sit down. She's shaking, Alec." His tone was reproachful.

"I . . . I wouldn't break the damn vase," Kendra muttered, sitting. She *was* shaking, she realized. And she was cold, so cold. Her teeth would be chattering any second.

"Of course not."

"For God's sake, Duke—it's a *Ming*. It's over two hundred years old! A face, no matter how comely, isn't worth losing such a treasure. She is a servant—and, I suspect, a thief."

"Alec!"

"Lady's maid," Kendra corrected automatically, and scowled at the green-eyed man. "I was hired as a lady's maid."

"Which Lady?"

"What?"

"For which Lady are you attending?"

"I . . ." She frowned. It had only been a role, but she'd been given a name. "Claire . . . or Clara." God, she couldn't *think!*

He slanted the other man a look. "She doesn't even know who she's been attending."

"And you don't even know your Ming Dynasty," she shot back, and felt the heat of anger warm over the core of ice developing inside her. It felt good. "Two hundred years old. More like over five hundred years old! The Ming Dynasty was from 1368 A.D. to 1644 A.D. That particular vase appears to be from the Jiajing Empire . . ." Her words trailed away when she realized that both men were staring at her like she'd grown two heads. Oh, God, she was babbling. She needed to get out of here.

"Who are you?" The younger man snapped out the question. "You're not English."

It was too late to pretend to be Marie Boulanger. "I'm from the United States."

"A bloody American." He sounded contemptuous.

"Oh, for God's sake, Alec, the war's over," the older man sighed. "The Treaty of Ghent was signed months ago."

Kendra blinked. "Oh, my God, you guys are taking your roles a bit too seriously, aren't you?" The realization almost made her laugh. The only thing preventing her was the cold dread whispering uneasily up her spine.

"Roles?"

The older man seemed genuinely baffled. Kendra clasped her hands together on her knees until the knuckles turned bone-white. She drew in a deep breath. "Look, I don't know what's going on, but enough is enough. I need to leave . . ." *Where was the damn body?* she wondered again. "I need to leave."

"You need to rest, Miss Donovan. Alec, could you please ring for Mrs. Danbury?"

"Duke, the chit says she wants to leave—"

"And I say she is too ill to leave." Up until that moment, Kendra would have sworn the younger man was in charge. But the steely note in the older man's voice had her hastily revising her earlier opinion. She slid a look at the other guy, who met her gaze with a scowl. But he didn't protest his friend's edict, striding toward the door. He pulled a cord in the wall, turning around to stare grimly back at her.

"Mrs. Danbury will take care of you, my dear."

Kendra switched her gaze to the man called Duke. "This is a joke, right? You're going to tell me this is all a joke."

There was a concerned frown behind his blue eyes. "I'm afraid I fail to see the humor, Miss Donovan."

Dammit, she'd *known* he was going say that. She shivered, because she was beginning to think the unthinkable, imagine the unimaginable. It was only when her fingers touched something smooth that she realized Duke was pressing a glass into her hand. He smiled. "You look like you need a restorative."

"And if you maintain your aversion to claret, please refrain from pouring it on His Grace," Alec said dryly. "That would be a waste of an excellent vintage."

Kendra ignored him, looking instead at the older gentleman.

"Thank you," she whispered, and this time she lifted the glass to her lips and drank. If it was poisoned . . . well, that would almost be preferable to this crazy situation, she decided. At least she'd understand it.

The claret burned smoothly down her throat. *It tastes real*, was all she could think as she sipped, and tried not to let her eyes dart to the candles that shouldn't be there, to the fireplace that should have a crater in it from the bullet, the vase that should be lying in shards.

"What were you doing in the passageway, Miss Donovan?" Alec demanded abruptly. He walked over to the decanter, poured himself another glass of claret. "If you are, as you claim, a lady's maid, pray, what were you doing in *there*?"

"I . . ." What could she say? Her stomach churned, and she had a momentary regret over drinking the claret. Not because it was poisoned, but because she thought she might disgrace herself by throwing up.

It was this damned situation. She didn't understand it. What was going on? Mind games? An illusion? *A delusion?* The last thought made her go cold with fear.

She glanced at the older man, but any hope that he'd rescue her from his friend's inquisition disappeared when she saw the interested light in the blue-gray eyes. What could she tell him? Nothing that made sense. In fact, the less said, the better. At least until she figured out what the hell was going on.

"I . . . got lost."

Alec snorted derisively, making no attempt to hide his disbelief. Duke's eyes sharpened, almost imperceptibly. He didn't believe her, either. She couldn't blame them.

"*How* did you get into the passageway?" Alec snapped out the question.

Kendra glanced at the tapestry that had been pushed aside upon her stunning exit from the passageway. The door had closed, its very existence once again hidden from view. There was no way she could've gotten "accidentally" inside the passageway. She knew it; they knew it.

She shook her head. "I don't remember."

If looks could kill, she thought as she caught Alec's gaze, all that'd be left of her would be a pile of smoking ash coming out of the ugly half boots. Her nerves tightened. She really wasn't up to a verbal battle, not until she had a chance to think this through. Relief rushed through her when someone knocked at the door, and a moment later a tall, thin woman wearing a black gown and white linen cap, swept in.

She dropped into a graceful curtsy. "Your Grace. My Lord." Except for that first glance, she didn't look at Kendra. "How may I assist you?"

Despite the old-fashioned gown and cap she wore, she reminded Kendra of a college professor she'd once had: cool, calm and, above all, competent.

"Mrs. Danbury, Miss Donovan seems to have gotten *lost* in the passageway," Alec commented, and there was no mistaking the disparaging note in his voice.

"Oh?" Mrs. Danbury turned to study Kendra with frosty gray eyes.

"She claims that she was hired as a lady's maid."

Mrs. Danbury opened her mouth, but before she could issue a denial, the other man said mildly, "I'm certain Mrs. Danbury knows this, Alec. While there may be quite a crush for Caro's house party, I have full confidence in Mrs. Danbury and Mr. Harding's control of the staff."

Put like that, Mrs. Danbury could only bow her head. "Thank you, Your Grace."

"Miss Donovan is feeling ill," he continued. "As the ladies have retired for the evening, Miss Donovan's services are no longer required. Perhaps you could escort her to her room?"

"Of course, Your Grace." The woman's skirts barely made a sound as she moved to the door. She glanced back at Kendra. "Miss Donovan?"

Kendra hesitated. She knew what was expected of her, knew she was being asked—no, ordered—to go with Mrs. Danbury. Anxious knots twisted her stomach as she weighed her options. She had none. She had no choice but to leave the room.

"I wish you good evening, Miss Donovan." The twinkle in the older man's s blue eyes was impossible to decipher.

"Good evening, Duke," she finally managed, and was already walking out the door so she didn't see the expressions that ranged from surprise to outrage flash in the eyes of the room's occupants. When she stepped out into the hall, she felt only a numb acceptance of the wall candles there.

"Miss Donovan, you will *never* address His Grace as Duke again," Mrs. Danbury said as soon as they were out of earshot of the study. "He is *Your* Grace, or the Duke of Aldridge, or sir. And you will curtsy when you leave a room with one of your betters. Is that understood?"

Betters? Kendra swallowed hard, but nodded. She ignored the look, bright with suspicion, that Mrs. Danbury slid in her direction. She needed to keep her mouth shut. Duke—*the* Duke—had given her a reprieve. No one was going to toss her out. Not yet, anyway.

She still had time to figure this crazy situation out.

Time . . .

Kendra shivered. That was the one question she'd deliberately not asked during the bizarre episode: time. The date, the month, *the year.* Because she was very afraid of the answer.

"She's a forward bit of baggage," Alec commented as he settled into a chair, sipping the claret with a frown.

The Duke—Albert Rutherford, the seventh Duke of Aldridge, and Alec's uncle—picked up the clay pipe he'd been packing with tobacco before the girl had begun banging on the hidden door. With a thoughtful expression, he lit a taper from the fire, carrying it to the pipe bowl. As he puffed, his eyes lifted to the oil painting above the fireplace, depicting a woman and child.

It had been twenty years, but the grief was still there. Sometimes it was as raw and fresh as the day it had first been inflicted. Other times, like now, it was a weary sort of pain, the sharpness dulled into a nostalgic ache.

Alec followed his uncle's line of vision to the painting of Aldridge's long-dead wife and child. Arabella had been a vision, both in life and captured in oil. Even though he'd been but a lad of twelve at the time of her death, Alec remembered her beauty, the black hair and brown eyes, her gregarious warmth.

The times he'd visited, his aunt and uncle's relationship had always struck him as idyllic. But that could've been because his own life had been so far from idyllic. Since he preferred not to dwell on that, he shifted his eyes to the child, a pretty little thing who resembled her mother in coloring and, if the artist's rendition was accurate, would one day rival her in beauty.

Only five when the painting had been commissioned, she'd be dead less than a year later, her body swept out to sea in the same sailing accident that had brought the mother's broken body in with the tide.

He glanced at the Duke, saw him looking at the child, too, and something inside him tightened. "She's not Charlotte, sir."

"She would be around Miss Donovan's age. And they have the same coloring."

"Charlotte's dead," Alec said more harshly than he intended. "She died twenty years ago."

The blue eyes came around, the sadness unmistakable. "I could remind you that her body was never found . . ." He lifted a hand when Alec opened his mouth to protest. "I'm not a lackwit, Alec. I know Miss Donovan is not my Charlotte, but she interests me nevertheless."

Alec's mouth tightened. "She's a liar and most likely a thief."

Aldridge frowned. He'd seen a multitude of emotions play out across the woman's face. Disbelief, anger, fear. But more than anything, it was the lost look in those big dark eyes that tugged at something inside him.

"She lied, yes. But I don't think she's a liar or a thief," he responded slowly, and glanced at the Ming. "She's right, you know. That particular vase was produced during the Jiajing Empire."

"I didn't say she was not clever, even if her mathematical skills are poor," Alec countered, his expression grim.

"Hmm."

"You should have let her leave. She wanted to leave."

"No." He recalled the flash of helpless terror he'd seen in her eyes before she'd controlled it. "She did not want to leave, Alec. She has nowhere to go."

Alec sighed, and set down his empty wineglass. He rose to his feet. His uncle had made his decision, God help them. "I see. Well, 'tis late, and I must go to bed."

That announcement brought the Duke of Aldridge back to the present. "Is it your bed you'll be seeking, Alec?" he asked with a trace of indulgent amusement. "I have heard talk of you and the lovely Lady Dover."

He and the beautiful widow had done more than talk, Alec thought, but merely smiled. "A gentleman never tells." He paused at the door, glancing back at his uncle. His expression turned serious. "One word of warning, Duke. If Miss Donovan stays on, I'd suggest you have Mrs. Danbury count the silver."

Kendra's sense of unreality deepened as she followed Mrs. Danbury down a hall and then up two flights of servants' stairs. The single lantern the woman had picked up to guide their way turned the walls into a horror house of twisting shadows. Kendra wondered if any of it was real. Stiffening her spine, she battled back the bubble of panic that was threatening to engulf her. Whatever was happening, whether it was a psychosis or something paranormal, panicking wouldn't help.

Mrs. Danbury stopped outside a wooden door. "I shall deal with you tomorrow, Miss Donovan." The tone was steely and suspicious. "Tonight, you may share the bedchamber with Rose." With that, she gave the panel a brisk tap and opened the door.

The light from the single lantern spilled across the threshold, illuminating a tiny room tucked under the eaves. A large oak armoire was positioned against one wall, opposite two narrow single beds separated by a nightstand. One of the beds was occupied. As Kendra watched, the covers moved, a pale hand lifted, and two big brown eyes, under the ruffle of a white nightcap, squinted toward the doorway.

"'Oo's there?"

"'Tis I—Mrs. Danbury."

"Mrs. Danbury?" The girl yawned. "Ma'am, w'ot time is it? W'ot's wrong?"

"Nothing is wrong, Rose. I am sorry to disturb you, but Miss Donovan needs a place to sleep. Good night." She withdrew, taking the light with her.

Kendra blinked as her eyes adjusted to the darkness. Moonlight streamed through a tiny window on the far wall. There was a flurry of movement from the bed, then steel striking flint, and sparks. A stout candle on the nightstand emitted a small circle of light.

The girl looked at her. "'Oo are you?" she asked bluntly.

"Kendra Donovan." Because she was feeling queasy again, she sat down abruptly on the unoccupied bed.

"W'ot 'appened to your 'air? 'Ave you been ill?"

"That would explain it."

In the faint glow, they studied each other. The girl couldn't be much older than fifteen or sixteen, Kendra decided. She was pretty, with big, Bambi eyes, bright with curiosity, in a round face, framed by her old-fashioned nightcap and tumbling dark curls.

"Are you 'ere for the 'ouse party?"

"I . . . yes. I was hired as a lady's maid." Again, Kendra could feel the panic tickle at the back of her throat, trying to work its way free. She could tell herself that this was impossible, that she couldn't be sitting on this hard little mattress in the candlelight, talking to a girl who looked like she belonged in a history book. Yet she was having an increasingly difficult time dismissing what she was seeing, smelling, feeling.

And that terrified her more than anything.

"Ooh," the girl said, impressed. "Me sister bettered 'erself by becoming a lady's maid in London. She was a scullery maid 'ere at the castle. Me ma says I only need apply meself. I'm an 'ard worker. Last year, Mrs. Danbury upped me to a tweeny when Emma became an 'ousemaid and Jenny ran off to Bath." She stopped suddenly, and blushed. "Look at me, runnin' on. You must be tired, 'aving been ill and all." She frowned as she glanced around. "Do you 'ave a bag, Miss Donovan?"

"Kendra. Please call me Kendra," she said automatically, and looked around, as though her bag would miraculously appear. She'd left her purse on the floor of the study, she remembered, before fleeing into the passageway. Of course, that, along with Sir Jeremy's body, had disappeared. "I'm afraid not. My bag was lost."

"Well, never you mind. Mrs. Danbury'll set you up. I'm Rose. Do you need 'elp getting undressed?"

"What? Oh. Thank you." Kendra stood, and turned her back to Rose, much as she'd done to Sally. The recollection brought on another shiver.

"'Ere, now, get under those covers. You're cold!"

Kendra sat down, bending to loosen the ties on her half boots. Rose knelt before her, and helped her out of them, setting them aside.

"Where do you come from? You don't sound English."

"I'm from the United States."

"Ooh, America. I've 'eard such tales," she said as she scrambled back into bed. "Me pa says the colonists are a bunch of 'eathens. No offense, mind you."

"We've been called worse." Kendra stood and stripped down to her shift. By the time she slipped between the sheets and pulled up the thin blankets, she was trembling from more than shock and fear; it was actually cold. The room, she decided, was like a refrigerator.

Rose smiled at her, before leaning over to blow out the meager candle flame. "Good night, miss."

Kendra said nothing for a moment, as she stared at the shadowy slanted ceiling. She could hear the girl settle into the other bed, hear her light breathing. Other than that, the silence seemed absolute.

"Rose?" she whispered.

"Aye?"

"What . . . what year is it?"

Kendra couldn't see Rose's face, but sensed by her sudden stillness that she'd shocked the girl. She couldn't blame her. If someone had asked her that question, she'd have thought the person was off their rocker.

"You mean, w'ot day?" the girl asked cautiously.

"No . . ." Her throat felt tight with apprehension, but she managed to push the words through. "I mean, what year is it? I've been ill, remember?" she added lamely.

"Oh. Of course." Still, Rose hesitated, as though trying to deduce what illness could possibly have wiped away someone's memory to such a degree. "'Tis 1815," she finally replied, her voice soft and anxious in the darkness. "Do you remember now?"

"Yes . . ." she lied, closing her eyes against the reality that she refused to accept.

"Sleep well, miss."

Kendra said nothing. She doubted whether she'd sleep at all. But exhaustion soon weighed her down, pulled her under, and she slept, dreaming of madness and murder.

8

Kendra woke to the rustling of clothes, the padding of feet, and the general hustling of movement. For just a moment, she thought she was back in the hospital, and the never-ending rotation of pill-prodding nurses.

"Annie?" she murmured, rolling over and opening her eyes to the gray light of morning.

"Nay. My name's Rose. Remember?"

"Jesus Christ. You're not a figment of my imagination?"

"You shouldn't take the Lord's name in vain," Rose reprimanded primly. Yet when she glanced in her direction, she softened the words with a smile. "You'd best 'urry, miss. Mrs. Danbury'll wanna speak with you before you attend your Lady."

My Lady?

"What time is it?" Kendra pushed herself to a sitting position, warily watching Rose, who was already wearing a cotton blue floral-print dress, unbuttoned down the back. She moved to an old-fashioned washstand that Kendra hadn't noticed last night tucked between the armoire and wall. Briskly, the girl poured water from the pitcher into the washbasin. Her eyes sought Kendra's in the small swivel mirror.

"'Alf-six," she answered, splashing water on her face. "The staff usually breakfasts at 'alf past eight, but Mrs. Danbury changed our schedules for the party." Snatching the towel draped across the washstand's inbuilt rack, Rose blotted away the moisture. She brushed her teeth using what looked like a primitive toothbrush that she wet and dipped in a jar filled with white powder. Then she pulled out and unfolded a small screen, which baffled Kendra for a moment until she saw Rose reach under the washstand for the chamber pot.

Kendra turned away to give the girl some privacy, and tried to ignore the tinkling sound of nature's call. Grimacing, she realized that she'd have to make use of the chamber pot as well.

A chamber pot, for God's sakes!

"If you button me, I'll do the same for you," Rose offered as she popped back around the screen, brushing her tumbling dark brown hair. With an efficiency born of practice, she twisted the mass into a tidy bun and began stabbing long, lethal-looking hairpins into it.

Swinging her legs over the side of the small bed, Kendra stood and shivered, both from the chilly morning air and the fact that her delusion was still going on.

"Ooh, whatever 'appened, miss?"

Kendra glanced around and saw that Rose was staring at her scars. She shrugged. "You might say they're reminders."

"Reminders of w'ot?"

"To be more careful."

She ducked behind the privacy screen and awkwardly used the chamber pot. Afterward, because she had nothing else, she dressed in the same garments as yesterday, turning obediently so Rose could button her.

"Maybe I have a brain tumor," she murmured, staring at the wall.

"W'ot?"

She sighed. "Nothing. I'm just babbling. Trying to fight off hysteria."

"May'ap you shouldn't. Babble, I mean. I know you're from America, but . . . may'ap you shouldn't."

"You might be right. They'll lock me up in a loony bin, if I'm not there already. Turn around." The buttons on Rose's dress were like smooth pebbles against her fingertips as she pushed them through the buttonholes. Sighing again, she sat down to lace up the half boots. "Figment or not, you're a nice girl, Rose."

Rose smiled uncertainly. "Thank you. And, um, may'ap . . ." she hesitated.

Kendra lifted a brow. "Spill it."

The girl looked confused, glancing around. "Spill w'ot?"

"Oh, God—sorry. I meant, go on. I know you have something else to say."

"Aye, well, may'aps you shouldn't ask people w'ot year it is, either."

"Good point. Thanks."

This time the maid's smile was tinged with relief. "I know you've been ill, but if you say such things, folks'll think you're a bit daft."

Kendra refrained from admitting that she was feeling a bit daft, simply nodding instead and picking up the abandoned hairbrush as she wandered to the window. It was small and not all that clean, but it offered a sweeping view of the English landscape that rolled gently into the distance, seamed with hedges and dotted with thick copses. An early morning mist clung to the ground, offering its own enchantment. In normal circumstances, she would've enjoyed the view.

These were not normal circumstances.

After brushing her hair, she turned to the washbasin, using the water already in the bowl. It felt icy cold against her skin. Did delusions *feel* this real? She stared at her reflection in the pitted mirror. She was paler than normal, making her eyes, below the blunt cut bangs, appear even darker. She didn't like the fragile look of the woman before her, the shimmer of panic twining with fear in her gaze. *Show no weakness.*

Behind her, Rose scurried around the room, quickly making the beds. "Did you come with one of the ladies, or did Mrs. Danbury 'ire you for the party?"

"Duke . . . I mean, *the* Duke wanted me to stay," Kendra said carefully. Since there was nothing else she could do with her hair except let it swing straight and silky to her jaw, she set down the brush and picked up the jar filled with white powder. Sniffing, she realized it was baking soda. She wet her finger, dipped it into the white powder and then scrubbed her finger against her teeth.

"'Is Grace 'imself 'ired you?"

From the girl's thunderstruck expression, Kendra deduced that wasn't normal. Yet Rose recovered quickly, shrugging as she donned her heavy apron, tying it behind her back, "Ah, well. The Duke's known for 'is peculiarities. Oh." She glanced back at Kendra as she headed for the door. "I didn't mean no insult, miss."

Was it possible to be insulted by a hallucination? "Right now, Rose, being called peculiar," she managed to say truthfully, "is the least of my worries."

The human mind can handle only so much stress. It's why men, women, and children eventually resume their daily business in war zones, shopping while bombs dropped. So it didn't surprise Kendra when the terror and sheer disbelief shrank and transformed into sort of a surreal amazement as she followed her new roommate down the backstairs to the servant's hall. Still, she was grateful that she wasn't required to make small talk as

Rose chattered excitedly about the house party. Kendra didn't bother to follow the thread of conversation, but she made the appropriate noises to encourage the girl. Better to have Rose talk, she figured, than to start asking questions. Besides, the one-sided conversation freed Kendra up to concentrate on the problem at hand, which, as she saw it, was one of three possibilities: someone was playing an elaborate hoax on her, she'd had a complete psychological break, or she'd actually been sucked back in time or into another dimension, à la string theory.

She'd almost ruled out the first possibility. Not only couldn't she come up with the *who*—CIA? MI5? KGB?—but she couldn't decide on the *why*. Why would anyone go to the trouble? Why, for Christ's sake, would anyone do it? The conspiracy of people involved and the implementation of such precise details made the whole idea preposterous.

The second possibility, some form of psychosis, sent a shudder through her. The mission she'd given herself—to dispense justice on Sir Jeremy Greene—had been stressful, certainly, and had, in many ways, gone against her own moral code. Had her mind snapped in response? Could she be sitting in some psychiatric ward, her body confined to a straitjacket, while her mind conjured up this alternative reality?

Even as she considered that horrible prospect, everything inside her rebelled. If she'd had some sort of psychotic break, could her mind actually fill in the minutiae that she was seeing now? The young maids busily sweeping the carpets—with whisk brooms, for the love of God—and polishing the heavy furniture in the hallways. Or the footmen in their embroidered, deep blue uniforms and white powdered wigs, carrying in kindling for the fireplaces. She'd concede hallucinating about this period given the costume party, but could she cull from her imagination the sights, the sounds, the *smells*—lemon, linseed oil, and beeswax—that she was experiencing now?

"What's a tweeny?" she asked abruptly, cutting Rose off midsentence.

"Pardon?"

"What is a tweeny?"

"Oh. I told you—*I'm* a tweeny."

"I mean, what do you *do* as a tweeny? We, ah, don't have that position in America."

Rose appeared to find that difficult to comprehend. "'Tis a between maid. I 'elp Cook and the kitchen maids, and the upstairs maids with their duties. 'Owever do your grand 'ouseholds go on without tweenies?"

"I have no idea."

Kendra remembered that there'd been a line yesterday for tweenies, but she hadn't known what they were. Could her brain access information that it didn't have? Assuming, that is, the information was correct, and she wasn't simply making it up along with the girl who was supplying the information. This kind of thinking would drive her crazy—if she wasn't already there.

She could feel her chest tighten, the flutter of hysteria in the pit of her stomach. With an effort, she pulled herself back from a full-scale panic attack, and concentrated on breathing. In and out. *Keep calm. You're not crazy. There has to be a logical explanation.*

She focused on her surroundings. They'd entered the servant's wing, where she'd been yesterday. Like the study last night, the area was both the same and different. The same walls, the same flagstone floor, the same flurry of activity with people running around. But the fixtures and furnishings had changed here, too. The faces had changed.

She paused abruptly in the doorway of the room that yesterday had been converted into the temporary girls' locker room. Today, it had cupboards and shelves filled with what looked to be pressed linen, a long table, and a few odd looking pieces of equipment.

"What's this room?"

Rose glanced back, frowning. "'Tis the linen room. Don't you 'ave that in America, either?"

"Not where I live," Kendra answered truthfully.

A moment later they entered the room that yesterday had been ground zero for Stark Productions. Today, it was exactly what it once had been: a dining room. There was still no fire in the enormous fireplace. The long sweep of table was covered by a crisp white tablecloth, which probably had been in the linen room only minutes before. Two maids, dressed in a similar style as Rose, were in the process of setting the table.

"And Oi 'eard, as bold as brass she was, calling 'is Grace *Duke*," one of the maids was saying.

"Go *on*!" The other girl sounded deliciously horrified.

"'Tis true! And she 'as hair as short as a boy's—" She broke off suddenly as she spotted Kendra and Rose in the doorway. A fiery blush swept up her cheeks. "Oh, Oi didn't see yer there, Rose." Her eyes met Kendra's, and then flitted guiltily away.

"Good morning, Tess, Mildred," Rose greeted easily. "This 'ere's Kendra Donovan. She's a lady's maid 'ired for the party."

"Mrs. Danbury's looking for 'er."

"Thank you, Tess." Rose cast Kendra an apologetic look once they were out in the hall. "Never you mind them. Tess is an 'orrid gossip."

Kendra suspected it wouldn't only be Tess gossiping about her, but kept quiet as they walked down the hall to a short flight of steps. After descending, Rose stopped to knock at the first door on the right. Mrs. Danbury's crisp voice invited them inside.

Again Kendra was reminded of her former college instructor. Dressed in similar attire to that which she'd worn the night before—white cap and black gown—Mrs. Danbury sat behind a large oak desk, its surface polished and everything on it arranged in such a precise way that it made more of a statement about the housekeeper than anything else in the small, tidy office. They stood waiting while she ignored them as she carefully dipped a quill pen into an inkstand, scribbling on a thick sheet of paper. Silence pooled in the room, broken only by the scratching of nib against parchment paper, and the slow, steady tick of the pendulum clock in the corner of the room.

Kendra found herself holding her breath. Mrs. Danbury finally laid the pen down in a wood stand. Still she didn't look at them. Rather, she picked up a small glass vial, tipping it and lightly sprinkling the parchment with sand, before blowing the grains away.

Ritual done, she lifted the sheet of paper to Rose. "Please give this to Monsieur Anton, Rose. We have a change in the dinner menu."

Rose went pale. "Ooh, 'e's not gonna like that one bit, ma'am."

"No, he's not," Mrs. Danbury conceded. "The chef is temperamental and difficult. One must expect such a disposition from the French, Rose. Nevertheless, Lady Atwood herself made these particular changes. Monsieur Anton must accommodate the countess' wishes, regardless of his own personal desires."

Rose did not look any happier with that announcement, but appeared resigned. "Aye, ma'am."

Mrs. Danbury nodded. "Thank you, Rose. You may go—close the door behind you."

Rose exchanged one quick look with Kendra before bobbing a curtsy, and, list in hand, leaving the room. Mrs. Danbury waited until the door snicked shut before turning those cool, appraising gray eyes on Kendra.

"Well, Miss Donovan . . . you've certainly put me in an awkward position. His Grace is under the impression that you are at Aldridge Castle as a lady's maid. Of course, we have several lady's maids currently under our roof, but most arrived with a Lady. Did you arrive with a Lady, Miss Donovan?"

Even though her heart had begun thudding, Kendra looked the woman in the eye and managed to say calmly enough, "No . . . ma'am."

"I could attribute your presence here as being part of the temporary help," she went on. "As you may know, several lady's maids were hired to accommodate our guests who were not fortunate enough to bring their own. However, as *I* was the one who hired the temporary lady's maids, this leaves me baffled, Miss Donovan. I do not know you. I did not hire you. If you did not arrive with a Lady, and I did not hire you to be a lady's maid, how did you come to Aldridge Castle? It fairly boggles the mind."

"You can say that again."

"I beg your pardon?"

"I don't have an answer for you, Mrs. Danbury."

"Indeed." The housekeeper's lips tightened. "And yet you had an answer for His Grace last night. You insisted that you were hired as a lady's maid."

"I *was* hired as a lady's maid."

The expression in Mrs. Danbury's gray eyes turned even more glacial. "That is not possible, Miss Donovan. As I have stated, Mr. Kimble gave me the responsibility to hire the temporary female staff. And I did not hire any Americans. I did not hire *you*."

"I was hired by another woman."

"*No* other woman has that authority! What is her name—this woman who hired you?"

Kendra thought of the woman from Stark Productions. "Mrs. Peters."

"There is *no* Mrs. Peters at Aldridge Castle."

Why didn't that surprise her? Because she could offer no other explanation—how do you explain the unexplainable?—Kendra remained silent, staring at the housekeeper.

Mrs. Danbury studied the young woman who met her eyes so brazenly. If it had been her decision, she would have sent the bold creature packing—without references. But earlier, Mr. Kimble had knocked on her door with orders from the Duke himself that Kendra Donovan was to stay. It was galling, simply galling.

"Miss Donovan, I do not believe you. Moreover, I do not trust you." Noticing the grains of sand across the desk, she swept her hands over its surface, clearing away the letter-making debris. "I shall, however, give you a temporary reprieve. As it so happens, we do have two ladies staying with us who could use your assistance. Miss Georgette Knox and Miss Sarah Rawdon. You will attend breakfast, and then see to your duties."

Relief loosened the tight knot of fear inside her chest. Whatever was happening, Kendra knew that she couldn't leave the castle. This was ground zero. "Thank you, Mrs. Danbury."

The housekeeper's eyes narrowed. "I shall be watching you, Miss Donovan," she warned. "That will be all."

Dismissed, Kendra moved out into the hall. There she paused and pressed a hand to her stomach. Her present emotional state appeared to be swinging between incredulity and full-on fear. She straightened when she heard someone coming: a young maid, no more than nine, carrying a bucket. The little girl gave her a curious look as she passed.

Composing herself, Kendra made her way to the kitchen. The room was much larger than the dining area, with high ceilings and high windows that allowed natural light to flood in. A chandelier, its tapers unlit, hung from the center of the ceiling on chains as thick as a man's wrist. Below the windows, long shelves carried the gleam of pots and the soft sheen of cookware.

It reminded Kendra of a hotel kitchen, albeit one placed squarely in what she understood to be the early nineteenth century, with at least a dozen helpers busy in several workstations. There were two fireplaces, both lit, the flames heating the blackened bottoms of bronze cauldrons hanging within. A monstrosity—a black cast iron range—took up a good portion of the other wall. An iron grid above the stove dangled with copper pots, big and small, and an assortment of utensils. A small, dark-haired man wearing a chef's hat was stirring two large pots simultaneously, muttering angrily in French. From the snippet she overheard, Kendra ascertained that the changes in the menu had not, as Rose predicted, gone over well.

Kendra spotted Rose at one of the tables, peeling, coring, and chopping apples. Moving in her direction, she caught the scent of sizzling meat steeped in savory spices. Overlaying that was the strong yeasty smell of baking bread. Kendra realized suddenly that she was hungry. Could you be *hungry* in a delusion?

The paring knife Rose held flashed as she sliced fruit into a bowl. The last slice, however, she popped into her mouth, which drew a snort from the woman next to her, who was pummeling a shapeless blob of dough roughly the size of a deflated basketball.

"Wicked girl—ye've eaten at least two apple pies by yer thievery," the woman admonished, wagging a finger dusted with flour.

Rose giggled, apparently unconcerned with the woman's reprimand. Spotting Kendra, she smiled. "Miss—over 'ere! Cook, this 'ere is Miss Donovan. She's sharing me room now. She's a lady's maid."

"Ah. Ye're one of the temporary lasses hired for Lady Atwood's party, then?"

Kendra judged the woman to be around Mrs. Danbury's age, but, thankfully, she did not seem to share the housekeeper's disposition. She was short, with a comfortable figure that filled out her pale blue dress and white apron. Her face was round and pleasant, with pale wisps of light brown hair escaping the mop cap she wore. The dark blue eyes took Kendra's measure, but without any animosity.

"Yes. Please call me Kendra."

The woman's lips curved into a smile as she continued to shape the dough. "Me name is Mrs. Acker, but everyone calls me Cook. Who will ye be looking after then?"

"Um . . . Georgette Knox and Sarah Rawdon." Kendra wondered if she could ask for a cup of coffee. Preferably one strong enough to wake her from this nightmare.

"Ye'd best have yer breakfast then," Cook said. "The ladies will be wantin' their chocolate and tea soon, I expect."

"Oh. Okay."

Rose intercepted her glance, and shook her head. "Not 'ere, Miss. You're to 'ave your breakfast in the upper staff dining room."

"What about you?" asked Kendra.

One of the other girls nearby giggled. "Ooh, la, Miss Rose. Shall I serve ye tea?"

"'Tis the *upper* staff dining room for *upper* staff. I'm a tweeny."

It was protocol, Kendra realized. She understood the need for protocol, for procedures and practices. Hell, she was an FBI agent. You couldn't get through the FBI without understanding protocol. But why would her mind separate the upper staff from the lower staff servants? It was crazy.

She was crazy. Or she wasn't. And for just a moment, Kendra didn't know which terrified her more.

The dining room was already crowded with people of varying ages. Mrs. Danbury stood ramrod straight near the head of the table, next to an older man who appeared almost as stiff as the housekeeper.

Kendra walked to one of the empty places at the table. Since everyone remained standing, she stayed on her feet as well, aware of the curious eyes that were trying not to openly stare at her. A sharp-featured woman, apparently less polite, appeared at her side, frowning.

"You've mistaken your seat, miss," she informed Kendra with an air of condescension.

"What?"

"Miss Beckett is Lady Atwood's personal maid, Miss Donovan," Mrs. Danbury explained in frosty accents. "At Aldridge

Castle we maintain the proper hierarchy at our table. As the highest-ranking lady's maid, Miss Beckett is entitled to sit in that chair. You may sit down the table."

Protocol, she reminded herself. Like the military. A private wouldn't sit next to a four-star general during a meal.

Ignoring Miss Beckett's smug look, Kendra moved down the table to another seat. Mrs. Danbury and the man sat down. Apparently it was a signal, because everyone followed suit.

Conversation was a low murmur around her as porridge was slapped into earthenware bowls. Cream was poured from clay pitchers. Hot cross buns, bigger than a fist and lighter than helium, were passed around the table. Honey, butter, and jam also made the rounds to the tune of clicking spoons and knives.

Kendra sampled the porridge. Although it wouldn't have been her first choice, she found it unexpectedly delicious, especially with a dab of honey and a dollop of cream. She would've preferred coffee, but the tea, she had to admit, was strong and fragrant. And the golden brown bun, smeared with butter and marmalade, was the best she'd ever eaten.

"Where do you hail from, Miss Donovan?" asked the pretty brunette seated on her right.

Kendra hesitated. "America."

"Where in America, Miss Donovan?" the woman on the other side of the brunette asked, and Kendra found herself again the focal point of everyone at the table.

"I live in Virginia." Maybe she was there right now, in a psych ward, in a catatonic state. Maybe she'd never recovered from being shot the first time. Maybe—

"I've never met anyone from America before," admitted a young man in footman livery, sitting across from her.

"How'd you ever get to England, Miss Donovan?" inquired a woman seated on her left.

"I don't suppose you'd believe me if I told you I flew?"

The woman laughed. Despite the length of the table separating them, Kendra felt Mrs. Danbury's disapproval like the lash of a whip.

"Only if you show us your wings, Miss Donovan!" the woman declared.

"You must have arrived late last night, Miss Donovan," the brunette commented. "I never saw you yesterday. Of course, we were in such a mad state to settle everyone. These parties are quite exhausting, are they not? I'm Miss Stanton, by the way. And this is Miss Burke." She nodded at the other woman. Her introductions opened up the door for others to chime in. Kendra nodded politely, but her head was spinning. Even though she'd never had a problem with her memory, she wondered if she'd remember anyone's name in five minutes. Was that a symptom of mental instability?

"Who is your Lady?" Miss Stanton asked her.

"What? Oh. Um. I've got two—Georgette Knox and Sarah Rawdon."

"Oh, dear." The other woman's expression turned sympathetic.

"That bad, huh?"

"I daresay it could be worse."

Great. Kendra wondered if Mrs. Danbury had deliberately given her the worst of the bunch, hoping she'd quit.

After a time, at the head of the table, the butler—Mr. Harding, Kendra had learned during the course of the meal—and Mrs. Danbury rose in quiet formality. Another signal. Everyone pushed themselves to their feet. Kendra followed the other lady's maids into the kitchen, and five minutes later, was bearing a tray laden with two dainty cups and a pot of hot chocolate, trudging up two flights of stairs to the Blue Room shared by Miss Georgette and Miss Sarah.

By the time she located the room, with the help of several footmen en route, she'd finally, reluctantly, begun to consider the third possibility regarding her predicament, as unbelievable as it may be.

Somehow, in some freaking way, she'd slipped back in time.

9

Because she felt shaky, Kendra made sure she had a firm grip on the tray when she eased open the door to the Blue Room. It took every ounce of her self-control to *not* think about her circumstance, to concentrate only on the duties assigned to her. Once she'd taken care of this lady's maid stuff, she'd find a quiet place to think, to figure a way out of this bizarre situation—*if* she could find a way out of this bizarre situation.

That uncertainty sent fresh panic skittering through her. But goddamn it, she wouldn't go there. Since she'd turned fourteen, she'd managed to take care of herself. She could handle this. She just needed to *think*.

She drew in a deep breath, and then let it out, focusing on her surroundings. The room was still semi-dark, and four times as big as the one she'd shared last night with Rose. Two canopied single beds draped in thick velvet curtains, partially drawn, revealed its sleeping occupants.

Not entirely sure what to do, she set the tray down on a nearby table. When nobody stirred, she crossed the room to push open the heavy drapery. The fog, she saw, had lifted, and the flower garden below was gilded in the soft light of the morning sun.

Finally, a bed squeaked, and someone yawned. Kendra turned to see one of the girls push herself into a sitting position. She wore a nightgown buttoned primly up to the neck and a nightcap on her head. Blond hair, twisted in rag curlers, stuck out below the cap's lace.

"Georgie—wake up," she ordered the other bed's occupant. She glanced at Kendra. "Who are you?"

"I'm Kendra Donovan. Your lady's maid."

"I want my chocolate."

The imperious tone scraped Kendra's already raw nerves, but she went to pour a cup of the hot chocolate.

"I shall wear my yellow muslin," the girl said as she accepted the cup and saucer.

"I want my chocolate, too," the other girl—Georgie—said, when Kendra made a move toward the wardrobe.

Veering back to the pot of chocolate, Kendra poured another cup. She brought it to the girl, who was wearing a similar nightgown and cap as her roommate.

"What shall I wear this morning, Sarah?" she asked as she sipped her chocolate. "I thought the blue morning dress Papa bought me. It's ever so fine."

"Hmm. I think you ought to wear the green muslin."

"Oh. But what of Lady Louisa? She has a prodigious fondness for green."

"Lady Louisa looks like a toad when she wears green." Sarah dismissed the unseen woman with cool contempt. She lifted the china cup, and her blue eyes gleamed maliciously as she took a sip. "Speaking of toads, I can scarcely believe that Lady Rebecca was bold enough to show herself at dinner last night. I nearly cast up my accounts when I was seated opposite her!"

Georgette giggled. "I believe she's the Duke's goddaughter."

"Nevertheless, they should be more considerate of their guests." Sarah shifted her gaze to Kendra and arched a brow. "Pray, what are you doing, standing there like a simpleton? I told you—I want my yellow muslin."

This had to be real, Kendra decided, as she walked to the wardrobe. Or she was a masochist to create such a delusion.

Opening the wardrobe's heavy doors, she scanned the numerous frothy gowns crowded inside on hooks. Odd, how something as insignificant as the absence of coat hangers could send her heart hammering again in her chest. But a memory—something she'd read or heard—surfaced on how wooden hangers hadn't become commercialized until 1869. And wire hangers wouldn't put in an appearance for another ninety years. If she were having a mental breakdown, would her mind be so historically accurate?

Oh, God, she didn't know. She pulled out the first yellow dress she saw.

"I said the yellow muslin—the yellow *muslin*, you stupid girl!"

Keeping her temper in check with an effort, Kendra replaced the yellow gown, and skimmed through the rest of the clothes. Finding another bright yellow dress, she pulled it out. "Is this the one you want?"

Sarah rolled her eyes. "Naturally. What kind of lady's maid are you? You're not even French." She looked at her roommate. "One would think someone as powerful as the Duke of Aldridge would hire a French lady's maid for his guests. At the very least, a Swiss one."

Georgette made a sound of agreement. "And I shall wear the green muslin." While she couldn't pull off the same imperious tone as her friend, it was close enough.

If the situation weren't so serious or bizarre, Kendra would've laughed at the irony. Here she was—onetime child prodigy, the youngest agent ever to make it through Quantico—taking orders from two snobby debutantes.

The girls got out of bed and disappeared behind the privacy screen. When they emerged, Kendra had found the green dress. She waited until they discarded their nightgowns and put on their undergarments, stockings, and garters. She had to lace up both girls' stays before helping them into their dresses. After she finished buttoning them, Sarah flounced over to sit in front of the mirrored dressing table.

"Well?" She glanced at Kendra in the mirror. "For heaven's sake. Stop woolgathering! I need my hair put up."

Kendra froze. *Put up*? What the hell did she know about being a hairdresser? Her own hair, thick and straight-as-a-pin, required very little maintenance. Before the shooting, she'd worn it in a ponytail. Afterward . . . well, she hadn't done anything except wait for it to grow, and then have it styled by Mr. Gerry at his swanky salon in Georgetown.

"*What* are you waiting for, you stupid girl?"

Where are the manners in this era? Kendra wondered, jaw tightening. She went over to Sarah, and began unwrapping her hair from the rag curlers. How hard would it be to pin up a few curls, for Christ's sake?

Forty-five minutes later, Kendra admitted to herself that she was no Mr. Gerry, and would rather face a dozen psychopaths than endure another session struggling to subdue wayward curls with only a few ribbons and old-fashioned hairpins that were little more than long, thin wires, all the while suffering verbal abuse from a girl who probably couldn't do basic math.

Goddamn it, she cursed mentally when one more wispy strand escaped the Grecian knot she'd been attempting on Sarah.

"Lud! What kind of lady's maid are you?" Sarah declared angrily. "If you were in *my* household—"

"Shut up." The words were out of her mouth before she realized it. Although talking back probably wasn't the smartest thing to do, some of the tightness eased from the center of Kendra's chest.

Sarah's eyes bugged out of her head. "How dare you! How dare—"

"I said, *shut up.*" In for a penny, in for a pound, Kendra decided. "If you want to make it down in time for your breakfast, you'll keep quiet so I can finish this. And for God's sake, stop squirming!"

"Ouch!"

"I told you to stop squirming."

"I—"

"There!" Kendra stabbed in the last pin and eyed the hairstyle grimly. Maybe it was a little lopsided, but if the idiot didn't jiggle around too much, it *should* stay put. "I'm done!"

Sarah stood up with a swish of skirts. "You *shall* be done," she promised, eyes flashing. "After I speak with the countess—"

"I told you to shut up." She pointed the hairbrush at Georgette. "You, *sit.*"

Georgette stared at her wide-eyed.

"Now!"

The girl sat.

"How . . . how dare you speak to us like that!" Sarah sputtered.

Kendra ignored her as she removed Georgette's rag curlers. "I'm out of pins so I'll tie your hair back with a ribbon."

"But—"

"Take it or leave it."

"But—"

"This is outrageous!" Sarah crossed her arms, toe-tapping furiously, glaring at Kendra.

Kendra ignored her, concentrating instead on brushing out Georgette's curls. When she snatched up a ribbon, the girl whined, "But that doesn't even match my dress!"

"Oh, for Christ's sake!" Kendra dropped the ribbon, grabbed a green one, and tied the girl's hair back into a ponytail.

"The countess *shall* hear about this!" Sarah threatened. "You shall be dismissed—without references! You shall be begging in the streets! You shall be sent to the workhouse! You—"

"Yeah, yeah. I get it. Your breakfast is probably getting cold," Kendra snapped, and felt a petty satisfaction at watching the girl's bosom swell in indignation. Her face was so red with temper that if she'd been older and heavier, Kendra might've worried about a stroke.

"Come along, Georgie!" Sarah practically snarled, and stormed out, her hair bobbing precariously.

Kendra waited until the girls had left before sinking into a chair. She put her throbbing head in her hands. She wanted to wake up from this nightmare. *Now.*

"Miss Donovan?"

She lifted her head, glancing around to meet the sympathetic eyes of Miss Stanton as she poked her head into the room.

"Oh, dear," she clucked her tongue, and came all the way into the room. "I saw the girls leave. Were they simply horrid? You look done in."

Kendra threaded her fingers through her hair in agitation. "It probably could've been worse." She didn't know how. "But I'm glad it's over."

Miss Stanton lifted her brows in surprise. "Over? My dear, Miss Donovan, it's only begun."

Kendra's stomach sank. "What do you mean?"

"Your duties, Miss Donovan. The day has scarce begun. If the ladies want to stroll in the garden, they undoubtedly shall need to change into their walking dresses. At the very least, they'll need their bonnets and shawls. If they want to go riding, they'll need you to assist them with their riding habits. Then they shall most likely wish to change into their afternoon gowns before the full dress of evening.

"And you, Miss Donovan, will need to assist them," continued Miss Stanton. "You will be required to mend and press their clothes, and redress their hairstyles."

Kendra shuddered as what Miss Stanton was saying hit her with the force of a baseball bat between the eyes. For a horrifying moment, she envisioned being a lady's maid for days, weeks . . . *years*.

No fucking way.

"Where are you going, Miss Donovan?"

Kendra hadn't even realized that she was up and moving until she felt the doorknob under her hand. She glanced back at the lady's maid—God, how did she live like this?—unaware of the stark desperation darkening her eyes.

"Home. I need to go home."

Thankfully, the study was empty. Kendra made a beeline for the hidden door. Her hands shook as she pushed aside the tapestry. It was only when the door swung open that she found herself hesitating, a spidery sense of fear crawling up her spine.

Time travel. It was absurd. Unbelievable. Yet here she was, smack in the middle of the unbelievable. Having ruled out a brain tumor, psychotic break, or hoax, Kendra had to believe that she'd just spent the morning in the early nineteenth century.

In theory, time travel *was* possible. Albert Einstein had theorized if gravity was strong enough, it could conceivably cause a curvature in the space-time continuum, forcing time to literally loop back on itself. There were some science fiction freaks who even believed that there were natural gravitational hot spots in the world that could create such a vortex of space-time, allowing people to travel through time. But that was science *fiction*, for Christ's sake.

Of course, there'd been experiments that had basically proven that time travel was possible. In 1971, scientists J. C. Hafele and Richard E. Keating had placed amazingly accurate atomic clocks—each with the capacity to measure time to the billionth of a second—on jets flying at 600 miles per hour. Using the atomic clock at the U.S. Naval Observatory as a reference point, they'd documented that nanoseconds of time had been both gained and lost on the clocks onboard the jets. In effect, anyone onboard the jets had leapt a nanosecond into the future and back to the past.

But there was a big difference between traveling *nanoseconds* in time and *centuries*. This shouldn't be possible. But since she was standing here, maybe she'd encountered one of those alleged gravitational hot spots. Could that explain the unnatural darkness, the vertigo, the pain . . . the way her flesh seemed to bubble, dissolve, *disappear* . . . ? And if the passageway housed one of those vortexes, this would be her ticket home.

There were a lot of things wrong with that theory, Kendra knew—like, if there was a vortex beyond this door, one would think the Duke would've encountered more people appearing suddenly, or inexplicably going missing. She didn't want to think about it. *I just want to go home.*

Still, Kendra hesitated before stepping through the door. Greasy knots of anxiety made her stomach clench. Physically, the experience had been agonizing. Excruciating. But that wasn't what made her vacillate. She'd endure the pain if she knew she'd return home.

That was the problem: would she return home? Or would she be flung deeper into the past, or even further into the future? The future she could handle. But what if she ended up in the seventeenth century? The fifteenth century? This century, at least, was the beginning of the modern era.

Again, Kendra was struck by the sheer absurdity of her thoughts. Yesterday if anyone had told her that she'd worry about being transported somewhere in time, she'd have laughed and wondered about their sanity. Now it was *her* sanity that was in question.

She raked her fingers through her hair, and then straightened her shoulders. *Stop stalling.* She inhaled deeply and walked through the door.

10

The stairwell was dark.

But not the absolute, unnatural darkness that she'd encountered last night.

It was also cold.

But not unusually so.

Slowly, she climbed the stairs, willing the darkness to thicken, the temperature to drop, the stairwell to take on that strange supernatural element that she'd sensed, but hadn't really understood, before.

Feeling a little like Dorothy clicking her ruby red slippers, Kendra closed her eyes and held her breath.

There's no place like home—yeah, right. She'd given up her home when she'd created new identities and bank accounts for herself, when she'd made it her mission to kill Sir Jeremy Greene. Was this some sort of karmic payback?

She was beginning to feel a little light-headed. Hope surged . . . until she realized the slight buzz in her ears wasn't caused by some paranormal electromagnetic charge in the air, but because she was still holding her breath. Feeling as stupid as Sarah had accused her of being, she let it out with a whoosh, sagging against the cold stone wall. Anger replaced the dizziness.

"This is *insane*! Absolutely fucking insane!" She climbed more stairs, and then slapped a frustrated palm against the stone wall. *"Goddamnit!"*

She pushed herself upward, paused. Closed her eyes. Nothing.

"Where the hell is that damn vortex? C'mon!" She thought of her mother, Dr. Eleanor Jahnke, currently trying to unveil the secrets of the universe in Switzerland. "Oh boy, oh boy . . . Mother, I've got a doozy for you. You'd love this. You'd—"

"Ahoy. Who's there?"

Kendra froze. The voice echoed from above. Footsteps approached.

She considered the odds of escaping. *Not good.* A second later, light bounced off the wall, and then the Duke of Aldridge rounded the curve, holding an oil lamp.

"Miss Donovan?" He stopped, raising his brows as he studied the young woman poised on the spiral steps below. Because she looked frightened, he gentled his voice. "This is a surprise."

"I'm sorry, I . . ." Kendra wondered how she could explain her presence in the passageway. Once was bad enough. But twice? That was bound to raise suspicions.

Aldridge looked at her curiously. "Do not apologize. 'Tis serendipity. Would you like a cup of tea?"

Kendra blinked in confusion. "What?"

"Tea. I rang for some. Come along, my dear." He didn't wait, but began ascending the stairs. "Don't dawdle, Miss Donovan," he said cheerfully, not looking back.

A little bemused, Kendra followed him through the doorway. The last time she'd been in this room, she remembered, it had been empty, save for the fireplace. Today, the hearth was filled with burning logs, adding a hint of smoke to the air. Above the mantel were two oval paintings, portraits of a woman and child. The same woman and child, Kendra realized, that graced the oil painting in the study.

Except for the mullion-paned windows that allowed in natural light, the other walls were lined with bookshelves. There was a desk, less elegant than the one downstairs, its surface smothered beneath stacks of books and sheaves of papers. A couple of wooden chairs were positioned around it. Yet it wasn't the desk, but the two long worktables that drew the eye. They carried an odd and untidy assortment of equipment, instruments, and tools. Kendra caught the gleam of brass, the polish of bronze.

With a sinking feeling, she scanned the old-fashioned microscopes; the mortar and pestle bowls; the pottery filled with chunks of rock and bits of what looked like bone; and jars filled with liquid. On the floor was a beautifully designed armillary sphere, representing the celestial bodies. A large telescope, as tall as she was, stood beside it.

"You're a scientist," she observed, and couldn't control a tiny shiver. The irony didn't escape her. She'd been born—bred, really—as a scientific experiment. For the first fourteen years of her life, she'd been treated with awe by some, suspicion by others, and careful clinical detachment by her parents. Was it some cosmic joke that she'd been transported back in time only to find herself employed by an aristocratic scientist?

"Scientist." The Duke of Aldridge said the word now, and in such a way that he seemed to be testing it on his tongue. "I am not familiar with the term."

Kendra stared at him in his old-fashioned clothes, and it took her a moment to remember that the word *scientist* wouldn't be coined for another twenty-five or so years. Language, she reflected ruefully, was a lot like a living organism: words were born, they thrived, sometimes died or evolved into new words, new meanings. It would, she suspected, be her greatest challenge while she was here. *Oh, God, please don't let me be here long.*

"I meant," she said slowly, even as her stomach twisted, "you're a man of science." Aware that he was staring at her—*studying* her—she moved toward the armillary sphere and telescope. "You're interested in astronomy?"

He smiled. "Like my father before me, I have an avid interest in natural philosophy and the arts." He touched the sphere reverently. "I was only a lad of twenty-two when Sir William Herschel discovered the planet Uranus. Such a discovery . . . And only four years ago, the Great Comet was observed streaking through the sky. What else is out there to be discovered, among the stars, eh, Miss Donovan?"

"Those to whom the harmonious doors,/Of Science have unbarred celestial shores," Kendra quoted unthinkingly, offering a tentative smile. It had seemed apropos, but she instantly regretted it when the Duke stared at her.

Fascinated, Aldridge said carefully, "Are you an admirer of the poet?"

Kendra shrugged uneasily. "He was . . . is . . ." She tried to remember when William Wordsworth had died. Mid-1800s? "Ah, remarkable."

"He is." The Duke's blue-gray eyes twinkled, even as he clearly wondered at the woman's sudden discomfort. "Like many of my contemporaries, I've tried my hand at poetry. But my efforts fall far short of Mr. Wordsworth's genius. He knows how to explore a man's soul, eh? I prefer to explore those celestial shores, or divine the secrets of the earth. There is much to be explored, is there not, Miss Donovan? You would, of course, understand. Being an explorer yourself."

Kendra went pale, her eyes wary as she looked to Aldridge. "What do you mean?"

"You are an American," he pointed out, deliberately keeping his tone mild, though her reaction had piqued his curiosity. "You were enough of an explorer to sail across the Atlantic."

"Oh, yes. Yes, of course." Her brow cleared. Biting her lip, she rubbed her clammy palms against her arms. Unable to meet the intensity of his gaze, she looked around. The messy sheaves of paper caught her attention. Smoothing out one curling paper, she studied the graphs and notations with interest.

"I chart the night sky," Aldridge explained. "These are my observations of last evening."

"There was a full moon?"

"Yes," he said, giving her a questioning look.

Kendra missed it, too busy considering the implications of a full moon on her own bizarre circumstance. Was there a connection? Not because of the myth that mysterious and magical things happen under a full moon, but for the purely scientific reason that the gravitational pull was strongest during that phase of the lunar cycle. And perhaps a stronger gravitational pull might influence the vortex . . .

Jesus Christ. Would she be marooned in this dimension, this time rift, for a full *month*?

"Are you quite well, Miss Donovan?"

"Oh . . . yes. I'm fine." Yet she couldn't stop shivering. It didn't make sense. Full moons didn't occur on the same day every month. *Her* full moon, in her own time, wouldn't necessarily be the same as the Duke's.

She rubbed her arms and paced aimlessly along one worktable, staring at the objects jumbled across it. There was no order or specialty. The Duke of Aldridge's interests, it appeared, were wide-ranging and eclectic. He was a true Renaissance man. She paused next to four squat jars connected with metal wires and rods.

"That's a Leyden Jar," the Duke identified, noting her interest. "Rather primitive electricity toys, but when I was a boy it was quite the thing. Do you have an interest in natural philosophy and astronomy, Miss Donovan?"

Kendra slanted him a look. She was a servant, she reminded herself. Did servants in the nineteenth century have an interest in natural philosophy or astronomy? "I suppose they're interesting subjects," she replied carefully.

"They are indeed." He picked up the pipe he'd left on the table. "How'd you find yourself on these shores, Miss Donovan?"

"What?"

Crossing the room to the fireplace, he lit a long taper and brought it to the clay pipe bowl. "England, Miss Donovan," he prodded gently as he puffed. His expression was genial but his gaze was sharp as he surveyed her through the smoke. "How'd you come here, pray?"

Kendra thought of the answer she'd glibly given that morning. "By ship," she said instead.

He smiled. "I didn't think you came by air balloon. Perhaps a better question would be: What brought you to England?"

"I . . ." Oh, God, what could she say? "I had . . . something to do. Business. And, ah, you might say I got stuck here." It was the truth.

"Stuck?"

"Unable to leave."

His expression was thoughtful as he drew on the pipe. "I see. Because of the war?"

That, Kendra decided, was as good a reason as any. "Yes."

"I certainly understand you not being able to travel back to America during the hostilities. But, what of now? The war's been over for months."

"I don't have any money," she improvised.

"I see. And once you acquire the funds to obtain passage to America, you'll be leaving us, then?"

"I need to go back home," she said with complete honesty.

His gaze moved beyond hers to settle on the two paintings above the fireplace. "Do you have family, Miss Donovan?"

Kendra thought of the parents she didn't speak to, the half-siblings that she'd never bothered to meet. "Not really. But I . . . don't belong here."

It wasn't the words, but the underlying desperation in her voice that caught his attention. "When did you arrive in England?"

"When?"

"Yes."

Her chest tightened, but she answered calmly enough. "I already told you—before the war."

"So you've been in England for four years?"

"Y-yes."

"'Tis a long time." He puffed on his pipe. "What month did you arrive?"

Apprehension prickled along the back of her neck. Sweat dampened her palms. Despite the gentle tone, she knew when she was being interrogated. "Um . . . May."

"May of 1812, then?" He nodded, taking her silence as agreement. "A time of great upheaval," he murmured. "Upon which ship did you travel?"

"Why?" She heard the hostility in her own voice and struggled to rein it in. She'd never studied this era specifically, but she was pretty sure servants weren't supposed to fight with the aristocracy. "It was so long ago—four years, like you say—that I can't think why it matters."

He smiled slightly. "I've always been a curious man—as you can see by my interest in natural philosophy. I also have financial interests in a few shipping companies; maybe you traveled on one of those."

"I don't remember." *Lame, Donovan.*

"You don't remember the ship you booked passage, the ship you spent weeks crossing the ocean?"

Kendra swallowed. If she'd had someone in interview giving her such evasive answers, they'd have shot to the top of the shortlist for whatever crime she was investigating. But she had no choice. Telling him that she was a time traveler wasn't an option. He wouldn't believe it. Hell, *she* didn't believe it.

"I'm sorry. I really don't remember," she said, and felt a wave of relief when the door opened, and a maid came in carrying a serving tray. Her eyes widened when she saw Kendra standing next to the Duke, but she quickly averted her gaze, depositing her burden on a side table.

Aldridge approached, rubbing his hands together. "We'll need another cup, as I'm expecting—" He broke off as the door swung open again, and the man Kendra recognized from the night before strolled into the room. "Ah, Alec. You are right on time."

Alec lifted a brow. "On time for what?" He stopped abruptly, his brow darkening as he spotted Kendra. Unlike the maid, he apparently had no intention of pretending she wasn't in the room. "What the hell is *she* doing here?"

"Alec, your manners are abominable," the Duke admonished gently. "Miss Donovan and I were discussing natural philosophy and astronomy. And about to have tea."

"You're bloody joking."

"I never joke about tea. And don't swear. If you'll be so good as to bring another cup for my ill-mannered nephew," he said to the maid, who immediately dropped into a curtsy.

"Yes, Your Grace."

Kendra didn't have to see the other girl's face to know that the Duke's statement had shocked her. And infuriated Alec. She was, after all, a lady's maid. While she still had a lot to learn about the customs of the early nineteenth century, she suspected a lady's maid taking tea with a Duke wasn't normal. "No, thank you," she said hurriedly, following the maid to the door. "In fact, I need to get back to my duties."

"Oh. Are you quite certain, Miss Donovan?"

"Yes. Thank you."

Aldridge knew he could insist that she stay and take tea with them. But for all his well-known eccentricities, he wasn't given to coercion of that sort. He smiled at her and said, "Another time perhaps?"

"Yes, perhaps." Aware of Alec's eyes on her, Kendra hurried out the door.

Alec waited for the door to close before turning slowly to face his uncle, who was already pouring two cups of tea into the delicate Wedgwood cups. "I obviously interrupted your cozy *tête-à-tête* with Miss Donovan."

Calmly, Aldridge added a lump of sugar to one of the cups, stirred, and handed it to his nephew. "Here, Alec. This may sweeten your disposition."

"I don't need any sweetening." Still, Alec took the teacup. "What's going on between you and that woman?"

"Nothing more than an interesting discussion."

"How charming," Alec said sarcastically. "The master and his servant, having tea and scones."

"The tea was for you and me. Miss Donovan simply happened along." He decided not to mention to Alec that the girl had been in the passageway again. Or her slippery manner when he'd quizzed her about her background.

"I don't recall receiving an invitation to tea."

The Duke grinned. "Alec, we may be only one day into Caro's house party, but I haven't forgotten the previous one. Or the one before that. Nor have I forgotten your desperate need for . . . sanctuary. As both a marquis with deep pockets and my heir, you are as in demand as a red fox in a hunting party. And since my laboratory is sacrosanct by everyone but invited guests, this is where you go to ground." He cast a glance at the clock on the mantel. "Around this time, too. I only thought you might enjoy some refreshments."

Alec gave a reluctant laugh. "I don't know if I particularly like the comparison to a fox, sir. My sympathies may lie with the creature next time the hunt is on."

"Indeed." Aldridge added two sugar lumps and a drop of cream to his own cup. "It's always a delicate issue dealing with the hopes, dreams, and desires of young ladies."

Alec sank into a chair, stretching his long legs in front of him. He regarded his uncle steadily. "And what of the hopes, dreams, and desires of Miss Donovan?"

Aldridge's smile faded. "What exactly are you implying?"

"You've never been one to play fast-and-loose with your servants—"

"No, I have not."

"Nevertheless," Alec went on doggedly, ignoring the icy snap in his uncle's voice, "you seem remarkably cozy with Kendra Donovan. I ought to remind you that you don't know anything about her character. Not to mention that she's a *servant*, Duke. One instructs a servant, is cordial to a servant, but it is never wise to forget that they are—that Miss Donovan is—still among the lower classes. She is a simple servant."

Aldridge remembered the look in Kendra Donovan's eyes as they scanned his instruments and specimens. She hadn't been baffled by what she saw. She'd even appeared to understand. She'd certainly understood the chart of the night sky.

And she could quote Wordsworth.

"You are usually more astute, Alec," he murmured finally. "Miss Donovan is a lot of things, I suspect. But a *simple* servant? I think not."

"Mrs. Danbury is looking for you."

Kendra's stomach sank as she regarded Rose. "Why?"

"I dunno, but . . ." She leaned forward and whispered, "Were you really 'avin' tea with 'is Grace?"

Wow. Gossip traveled fast, even without Facebook. "I didn't have tea."

"But you were with 'im in 'is laboratory?"

"We talked. Is that so wrong here?"

The girl seemed to ponder that. "I don't much know if it's wrong. But it's not w'ot you'd consider proper."

Rose looked like she wanted to say something more, but Cook hurried over, dumping a tub of potatoes on the table in front of her. She gave Kendra a once-over. "Mrs. Danbury wants ye."

"Yes, ma'am."

"Well, then—"

"Quand est-ce que ces pommes de terres seront prêtes?" Monsieur Anton approached, gesturing madly. *"J'ai besoin de ces pommes de terre!"*

Cook put her hands on her plump hips in such a way that made Kendra think that the two had been through this scene before. "What are ye yammering on about, ye bloody froggy?"

"J'ai besoin des pommes de terre, femme stupide!"

"I don't speak French, as well ye know. 'Course, if yer wantin' to know when we'll be done with these here potatoes, we're peelin' and choppin' as fast as we can."

The chef sniffed, and retreated. Kendra caught him muttering an unflattering description about the cook's ancestry. She looked at Cook, who winked. Kendra couldn't help but smile.

"For someone who doesn't speak French, Cook, you seem to understand him very well," she said.

"We manage, in our own way. Now, ye go on, miss. Go to Mrs. Danbury. Ye need to manage in yer own way, too."

Easier said than done, Kendra thought uneasily, especially when she was sitting across from the housekeeper five minutes later. She didn't think it was possible, but the woman looked even less friendly than before.

"Miss Donovan, I am . . . I am *without words.*" Mrs. Danbury drew in a deep breath, her small bosom swelling in the black bombazine gown. "When you attended Miss Sarah and Miss Georgette this morning did you tell them to *shut up*? Did you shout at them? Swear at them? *Threaten* them?"

For someone who was without words, she was doing an excellent job of getting her point across, Kendra decided. "I . . . don't remember threatening them."

Mrs. Danbury's eyes narrowed. "This is not a *jest,* Miss Donovan."

"I lost my temper," Kendra admitted.

"You . . ." Mrs. Danbury seemed stunned by the confession. She straightened her shoulders. "Miss Donovan, a lady's maid cannot afford to lose her temper. *They are your betters!*"

Kendra had to bite her tongue. Sarah and Georgette were a lot of things, but they weren't her betters. She doubted if they'd be able to pass sixth grade.

"It is quite clear that you are not suited to be a lady's maid," the housekeeper went on coldly. "Miss Sarah and Miss Georgette have already voiced their complaints to Lady Atwood, who, of course, brought those complaints to my attention." Though Kendra didn't know it, Lady Atwood had also ordered Mrs. Danbury to send her away, and though Mrs. Danbury had fully expected to comply with the countess' orders, there was also the matter now of Miss Donovan having taken tea with the Duke of Aldridge. While she didn't know what was going on between the Duke and the American, it was painfully obvious that she must bide her time before dismissing the creature.

"You are not a lady's maid, Miss Donovan."

"I—"

Mrs. Danbury's hand shot up in warning. "I'm not finished. You are *not* a lady's maid. You will join the lower staff."

"I'm not, er, discharged?"

"Did I say you were?" the housekeeper countered testily. She hesitated, appearing a little nonplussed by her own anger. Mrs. Danbury, Kendra suspected, did not lose control often. Or ever. "Your duties will now be that of a downstairs maid," she began again. She folded her hands, surveying the young woman coldly. "You will be given a morning and an afternoon uniform to do your duties. Naturally, the cost will be deducted from your wages, which will be adjusted according to your new position.

"You will," she continued briskly, "change immediately. Lady Atwood has requested a nuncheon to be served alfresco by the lake. Your services will be required for this endeavor. Rose will help you find more appropriate attire."

Slowly, Kendra stood.

"Miss Donovan? Like a lady's maid, there are standards of behavior which are expected of a downstairs maid. You will not tell your betters to . . . to *shut up.* Is that understood?"

"Yes, ma'am."

"You will not *speak* to your betters unless they ask you a specific question. You will, in fact, blend into the background. A good servant, the *perfect* servant, is not noticed. Is *that* understood?"

"Yes. I promise no one will even know I'm there."

Kendra didn't dare smile, but she left lighter, as though a burden had lifted. Helping serve a meal outside didn't sound too bad. Much better than being a lady's maid. Maybe things were looking up.

She never dreamed her promise would be broken just as quickly as it had been given.

11

The heat struck Kendra like a punch to the face when she returned to the kitchen. In the short time that she'd been gone, the temperature had shot up at least ten degrees, along with the noise.

For just a second, she leaned against the doorjamb and watched the maids and footmen race around the kitchen. She could smell the savory odor of roasting meat and garlic mingled with the odd smell of burning feathers. The latter she traced back to one of the workstations, where two maids were busy plucking and burning the feathers off of beheaded pheasants that were stacked on the counter like gruesome cordwood.

Monsieur Anton was almost maniacal as he hopped between the stove, fireplaces, and counters, issuing orders in a mixture of French and broken English as he stirred, seasoned, and tasted whatever was simmering in the kettles and cauldrons.

This is real. It's not possible but it's real.

Aware that she was beginning to draw attention, Kendra straightened and crossed the room to where Rose was standing on her tiptoes, reaching for a large serving bowl.

"Mrs. Danbury told me to join the lower staff."

Rose set the bowl on the cupboard with a clatter, spinning around to stare at her in dismay. "Oh, miss—*no!* W'ot 'appened?"

"What? Oh. Nothing." It took Kendra a moment to realize how that might sound to Rose. From lady's maid to the lower staff. It probably looked like a demotion. Hell, it *was* a demotion—her first ever.

"Are you all right?" Rose's brown eyes brimmed with sympathy.

"I'm fine." At least, she was fine about her change of employment status here in the nineteenth century. She just wasn't fine about being *in* the nineteenth century. She forced a smile when Rose still looked worried. "Honestly. It's not that big of a deal."

"If you say so, miss." Clearly the maid didn't believe her.

"Mrs. Danbury told me to help with lunch, but apparently that requires a change in clothes."

"Oh. Aye. Come along then." Rose picked up the bowl, and brought it to another girl. "'Ere, Beth. Cook needs this for 'er tarts."

Following Rose out of the kitchen, Kendra marveled again at the warren of rooms in the servants' hall, and the vast number of employees. It was like a beehive: constant people, constant movement.

"How many work here at the castle, Rose?"

"Aldridge Castle's one of the oldest an' grandest 'ouseholds in these parts," the maid said with unmistakable pride. "We 'ave round four thousand servants in and about the castle."

"Four *thousand*?"

"Aye, miss. And that ain't includin' outside 'elp for the 'ouse party."

"Good God."

"'Ere we are." Rose opened a door and entered a room that looked like a cross between an old-fashioned seamstress shop and a medieval laundry. On either side of the stone fireplace were walls lined with open cupboards containing neatly folded fabrics, spools of thread and trimmings. In the center of the room was a wooden counter with a thick blanket tossed over it, and a dress laid over that. It was, Kendra realized, a primitive version of an ironing board. An older, heavyset woman was running an iron that looked like it weighed a ton across a brown dress, while the younger maid helped by keeping the material smooth.

The older woman flashed them a hard look. "We're a mite busy today, Rose," she said, and handed the iron to her assistant, who immediately transferred it to the hearth to heat up again.

"Aye, Mrs. Beeton." Rose nodded. "But miss 'ere needs a dress."

Mrs. Beeton wiped the sweat from her brow. "What kinda dress?"

"Maid's dress."

"We don't have time to sew a new dress."

"She can 'ave Jenny's old dress. Since she ran off to Bath with Mr. Kipper and all."

"Ooh. And a right scandal that was. Not even a by-your-leave!" Mrs. Beeton sniffed, and gave Kendra a measuring look. "You part of the temporary help?"

"Well—"

"She's been 'ired on," Rose put in.

"What happened to your hair? You been ill?"

"I—"

"She's better now," said Rose.

"What's your name?"

"Um—"

"Kendra Donovan. She's an American."

"You're a right chatterbox, Miss Donovan, ain't you?" Mrs. Beeton remarked.

Kendra smiled.

Mrs. Beeton went over to a drawer, shuffled around, and pulled out a pale blue dress. Holding it up, she surveyed both the dress and then Kendra with a sharp eye. "It'll do," she pronounced. "But it needs ironing."

"Oh, but we're in an 'urry, Mrs. Beeton," Rose protested. "Mrs. Danbury—"

"Would want her staff to look respectable."

Recognizing defeat, Rose let out a breath. "Oh, aye. But Mrs. Danbury says she's to 'elp with the nuncheon. And Lady Atwood 'as a bee in her bonnet to set it up down by the lake. Monsieur Anton is anxious about the 'ole thing."

"Monsieur Anton is usually anxious. He's French." Mrs. Beeton briskly exchanged the dress on the counter for the maid's uniform. "You'll find a cap and apron in the third drawer, Rose. Maggie, bring me the iron."

Kendra didn't know much about ironing—she'd always dropped her laundry off at the dry cleaner around the corner from her apartment—but she realized this was a far more laborious process. Without electricity, the iron had to be constantly reheated in the fireplace. Rose was beginning to look anxious by the time the uniform finally met Mrs. Beeton's approval. She removed it from the counter and handed it to Kendra.

"You can come back for alterations when there's time. You're a mite smaller than Jenny, so we'll need to nip in the waist. Jenny did love Cook's cakes."

"Thank you, ma'am." Rose was already at the door. "Come along, miss."

In the bedchamber, Kendra changed into the new uniform. While Rose hung up her discarded gown, she put on the apron and mop cap. Unable to resist, she looked at herself in the small swivel mirror, and nearly sighed.

"You look a proper maid," Rose said with an encouraging smile.

"My parents would be so proud."

"W'ot?"

"Nothing." She pressed her thumb and index finger to the bridge of her nose. *Stay calm. Stay focused.*

"How long have you been at Aldridge Castle, Rose?" she asked as they went back down the servants' stairs.

"Ooh, since I was ten. Me sister worked as a scullery maid, and when she bettered 'erself, I got 'ired on by Mrs. Danbury."

"Where's your family?"

"They live down the road. Me pa has a field he tends for 'Is Grace. Me brothers 'elp 'im. I miss me sister, who went off to London. I 'ave another sister that married an officer in the army, and lives in Colchester now. Then there's the wee ones—"

"Good God. How many brothers and sisters do you have?"

"Fourteen. I 'ave six brothers and eight sisters. 'Ow many brothers and sisters do you 'ave, miss?"

"None."

Rose looked astounded. "No brothers and sisters! Not a one? Was your ma ill, too?"

"No. Busy. She and my father divorced. He remarried and has two children by his second wife. So I suppose I do have siblings. A brother and sister."

"Divorced?" If anything, Rose looked even more astounded. And a little appalled. "I don't know anyone 'oo's divorced!"

Kendra realized she was talking too much. Life, societal mores, and people would change in the next two hundred years in ways that Rose could never hope to understand, and that Kendra could never hope to explain.

She was grateful when they arrived again at the kitchen. Cook immediately homed in on them, directing Rose to the pastry room and Kendra to the lower staff dining room. "Eat now, 'cause Mrs. Danbury'll want everything ready by the lake in an hour."

The lower staff dining room was down the corridor from the upper staff dining room. At least a dozen maids and workmen were already sitting around the table, eating. As soon as she sat down, a maid materialized with a plate, silverware and—shockingly, Kendra thought—a glass of beer. And not the lite version, either, she realized, as she sipped the fermented brew.

Unlike breakfast, lunch was a speedy affair, with everybody racing through the meal that consisted of boiled potatoes and freshly picked peas, slabs of roast beef, lashings of gravy, and thick, lighter-than-air slices of bread with generous pats of butter. Real butter. Real bread. Not a preservative in sight. The meal was unpretentious and filling, and Kendra was surprised that, like breakfast, she finished it all—and enjoyed it. At this rate, she wouldn't need Mrs. Beeton to take in her dress; she'd be filling it out in no time.

"So . . . what's next?" she asked the young maid seated next to her.

"Lady Atwood's gipsying."

"Gipsying?"

"Aye. We'll need to bring the lot down to the lake."

The lot, Kendra soon realized, was four long wooden tables and several dozen chairs, which were loaded into a horse-drawn wagon, along with enormous wicker baskets carefully packed with starched, hemstitched linens, polished silverware, china, and cut crystal. Smaller linen baskets, laden with food, spices, liqueur, and wine, were carried out under the watchful eye of Mr. Harding and Mrs. Danbury. Kendra found herself in charge of one of them, and joined the procession as it marched out the servant's door and down a flagstone path flanked by hedgerows, winding its way around one of the many gardens.

For just a moment, Kendra allowed herself to forget about her crazy situation and drink in the sheer physical beauty surrounding her. It was nice to be outside, to feel the sun beating warmly on her face and the faint breeze that carried the perfume of honeysuckle and rose, lilac and peonies. Beyond the ebb and flow of conversation and steady shuffling of feet around her, she could hear the drone of bees, the chirp of birds, the rustling of shrubs, and long blades of grass. It wasn't silent by any means, but Kendra was keenly aware of the lack of twenty-first-century noise. This was a world with no automobiles or airplanes. No jets would streak across the sky. There was no mechanical thrum of tractors plowing across the fields or cars moving along the country roads. Steam locomotives were in their infancy, with another ten years to go before England developed its first public steam railway. On water, steamboats were just beginning to chug their way into a territory dominated by sails.

Oh, God. Had it only been two days ago that she'd jumped on a Boeing 747, flying 567 miles per hour, touching only clouds?

The flagstone path fell away, replaced by a ten-minute walk up a gently sloping hill before curving down into a forest. Kendra could feel the strain in her muscles as she shifted the wicker basket, but she doggedly kept pace. No one else seemed to find it an effort.

The floral scent of the garden gave way to the more loamy smells of the forest. Shadows, cast by tall pine trees and ancient oak and elm, dueled with the sun's light. Between the tall, spiky weeds and woods, Kendra saw the gleam of blue, heard the splash and murmur of moving water. She caught herself from stumbling over exposed roots and pushed forward. Again, she shifted the basket to relieve the dull ache in her arms. Two minutes later, they arrived at their destination, a picturesque dell ringed by trees and rock formations and a lake. Water cascaded down sheer rocks at the far end.

Kendra saw that the horse-drawn wagon was already parked (could you park horses?) on the other side of the trees so as not to ruin the tranquil ambience of the area. Mrs. Danbury and Mr. Harding must have come with the wagon, because they were already there, keeping an eye on the footmen who were setting up the tables and chairs.

It was like a Ralph Lauren ad come to life. Somebody had even produced—and lit, for heaven's sake—heavy brass candelabras on the tables. Lady Atwood may have wanted to dine alfresco—gipsying, as the maid had called it—but that didn't mean she wanted a picnic, Kendra reflected wryly as she helped shake out the white linen tablecloths and napkins.

Footmen uncorked bottles of fruity white wine and set them in the lake to chill. Bottles of red were kept to the side. The servants congregated around two of the tables that were laden with plates of food that would be served: baked trout swimming in cucumber sauce; roast beef and ham so thinly sliced it was almost transparent; baby asparagus salad as a side dish. Butter cakes were set alongside fruit stacked like pyramids.

Mrs. Danbury checked her pocket watch, and nodded to Mr. Harding. There was a military precision to planning such an event that Kendra hadn't appreciated before. She'd been to similar functions, but always as a guest.

"'Ere they come," whispered one of the maids, who apparently had ears like a bat. Half a second later, Kendra heard the voices interspersed with feminine laugher and masculine chuckles.

They were an exotic parade, thirty men and women in total. The Duke of Aldridge led the way. On his arm was a small, plump woman in a vivid blue dress and bonnet decorated with an enormous peacock feather. Alec was right behind him. He looked more handsome than the last time she'd seen him, probably because he wasn't scowling. Instead, he seemed relaxed, smiling at the woman he was ushering into the clearing. Kendra couldn't see the woman's face, since it was angled toward Alec, and obscured by the bonnet and gauzy white veil she wore. *Wife or girlfriend?* Kendra wondered as she observed the intimacy between them.

She nearly jumped when Alec turned his head suddenly, looking straight at her. Even from that distance Kendra could see the green eyes narrow in suspicion. His companion turned, too, and looked at Kendra.

She wasn't beautiful, Kendra noted with some surprise. That, she supposed, was her own prejudice. Guys who looked like Alec usually had a beautiful woman on their arm. This woman—Kendra pegged her to be in her early twenties—had pleasant enough features, but her skin was severely pockmarked, destroying any hope of beauty.

When the woman turned back to say something to Alec, drawing his attention, Kendra deliberately shifted her gaze to the rest of the group. It was odd that there were more women than men. Societal mores, she'd have thought, would have paired up the sexes.

She spotted the brats, Sarah and Georgina, at the end of the procession, dangling off the arms of two young men who were dressed like the other men in the party—cravats, shirts, vests, coats, breeches, and boots—except the points of their collars were so starched and exaggerated, their cravats so elaborate, that their chins were swallowed up in yards of fabric.

"Lady Atwood, you've simply outdone yourself," trilled an exquisitely lovely blonde in a sugary pink-and-white striped dress and matching coat and hat. She paused to admire the table settings. "'Tis absolutely delightful."

"You are too kind, Lady Dover." The woman on the Duke's arm gave a gracious nod. "Thankfully, the weather is cooperating. 'Tis been a dreadfully chilly summer."

As the nuncheon began, Kendra concentrated on her duties, but couldn't help but overhear snippets of conversation. In many ways, this was no different than social gatherings in her own time. Chatter centered around mutual acquaintances and the latest gossip from London. Yet she nearly dropped a plate when someone mentioned the health of King George and the political intrigue surrounding the Prince Regent.

Sweet Jesus. *Mad King George*. The guy America had revolted against. He was freaking *alive!*

"Careful with the dishware," one of the maids whispered.

"Sorry." She shook off her sense of amazement, and tried to pretend she was watching a period play. There was a lot of flirting going on, plenty of fluttering of ivory fans and eyelashes. It was weird to think that in another two hundred years people would flirt by pole dancing, twerking, and sexting.

The lunch seemed to stretch on interminably. But maybe that was because the maids were required to stand silently in the background. The footmen had the more active job, replenishing wineglasses under Mr. Harding's direction, and serving the food under Mrs. Danbury's eagle eye. When one of the young ladies dropped a spoon, Mrs. Danbury snapped her fingers, and a footman scooped it off the ground and replaced it with a clean spoon within seconds. If this had been a restaurant, it would've registered five stars.

The fruit and cheese were offered at the end of the meal, along with glasses of Madeira. Kendra finally understood the purpose of the extra ladies when several of the young men approached for permission to walk with the young ladies around the area.

Chaperones. This was an era where ladies were practically kept under glass until they could be wed off.

Shaking her head—if she'd been dropped in the middle of Mars, she couldn't have felt more alienated—Kendra turned her attention to the mundane task of scraping off remnants of food from the china plates, and stacking them in the wicker baskets so they could be carted back to the castle for washing.

The scream that cut through the idyllic atmosphere was so shocking that, for the second time, Kendra nearly dropped the plate she held. Everyone froze. Then instinct and training kicked in. Kendra put the plate down and began running in the direction of the screams. She made an instinctive movement for her service weapon, her fingers brushing her skirt.

Goddamnit!

"Get back!" she shouted as she rounded the rocks and shrubbery. She saw a girl—Georgina, she recognized—shaking and crying in the arms of an ashen-faced man.

"What is it?" she demanded, scanning the area. What kind of wildlife did they have in these parts? "What's wrong?"

The man gave her a blank stare. Georgina continued wailing, hysterical. Kendra considered slapping her, but thought she'd enjoy it too much. Instead, she reached out and shook the arm of the man. "What happened?"

"T-there! Over there!" he gasped and pointed to the water.

Warily, she inched toward the edge of the lake, and caught the pale glimmer in the dark water. It could've been a dead fish, but she knew it wasn't. She knew what it was even before she saw the hair floating like flotsam on the surface of the water, the cameo blur below, the wide, dark eyes. Most likely, the girl had been pretty. Yet nature, as brutal as it was beautiful, had taken its toll. Now she was just dead.

12

Kendra studied the nude body that had been caught and anchored in the cattails and weeds along the shore.

"My God!" The Duke of Aldridge's voice came from behind her, sounding shaken. "My God. Is that . . . ? We need to get her out of there. We need to help her!"

"She's beyond help," Kendra stated matter-of-factly, and shifted her gaze to the surrounding area. It was as idyllic from this angle as it was from where they'd set up the nuncheon. Green trees, lush shrubbery, slate-gray rocks, and the waterfall created a private oasis of which Georgina and the young man no doubt had wished to take advantage. Instead, they'd found death—and, she could see, not an easy or a natural death. Her practiced eye scanned the body, noting the dark bruises circling her throat, the ligature marks at her wrists, and the lacerations running across the torso. Something tightened inside her as her gaze fell on what she considered the most damning of all—the injury on her left breast.

Alec crouched down beside her, his face grim as he stared at the figure under the water. "We still need to get her out of there."

"No. We need to . . ." *Preserve the crime scene.* It hit her like a two-ton brick that those words had no meaning here. What the hell was she going to do? Call the coroner, the cops, the CSI team? She'd never studied this particular time period, but she sure as hell knew that the tools she was so familiar with in the twenty-first century were either rudimentary now, or nonexistent.

Alec eyed her curiously. "We need to . . . what?"

"Nothing," she mumbled and rubbed her hands over her face, trying to organize her thoughts.

"What happened? Did she fall in?" A man stepped to the edge of the lake so he could get a better look.

"Most likely she was bathing, slipped, and drowned," suggested another man.

Kendra shot him an incredulous look. Would they write this off as a *drowning*? She couldn't let that happen. "Not unless she walked naked through the forest to get here. You don't see any clothes, do you?"

Alec frowned as he did a narrow-eyed scan. "This area is a watershed, with a network of tributaries, one of which feeds this lake. The main river flows toward the ocean, but her body could've been swept downstream and carried here."

"That may be how her body got here, but that's not how she died." Kendra stood up abruptly. "She was murdered."

For the space of about three seconds, there was a shocked silence.

Then someone denounced shrilly, "That's outrageous!"

Kendra glanced around. The rebuke had come from the woman in the vivid blue dress who the Duke had escorted to the nuncheon. She glared at Kendra like she was responsible for the dead woman. "Who is this creature, Bertie?"

That seemed to rouse Aldridge. He still looked deathly pale, and his hands shook visibly as he brought up a handkerchief to wipe the sweat from his brow. But he made an effort to pull himself together. "Caro, you and the other ladies must return to the castle. Harding? Mrs. Danbury? Please be so good as to escort the ladies home."

The butler moved forward. "Of course, Your Grace."

"I'll be happy to lend my assistance to the ladies, sir." The offer came from the young man who was still holding the whimpering, red-eyed Georgina. Sarah had raced to her friend's side, and was now casting curious glances at the lake. She didn't look eager to leave. In fact, Kendra thought several of the ladies looked undecided, wanting to display the proper horror even as they strained to get a glimpse of the body. As they were standing several yards away from the lip of the lake, Kendra doubted whether anyone could see anything. Georgina was probably the only woman who'd gotten a good view of the corpse.

Kendra caught the hard look Mrs. Danbury shot her. The housekeeper's expression would've been understood even in the twenty-first century: *Get your ass over here, now!*

Her heart sank. This was outside her jurisdiction. *Way* outside her jurisdiction. Like, two hundred years outside her jurisdiction. But she couldn't force her feet to move.

They'd probably shrug the girl's death off as an accident. And why should she care? She didn't belong here. Her only concern was to get back to her own time line.

But what if the two incidents were connected? Like most people in law enforcement, Kendra wasn't a big fan of coincidences. She'd been thrown back in time, and now she was presented with a murder victim. And, God help her, the violence that had been done to this poor girl piqued every one of Kendra's instincts.

She'd probably pay for her insubordination, but she ignored the housekeeper. "The Duke's right. We need to clear the area, secure the scene," she said in a low voice to Alec.

He gave her an odd look, but before he could respond, the woman with the pockmarked face separated herself from the group of ladies that Mr. Harding and Mrs. Danbury were trying to hustle out of the area.

"Bloody hell," Alec muttered under his breath, and moved forward to intercept her. Kendra couldn't hear what was being said, but from the woman's body language she was making an appeal to stay while Alec was ordering her to go. The woman gestured to the lake, even stomped her foot, but Alec won the argument. The woman shot Kendra a disgruntled look, then whirled around, skirts belling out as she rejoined the departing procession.

"Now, Miss Donovan," Alec said, returning to Kendra's side. There was a tic along the clean line of his jaw; impatience deepening the green of his eyes. "You need to explain yourself."

Kendra had the oddest sense of déjà vu. A handful of men had stayed behind and were now staring at her. Once again, as in her life in the twenty-first century, she was the only woman . . . and a freak.

"No." Aldridge stepped forward. "Alec, we need to get that poor girl out of the water. Now."

Alec exchanged a look with the Duke, and nodded. "Yes, you are correct, Your Grace. I trust you have no objections, Miss Donovan?"

He was being snide, she knew, but she answered anyway. "She wasn't killed here, so you won't be destroying any trace evidence." Not that it would matter if there was trace evidence, she thought bleakly. She wouldn't be able to examine it, anyway.

Again she felt a wave of helplessness. What could she do here? Christ, even something as simple as fingerprinting was beyond the scope of these people. Fingerprints *had* been used as a source of identification as early as the T'ang Dynasty in China, and there'd even been a murder case solved in ancient Rome by identifying a bloody handprint, but that was an anomaly. The distinctive ridges in fingerprints, she knew, wouldn't be accepted as a crime-solving tool for another fifty years.

She stepped back while Alec took charge, ordering two footmen to wade into the water to disentangle the body from the weeds. During the grim process, the younger footman began to look so green that Kendra feared he was going to throw up on the corpse at any moment. Thankfully, they managed to get her limbs free and carry her to the shore before anyone got sick. Alec was already stripping off his coat to cover her in a belated attempt at modesty.

Kendra saw the look in his eyes, knew that he understood. He'd seen what she had. That close to the body, it would've been impossible to miss.

"She's been strangled," he said.

"Yes." Kendra knelt, scanning the girl's white face. "God, she looks so young. Fourteen. Maybe fifteen," she murmured softly, feeling a tug of pity. She cleared her throat. "She hasn't been in the water long. Less than twenty-four hours, I'd say."

"What, are you a bloody body snatcher?" laughed one of the loitering young men, earning a few uneasy chuckles from his peers.

A man with ash blond hair and soulful brown eyes came forward, squatting down beside her and Alec. "I may be of some help. I was a surgeon. Simon Dalton," he introduced himself, meeting Kendra's eyes. He shifted the jacket aside. It took Kendra a moment to realize he was being careful to preserve the girl's modesty before lifting her arm. "She's still in rigor mortis."

"The water's cold, so rigor mortis could be slowed."

"You seem remarkably well-informed, ah . . . ?" That was from the tall, russet-haired gentleman standing next to the Duke. He was handsome—not quite in Alec's league, but there was something compelling about his dark blue eyes in the tanned, raw-boned face as he stared down at her.

"Kendra Donovan. I've had some experience."

He lifted an incredulous brow. "In murder? Forgive me, but you are a woman. A maid!"

"So?" Since that response seemed to flummox him, Kendra went back to studying the dead girl. "I suspect we'll find the hyoid bone and the thyroid and cricoid cartilages compressed from manual strangulation." She glanced up at Simon Dalton. "And look at the eyes, Doctor—subconjunctival and petechial hemorrhage."

Surprisingly, he flushed. "I'm not a physician; I'm a *surgeon*."

She frowned. What the hell was the difference?

"I noticed," he continued, in response to her observation, and then explained to the group at large, "Petechiae is when the blood vessels around the eye rupture due to asphyxiation."

Alec scowled. "Does anybody recognize her? Is she from the area?"

Flies, ever in tune with the scent of death, began to arrive. Alec waved his hand impatiently to disperse them, a temporary reprieve, as they simply buzzed back in greater numbers.

The men surged forward to get a better look at the dead girl. Kendra got the impression that it was curiosity that drove them, not a desire to help. One of the young men made a noise low in his throat and stumbled back.

"Watch it, Gabriel!" another man grumbled, pushing lightly at him.

"Have you seen her before?" Kendra asked Gabriel sharply. He looked to be around her age, good-looking with tousled dark brown hair and hazel eyes. His reaction could've been the shock of seeing a dead body. Or something else.

"No . . . No . . ." Gabriel moved away. As Kendra watched, he reached into his coat and pulled out a silver flask, unscrewing the lid and drinking deeply. Judging by his flushed face and somewhat glassy eyes, she suspected this wasn't the first time he'd used the flask today.

Alec was watching, too. "Try avoid getting foxed, Gabe."

The younger man stiffened, shooting Alec such a blistering look that Kendra was surprised she couldn't feel the heat of it.

"It's difficult to tell . . . but she doesn't appear familiar," Aldridge murmured, rubbing the back of his neck as though it ached. "No word has gone around about a missing girl. Have you heard anything, Morland? The local magistrate is usually the first to hear such things."

"Eh?" The man with the russet hair—Morland—gave a start, then shook his head. "No, Your Grace. I've heard nothing."

Aldridge stared down at the girl somberly. "Somebody had to have been mad with rage to strangle this poor child and throw her into the river."

Kendra hesitated, chest tightening. Again, she considered letting this go, just agreeing with whatever they said . . . dammit. She *couldn't*.

"This wasn't rage," she said slowly. "It was calculated. Cold and calculated. The man who did this did it deliberately."

Again there was a stunned silence. Then the man named Morland demanded, "What the devil are you saying?"

"I'm saying this girl wasn't just strangled. She was strangled *repeatedly*. The pattern of bruising round the neck is large, irregular, meaning he strangled her and then allowed her to breathe again. He then brought his hands back, the position slightly different—see?" She pointed to the irregular shadowy smudges around the victim's throat. "And he strangled her again. And again."

Morland glared at her. "That is utterly preposterous! *Who* are you? Really, sir." He turned to the Duke. "You can't expect us to swallow such a preposterous tale. And from a mere servant . . . from a . . . a *woman!*"

Kendra had to bite back a scathing reply. *This is not my era*, she reminded herself. If they didn't believe her, she'd have to let it go.

Still, her mouth felt dry as she shifted her gaze to the Duke of Aldridge. His brow was furrowed, but she couldn't read him. Would he dismiss her findings because she was a woman?

He shook his head. "'Tis not the time to argue about it, Morland. We need to do something with this poor girl."

Kendra let out the breath that she hadn't realized she'd been holding. He wasn't calling her crazy. *Yet.*

That test would come when she told the Duke what she knew, what she suspected.

She could only pray that he'd believe her.

Kendra hung back while they discussed where to bring the body—the castle's icehouse was the final consensus. Then they had to figure out the best way to get her there. It was finally decided that a couple of footmen would carry her to the clearing, and a wagon would transport the victim the rest of the way to the castle.

The process was cumbersome. First, the remaining footmen were squeamish about touching the body any more than they had to. They balked at her suggestion that they relinquish their fancy livery coats to wrap around the victim, and only did so after Alec ordered them.

Kendra couldn't really blame them. Hell, she wasn't happy with the situation either. It didn't matter that this wasn't the kill site, or that the body had been washed thoroughly by the river and lake, or the fact that even if she could find some trace evidence, she didn't have the equipment or forensics experts to give her the answers that she needed. She still kept track of every forensic violation that was made.

"We must summon the local constable," the Duke said as they began their trek back through the forest.

Alec snorted. "Much good that'll do. The worst Roger Hilliard has had to face is catching a poacher now and then, and breaking up fights between farmers, because a cow got into somebody's field and ate their bloody grain."

"So . . . in terms of law enforcement, you only have a local constable?" Kendra asked, the sinking feeling in her stomach getting worse.

"Morland's the magistrate," someone pointed out.

Alec scowled. "You don't have any experience in this matter either, Morland."

Kendra caught the flash of anger in Morland's eye. Alec wouldn't win points for diplomacy, but she silently agreed with him. None of them had any experience in this matter.

Except for her.

"What do you suggest, Sutcliffe?" the other man challenged. "Bring in a Bow Street Runner?"

Alec's jaw tightened. "Perhaps."

"I don't like bringing in someone from the outside," Morland scowled.

Both the sentiment and the sour tone nearly made Kendra smile. It was almost exactly the same words, certainly the same inflection, that she'd heard from countless cops when the FBI was called in to investigate homicides. Maybe things weren't so different here after all.

Then she remembered what Morland had said to the Duke. *You can't expect us to swallow such a preposterous tale. And from a mere servant . . . a woman.*

It wasn't like she hadn't faced discrimination before. But dealing with a stubborn local sheriff or a surly police officer who resented the FBI's input—whether she was a woman or not—was a far different situation than *this*. She shivered suddenly, rubbing her arms.

"Are you all right?"

Kendra glanced up at Alec, surprised by the concern she heard in his voice. "I've had better days."

His mouth curved at her dry tone, but the smile was fleeting. He reached out automatically to hold the tree branches back from slapping her in the face. The action was surprisingly chivalrous.

"There's no need to be afraid, Miss Donovan," he assured her, surprising her even more. "You'll be safe at the castle."

Kendra blinked. He was, she realized, actually trying to be nice. Except he didn't know what the hell he was talking about.

Some things weren't so different in this time line. In fact, some things, she thought, never changed. Like murder. And monsters.

"You're wrong, you know," she said solemnly. "We should be afraid . . . because it's going to happen again."

13

The icehouse was a large, low, windowless building of gray stone, with its entry point—thick oak double doors—facing north. The squat appearance was deceptive, Kendra realized, as they went through another set of doors that led down, below ground level. It was clever, making use of the earth to keep the temperature cool. There were four rooms, the largest being where the ice itself was stored, giant slabs that had been cut from lakes and ponds during the winter months and carted here to be stored year-round.

The other three chambers had a variety of uses. Two were used for storing perishables like milk and butter, and vegetables. The third, the one they crowded in, was obviously where the fresh game hunted on the estate was skinned and deboned. A handful of pheasant and quail, and several rabbits hung by their feet on hooks in the ceiling, near the white tiled wall at the far end of the room. Though lanterns had been strung around the room, thick shadows seemed to crouch and wait in the corners. The air smelled of smoke, earth, gamey meat, and raw blood.

Dalton tossed a coarse wool blanket over the long worktable in the middle of the room before the girl was laid on it. Kendra unbuttoned and unwrapped the footmen's livery, leaving the girl exposed, her flesh no longer marble-white, but artificially golden in the lamp-lit room, the bruises and cuts on her body appearing darker, more grotesque.

Alec was surprised at the flicker of embarrassment he felt. He was no stranger to a woman's body, albeit they'd all been very much alive when he'd viewed them. He'd also seen his share of death during the bloody campaign waged against Napoleon. But this seemed . . . *wrong.* Kendra Donovan's presence seemed *wrong.*

The Duke apparently felt the same way, and cleared his throat uncomfortably. "Mayhap we ought to put a blanket on the poor girl, Miss Donovan, to preserve her modesty."

Kendra looked up with a frown. It took her a moment to realize the expression that she saw on their faces was discomfort. She correctly surmised that most of the men's unease came not from the dead girl in the room, but the living one. If she was going to be involved in the investigation, she needed to set the parameters now. "She's beyond modesty," she said flatly. "Right now, the truth is more important."

"The truth?" Alec raised his brows. "Such as your pronouncement that whoever did this will kill again? Pray tell, how could you possibly know that, Miss Donovan? Do you have the sight?"

"The sight?" Then she understood. "Oh. Like being psychic . . . or a soothsayer, you mean?"

"Yes, Miss Donovan." Impatience thinned his lips. "A soothsayer. Someone who claims to know the future."

Kendra was instantly struck by that notion. She *did* know the future. Their future was her past . . . or, rather, her history. It was an odd thought. And a distracting one. She pushed it aside.

"I must agree with Lord Sutcliffe," Morland put in, stepping near the table so that the lamplight limned his features and brought out the red highlights in his hair. Suspicion glinted in his eyes. "How can you possibly know the future, pray?"

Kendra hesitated. This was the tricky part. In seventy-three years, Jack the Ripper would hold London in thrall with his brutal slayings of five prostitutes, but the term *serial killer* would have little or no meaning to the public-at-large until the 1970s. By the time the twenty-first century rolled around, people would not only know about serial killers, society would practically celebrate them in prime-time shows, made-for-TV movies, feature films, documentaries, and a slew of books devoted to the subject.

"Well, Miss Donovan?" Alec raised his brows.

She shifted her attention to the Duke. He was the one with the power, she knew. In this society's pecking order, he was the one she needed to convince.

"Where I come from . . ." she began, then paused, frowning slightly as she tried to organize her thoughts. Even in her own time, one dead body wouldn't bring in the FBI. The magic number was three. That proved a pattern, that was the formula suggesting a serial killer was on the loose. Yet what she saw here on the victim was compelling evidence suggesting that was exactly what they were dealing with.

"We . . . we've dealt with murderers like this one. They're not normal." *Clumsy, Donovan,* she thought, as Aldridge's eyebrows shot up. "I know that murder is *not* normal. But there's often a motivation. Profit or greed. Anger or jealousy. But this . . . this is more." God, she was bungling it. A more pragmatic approach was required. "Look at the wound on her left breast."

Aldridge frowned, then leaned forward for a closer inspection. "A bruise."

"No. Look closer."

"Ah. A bite mark."

"Yes."

"An animal of some sort," Dalton suggested, frowning. "A wild dog, mayhap."

"No. If you look at the impression, it's not canine. They're human."

Morland stared at her. "You cannot know—"

"Yes, I *can*." Her eyes flashed impatiently. "Can anyone tell me what animal would take one bite and leave the rest of the vic alone?"

"The vic?" Alec wondered.

"Victim. *The girl*."

The Duke straightened. "Miss Donovan is correct. If an animal did this, she'd have been mauled. A wild beast would not leave one single bite mark."

She moved down the victim. She wasn't a medical examiner, but she knew what she was viewing. Would they see the same thing?

"She has contusions and cuts around both her wrists." Although she wished she had latex gloves on, she picked up a hand and ignored its cold, waxy feel as she studied the fingers and then palms. "No visible defensive wounds. Under attack, human beings will instinctively defend themselves. We put up our hands, try to return the attack." She scanned the circle of skeptical faces. "This woman did not. She was held immobile throughout the attack. Based on the lacerations on her wrists, I'd say it was metal, most likely handcuffs. Rope would have created more of an abrasion."

"Good God." Aldridge's eyes filled with horror. "What are you saying?"

"He tortured her. I'd need a magnifying glass, but these look like cuts, most likely by a knife." She frowned as she studied the bruised, cut flesh along the torso. "It looks as though he spent time cutting her."

"Jesus Christ," Alec breathed, affected.

"There's more." While the victim had been in the water and the dark mane had been wet, it hadn't been as obvious. Now Kendra threaded her hands through the girl's hair, fanning the long dark strands out so they could see chunks behind the ears and back of the head had been clipped, sometimes close to the scalp. "He took pieces of her hair."

"Why? *Why* would he do such a thing?" Morland asked, sounding fascinated, despite himself.

"A trophy. They sometimes take souvenirs from their victims to relive the moment over again."

Aldridge stared at her. "*They*?"

"This type of killer," she answered slowly. "This girl wasn't killed because of robbery or greed or jealousy. This type of killer can't control himself, even though control is a big issue with him. Control. Power. Domination. I . . ." *Need time to work up a full profile,* she thought. But she couldn't say that. She'd probably already said too much. "I don't know who killed this girl, but I can tell you two things: this isn't his first kill, and he *will* do it again."

There was a stunned silence, and then Kendra turned to Dalton. "You said you are a surgeon. Will you handle the autopsy, Dr. Dalton? Unless there's someone else . . . ?"

Again, the man flushed. "It's *Mr.* Dalton. And I said I *was* a surgeon."

Oh, God, had his license been suspended, revoked? Maybe he was incompetent. Was that why he reacted so strangely whenever she called him a doctor? "I'm sorry. If you're no longer practicing—"

"No, I'm not, but . . ." He shook his head, and glanced over at the Duke. "Your Grace, with your permission, I would be willing to conduct the postmortem."

"Thank you, Mr. Dalton. Your assistance would be invaluable." Aldridge sighed as his gaze returned to the dead girl. "We must get her description out in the community. Someone has to know who she is. We shall have to bring in that Runner, Alec."

"I'll dispatch a note to London at once."

The Duke nodded and sighed, "We've done all we can do here. Mr. Dalton, you'll need to send around for your tools. Miss Donovan, I shall escort you back to the castle."

As he drew her arm through his, Kendra caught the distrustful looks on the faces of the other men. *Thank God I didn't end up two centuries earlier, because they'd be burning me as a witch.*

Outside, the Duke murmured, "'Tis good to feel the sunshine, is it not, Miss Donovan?"

Kendra forced herself to ignore the disbelief she could feel emanating from the trio behind her. She lifted her face.

"Yes," she answered Aldridge. And it did feel good. The breeze, redolent with flowers, chased away the scent of death from the gloomy, cold, cave-like room.

But the sunshine couldn't dispel the chill in her heart. Because she knew that somewhere out there, in this sunshine-filled world, there was a monster masquerading as a man. And he was probably already stalking his next victim.

She wondered if it was already too late.

14

"We'll send for Hilliard, of course," Aldridge said. "At the very least, he can be responsible for circulating a description of the poor girl."

They'd entered the castle's enormous, atrium-style hall. The ceiling was interlaced with wooden beams. Hanging from the center was a massive, ormolu chandelier with more than a dozen tapered candles, currently unlit. Daylight streamed in through the long, skinny windows flanking the entrance. The half-moon stained-glass window above the double doors splashed a pretty prism on the black-and-white marble tiled floor. On the far wall, a wide staircase, its balustrade made of heavy wrought iron, wound upward. The walls were dotted with oil lamps set in ornate mirrored sconces, and decorated with medieval tapestries, weapons, and the mounted heads of rams and deer.

She saw the Duke's gaze flick toward the big glassy eyes of the long dead animals and knew what he was thinking. *Trophies.*

"Your Grace, gentlemen . . ." Mr. Harding materialized out of one of the shadowy corridors. His eyes rested on Kendra briefly, appearing at a loss for words. He recovered, ignoring her completely by shifting his gaze back to the Duke. "The countess is in the Green Salon, sir. She sent word that she'd like to speak with you when you returned."

"Thank you, Harding."

The butler sketched a bow, cast an indecipherable look in Kendra's direction, and disappeared through an arched doorway.

Aldridge said, "I must see to Caro. Alec, if you'd be so good as to send for the constable and dispatch that note for the Runner. I suggest we meet in my study again . . ." He consulted his pocket watch. "Say, at half past five? That should give Mr. Dalton enough time to conduct the postmortem. Until then, I'm certain my sister has arranged some activity for the guests that ought to keep you well occupied, Mr. Morland."

Morland inclined his head. "Thank you, sir."

Kendra held her breath as the Duke's gaze came to rest on her. "You shall, of course, join us, Miss Donovan."

Relief loosened the knots in her stomach. "Thank you, sir." She hesitated. "Well, I . . . should get back to my duties."

"Until half past five then." Aldridge smiled.

Although she could feel their eyes drilling holes into her shoulder blades as she crossed the hall, Kendra resisted looking back, slipping through one of the doors that, she hoped, would take her back to the kitchens.

Alec waited until she was gone before raising a brow at his uncle. "And what duties are those? Last evening she said she was a lady's maid. Today, she clearly is not."

Aldridge smiled. "Last evening you thought she was a thief."

Morland seemed bemused by their conversation. "The woman is a thief?"

"Most certainly not."

Alec's mouth tightened. "You cannot be certain, Duke. I also said she was a liar, most certainly a liar. Do you believe her about the girl?"

The Duke's smile faded, and his gaze moved to the trophies decorating the wall. The girl's hair *had* been cut. Someone had bitten her, for heaven's sake.

"I don't know what to believe, my boy, but, for now, we should keep an open mind."

Kendra had never felt more like a freak than she did as she made her way back to the kitchens. She knew she was under surveillance, recognized the furtive looks cast in her direction. A few servants even stopped their work to openly stare as she passed.

A headache began brewing at the base of her skull. It didn't help that the kitchens were now boiling hot and even noisier than before, or that here, too, people paused in their work and stared until Monsieur Anton, noticing, began to yell at them in French.

"Oh, miss!" Rose ran toward her, and grabbed both her hands. "Wot 'appened? We 'eard there was a murder!"

Another maid came forward. "Aye—and the fiend is on the loose!" That declaration caused several gasps of fright to ripple through the crowd of young maids gathering around Kendra.

"We'll be murdered in our beds, we will!"

"Nonsense." Cook came over to disperse the knot of young maids. "Everyone back ter work. Now! Dora, those chestnuts won't blanch themselves!"

"But Cook—"

"Go on with ye!" She made a shooing gesture and then turned back to eye Kendra. "Well, miss, ye've caused quite a stir. Word's goin' 'round on how ye had all these things to say about the dead lass. On how she'd been murdered. Ye're not touched, are ye?"

"Touched? Oh. Crazy. I've been wondering that myself lately." She attempted a smile that fell short of its mark, and disappeared altogether when Mrs. Danbury's voice came from behind her.

"Miss Donovan. A word, please."

She turned in time to see the black flutter of the housekeeper's skirt disappear around the corner. Some of her dismay must have shown on her face, because Cook patted her shoulder sympathetically. "Best go on, Kendra. Mrs. Danbury's a good woman, but ye've been a bit of a surprise to her. An' she don't like surprises."

"I've discovered I'm not too keen on them myself." Anxiety made her stomach churn as she walked the now familiar path to the housekeeper's office.

"Sit down, Miss Donovan."

"I'm sorry—" she began, hoping to stave off another lecture, but the housekeeper whipped up a hand for silence.

"Don't, Miss Donovan . . . *don't.* Your apology strikes me as false, since you are well aware that your behavior is highly irregular. In point of fact, it is *outrageous.*" She seemed to be warming to her topic. The gray eyes, which often seemed like chips of ice, flashed with heat. "I have never been so . . . so *mortified*. Mr. Kimble may be responsible for distributing your wages, but you are under *my* authority. Your conduct reflects upon *me.*"

Kendra pressed her clammy palms together. This scene was familiar. Too familiar. How often in her childhood had she stood in her father's study much this same way, while he criticized that some test or performance hadn't been up to par?

We expected better of you, Kendra . . .

Are you deliberately trying to embarrass your mother and me?

"Lady Atwood is furious with this situation," Mrs. Danbury continued. "Her house parties are renowned by the ton, Miss Donovan. *Renowned*. To find that girl, to say she was killed—"

"She *was* killed." Kendra clenched her hands. "And I didn't find her. I didn't *kill* her."

"You made a spectacle of yourself in front of your betters! I do not know how things are done in America, but this is *not* done here," she said in ringing accents. "*Here* you will behave in the proper fashion. Until I can decide what ought to be done with you, you shall be confined to below stairs. You shall have no contact with the guests or—"

"The Duke requested my presence in his study at five-thirty." And, yes, Kendra derived a petty satisfaction at the housekeeper's dumbfounded expression.

Mrs. Danbury regained her composure. "I see. We, of course, must acquiesce to His Grace's wishes. Until that time, though, I expect you to attend to your duties in the kitchen." An ice cube would've been warmer than the housekeeper's tone. "And Miss Donovan? I shouldn't get too complacent if I were you. Lady Atwood is the Duke's sister. They are quite close. The countess is *not* happy with your behavior today. His Grace may be amused by you, but mind your step. Your footing here at the castle may not be as solid as you think."

"She must be dismissed, Aldridge!"

From his position on the Grecian couch, the Duke of Aldridge observed his sister pace off her agitation. At fifty-three, two years his junior, she was still a pretty woman, he thought. She'd gained weight since the time she'd taken London by storm in her first season, thirty-five years ago, but it only served to smooth out the lines on her face. Her hair might not have been as golden, threaded as it was with silver, but she still styled it to the height of fashion, an elegant updo with a Spanish comb to anchor the topknot in place. Her blue eyes still sparkled, although at the moment, that sparkle had more to do with temper than vitality. In the last three years, he'd noticed that she'd begun applying rouge to her cheeks. Today, she could have done away with that artifice, since temper added a becoming flush to her countenance.

"Are you *listening* to me, Aldridge?" She paused, settling her hands on her hips, glaring at him.

He sighed. Caro only called him by his title when she was in high dudgeon. "I'm listening, my dear. But I fail to see why Miss Donovan should be dismissed."

"For heaven's sake. She said that girl was murdered! In front of everyone. She ruined my nuncheon!"

"I suspect the dead girl did that."

"Don't be flippant, Bertie!"

Instantly, the Duke sobered. "You're absolutely correct, Caro. This is not amusing. However, Miss Donovan had the right of it; that poor girl was murdered. If you only knew what had been done to her . . ." His eyes darkened as he remembered the bruises, the cuts . . . the bite mark. What sort of vicious animal were they dealing with? Abruptly, he stood and put his hands on his sister's shoulders to still her agitated movements. He stared down into the blue eyes so similar in shape and coloring to his own. "It's not for a lady's ears. Suffice to say, the girl deserves justice. She most likely has a family out there. They need to know what happened to their girl."

"Oh, Bertie!" Lady Atwood's anger evaporated, replaced by a flood of sympathy. Because she knew he wasn't only thinking of the girl in the lake.

Recognizing the concern, he pressed a kiss to her forehead, squeezed her shoulders once, then let her go. "I'm sorry, Caro. I know this is unfortunate timing with your party. But we cannot ignore it. I've sent for a Bow Street Runner."

"A Runner!" She put a hand to her throat, appalled. "Whatever will our guests think?"

"I'm certain they will be deliciously entertained."

"They will *not*!" Yet she couldn't meet her brother's eyes, because she suspected that he was correct. Even now, she knew, many of the women were comfortably ensconced in the Chinese drawing room in the guise of working on their needlepoint, gossiping over what had happened down by the lake. Even that silly chit, Georgina, who'd discovered the body, seemed to be enjoying her newfound celebrity, repeatedly sharing her shock and horror. Lady Atwood was well aware that she'd given at least three different versions of the story; each time, her fear had magnified and the description of the dead girl had become more grotesque.

"And the woman—the maid. What did you call her? Kendra Donovan—Irish." Her lip curled. "Little wonder she's a troublemaker!"

"Actually, she's an American."

"Good heavens—that's even worse! How can she be so vital to your investigation? An *American*. A mere *servant*. A *woman!*" She sounded incredulous. "'Tisn't natural!"

"What are you objecting to, Caro? That Miss Donovan is an American, a woman, or a servant?"

The countess' mouth tightened. "Be reasonable, Bertie. If that girl was murdered—and I'm not so certain that she was—how can Miss Donovan possibly help you?"

"She appears to have some experience in these matters."

"How can that be? She can hardly be educated, given her station in life."

Aldridge pursed his lips as he considered what he knew of Kendra Donovan. "I don't believe we ought to underestimate Miss Donovan," he said slowly. "You must trust me in this matter, my dear."

"Bertie—"

"I shall be requiring Miss Donovan's assistance." He hesitated, then said, "And for the duration of this party, Caro, I'd prefer it if you didn't go about the park unattended."

That surprised her. "I'm a bit old for a chaperone, Bertie. And as I've been married—God rest Atwood's soul—I don't need one."

"Nevertheless, I must insist."

Lady Atwood felt a chill race up her arms that had nothing to do with the drafts in her family's ancestral home. "What's this about, Bertie?" she demanded, alarmed by the look in her brother's eyes.

Aldridge recalled Kendra Donovan's words. *I can tell you two things: this isn't his first kill, and he will do it again.*

He believed in trusting his instincts, but he was also a man of logic. An enlightened man. Was he mad for listening to the woman? Or would he be mad not to?

His stomach clenched as he thought of the dead girl. Mother of God, she'd been bitten, beaten, strangled. He looked at his sister now, his expression grim. "'Tis a nightmare, Caro," he said quietly. "A nightmare like I've never seen."

15

Maybe she *was* crazy. Maybe at this very moment she was locked in some psych ward in London, having succeeded in her attempt to kill Sir Jeremy. Or maybe she'd never recovered from the gunshot wound to her head. Maybe she was . . . somewhere else.

No! Kendra wasn't going to go down that road again. She didn't know what was happening, but she refused to believe that this wasn't real. That girl on that wooden table in that odd, old-fashioned building had been *real*. At the very least, the revolting paste made out of water and ash that she was now using to polish the silver teapot in her hand was all too real.

Frowning, she rubbed harder. Her distorted face was reflected back at her in the silver surface, unfamiliar because of the mop cap on her head. Mrs. Danbury had stuck her in one of the back-rooms of the kitchen, helping Rose and another tweeny named Molly with the household silver. No doubt she'd meant it as a punishment, but it wasn't so bad. The work itself was kind of soothing. And it gave her the opportunity to question the girls about life in the castle, and, more importantly, the nineteenth century.

She broached something that had been puzzling her. "Simon Dalton—he's not a doctor?"

"Mr. Dalton? Oh, nay. 'E's a *surgeon,*" Molly supplied.

"A surgeon, but not a doctor?" She set the teapot down. "What's the difference?"

Molly blinked at her. "A doctor is ever so much more important! 'E wouldn't *think* ter poke around in somebody's innards like a sawbones!"

"That's a bad thing?"

They looked at her like she was crazy. "'Tisn't proper," Rose said, "'Course, Mr. Dalton ain't a sawbones now. 'E resigned 'is commission in the army when 'is aunt, Lady 'Alstead, cocked up 'er toes. Now 'e lives at 'Alstead 'All."

"Doing what?"

Rose shrugged. "Being gentry."

Kendra supposed that meant he either rented out parcels of land to local farmers or he hired locals to tend to the land he'd inherited.

"The Duke seems . . . nice," Kendra remarked casually, picking up a pair of serving tongs to polish.

"Oh, 'e's an oak. And ever so clever. 'E's always up on the roof, studyin' the stars and such. 'Tis a shame w'ot 'appened with 'is wife an' child."

"What happened?"

Rose said, "'Twas before I was born, but me ma told me 'ow the Duchess took the wee one sailing. Davy Jones's Locker got 'em, 'e did. 'Twas a clear day. No one knows w'ot 'appened, but 'is Grace found 'is wife on the beach; Lady Charlotte forever swept out to sea."

That explained Aldridge's strange behavior with the victim in the water, Kendra thought.

Molly shivered. "Oi 'eard that 'is Grace went mad."

"Aye," Rose agreed in a hushed voice as she buffed and polished. "'E's always 'ad strange notions—speakin' no disrespect. But me ma said 'e locked 'imself in 'is study. The only one 'oo could 'elp 'im was the marquis."

"The marquis?"

"'Is Grace's nephew—Alexander Morgan, the Marquis of Sutcliffe. An' 'e was only a young lad."

"Ooh. 'E's a fine-looking bloke, ain't 'e?" Molly sighed.

"'E's far above your touch, Molly Danvers!"

"Oi didn't say 'e wasn't. But Oi got peepers, don't oi?"

Kendra changed track. "Have either of you heard of any girls from around the area who have gone missing?"

They exchanged nervous glances. "Do you think the monster lives around 'ere?" Rose asked.

"I don't think anything yet."

"Nay. Jenny went off ter Bath, but Oi dunno anybody missin'," Molly whispered.

They lapsed into an anxious silence. Kendra regretted being responsible for the fear she saw on the tweenies' faces.

At five-fifteen, Kendra excused herself to go to the chamber she shared with Rose. She washed her hands and face, and used the chamber pot. As an afterthought, she took the mop cap off her head, tossing it on the bed, before heading to the Duke's study.

The Duke, Morland, and Dalton were seated, along with another man. Alec had taken up his familiar, negligent position, leaning against the fireplace. Each man was holding a heavy lead crystal glass filled with brandy. The candles had been lit, a fire crackling in the grate. They stood as she entered, a courtesy that she only sometimes received in the twenty-first century.

Aldridge smiled. "Miss Donovan, allow me to introduce you to our constable, Mr. Hilliard."

Kendra surveyed him as she stuck out her hand. Fortyish, she judged, with thinning brown hair, a round, florid face, stocky build. He seemed a little bewildered, but she wasn't sure if that was because he was surprised to shake her hand, or because he was being introduced to a servant, or because he was in the Duke's study, drinking brandy. She suspected the last was not a usual occurrence, noting that the man's clothing was inferior to the other men in the room. In social ranking, Hilliard was well below the titled gentry. But, Kendra reflected wryly, probably still several tiers above her current position.

"Miss." He nodded diplomatically.

"Mr. Hilliard."

Aldridge asked, "Would you care for a drink, Miss Donovan? Perhaps sherry?"

"No, thank you." She could hear the disapproval in her voice, and had to remind herself that she wasn't standing in an FBI war room surrounded by professionals. God help her. This was long before the vast network of specialized law enforcement agencies would spring up to protect its citizens. In fact, there wouldn't be any true concept of a police force here in England for another fourteen years, not until Sir Robert Peel introduced the Metropolitan Police Act in London. Centuries later, tourists to England might not have heard of Robert Peel, but they would know the police who'd been nicknamed after him—Bobbies.

"We've sent for a Runner. He ought to be here tomorrow morning." Returning to his seat behind his desk, the Duke picked up his pipe, but didn't make any attempt to light it. "Miss Donovan, please sit down. We ought to begin." He waited until Kendra had taken a seat on the sofa next to Hilliard. "Mr. Dalton, what are your findings?"

"Miss Donovan was correct." He gave her a slight nod to acknowledge that fact. Kendra was aware of the veiled looks from everyone but the Duke. "The female had a crushed hyoid bone, thyroid, and cricoid cartilage. There was no water in her lungs. She died of strangulation, not drowning."

"Strangled repeatedly as Miss Donovan suggested?" Alec asked, although he'd viewed the evidence with his own eyes.

"My findings support Miss Donovan's theory. Although it's impossible for me to determine the exact time of death, based on the degree of rigor mortis, I believe she died in the early morning hours, sometime between three and four, but that is only conjecture. Her stomach was empty; she hadn't eaten for hours before that.

"I counted fifty-three cuts on the girl's torso. Based on my measurements, we're dealing with four different knives. And all fifty-three wounds were inflicted premortem."

"Holy Mother of God," Hilliard breathed.

"Whoever did this must be utterly mad," Aldridge said, looking shaken.

"Yes and no," Kendra said quickly. "His psychosis—his *madness* is internal. To all outward appearances, he will appear normal."

Mr. Hilliard's eyebrows rose. "How'd'ya know that?"

"Because . . . he's organized. He's done this before. He knows how to blend in."

"We've never found a girl dead like this," Morland protested.

"He may have worked outside this area. Or we were never supposed to find this girl." She thought back to when she first came to the castle—a couple of centuries in the future—and the surrounding geography. "The ocean is, what? Two miles from here?"

Alec surveyed her with hooded eyes. "Thereabouts."

"You said this area is a watershed. The killer could've dumped the body in the river, expecting the current to take it out to the ocean."

"That was rather careless of him, wasn't it? Why not bury the girl? Dispose of her in some way where she would not be found?"

"I don't know." And that bothered her. It *was* careless. "The unsub may be—"

"Unsub? What is an unsub, pray tell?" Aldridge eyed her curiously.

Oh, God. In spite of everything, she'd forgotten where she was. *When* she was. "Unknown subject," she identified. "The murderer. He may be getting complacent. Or he may have wanted her to be found." She looked at Dalton. "Was she raped?"

He flushed, unable to meet her eyes. "Yes."

The Duke looked grim. "He is a monster."

"Yes. But he won't *look* like a monster. It's very important that everyone understand that." She scanned the faces in the room. "He will look no different than you or me."

"Jesus." Hilliard drank the rest of the brandy in one gulp.

"Right now the victim is our only connection to the killer," Kendra said. "We need to find out her identity."

"I don't believe she's from the area. She wasn't a farmer's daughter, a servant, or of the working class," Dalton said slowly.

Kendra looked at him. "Why do you say that?"

"Because of her hands. The palms were not rough. No calluses. No indication she did manual labor."

Kendra raised her brows, surprised. Soft, smooth hands were so much a part of her world that she hadn't considered it an anomaly during this time period.

"Could she be a Lady?" Morland wondered, sipping his brandy.

"Doubtful," said Alec. "If a peer of the realm's daughter disappeared, there'd be hue and cry by now."

"Unless the peer in question is afraid of the ensuing scandal," Morland countered.

Aldridge frowned. "You gentlemen are out and about in society. You didn't recognize her?"

"She struck me as a bit young to have come out, Duke," Alec commented.

"She could be some cit's daughter," Hilliard speculated.

"No. I don't believe so." Dalton cleared his throat, looking uncomfortable again. "I believe she was a prostitute."

"I say—how'd you know?" The constable's eyebrows shot up.

"The girl—I estimate her age to be around fifteen—she'd been pregnant, but the child was not brought to term."

"I see," Aldridge said slowly.

Alec straightened. "Miscarriage or abortion?"

"Abortion."

"That would make her a prostitute?" Kendra asked.

All four men seemed to find her question shocking. "Miss Donovan, gently bred women do *not* procure the services of an abortionist," was all the Duke said.

Kendra wondered if that was true. In her opinion, if a woman was desperate enough, scared enough, it would drive her to do anything, regardless of laws or societal restrictions.

Dalton continued, "Like her hands, her feet were soft, well-maintained. No calluses, bunions, or other imperfections."

Morland lifted his brandy glass and muttered, "Sounds like a woman who worked on her back."

Hilliard was the only one who found his crude jest amusing. Catching the Duke's reproving stare, he transformed his laugh into a cough, straightening in his chair. "My apologies, gov—er, Your Grace."

"She was not a street prostitute," Dalton went on. "She was too . . . soft, I'd say. Streetwalkers are tough and rough. No sign she relied on the drink—or anything else for that matter."

"Could've only begun plying her trade," Alec suggested. "She's young enough."

"By my estimation, the scarring from the pregnancy and abortion is at least two years old."

"She'd have been only thirteen," murmured Kendra.

"She probably worked in an academy," Dalton said.

Kendra looked at him. "An academy?"

"Ah, it's um—"

"A brothel," Alec said impatiently. "Or she was some man's mistress."

Kendra decided not to comment on what she thought of a man taking a thirteen-year-old mistress. Instead, she said, "Okay, we'll go with the assumption that she worked as a prostitute. This is as good a starting point as any." She paused, a little surprised that what she said was actually true.

She had very few expectations when she'd first entered the study. Certainly she wouldn't be able to rely on her usual arsenal of tools—forensics, FBI databases. Even the media. While the latter could be annoying, it served a purpose—photos of victims could be released in the hope that a John or Jane Doe would be identified.

Her eyes fell on the portrait of a woman and child above the fireplace. An idea occurred to her. "Is there any way we could have someone make a sketch of the victim?" she asked. "If we did that, maybe we could get it to the local newspaper. Someone might recognize her, come forward."

"Lady Rebecca—" Dalton began.

"Impossible." Alec gave him a quelling look. "She'd have to view the body to sketch it."

"Who's Lady Rebecca?" Kendra asked.

Alec scowled. "A *Lady*."

Kendra frowned, although she knew his attitude was the norm in this world. Women of rank were treated little better than china dolls. She remembered reading once that it was not unheard of for ladies to be banned from attending funerals, for fear their delicate sensibilities would shatter.

"That is neither here nor there," said Aldridge. "No reputable newspaper would publish a sketch of an Unfortunate Woman. We shall have the Runner take the girl's description and make inquiries around London."

"Assuming the whore was from London," Morland pointed out. "London is scarcely alone in having brothels. She may have come from an academy in Bath or Manchester or Glasgow."

"London is the closest city," Kendra pointed out. "Why would he search farther for his victim?"

Morland eyed her over the rim of his brandy glass. "If we should discover the chit's identity, pray tell, how will that help us identify her murderer, Miss Donovan?"

Kendra gave a slight shrug. "It's a lead. If she belongs to an . . . academy, he may be a client. Someone else at the brothel might know who he is."

The Duke's gaze was troubled as he met hers. "And you really believe he will kill again?"

"I know he's killed before. I know he'll kill again. And . . ." she hesitated, and licked suddenly dry lips. She couldn't tell if he—if any of the men—accepted what she was telling them. The next bit, she knew, would be even more difficult. "And," she said firmly, "you probably know him."

She didn't have to wait long for a reaction. Morland looked indignant. "That's preposterous!"

Hilliard gaped at her. "I say!"

Even Dalton shook his head. "No . . .Whoever did this is a . . . a . . ."

"A madman. A monster. Yes, we've already been over this," she said impatiently. "I told you: he'll be quite ordinary. You could talk to him, and never really know *him*. His nature. What he's done. He most likely lives in the surrounding area, or at the very least, he's familiar with it." She saw their disbelief, and couldn't really blame them. Hell, the idea of having a serial killer living in one's community was difficult to digest even in the twenty-first century.

Everyone was silent, staring at her, at each other.

The Duke sighed, then stood. "Well, you certainly have given us much to consider, Miss Donovan. The Bow Street Runner ought to be here tomorrow."

Aware that it was a dismissal, everyone stood. Aldridge came around the desk and laid a detaining hand on Kendra's arm as all the men, with the exception of Alec, filed out of the room.

When the door had closed behind them, Alec lifted his glass in a mocking salute. "Well, Miss Donovan, you *do* liven up what would've been an otherwise tedious house party."

She shot him an exasperated look, and then turned to the Duke. "Do you believe me?" she asked bluntly.

"I don't want to," he admitted. "But I saw what was done to that girl. I cannot disregard what you have told us. We shall see what the Runner has to say."

Kendra frowned, and wondered what that meant. Would the Duke turn the entire investigation over to the Bow Street Runner? A detective, perhaps, but a *nineteenth-century* detective.

Her stomach clenched. There was still one thing she could do.

"Do you have a chalkboard, by any chance?" she asked.

The Duke seemed puzzled by the question. "Chalk . . . board?"

"Yes." Oh, hell, when was the chalkboard invented? She didn't know. But from the Duke's reaction, obviously not now. "Something to write on." She pantomimed the activity. "You know, children use it in school."

"I believe she's referring to a slate board," Alec offered, sounding amused.

"Ah. Yes, we've a slate board in the schoolroom. Why?"

Kendra considered the question. "In your laboratory, you make notes regarding your observations of the night sky. It allows you to extrapolate data and come up with theories. Edmond Halley used Newton's law of gravity to identify his comet and predict its orbital pattern. I need to organize my observations in a similar manner."

Aldridge eyed her with interest. "You expect to predict a pattern for our killer?"

"Yes. And if we're lucky, we can use it to catch him before he kills again."

16

There was no question about it: Kendra Donovan was a bold, brazen creature, Alec thought, as he leaned against one of the Carrara marble columns near the entrance of the ballroom, where his aunt had organized the evening's entertainment of dancing. Could Kendra's calculations possibly predict the mind of a madman? He very much doubted it. Who had ever heard of such a thing?

"Is it true?"

Straightening, he glanced down into the intelligent cornflower blue eyes of Lady Rebecca Blackburn as she came up beside him. He'd known her since the day that she'd been born. As the Duke's goddaughter and the Earl of Kendall's only child, she'd often visited the castle, and many of her holidays had coincided with his own sojourns. He'd been as devastated as the Duke and her family when she'd been stricken with smallpox at the age of seven. No one had expected her to live. She'd surprised them all by surviving, although not without consequences.

Her face was badly disfigured by the pockmarks that accompanied the disease. Because of it, she'd endured long stretches of being either teased or shunned. Not surprisingly, she'd decided to forgo a London season, preferring her art and country life, and at twenty-three was considered quite on the shelf, with no prospects for marriage except for rogues attracted to her sizeable inheritance, rather than her person. The mischievous, affectionate child he'd known could easily have become embittered by her unfortunate circumstance. Instead, she seemed at peace with herself. Which, Alec reflected ruefully, was more than he could say about himself.

"Well?" she persisted.

"Is what true?"

"Don't be a goose, Sutcliffe!" Rebecca gave his arm a playful rap with her ivory fan. "Everybody's talking about the murder! They say the murderer is still about."

Though the crowd around them was well occupied with their own conversations and dancing a lively quadrille, Alec lowered his voice. "And when did you start believing in gossip, Becca?"

"Since a dead girl was found in the lake," she answered pertly. "Don't evade, Sutcliffe. You already bullied me once today. I shall not let you do it again!"

"If you're referring to my not letting you view the body, I had your best interest at heart."

Rebecca rolled her eyes. "*I* have my own best interest at heart, thank you very much. And I'd be pleased if you remembered that. I noticed that you did not order *all* women away." When he remained silent, she gave him another rap. "Who is she, Sutcliffe? The maid with the short hair?"

That was an excellent question. "She is an American, which may explain her peculiarities, including her hairstyle."

Rebecca laughed. "Caroline Lamb cut her hair short."

"You make my point. Caroline Lamb is an eccentric who is making a cake of herself over Lord Bryon."

Since she couldn't argue with that, she merely waved her fan. "They say that the madman did the most horrid things to the girl."

Alec scowled. "'Tis not something that should be consumed for the amusement of the Beau Monde."

"And yet the ton is so easily amused," she murmured dryly.

"What else are they saying?"

"That the girl was a prostitute."

Alec's scowl deepened. Hell and damnation. The fact that Becca had heard that particular tidbit meant that either someone in the study had gossiped, or a footman had been listening at the door. Both scenarios were entirely possible.

"Who did you hear that from, pray tell?"

"Mary, my maid, of course—although it's being bandied all around the castle. I daresay, all around the village. She also told me that you sent for a Runner." She gave him a speculative look. "And that the maid from this morning is assisting the Duke in finding the murderer."

Alec pressed his lips together in annoyance. He noticed, across the room, Gabriel weaving toward the doors that led off to the garden. In his cups. *Again.* At the last moment, his friend, Captain Harcourt, steered him clear of a large urn in his path.

"Well?" Rebecca pressed. "Is the maid really assisting His Grace?"

"Miss Donovan appears to be remarkably well-informed about criminal behavior."

Rebecca peered at him closely. "Are you joking?" When he remained silent, she murmured, "How very interesting. She sounds like an Original."

"That kind of originality is nothing to aspire to, my dear."

She grinned. "If not an Original, what then?"

"Minx."

She hesitated, and her smile vanished. "Sutcliffe, there is something else being said."

"Yes?"

Instead of answering immediately, she shifted her gaze to the familiar faces circulating around the ballroom that had been redesigned by none other than the great John Nash himself. An inexplicable chill danced up her arms.

"'Tis being said that the murderer is someone we know," she said slowly, and then looked up at the marquis, her gaze troubled. "That *must* be a Banbury tale. Is it not, Sutcliffe?"

"It certainly sounds ridiculous enough to be a Banbury tale."

"That is not a definitive answer."

Alec sighed, and wished, for the first time, that she wasn't so bloody perceptive. "There's the rub, my dear. I have no definitive answers. I have only many questions." Beginning, he thought grimly, with Kendra Donovan.

By eleven-thirty that night, Kendra decided that being a servant in the nineteenth century was damn hard work. All her muscles were throbbing like she'd undergone a week's worth of workout sessions with the Terminator in one day. She estimated that she'd probably logged ten miles sprinting up and down the backstairs, restocking guest rooms with supplies and hot water for bathing, and later bringing up platters of food for the liveried footmen to serve during the dinner at eight.

Two hours later, she was one of the team of maids that cleared the table and cleaned the dining room, after the guests had moved to the ballroom for dancing. The only servants who had it worse, she believed, were the scullery and chambermaids. The former were required to scrub the giant pots, pans, and plates used for the evening, their hands left raw and red, and the latter had to collect, dump, and replenish all the chamber pots in the castle.

Earlier, she'd learned that the castle's garderobes, or privy chambers, still functioned, but for some reason, everyone seemed to prefer the chamber pot. The Duke, she'd been told, had begun installing Bramah's closets, which, she deduced, were primitive toilets that had actually been invented years before. Still, those closets had yet to make an appearance in the servant's quarters. And Rose was just fine with that, viewing the contraption with a great deal of suspicion.

Of course, the only plumbing that Kendra would've been really interested in at the moment would be a Jacuzzi.

"You're not human, Rose," she groaned as they climbed the stairs. "My muscles are screaming."

The tweeny giggled. "'Twas a normal day, miss. I expect you, 'avin' been a lady's maid, ain't used to it."

"Yeah. I'm not used to it—any of this."

They were both holding candles, the light bouncing madly against the wall. Even though she was bone-weary, Kendra paused when they reached the first floor, which, by American labeling, would be the second floor.

"Rose, where's the schoolroom?"

"The schoolroom? W'otever for, miss?"

"I need to work."

"But we finished our work!"

Kendra smiled weakly. "I need to organize my thoughts, and I'd like to use the slate board to do it."

"Is this about the murder?"

"Yes."

Rose hesitated.

"The Duke gave me permission," Kendra pressed.

The tweeny shrugged. "Come along then."

The schoolroom was located in the east wing of the castle, down a little-used corridor that didn't even have the benefit of wall sconces to light the way.

"There 'aven't been any wee ones in the castle since Lady Charlotte," Rose whispered. "There's the nursery and the governess' room." She pointed to two closed doors, and then opened a set of double doors. "'Ere's the schoolroom."

Four ceiling-to-floor multi-paned windows graced one wall. The moon loomed high, its rays strong enough to bathe the room in an icy light. Otherwise, Kendra suspected, their meager candles would never have penetrated the thick shadows.

She saw five desks, four child-sized and one adult. Bookshelves lined another wall, opposite a fireplace. There was a sturdy wood table and an assortment of other objects around the room, including a globe, several yellowed maps, an empty easel, and paintbrushes and small pots. Hanging on the wall behind the larger desk was the chalkboard—*slate board,* Kendra corrected herself.

There was a musty scent in the air and a general aura of disuse. Kendra felt as though she'd found the toy of a child who'd long since grown into adulthood. It had that same sad, abandoned feel.

Rose shivered beside her. "Some of the servants 'ave said they've 'eard the sound of a child weeping when they pass by this 'ere room late at night."

Kendra paused in picking up one of the jagged, thumb-sized pieces of slate, and glanced over at the young girl. "It's probably the wind, Rose. Or their imagination."

"Aren't you 'fraid of spirits, miss?"

"Can't be afraid of something you don't believe in." Experimentally she drew a line on the board. The result was similar to what chalk would have produced.

"You don't believe in spirits, then?"

She grinned at the girl. "Only the kind you drink." She used her apron to erase the mark she'd made, and frowned when it didn't come off. She rubbed harder.

"You need to wet it," Rose said from behind her.

"Oh." She turned to find the maid eyeing her oddly again. "Thanks, Rose."

Rose hesitated. "Will that be all, miss?"

"You know, you can call me Kendra."

"Aye, miss."

Kendra had to smile. "Go to bed, Rose. I'll be up soon. I just need to work on a couple of things here."

When Rose left, she took her candle with her, reducing the light to Kendra's single flickering flame and the glow of the moon. Briefly, Kendra looked around for more candles or an oil lamp, but found nothing. She supposed the thrifty Mrs. Danbury had taken all useful items from the room before shutting the doors.

Setting her candle on the desk, Kendra went to work. On the slate board, she drew three vertical lines. In the first section she wrote: *Unsub*; in the middle section: *Victimology*; in the third: *Forensics/Pattern*.

She started in the middle. Victim—Jane Doe; Age—approximately fifteen; Race—Caucasian; Hair—brown; Eyes—brown.

Height . . . Kendra closed her eyes to bring up a mental image of the girl. She was small. Five-one, maybe, or five-two. As for weight, Kendra doubted if the victim would have tipped the scales at more than one hundred to one hundred and five pounds. She opened her eyes and jotted the information down. Satisfied, she moved on. Profession—Prostitute (likely).

Kendra paused, considering that. It wasn't surprising. Even in the twenty-first century, prostitutes were the primary targets of serial killers. They were society's throwaways. A dead hooker never registered the same on the horror meter or had the same cachet with the media as a dead housewife. Still, the way the men had talked, this girl had been a part of a brothel, not a street whore. That made her more likely to be missed.

There was easier prey. Why *this* girl?

Moving to the third section, Kendra began ending sentences with a question mark. Body dumped in the river—deliberate or discarded? Did the killer want Jane Doe found? Or had he expected the body to be carried out to sea?

The hair cut off in sections—a souvenir?

Single bite mark on the breast—sexual?

Many serial killers were biters, she knew. *The mark of the beast.* That's what Keith Simpson, Britain's first professor of forensic pathology, had labeled the bites inflicted by killers in the twentieth century.

The fact that Jane Doe had only one bite mark was interesting, though. Most likely part of a fantasy developed over time.

Jane Doe had fifty-three cuts on her torso made by four different knives. Kendra wondered if there was any significance to the number of wounds or variety of knives. The victim had been handcuffed. She was petite, so she could have been easily controlled. Unless the killer wasn't a big man himself.

The victim had been raped repeatedly. Strangled repeatedly. Did the killer get sexual gratification by maximizing the girl's terror?

Based on the bruising and decomposition, the girl had been killed last night. Kendra thought of the Duke's charts, and wondered if there was any significance to the full moon, if that was part of the unsub's pattern.

Kendra returned to the first section. The unsub. The big unknown.

Slowly, she lifted the hand clutching the piece of slate, and wrote: *Mission-oriented killer, or power-and-control killer?*

Not mission-oriented. She lifted her apron to scrub that away, then remembered she needed to have a wet cloth. She ended up drawing a line through "mission-oriented," and circled "power-and-control." That's who they were dealing with—someone who fed off his victim's terror, who relished their suffering, wanted to hear them scream.

And scream.

A chill raced up Kendra's arms. It was always this way, brushing up against evil. She'd fought hard to be a field agent, but she remembered her first case, when several teenage girls in Kentucky had been found dead, their bodies dumped along the Appalachian Trail. Their throats had been cut, but the fatal wound had been hidden by the pretty pink bow the killer had tied around their necks. Each victim's feet had been severed and taken as souvenirs. She recalled how her stomach had knotted, and she'd just managed to stumble to a ravine before throwing up.

Over the years, she'd gotten used to the gruesome, unspeakable images, to the buzz of flies, to the sickening, rotting scent of death. But she would never get used to the twisted mind that could commit such atrocities. *Thank God.*

"Who are you, you sick son of a bitch?" she whispered, staring at the section that had the least words written in it. She lifted the piece of slate again, and wrote: *Male; familiar with the area; intelligent; organized.*

A cloud passed over the moon, leaving only the meager light from the one candle. The shadows around her deepened and crept up the walls like tormented souls escaping the underworld. Tension pricked at her nape. Her heart rate escalated as she thought of Rose's ghost story of the weeping child. *Get a grip, Donovan.* She didn't believe in ghosts.

Then again, she hadn't believed in time travel, either.

She found herself holding her breath, letting it out in a rush of relief when the moon reappeared and flooded the room again in its silvery light.

Silly. She was being silly. And fanciful. Two words that rarely applied to her. She drew in a deep breath and let it out slowly.

She didn't believe in ghosts, but she did believe in evil—the two-legged kind.

Dropping the slate on the desk, she did a couple of yoga stretches to loosen up her tight muscles. Picking up her candle, she moved to the door. She paused, glancing back at the notes she'd made. In the gloom, she couldn't see them anymore. The darkness had swallowed them up.

Though that didn't mean they weren't there—*like him,* she thought. He may be in the shadows, but she knew he was out there. Hunting.

This time when the tension coiled inside her, pricking at her nape, it wasn't because she was being fanciful. It was because she knew she was right.

The little whore had been found. He hadn't anticipated that, couldn't like it.

And yet . . . there was no denying the sweet, hot rush of pleasure he'd felt upon her discovery. To listen to the whispers of those around him, to hear the shock and terror and trembling disbelief in their voices. It was exhilarating to know that when they went to bed tonight, they'd be thinking of him.

Fearing him.

He hadn't anticipated that, either. The excitement of holding society in thrall. Fickle, feckless society, who would turn on him in a heartbeat, if they knew what he really was. He couldn't risk exposure. He'd be swinging at Newgate for certain.

But his work was another matter.

He'd never consider that possibility before. In a way, it would be like breathing new life into the dead harlots, extending their purpose beyond his own.

The thought amused him. Intrigued him. *Inspired* him.

He'd still have to be very careful. He was no fool. The Duke's decision to bring in a Runner was a complication. Still, if it proved too much of a nuisance, he'd simply have to take care of the matter. Until then, though, he'd enjoy pitting himself against his opponents.

He thought of the woman. Again, he felt a stirring deep inside himself, a shivery kind of excitement and anticipation. It reminded him of the feeling that possessed him right before he took one of the whores for his pleasure.

Kendra Donovan.

He whispered the name, enjoying how it sounded on his tongue. Like an exotic liqueur, sweet and tantalizing. She was only a woman—less, really, given her servant status. She was undoubtedly a whore, clever enough to insinuate herself next to the powerful Duke of Aldridge. The old man had always been queer, and like any daughter of Eve, the maid had recognized his eccentricity and exploited it, manipulating it to her advantage.

As a woman, she couldn't be considered a true opponent. However, he couldn't deny she added an interesting element to the game. He would enjoy her participation, enjoy parrying with her. And when the time was right, he'd enjoy killing her.

17

At six-thirty the next morning, Kendra woke with a start, her heart pounding, her ears attuned to the same noises that had woken her the previous morning. For one moment, she had the wild hope that she'd dreamed the last forty-eight hours. Yet the first thing she saw when she opened her eyes was the candle on the nightstand, which brought her back to reality.

Well, her current reality: she was in the early nineteenth century. And a serial killer was hunting prostitutes.

She wanted to pull the thin blankets over her head and go back to sleep. She wanted to *will* herself back to the twenty-first century. Instead, with an effort—her muscles were so stiff—she pushed herself to a sitting position just as Rose emerged from behind the privacy screen, and smiled at her.

"Mornin', miss."

"My God. I used to think I was in shape," Kendra muttered. She forced herself to stand, and do some yoga moves in the small space.

"W'otever are you doing?" Rose watched her, perplexed.

"Downward facing dog."

"W'ot?"

Kendra straightened. "It relaxes me."

"If you say so, miss. Don't you 'ave a nightdress?" Rose eyed the chemise that she'd stripped down to again last night.

"No." She slipped behind the privacy screen, washed her face and scrubbed her teeth by the same method she'd employed yesterday. By the time she emerged, Rose was already dressed and waiting to be buttoned up.

"We 'eard 'is Grace 'as called in a thief-taker from London."

"Thief-taker?"

"A Runner. The gentry 'ires them to find villains."

"Oh. The Bow Street Runner. Yes. The Duke sent for one."

"Does that mean you're no longer gonna be 'elping 'is Grace?"

If this was the twenty-first century, she'd be driving to the Bureau or setting up a war room in whatever police station in the country required the FBI's assistance. There'd be a system to follow, and she'd know her place in that system. But what was her place here? In everyone's eyes, she was a servant. When she'd stepped outside that role yesterday, she knew it had confused and angered some people. She'd done what came naturally to her, but it was completely unnatural in this world.

"Miss?"

"What? Oh. Sorry. I'm sure I'll help the Duke." She frowned as they left the bedchamber and descended the backstairs, remembering Mrs. Danbury's orders. "But I suppose I'd better help in the kitchen until he calls for me."

"Aye, miss."

In the kitchens, two maids were scouring and black-leading the enormous stove. Fires were already lit in the fireplaces, heating up giant tubs of water. Monsieur Anton was muttering in French, casting the footmen loitering nearby an evil eye. It was pleasantly cool now, but by mid-afternoon, Kendra knew, the room would be boiling hot and more crowded than the Pennsylvania Turnpike on a holiday weekend.

Again, Kendra felt eyes turn in her direction as she followed Rose to the lower staff dining room, where a buffet-styled breakfast was offered—trays of cold meat, fresh bread, and pots of tea and—*hallelujah*—coffee. A few maids and footmen were already seated at the long pine table. They stopped their conversation, and stared at Kendra. It gave her a twitchy feeling, as she followed Rose to the buffet and filled a plate with cold cuts and two buns. She poured coffee into an earthenware mug, the fragrance alone making her happy.

"Do you know what's happening with the murder, miss?" a young footman asked her as soon as she sat down.

"Aye," another man put in. "D'ya know who did it?"

"Who was the chit?" a maid asked. "We 'eard she mebbe was a light-skirt from London."

"Oi 'eard she was from Glasgow."

Kendra drank her coffee, and nearly sighed at the much-needed caffeine jolt. "We don't know anything yet." She surveyed them over the mug. "Has this ever happened before? An unknown young woman found in, say, the last ten years?"

Like Rose and Molly yesterday when she asked that question, she saw the shock in their eyes, the automatic denial. "Nay! Never!"

"Me da says she was probably done in by gypsies," a young girl whispered, eyes round. "Ye know that the Duke lets them camp on the south side of the forest."

"Ooh—the devils will slay us all if we don't do somethin'!"

"They're a bunch of 'eathens!"

Kendra recognized the rising hysteria in the room. Really, it was no different than what she'd encountered in City Hall meetings, where citizens were quick to point the finger at a drifter or stranger in town. Better to think a murderer was a vagrant than a neighbor, someone they probably sat next to in church, or had coffee with at the local diner.

"Gypsies didn't kill this girl."

"'Ow d'ya know?" One of the footman squinted at her.

"Aye. Why should we believe you? We don't know *you*."

Hysteria and hostility. They went hand in hand.

Kendra picked up her knife and fork, slicing through the ham in a controlled motion. "True. You don't know me. But you know the Duke. He doesn't strike me as a fool. Am I wrong? Is he a fool?" That evoked a strong reaction, as she'd known it would.

"'Is Grace ain't no fool! 'Es got strange ways—but the gov ain't a fool."

She chewed the ham and waited for the furious mutterings to end. Then she said, "The Duke trusts me." *Please let that be true.* For all she knew, Aldridge could have second thoughts today and toss her out on her ass. Her stomach knotted at the possibility, but she was careful to keep her expression neutral. "He trusts that I have some expertise in this area. You'll have to trust me as well."

Although she could see that wasn't going to happen—their expressions remained suspicious—she didn't think they'd be picking up the pitchforks and torches to go after the gypsies. *Yet.*

Just another thing to worry about.

Sighing, she forced herself to finish her breakfast. Not easy when you had a dozen pair of eyes on you. It was a relief when she could push herself away from the table and follow Rose back to the kitchen, where Cook gave her a knife to peel and slice potatoes into an enormous copper pot.

For a second, Kendra stared blankly at the knife. Only then did it occur to her that she'd never peeled a potato in her life. For as long as she could remember, her parents had employed housekeepers, so they could concentrate on their work. And later . . . well, she lived in a time of takeout, prepackaged microwave dinners, and restaurants. In her world, the culinary arts were a desire, not a necessity, and like her parents, she'd poured her time and attention into her work, not the kitchen.

Yet how hard could it be, really? It was a damn potato. She'd graduated magna cum laude with a fistful of degrees in psychology, criminology, and computer science from Princeton when she was only three years older than Rose.

Twenty minutes later, she discovered that peeling potatoes was a lot like styling hair—it looked easier than it was. For every freshly skinned potato that she managed to plop into the giant pot, Rose did five, her hands almost a blur as she peeled and chopped. And Rose's potatoes were the same size post-skinning, whereas Kendra's own were whittled down like the after picture in a weight loss commercial.

Who knew that peeling a potato could make you feel inadequate?

"Miss?" Molly approached, and Kendra paused to listen. "'Is Grace is askin' fer ye."

The kitchen was a place of steady noise and movement, a constant din always in the background. None of that stopped, but Kendra was aware of the eyes that swiveled in her direction. Carefully, she laid down the knife on the counter, wiping her hands on her apron as she followed the tweeny out into the hall.

She expected Molly to usher her to the study, or even the Duke's lab. Instead, the maid brought her to the schoolroom, gesturing at the door.

"They're in there, miss."

Kendra nodded. "Thanks, Molly."

She rubbed suddenly sweaty palms against her apron, drew in a deep breath, and pushed open the door. Aldridge and Alec were standing in front of the slate board, but as soon as she entered, they swung around to stare at her. She tried to figure out what they were thinking. With Alec, it was impossible. He was frowning, but that was his normal expression, as far as Kendra was concerned. His green eyes hid his thoughts well.

The Duke was a little easier to read—he looked uneasy. "I see you've begun your observations."

Kendra moved into the room. "Yes, sir."

"'Tis a gruesome business that you've written."

Kendra wondered if she was being sensitive, or if there was a reproving note in his voice. But then he turned back to the slate board. "I see you crossed out 'mission-oriented.'"

"Yes, sir. Prostitutes are a common target of mission-oriented killers. They see them as blights on humanity. They believe they're doing God's work by eliminating them."

The Duke frowned. "That's absurd."

"It's a psychosis—but one we don't have to worry about here, because we're not dealing with that type of killer. We're dealing with something far worse." Because there was a chill in the room—at least that's what she told herself—Kendra hugged her arms across her chest. "The pain inflicted premortem was designed to torture the girl. The rape and strangulation, being handcuffed . . . it makes a statement: I'm in control here; I have power here. Power over *you*; control over *you*. For however many hours she lived, the killer was her whole world. She would've begged and pleaded, and that would have only excited him."

"Good God."

"He doesn't believe he's *helping* God. He believes he *is* God. He had the power of her life and death in his hands. What we're dealing with—" She broke off as the door to the schoolroom swung open again, and the woman with the pockmarked face that Alec had escorted to the nuncheon yesterday strode in.

She wasn't wearing a bonnet, so Kendra could see that her hair was a beautiful auburn, pulled into the style that Georgina and Sarah had demanded she produce the previous morning. Her eyes were a cornflower blue and held a determined gleam, especially when Alec hurried toward her.

"Rebecca! What the devil are you doing here?"

She smiled up at him. "I heard you were here, of course."

"How did y—"

"Mary."

He scowled. "The woman's a bloody gossip."

Rebecca grinned. "Naturally. 'Tis one of the prerequisites to being a lady's maid." She shrugged off his detaining hand, and came to stand before Kendra. "You are Miss Donovan."

Kendra was surprised by the woman's forthright manner, the laser-like directness of her gaze. Yesterday, Sarah and Georgina had looked *through* her most of the time. This woman actually saw her, studied her with frank curiosity.

"Yes. Kendra Donovan."

Alec's mouth compressed. "You are turning into a hoyden, Becca."

"My dear Sutcliffe, I have been a hoyden for *years*."

"Lady Rebecca, this is really not for your ears," the Duke offered his own protest. "Alec shall escort you—"

"Stuff and nonsense! My ears have spent hours in the stables. I'm not a green girl, you know." She turned toward the slate board. "This is about the girl who was killed, is it not?"

"Becca—"

"Oh, don't look so Friday-faced, Alec! If Miss Donovan is allowed to stay, I don't know why I should be sent from the room. I am not a child—I'm three and twenty." She gave both men an arch look. "And I seem to recall you applauding my study of Mary Wollstonecraft's work. You have always encouraged my artistic and intellectual pursuits."

"For God's sakes, Becca, we are not having a theoretical discussion in Duke's study or the drawing room," Alec argued impatiently. "This is not an exercise in women's rights."

"Oh, but that is exactly what it is, Sutcliffe!" She was no longer smiling, and her blue eyes narrowed. "For the first time, we can take the discussion out of the theoretical and apply it to the real world. Unless you were gammoning me."

Kendra had to admire the woman. She'd neatly turned the tables on the men. If this were the twenty-first century, Lady Rebecca would've made a good lawyer.

Alec gave a snort. "You are only here because of your lamentable curiosity."

"There's nothing lamentable about curiosity," she retorted. "You, my father, Duke . . ." She shifted her gaze to encompass the older man. "You taught me that. And you have always indulged my intellectual path. My dear Duke, you cannot find fault with my argument. If you turn me away now, I shall suspect you've only been patronizing me."

Good lawyer, hell. She'd have made a great one, Kendra decided. Acting on impulse, she said, "I think she should stay."

Alec's head snapped around, and he glared at her. "*You* have no say in the matter."

"Caro would be apoplectic if she found out." Aldridge rubbed his chin thoughtfully. "I'm not entirely certain this is a good idea, my dear. And, I warn you, none of this is pretty."

Some emotion flitted across her face, too quick for Kendra to define. And then it was gone, and Rebecca was smiling again. "I have never expected pretty." Abruptly, she pivoted to face the slate board again. "Miss Donovan, I do believe you were speaking when I arrived. Pray continue."

Kendra decided to ignore Alec's deepening scowl. She tapped the board with her finger. Maybe if she pretended she was in a war room, and everything was normal . . .

"As I was saying, we can rule out mission-oriented. We're dealing with a power-and-control killer. As for the victim, her being a prostitute, I believe, is significant. Killers tend to prey on prostitutes because they're dispensable."

Rebecca bristled. "That is a dreadful thing to say! They may be soiled doves . . . er, Unfortunate Women. But they are still human beings!"

"I'm not making a statement about their humanity," Kendra said. "I'm seeing her as the killer would see her. Why did he choose her instead of a village girl?"

"A village girl would be missed," Alec said tersely, clearly still not entirely comfortable with Rebecca being in the room.

"Exactly," Kendra nodded. "And by his choice of victims, we learn something about the killer. He's cautious. He doesn't want to draw the kind of attention a missing village girl would. Instead, he selects a prostitute. Not a street hooker, though," she murmured, almost to herself. "Why not? If he were really cautious, he'd take the one who'd be the least missed."

"Mayhap he doesn't wish to risk disease," Alec suggested. "Streetwalkers are notoriously filthy. They tend to be a coarse lot, often drunk, diseased."

"Yes." Kendra gave him a thoughtful look. "This girl was young. Soft. Maybe he doesn't want a girl who *looks* like a prostitute. Which means her appearance is a factor. I'd need more victims, though, before I can identify it as a signature."

"Signature?"

Kendra hesitated. She was giving them more information than maybe she should. Though in the latter half of this century Dr. Thomas Bond would offer up a profile on Jack the Ripper, she was introducing a lexicon that wouldn't be part of criminal investigative analysis for another century, at least. Was she changing the future?

Dammit. She didn't know. And she couldn't worry about it. If she was going to do any good here, she needed to think and act like an FBI profiler.

Shrugging aside her unease, she explained, "The psychological pattern of the killer. It's something that he does that has a special meaning to him. Like Jane Doe's appearance, or the bite mark on the breast—one very deliberate, very vicious bite mark. He didn't bite her to kill her. He had another, more personal reason to do it."

"What reason, pray tell?" Rebecca asked, fascinated.

"I don't know. What does the female breast represent? Sex. Desire. Life—mother's milk. A mother who dominated him. A lover who spurned him. It means *something*. And then there's the hair. Why did he cut portions of it? Like the breast, it's a female symbol. A woman's crowning glory." Unconsciously, Kendra threaded her fingers through her much shorter hair. "Female vanity. Did he do it to humiliate her? Or for another reason? I'll need to see the body again."

She turned to face her audience. "There's another difference between a streetwalker and a prostitute in—what did you call it?—an academy. Streetwalkers aren't very choosy."

"Neither are Birds of Paradise, if you have the blunt," Alec pointed out dryly.

"Yes. You have to have the . . . er, blunt. Does it cost the same to hire a street whore as it does a girl from an academy?"

"Hardly. Streetwalkers will offer their services in the alley for a shot of whiskey and a few shillings."

Kendra picked up the piece of slate and wrote "money" in the unsub column. "He paid for a girl from an academy. From London, most likely. Plenty of opportunities to hunt. Why go farther?"

Alec looked at her. "You speak as though killing the girl were sport."

"To him, it was. This was not the murder of a young girl. It was *more*."

"Dear heaven," Rebecca breathed.

"And he had to transport her here somehow." It was too early for trains. That left . . . stagecoach or horse?

Rebecca frowned, thinking. "A public stage?"

Alec's lips twisted. "Doubtful—not unless her benefactor made it worth her while."

"So *not* a tryst with a farmer," Kendra said slowly.

"He'd have to be a wealthy farmer. A bawd would never have let her go, and the girl would not have gone unless—"

"She could better herself," Kendra finished, earning a raised brow from Alec.

"I never considered it in that precise way, but yes."

"'Tis true, then," Rebecca said, staring at her. "The outrageous rumor that this madman is one of . . . of *us*."

"If you mean someone in the upper classes, then yes." Kendra noted the other woman's shocked expression and thought of the servants crowded around the breakfast table. "You thought he was a drifter—a gypsy, perhaps? Because the perpetrator *can't* be somebody you know?"

The blue eyes sparked, then went cold. "Mayhap *you* know such fiends, Miss Donovan." Her upper-class accent was so precise, it was like a slap. "*I* do not."

"Actually . . . you do."

Rebecca drew in a breath, the earlier friendliness gone. Now she looked every inch the aristocrat.

Kendra sighed, but maintained eye contact. "I think you could be very helpful to this investigation, but if you can't handle it . . ." She shrugged.

The other woman frowned. "I can . . . *handle* it."

The phrase was obviously unfamiliar to Lady Rebecca, but she'd gotten the gist of it. Kendra was beginning to like the Lady.

"Good. Otherwise . . ." She remembered what Dalton had said yesterday, and gave the other woman a speculative look. "Just how good are you at portraiture?"

The question threw Rebecca. "You want me to paint your portrait?"

"Not me—"

"Bloody hell. We already told you, that would not be proper," Alec snapped.

Kendra ignored him. "We plan to send out a description of the girl with the Bow Street Runner. It would be much more effective to have a photo—a sketch of some kind."

"You want me to paint the dead woman?"

"Charcoal or pastels would be faster." She glanced at the Duke. "I'm sorry, but it's the best way."

"This is beyond the pale—" Alec protested.

"I've never known you to be such a stuffed shirt, Sutcliffe," Rebecca interrupted him, her expression once again amused. Kendra caught the glimmer of excitement in the cornflower eyes. "I shall do it. When?"

Kendra's lips curved with an irony her audience would never understand. "I always say there's no time like the present."

18

Alec grabbed Kendra's arm before she could follow the Duke and Rebecca out of the schoolroom. The action surprised Kendra—almost as much as the electrical jolt she felt at the physical contact.

"Why are you involving Lady Rebecca in this?" he demanded.

He released her, and Kendra let out a breath. But it caught in her throat again when he put his hand up, palm flat against the wooden doorframe, and shifted his body, effectively caging her in. She was close enough to see the gold flecks around the pupils in his green eyes, close enough to smell his scent, a blend of clean linen, leather, some kind of soap, and a masculine underpinning that was unique to the man.

"Well?" he asked impatiently, when she remained silent.

She cleared her throat. "I already told you—I think she'll be helpful to the investigation. If she can sketch the dead girl's face, we'll have a much better chance at identification than sending out a verbal description." She paused, then shrugged. "And it wouldn't hurt to bring in a woman's perspective."

Alec frowned. "What the devil is *your* perspective?"

A twenty-first-century perspective, Kendra wanted to say. Instead, she shrugged again. "A woman from the aristocracy, then. As I said before, I think we're dealing with someone from your class, *Lord* Sutcliffe."

"Exactly what is *your* class, Miss Donovan?" he asked softly.

He was looking at her so intently that Kendra found herself fidgeting. She forced herself to stop and gestured to the clothes she was wearing. "I'm a servant."

"Odd. That is what I told the Duke." He smiled but it didn't reach his eyes, which remained a clear, cool green. "Exactly who are you, Miss Donovan?"

To Kendra, it seemed as though he were saying: *What* are you? But perhaps she was reading too much into that—years of being under the microscope, as it were, more science experiment than child, had left her sensitive.

She remained silent. She had no choice, really. She could hardly tell him the truth.

He straightened, stepping back. "I shall be keeping a very close eye on you."

Not for the first time, Kendra thought that, despite his elegant clothes, upper-class accent, lithe grace, and lineage, there was something dark, almost dangerous about the marquis. "That sounds almost like a threat," she said.

He smiled grimly. "There is no *almost* about it, Miss Donovan."

Kendra was relieved when they caught up with Rebecca and the Duke on the path leading to the icehouse. Aldridge was carrying Rebecca's art supplies. The other woman had also put on an ankle-skimming dark brown velvet coat, Kendra noticed. The gaze Rebecca turned in their direction was frankly speculative, but she didn't ask where they'd been.

"I've told Lady Rebecca if she has second thoughts about doing this, she may simply inform us," Aldridge stated.

Rebecca merely smiled. Her amusement vanished, however, when they entered the icehouse. *Good,* thought Kendra. She didn't want anyone involved who viewed this as some sort of novelty.

Propriety may have been tossed out the window, but the Duke and Alec still made sure that the nude body was covered to the neck with a coarse wool blanket before Lady Rebecca was allowed to enter.

Kendra immediately scanned Jane Doe. Dalton had closed her eyes, but otherwise hadn't touched the head. Normally, the M.E. would make an incision and pull down the scalp and cut open the skull to remove the brain, which was then weighed and measured. But this was the early nineteenth century. Maybe that wasn't part of the normal procedure. Or maybe Dalton had decided to forgo that part of the autopsy because it was clear that the girl hadn't died from a brain injury. Whatever the reason, it was probably for the best; Kendra doubted Lady Rebecca would've been allowed into the room if the girl's head had been sliced open like a tin can.

As Rebecca began setting up her art supplies, Kendra glanced around. Visiting morgues and viewing autopsies were all part of the job, but there was something really creepy about this room, with the cold seeping up from the stone floor, the dead animal carcasses hanging by hooks against the far wall, and the flickering light from the lanterns, staving off the perpetual gloom. The smell—dust and decay—seemed to have grown stronger.

She saw that Rebecca was also affected, but that might have had less to do with the atmosphere than it did with the corpse. For a long moment, Rebecca stared down at the dead girl, her expression solemn. Kendra thought she saw her shiver, but when she reached for the paper and pastels, her movements were brisk and sure.

Kendra didn't know what to expect, whether she'd get an accurate likeness of the victim or not. It wasn't as though Rebecca was a professional artist. Art was merely considered an appropriate activity for ladies of the era. At least she wouldn't get a woman with three noses, as modernism wouldn't take the art world by storm for several more decades. But Kendra was impressed with the woman's absolute focus, her face pulled into lines of concentration as she worked, her tongue caught between her teeth. For the next ten minutes, the only sound in the room was the whispery movement of pastels against sketch paper.

"What color are her eyes?" Rebecca asked, without stopping, without looking up.

"Brown."

She nodded, choosing a different pastel. Her fingers were smudged with color by the time she put the crayon down, and flipped her drawing tablet around to show them.

Kendra studied the portrait with an appreciation she hadn't expected to feel. Not only had Rebecca captured the girl's likeness, but she'd infused it with a liveliness that was obviously now absent. Maybe it was creative license, but Rebecca had added just the faintest smile to the Cupid's bow mouth, a healthy tint of pink in the cheeks, a coquettish gleam in the eyes.

"You're good. You're very good."

"Better than a death mask," Aldridge added, and then looked over at Kendra. "You were right to insist upon this, Miss Donovan."

"Do you really believe this will help?" Rebecca asked.

Kendra thought of what was said yesterday, that there were hundreds, if not thousands, of brothels in London—assuming the vic was even from a London brothel. She shrugged. "It can't hurt."

Gently Aldridge pulled the blanket up to cover Jane Doe's face.

"What will happen to her now, Duke?" Rebecca asked.

"We shall have to bury her soon. We can't keep her here forever."

"A day or two at the most," Alec agreed.

The Duke picked up Rebecca's art supplies, and gestured toward the door. "Shall we?"

"You can go," Kendra said. "I have one more thing I need to do."

She was already turning to Rebecca so she didn't see the humor that flashed in the Duke's eyes. It wasn't every day, Aldridge reflected, that he was dismissed by a servant.

"Could I borrow a pastel stick and some of your sketch paper?" she asked Rebecca.

Even though the other woman's eyebrows rose questioningly, she handed over the requested supplies. "What are you planning, Miss Donovan?"

"I need to view the body again. Make a record of the wounds inflicted. I should have done it before the autopsy, but . . ." *She'd still been reeling over the fact that she was in the nineteenth century.* "I'll need some assistance turning over the body."

"I will stay with Miss Donovan," Alec volunteered.

The Duke hesitated, looking as though he would've preferred to stay as well. But then he took Rebecca's sketches and box of pastels and ushered her from the room. The woman shot them a departing look that was impossible to interpret before the door closed behind her.

Ignoring Alec's presence, Kendra concentrated on drawing two crude outlines of the female form, front and back.

"Perhaps Rebecca ought to have stayed. Your artistic skill leaves much to be desired," Alec observed, seeing the results of her handiwork.

She made a face. "Likeness isn't important here. Location is—location of the injuries." She put down the paper and pastel stick, and pulled off the blanket.

Dalton had done the standard Y-incision, sewing up the ragged edges of flesh after he'd finished. The girl looked like a torn ragdoll that some tailor had attempted to repair, with gruesome results. Her skin had become more mottled, tinged greenish-red.

They were right; the cool temperature in the icehouse wouldn't delay the body from breaking down much longer.

Methodically, Kendra moved down the body with her visual examination, starting at the top. "No bruises, cuts on the face, other than petechiae around the eyes," she murmured. Was that significant? She retrieved the paper and pastel stick, drew a line through the neck area. "Manual strangulation. Several times. Ultimate cause of death. Bite mark on left breast." She made a corresponding mark on the drawing, scribbling notes in the margins. "Knife wounds begin beneath the breasts. Looks like shallow slashes on upper torso. Deeper, thicker cuts in the middle of torso following the path of the Y-incision to the pubis. Still—deliberate cuts. No stabbing. Nothing frenzied."

Alec suspected Kendra wasn't even aware that she was talking out loud. He watched her with a kind of appalled fascination as she marked up the crude drawing she'd made, carefully depicting each wound, and meticulously writing notes in the margins. In a strange way, her behavior, the intense look of concentration on her face, reminded him of the Duke when he was caught up in one of his experiments.

She paused, leaning back to glance at the drawing she held, comparing it to the body. "There are no cuts on her arms, and only a few on the legs, confined to the upper thigh area. The majority of injuries were inflicted below the breast but not *on* the breast."

"That is incorrect. Her arms and legs have cuts."

She glanced up, looking vaguely startled, as if just remembering he was there. "Those weren't caused from a knife. They're lacerations—postmortem. Probably caused by the river's current and rocks. Her inner thighs are bruised, most likely from when he raped her. I need to turn the body over."

Ironically, it was Alec who had no trouble touching the dead girl. Kendra was the one who had to swallow hard when she reached out to grip a shoulder. The flesh felt cold, waxy. Unfortunately, the victim was no longer in rigor mortis, leaving the body flaccid, and more difficult to turn over. As soon as it was accomplished, Kendra wiped her hands against her apron, feeling queasy.

Kendra studied the deep purple blotches that marred the flesh at the small of the girl's back and thighs. "She was lying on her back when she was murdered. This is lividity. When the heart stops, blood begins pooling at the body's lowest points."

Alec stared at her. *Who the hell is she?* If she hadn't been a woman, he'd have thought her a sawbones.

"He didn't bother to cut her here, either."

Alec pulled his eyes off Kendra to survey the lacerations on the dead girl's back and buttocks. "Those are from rocks, I assume."

"Yes." She returned to the girl's head, threading her fingers through the hair as she peered closer. Although she still wished that she had latex gloves, this didn't make her feel so queasy. Human hair, after all, was dead protein, even on a living person.

"There are scrape marks on the scalp consistent with where the hair has been cut. Looks to be postmortem, given there are no contusions in the scalp area. He wasn't careful, but this wasn't part of his need to inflict pain," she said quietly. "She was already dead. She had no more meaning to him. He was done with her." She made more notes on the sketch paper. "We can turn her back now."

They rolled the body over, and Kendra was wiping her hands on her apron when someone knocked at the door. Alec barely had time to toss the blanket over the dead girl before the door flew open. A boy of about ten stood there. His round eyes immediately went to the corpse. He looked disappointed that the body was covered.

Alec narrowed his eyes when he recognized him. "Dammit, Will! When you knock at a door, you need to wait until someone bids you to enter."

"Oh. Sorry, gov—er, me Lord. Oi was told ter fetch ye." The kid's eyes shifted from the covered body to Alec. Kendra caught the sparkle of excitement. "The thief-taker . . . Oi mean, the Bow Street Runner—'e's 'ere!"

19

"You think the dead lass was a bit o'muslin? Beggin' your pardon, m'Lady . . . ma'am." Sam Kelly, the Bow Street Runner, shot Rebecca and Kendra an apologetic look. If he thought it odd that two women, one a Lady and one a servant, were allowed to sit in on what must be considered an improper discussion, he didn't show it.

Kendra hadn't known what to expect from a nineteenth-century detective, but Magnum, P.I. he was not. He was a short plug of a man, with muscular arms and legs that strained the seams of his dusty gray topcoat, black waistcoat, and breeches. His face, framed by a mop of curly, reddish-brown hair and iron-gray sideburns, looked almost elfin, with turned up features that seemed incongruous on a man his age, which Kendra estimated to be early forties. His eyes were light brown, almost gold, and as expressionless as his face. *Cop eyes*, Kendra thought with a jolt of recognition.

"Should we summon Mr. Hilliard and Mr. Morland?" Rebecca asked from her seat on the sofa.

Sam glanced at the Duke. "Mr. Hilliard and Mr. Morland?"

"Mr. Hilliard is our local constable and Mr. Morland holds the position of magistrate—a mere formality, as the Duke is the largest landholder in the area," said Alec. "Neither gentleman has experience with anything like . . . this."

"I agree." Aldridge considered what Miss Donovan had written on the slate board. "'Tis no insult to the gentlemen in question, but we ought to keep our speculation amongst ourselves. Do you have any objection, Mr. Kelly?"

Sam considered the matter. The gentry were an odd lot. But the Duke of Aldridge was his client and paying the blunt. He shook his head. "Nay. Not a one."

"Excellent. As for the girl, we suspect she worked at an academy. Most likely London."

Sam glanced down at the sketch he held. It had been a clever idea to make use of Lady Rebecca's artistic talents in such a manner, he thought. It would make his job easier—if knocking on more than a thousand brothel doors in London Town could be considered easy.

"You found the lass in a local lake?" He lifted his gaze. "And you believe she was murdered?"

"She *was* murdered," Kendra answered. "Specifically, strangled. Before that, she was held for a period of time. The abrasions on her wrists are consistent with being restrained. Metal, not rope. She was strangled repeatedly. Raped repeatedly. And cut repeatedly. The latter were shallow cuts, nothing mortal. He wasn't trying to kill her, just hurt her."

She'd gotten the detective's attention, which was what she'd wanted. She also wanted to impress upon him the seriousness of the situation. Their eyes met for a long moment. She couldn't figure out what he was thinking.

He finally shifted his gaze back to the Duke. "Is what she's saying true?"

"Yes. I viewed the body myself."

"I'd like ter see the lass as well."

"Certainly. I'll escort you to the body, but Miss Donovan is giving you an accurate account."

Again the golden eyes flicked in her direction. They were still carefully blank, but Kendra suspected that he was wondering who the hell she was. She couldn't blame him. She'd be thinking the same thing if she were in his shoes. In his eyes, she realized, *she* was the civilian.

"He also cut off sections of her hair," she told him.

He frowned. "Why'd he do that?"

"I don't know," she admitted. "He has a reason, though. I think he has a reason he selected that particular girl. And there's a reason he bit her on the breast once, no more."

Sam leaned forward, fascinated. "He bit her?"

"Yes."

Aldridge asked, "Mr. Kelly, have you encountered anything like this before?"

Sam rubbed the side of his nose, thinking. "I've seen bawdy baskets bite each other and yank their hair almost clean outta their scalps when they get into flaming rows. Never what you're describing, though." His eyes dropped to the portraiture again. "Have you considered that a client of hers might've taken exception ter something the lass did or said?"

Instead of answering, the Duke glanced at Kendra.

Interesting, Sam thought. The Duke of Aldridge seemed almost deferential toward the maid.

"He's most likely a client, but this wasn't an impulsive attack," Kendra told Sam. "She didn't have any defensive wounds on her fingers and palms. I think she came with him willingly and the attack happened after she was restrained. She may have agreed to be handcuffed or he took her by surprise, so she didn't have time to fight back."

"Why in heaven's name would she agree to be handcuffed?" Rebecca asked, surprised.

Kendra caught the deer-in-the-headlights look of the men, and had to suppress a smile. "I'll explain it to you later."

"You will not!" Alec glared at her.

Rebecca in turn glared at him. "You shall not dictate my future conversations, Sutcliffe!"

Sam cleared his throat. "Ah, aye, well, you've given me an interesting case, Your Grace." He hesitated and then slanted another look at the maid. "Forgive me, Miss Donovan, but I must ask . . . who are you?" He spread his hands. "You appear ter have a bit of expertise in this area, which—if I may be blunt—is unusual enough for anyone, but especially for a woman."

Kendra tensed automatically, thinking, *Will I always be a freak?* Still, she understood his confusion. She *was* a freak here. Any woman from her era would be.

"I know that what I am saying may be unorthodox," she said slowly, fixing her gaze on him. "I can only hope you won't discount what I'm saying because I'm a woman."

Sam regarded her carefully, aware that she hadn't answered his question.

"Brava, Miss Donovan!" Rebecca declared, breaking the silence. "The contributions of women have too long been discounted. We have been treated like we have nothing but feathers stuffed in our heads! When I think of—"

"Hell's teeth, Becca," Alec interrupted, shooting her an exasperated look. "Now is not the time to discuss Mrs. Wollstonecraft's radical ideas, my dear."

Rebecca looked insulted. "That is the trouble, sir. There is no good time a *man* wants to discuss the rights of women. But there shall come a time, Sutcliffe! Someday women shall even be given the right to vote. Mark my words!"

"Yes, well. I think we need to concentrate on the matter at hand, rather than politics, my dear," Aldridge said mildly. "And, for the record, I have never adhered to the nonsense that women are ornamental creatures with no intellect." His gaze lifted to the painting above the fireplace. "My wife was a brilliant mathematician and astronomer. If the course of events had been different, I believe she would have rivaled Caroline Herschel in her contributions to science.

"So, you see, Miss Donovan," he added, smiling sadly at Kendra, "I shan't dismiss what you are saying because of some misplaced theory that a woman's brain is smaller than a man's."

"Aye. You needn't fear that I'll dismiss you out of hand, either, miss," said Sam. "Some of the most devious criminals I've ever encountered were women."

He grinned, but sobered quickly when he turned to the Duke. "Me and me men will begin making inquiries as soon as I return ter Town. If she worked for an academy, 'tis doubtful a bawd would've let her leave—not without brokerin' the deal."

"A bawd?" Kendra asked.

Sam gave her another look. Maybe they called them something else in America. "An abbess—brothel-keeper. I suspect that the lass didn't work for the more exclusive brothels in Town. We'd have heard if a Cyprian went missing," the Runner continued. "We'll begin at the mid-range academies. I warn you, Your Grace, this will take time. London brothel-keepers do a bang-up business."

"We understand we've given you no easy task, Mr. Kelly," Aldridge nodded. "I thank you for coming so promptly to my summons."

Sam controlled his wince as he thought of the almost two hours that he'd spent on horseback in order to answer the summons so promptly. He'd rather have hired a carriage, but that would've taken nearly twice as long. And he didn't like to keep the gentry waiting. Especially not someone as influential as the Duke of Aldridge.

He rubbed his chin thoughtfully, since that brought up a point. "The lass had ter get here somehow."

"Yes, we already discussed that," the Duke said. "We deduced a private carriage would be most likely, given the circumstance."

"I'll have me men interview the whips who might have this route, just ter be certain. 'Tis almost a four-hour journey by carriage. If she came by private carriage, they may have stopped ter freshen their horses, take a meal. Mayhap innkeepers and publicans would remember her."

"An excellent notion, Mr. Kelly."

Sam slapped his hands on his thighs and pushed himself to his feet. He wasn't exactly looking forward to the next part, but it was necessary. "If you'd be so good as ter take me ter the lass, sir. The quicker that's done, the quicker I'll be off."

"I've never seen the like," Sam confessed, studying the body on the table. Aside from the sawbones's needlework, the bruises that circled the throat stood out. As the American had said, she'd been strangled more than once. Pushed to the brink of death, and brought back, over and over again. What kind of madman would do that? "We get plenty of murders in Town. I recall all too vividly, sir, the hideous murders of the Marr household at the East End. Everyone, including the wee babe and Mr. Marr's apprentice, were bludgeoned, their throats slit."

The Duke's blue gaze darkened. "I heard about that crime. They caught the perpetrator, did they not?"

"Not then. A similar crime occurred almost a fortnight later, at the King's Arms Inn. John Williams, a sailor, was arrested for that heinous act. He hung himself later, so most likely he was the culprit."

"You have doubt?"

Sam shrugged. "Don't matter what I think. The fellow's dead. And the folks drove a stake right through his black heart so he could never rise again."

"Superstitious nonsense."

"Aye. But it made them feel better. And it must've worked as there've been no like crimes since." Sam grinned.

"Or it could mean he was the true culprit," Aldridge remarked dryly.

"Aye. That too." Sam reached to draw the wool blanket over the girl. "You know, I was among those at the first murder scene. It was a bloody mess. There's less blood here, but . . . this seems worse somehow," he said quietly. "This seems more . . . evil."

The Duke nodded solemnly. "I consider myself an enlightened man, but I agree with you, Mr. Kelly. What was done to this girl was evil."

He moved toward the door, glancing back at the Runner. "If we're done here, I'd like to return to my study. I have something else to discuss with you before you leave for Town."

Sam eyed the Duke warily, but said nothing until they walked into the study ten minutes later. "You are aware that your man of affairs in Town already gave me my terms, sir?" he asked, and held his breath. As the terms had been extremely generous, he hoped there hadn't been a miscommunication in that regard.

"Yes, I'm quite aware." The Duke moved behind his desk and sat down. "I have another matter to discuss with you."

"Oh?"

He hesitated. "I am afraid it shall add to your burden, Mr. Kelly. Naturally, I am prepared to pay. It will, however, require your greatest discretion as it is a sensitive matter."

A slow smile spread across Sam's face. The gentry were an odd lot, but there were reasons he enjoyed dealing with them.

"I am always discreet, sir."

20

Kendra couldn't say that she was getting used to being in the nineteenth century, but she now had a routine, which meant helping Rose again in the kitchens the next morning for another marathon of potato-peeling. God, if she never saw another spud—unless it was already baked, broiled, boiled, or mashed on her plate—she'd die happy. And Rose still managed to fill up three pots to every one she did.

Not that she was counting.

Around noon, she grabbed a couple of apples from a nearby barrel and escaped outside. The temperature was in the low seventies, but seemed cool after the stifling heat of the kitchens. She followed the pretty flagstone path that wound its way around the vegetable gardens. Aware that she was under observation from the gardeners, she veered off the path, up the gently sloping hill, into the shadowy forest.

Without the heavy basket she'd carried the other day, it took her less than fifteen minutes at a brisk pace to reach the lake, another ten to walk the perimeter. The waterfall wasn't big, but the cascade came over in a steady sheet, churning up the water at its base. Kendra could imagine Jane Doe being swept over, floating to the calmer waters of the shore before becoming entangled in weeds and cattails. If the nuncheon hadn't occurred, she wondered how long it would have taken to discover the body.

Careless or uncaring? she wondered. There was a difference. Careless meant the unsub had hoped that by tossing the body in the river, it would be carried to the ocean. Uncaring meant he didn't have a problem if the body was found. Careless meant he was getting sloppy. Uncaring meant he was getting bold.

She climbed the steep terrain to the top of the waterfall. The river widened to about sixty feet. On either side were Chest Wood trees, ancient oak and pine, tall weeds, and a scattering of wildflowers, their colors popping amid the greenery. Picking up her skirt, she followed the waterway for about half a mile before angling off to climb the hill. At the top, she did a slow scan of the surrounding countryside.

Pretty as a postcard—too pretty to carry the ugly stain of murder.

Impulsively, she clambered up a grayish-brown boulder the size of a Fiat. Sitting down, she leaned back on her elbows, tilting her head and closing her eyes to drink in the warm rays of the sun. A light breeze stirred the grass and branches around her, fluttered the leaves. Birds called to each other. Sometimes she'd hear weird clicking noises.

She could almost fool herself into thinking she was back home, lazing down by the community pool in her Virginia apartment complex. Except there was no squeal and splash from the neighborhood children. *And* she was wearing a maid's uniform. And she was in the freaking nineteenth century.

Sighing, fantasy destroyed, she sat up, and pulled the apples from the pockets that she wore. They did not look like the apples she'd buy at the store. They weren't as big or red or as perfect.

But they were pesticide-free, so she didn't have to worry about washing them. She polished them up before biting into the fruit, using the apron as a napkin to blot the excess juice that dribbled down her chin.

She caught a flash of brown and white, and turned her head to observe a rabbit sprinting across the clearing. Not a white rabbit, but she felt like Alice in Wonderland.

Alice in Wonderland—which wouldn't even be written for another fifty years.

Instead of falling down a rabbit hole, she'd fallen through a wormhole. While wormholes were really her mother's area of quantum physics, Kendra knew some of the theories. One of the more recent ideas floated in scientific circles was that the universe was filled with tiny wormholes that popped up and winked out of existence all the time. Of course, with her, it would've had to be a *big* wormhole.

But it was pointless to panic or speculate on how she'd got here. Better to concentrate on solving the murder, which, in her mind, had become linked with her bizarre situation.

Kendra knew her profile was weak, but it was a starting point. Every investigation needed one. And while Lady Rebecca might not like it, she stood by her profile that they were dealing with someone from the upper class. The good news was that the pool of suspects was considerably less than the working class. Maybe only a dozen or so men in the area, depending on how wide a net she wanted to toss. The unsub would also have to be familiar enough with London that it would be part of his comfort zone. But he lived locally, she was sure. Or at least he had a private place here. Privacy was essential to do what he needed to do.

Kendra would need help coming up with a list of suspects. They'd have to be interviewed, their alibis verified—basic, old-fashioned police work.

Sighing, Kendra finished off the apple as she surveyed the countryside from her perch—a haphazard patchwork of rolling green hills seamed with hedges and clusters of trees. From this vantage point, she could see Alec was right; the river wasn't a single flowing stream, but several branches. No telling where the girl had been dumped initially. The current should have carried the body downstream toward the ocean. It was just dumb luck that she'd been swept into the tributary that fed the lake.

She spotted a small stone building in the distance, next to the river. A mile or two north, chimney stacks rose above the treetops, indicating other houses. Simon Dalton and Kenneth Morland, she remembered, owned neighboring estates.

They fit the profile. So did Alec, for that matter. He'd been with the Duke on the night Jane Doe was murdered, she knew. It was unlikely that he'd slipped out of the castle to wherever the girl had been held afterward—unlikely, but not impossible. Could you slip out of a household like this without a servant or someone in the stables seeing you?

It was another avenue to pursue, she decided as she pushed herself to her feet and tossed the apple core down for the ants to feast upon. Jumping off the boulder, she began to retrace her steps down the hill, back to the castle.

Her mind circled back to the discovery of the body. *Careless or uncaring?* she wondered again. The more she thought about it, the more she suspected the latter. This was an age when people spent time outdoors. They weren't sitting in front of their televisions, computers, or Xboxes. The chances of discovery were high.

That boldness worried Kendra. Contrary to their portrayal in the media, most serial killers preferred to work in secrecy, never seeking notoriety from the press or police. Few escalated to the point where they wanted to share their work.

Kendra fought off a shiver, attributing the sudden chill to the fact that she'd entered the forest again. The big trees swallowed up the sunshine, leaving the woods in a perpetual shade. It made her uneasy. The space between her shoulder blades pricked with the sensation of being watched. The sensation deepened as she continued to walk. *Not good.*

She slowed to a stop and turned a full circle, scanning the forest, trying to probe beyond the trees and shrubbery thick with shadows. She made an instinctive gesture for the gun she no longer carried.

"Who's there?" she called out sharply.

Around her, birds continued to whistle; insects whirred and chirped. If there was something bad lurking in the woods, wouldn't the birds stop singing? Except she couldn't shake the creepy feeling of watching eyes. Maybe it was an animal, a deer or a rabbit. Or—*fuck*—a wolf or a bear?

Her fingers shook with a phantom itch to hold the comforting weight of her SIG Sauer. Heart beginning to hammer, she moved forward, keeping her strides long and even. Her ears strained to pick up the slightest sound—a footfall, the snapping of a twig—to pinpoint the direction of her hidden observer. She'd gone about fifty yards and thought she heard something in the two o'clock position. She stopped, swiveling to stare hard in that direction.

She was wrong.

He came at her from behind, making no attempt to cover the noise as he broke free from the trees. Spinning around, she saw a man with long, tangled, sandy brown hair and ratty beard rushing toward her, waving his arms and yelling something guttural.

Her entire body tensed. *Flight or fight.* A part of her wanted to run, but her training had her standing her ground, even as her heart leaped straight into her throat.

"Stop!" she ordered, but the man continued his headlong rush toward her, his hands conveniently stretched out in front of him. It was too perfect, and she lunged forward, grasping his hands and viciously yanking back his fingers. It was a classic policeman's restraining maneuver, and it worked as it was intended.

The man gave a sharp yelp and tried to pull away. Kendra completed the maneuver by twisting his arm behind his spine, and driving him to his knees.

"Okay, asshole! Who the hell are you?" she shouted, adrenaline rushing through her veins. She jerked his arm up higher, twisting it near his shoulder blades until he screamed in pain. "Why are you following me? *Tell me!* Tell me or I'll—"

"Miss Donovan!"

Her head snapped around. Alec was standing about twenty feet from her, having come from the direction of the castle. His expression was indecipherable as his gaze traveled from her to the man who was now whimpering on his knees before her.

"What, pray tell," he drawled finally, "are you doing to the hermit?"

21

"Hermit?" Kendra repeated stupidly, not sure she heard correctly. "You have a hermit?"

"Not I. The Duke. All the best households have them." Alec lifted one brow. "Mayhap you ought to unhand him. If you break his arm, he won't be able to fulfill his duties."

"Duties?" Was he serious? "You have a hermit. And he has duties."

Alec grinned suddenly, and it occurred to Kendra that this was the first genuine smile she'd ever seen from him. If she wasn't already feeling like someone had kicked her in the head, that might've done it. "I believe most hermits are required to leap out of bushes, frighten the ladies. Being ferocious and uncivilized, or brooding and poetic. Whatever the advertisement stipulated. I must say, you failed miserably with the ferocious part, Thomas. At least with Miss Donovan."

"She's breaking me bleeding arm!" the man cried out, sobbing.

Kendra let him go. He scrambled to his feet, eyeing her warily as he rubbed his arm.

"You actually advertised for a hermit?"

"Again, not I. Thomas is an ornamental hermit. The countess acquired him for the house party. It's quite the thing."

"It's absurd," she muttered. But was it any more ridiculous than millions tuning in to watch *Jersey Shore* or the Kardashians? Or cats on the Internet? People were freaking nuts, regardless of the century.

"The Ton delights in the absurd."

Kendra eyed the strange man. If you looked beyond the matted hair and filth—good God, he stunk to high heaven—she saw that he was young, probably no more than twenty-two or twenty-three. "You actually get *paid* to skulk about the forest and terrorize women?"

"I don't skulk. And the ladies *want* to be terrorized. I add a bucolic charm, the countess says. I'm an artist."

"Of course you are," Kendra said dryly. "Where do you live?"

He frowned, eyeing her suspiciously. "Why?"

"I'm curious."

He hesitated, then gave a jerky shrug. "In the stone hut near the river."

"Did you hear about the dead girl found in the lake?"

Thomas stepped back, his face becoming wooden. "Nay."

"That's odd. Everybody's talking about it."

Something flickered behind his eyes, then was gone. "Aye. Aye, I remember now. Word gets around."

"So you *did* hear about it?"

He wiped his palms on his grimy beige homespun pants, looking nervous. "Aye. Mayhap I heard something. About a doxy being found in the lake. I dunno anythin'. I had nothing to do with it."

"I didn't say that you did. But you live near the river. Somebody dumped the body in the river. Maybe you saw something, someone in the area."

"Nay. I don't know nothin'."

Alec considered him carefully. "If you did know something, Thomas, you would tell me or His Grace, wouldn't you?"

"Aye." His Adam's apple bobbed. "May I go, sir? I know nothin'."

Alec exchanged a look with Kendra, then nodded. "All right, Thomas. If we need you, we'll send for you."

He didn't wait, bolting back into the forest.

Kendra stared after him. "He's hiding something."

"Most likely the lice in his hair." Alec lifted a mocking brow. "I thought you were of the mind the murderer was one of my ilk? Not our poor hermit—and when I use the word *poor,* I mean it most literally. Thomas doesn't have two coins to rub together. And while I suppose women are sometimes drawn to the brooding artist, a Bird of Paradise has, shall we say, a bit more pragmatic disposition."

"I'm not saying he killed the girl. I'm saying that he's lying now. Or holding back."

"Why would he lie? If he saw something, why not tell us? I gave him the opportunity."

"In my experience, people like Thomas often don't like to get involved. Especially if it's his word against . . . one of your ilk."

"Exactly what *is* your experience, Miss Donovan?"

Instead of answering—and what could she say, really?—Kendra swung around and began walking. She was caught off guard when Alec grabbed her arm. He looked grim.

"You haven't answered my question. What do *you* have to hide, Miss Donovan?"

Oh, just a little thing like dropping in from the twenty-first century, she thought, and had to squelch the bubble of hysterical laughter that rose in her throat. Instead, she said in her most neutral tone, "I know what I'm doing. You need to trust me."

"As you trust me? You think I could be a murderer." He laughed without any amusement at her start of surprise. "You said the murderer was someone in my class, someone familiar with the area, someone who has the means to hire a London light-skirt and bring her to the country."

"I never accused you."

He gave her a wry look. "Not out loud, no. But you've certainly considered the possibility, have you not?"

Kendra stared at him warily.

His mouth twisted, and he lifted a finger, skimming the silky wedge of hair that swung against her jaw to the delicate jaw itself.

Kendra forced herself to stand still, again taken aback by the awareness that hummed between them. This was far more dangerous than if she thought him a murderer—a murderer she could handle.

"Tell me, Miss Donovan. Isn't it rather perilous for you to be out here with me, in the woods all alone?"

"I can take care of myself." She was pleased her voice was steady. Her knees certainly were not.

He smiled slowly. "Yes, I saw that myself. Who taught you that little trick you used on poor Thomas?"

She didn't know how to respond to that. It was a relief when she heard approaching footsteps. Alec heard them too, and dropped his hand, his expression once again becoming indecipherable as Kenneth Morland came along the path.

He hesitated when he saw them. "Ah, Sutcliffe . . . I was told you'd returned to the lake. I didn't realize you were here with Miss Donovan." He flicked a look at Kendra, then dismissed her. "Did you discover anything else?"

His question was directed at Alec, but Kendra answered. "I found a hermit."

Morland shifted his attention back to her. "A hermit, you say?"

"Miss Donovan had an encounter with the countess' ornamental hermit. He attempted to terrorize her, but she ended up terrorizing him."

"I didn't realize his job was to leap out of bushes," she muttered.

Morland laughed. "Oh, I see. All in good fun, of course. My mother had a fancy for one years ago, but my grandfather refused. Not that it's easy to hire one. Not a lot of hermits lying about, you understand. Especially with all the stipulations imposed on them."

Kendra had to ask, "What sort of stipulations?"

"I heard when Sir Jeremy Pellman hired an ornamental hermit for Pellman Park, he was required to grow out his hair and fingernails and to restrict his speech to growling and cursing at the guests. Sir Jeremy promised to pay him seven hundred pounds if he lasted the length of the contract, which, if I am not mistaken, was seven years. I heard Sir Jeremy sacked him after two months, when he learned his hermit spent his afternoons in the village pub."

"You're joking."

"I most certainly am not!"

"After our hermit encountered Miss Donovan, he ought to think twice about leaping out at the ladies. She may have quite ruined him," Alec drawled, his eyes gleaming with amusement. "But my aunt has less stringent requirements for a hermit than Sir Jeremy, so Thomas, I daresay, will stay on."

Morland gave them both an uncertain glance. "Aside from the hermit, have you discovered anything in regards to the doxy, Sutcliffe? I was told the Runner has been and gone."

A sour note crept into his voice. As magistrate, Kendra realized, he was the local law. And even though it appeared the role was more ceremonial than functional, Morland seemed to have the same territorial instincts as everyone she knew in law enforcement. Or maybe it was just the male ego. Either way, it was clear that Morland was not happy about missing the Bow Street Runner.

"As Mr. Kelly will be required to scour all the brothels in London, Duke thought he ought to begin his task immediately."

"'Tis an enormous task for the Runner. Do you think he will accomplish it?"

Alec shrugged. "Mr. Kelly seemed a competent sort."

"Then we're at a standstill until the Runner returns."

"The thief-taker's already gone?" a new voice demanded to know.

Kendra glanced at the two men striding down the hill. She recognized both from yesterday's nuncheon. The shorter man had a round, almost babyish face with wispy blond hair and blue eyes. The other was the good-looking young man who'd been drinking out of a flask. By the look in his bright eyes now, she suspected he was drinking again today. Or maybe he'd never stopped.

"Gabriel." Alec's voice was ice-cold. "What are you doing here?"

The good-looking man—Gabriel—scowled and threw out his arms. "You are not my keeper, Sutcliffe. Until His Grace cocks up his toes, none of this is yours yet. I am free to go where I please."

"You're bossy, as usual," Alec snapped.

"Gabe." The other man laid a hand on Gabriel's arm, shooting Alec an uneasy glance. "Mayhap we ought to return to the castle."

"Listen to Harcourt, Gabriel. And go easy on the port."

Gabriel flushed and shook off his friend's hand. "I suggest you mind your own bloody business, my Lord." His chin jutted out belligerently, his gaze hot. He took a step forward, and for a minute Kendra wondered if he was going to take a swing at Alec. Then Morland intervened, stepping forward and clapping a hand on Gabriel's shoulder. "I'll walk with you back to the castle, my boy." He had a forced jovial note in his voice. "'Tis too fine a day to be shadowed by bickering."

In an adroit maneuver, Morland and Harcourt flanked Gabriel, hustling him back up the footpath. Kendra glanced at Alec.

"What's going on between you? It's clear that the guy hates your guts."

Despite the grimness he was feeling, Alec smiled. "Miss Donovan, ladies do not mention one's innards."

"I'll make a note." They began following the trio at a more leisurely pace. She slanted him a curious glance. "Who is he? Jealous rival? Longtime enemy?"

Alec's smile faded; his face became shuttered.

"You might say that," he finally answered. "He's my brother."

22

Apparently families were as screwed up in the nineteenth century as they were in the twenty-first. Kendra wondered if simple rivalry was at the root of Gabriel's animosity. Or if there was something more, something even darker, more twisted than jealousy.

By the time the Duke sent for her, she'd gotten three blisters on her fingers from cutting vegetables. The wounds reminded her of Jane Doe's soft hands. Definitely *not* a servant.

She walked into the study, and stopped when she saw the slate board.

"Few people venture into the schoolroom, much less that wing of the castle, but I see no need to incite hysteria in anyone curious enough to go there," Aldridge said, rising from his chair and coming around the desk. "I thought it best to bring the slate board here."

She nodded. "That's a good idea. Some of the staff have already begun thinking gypsies are responsible. In fact, you might want to warn them. There could be trouble."

"No need, Miss Donovan. The Romani are gone."

She raised her brows. "You already told them?"

"Alec and I rode out to their camp, but they had already departed."

"How—"

"The Romani have been persecuted their entire lives, Miss Donovan. Whenever something befalls the countryside—a cow becomes ill, a field is devastated by blight—they are the first to be blamed. Despite our modern age, many fall back on superstition. The Romani are a pragmatic and clever people; they will leave at the first sign of trouble."

"Well, that's one less thing to worry about, I suppose."

He was silent as he surveyed the shadows beneath her eyes. "I can see that you have been worrying," he finally said.

Kendra shrugged. "There's a lot to worry about." *Time travel. Serial killers. An attraction to a man who's more than two hundred years older than I am.* She glanced at the slate board. "He's out there, you know. He'll kill again."

Aldridge frowned. "I fail to see what we can do until the Runner returns."

Panic tickled at the back of her throat. How long, she wondered, would it take the Bow Street Runner to conduct his inquiries? Days? Weeks? *Months?* London's population, even during this time period, had swelled to more than a million.

"We have a general sense of who this guy is. We know that he's either a member of the gentry or, at the very least, he's affluent. He lives in the area or is familiar with it. We also know the general time that Jane Doe was killed."

"What do you propose?"

"First, we need to come up with a list of suspects."

"Suspects," Aldridge murmured.

The way he said it, the word sounded ugly. She had no doubt that the Duke wanted the killer caught. But it was amazing how many people got downright pissy when their friends and family were questioned by the authorities. "Yes. Men who fit the profile. Is that a problem?"

"'Tis troubling to look at neighbors, acquaintances, perhaps even friends with suspicion."

"I'd think that it would be even more troubling to find another dead girl."

He gave her a wry look. "Rest easy, Miss Donovan. I have no intention of turning a blind eye."

"Good, because once we have the list of suspects, we'll need to interview them. Find out if they have an alibi for the night the girl was murdered." *Basic police work*, she thought again.

"Hmm. And if they do, we will be able to cross them off our list, I assume?"

"Yes."

The Duke's expression turned thoughtful. "'Tis a logical approach—if, that is, your assumptions are correct."

"They are."

He had to smile. "You are very confident."

"In this, I know what I'm doing."

"Interesting. That implies in other things, you do not."

"Well, I don't know how to peel a potato. At least not as fast as Rose."

"You surprise me, Miss Donovan."

"It's a lot harder than it looks."

He smiled. "I shall take your word for it. Sit down, Miss Donovan. Let us begin that list, shall we?"

The Duke identified at least two dozen men in a ten-mile area who fit the broad description of being affluent. They whittled that list down by eliminating men who rarely ventured outside the area. Jane Doe wasn't a local. Another handful of names were crossed out because the men were traveling abroad.

It was a tedious process, especially since she was the one writing the names down in a ledger by dipping pen in ink.

She refused—absolutely *refused*—to think about her kick-ass laptop back in the twenty-first century.

By the time the Duke left for dinner, they had eight names, including Dalton and Morland. She noticed that his nephews, Alec and Gabriel, were absent from the list. There were all sorts of blind eyes, she thought.

Still, eight names wasn't a bad starting point.

Alone, she turned her attention to the two crude drawings she'd made yesterday. The marks she'd made depicting each wound couldn't begin to convey the horror that had been inflicted on Jane Doe. Without that brutal overlay to shock and distract, she could get a sense of the wounds themselves.

Unfortunately, there appeared to be no discernible pattern: fifty-three stab wounds in total. Usually a number that great would indicate a frenzied attack, with the blades puncturing the flesh in what was often a simulated sex act. But not in this case. This, as she'd told Sam Kelly, was methodic *cutting*. Terrible control and a terrible desire to inflict pain.

Did he do it to punish someone—ex-girlfriend, wife, mother—or simply because he was a sexual sadist? Or both?

She glanced up when the door swung open, and Lady Rebecca came into the room. The Lady was already dressed for evening in an empire-waisted blue gown with tiny pearls sewn into the bodice. The skirt was narrow, but that didn't stop Lady Rebecca from making brisk strides to stand before her. She carried an ivory fan that she thumped against her open palm in what Kendra could only conclude was a sign of extreme irritation.

"You think Alec is a murderer!"

Carefully, Kendra slipped the drawings into the ledger. "He told you that?"

"He finds it amusing. I do not!"

"I can see that. Look, whatever—"

"I shall tell you a story. I expect you've wondered about my face."

"What? No," Kendra said. "I mean, I assumed you had smallpox."

"Yes. I contracted the affliction when I was seven." She wandered around the room as she told her story, picking up and setting down objects she found. Nervous energy. "I am certain my parents measured me for a shroud. Many children of the same age died, you see. I don't know why I did not." She fell silent, and shook her head. "I lived—but not without repercussions. As you can see."

"I'm sorry."

"I am not asking for your sympathy, Miss Donovan. Or pity." Rebecca set down the figurine she held and deliberately moved over to where one of the oil lamps was burning, positioning herself so that the light slid mercilessly over her disfigured face, so that she was grotesque.

"Children can be cruel. I may be the daughter of an earl, but that doesn't guarantee friendship. It did not stop the teasing and name-calling. Alec defended my honor with his wits and sometimes, his fists. It did not stop the viciousness when he was absent, but he was my white knight."

Kendra remembered the first morning, when Sarah had talked about getting sick because she had to sit opposite Rebecca. She suspected that the cruelty hadn't stopped with childhood, it had just become more underhanded. Human beings had an almost limitless supply of malice.

"I understand how protective you must feel toward Lord Sutcliffe," she said slowly.

Rebecca waved that away impatiently. "Mayhap I *do* feel the need to come to his defense as he always came to mine. But that is not why I'm telling you this. A young lad—Alec was sixteen at the time—who has the compassion to rescue a little girl from the evil taunts of her playmates, to spend time with her to alleviate her loneliness, could never grow up to be the man, the *monster*, you have described."

She walked to the slate board and stared at it for a few minutes before turning to look at Kendra. She used her fan as a pointer. "*This* is a man who hates women. This man could never have been the boy who provided succor to a young child in need."

"I agree."

Rebecca looked surprised. "You believe me?"

"It's not a question of me believing you. It's logistics. I saw Alec—Lord Sutcliffe—myself in this room on the night of the murder. It's highly unlikely that he'd have left here to torture and kill the girl."

"Highly unlikely, but not impossible."

"He fits the profile," she conceded. "And I can't afford to let personal feelings"—she thought of the sharp tug of attraction she'd felt earlier—"stop me from doing my duty."

"Apparently the duties of a maid are much more expansive in America," Rebecca remarked drily, then let out a frustrated sigh. "I confess, Miss Donovan, that I am finding it difficult to believe that someone from my class did this horrendous thing!"

"No one wants to think that someone they know is capable of cold-blooded murder," Kendra agreed, not without sympathy. "But we can't ignore the facts, either."

Rebecca scowled. "Facts. You don't have any *facts*, Miss Donovan. You—we—only have supposition."

"Based on deductive reasoning. We're looking for someone who has the means to hire a high-class prostitute, transport her to the country, and—"

"Yes, yes, we've already discussed this," Rebecca waved her hand holding the closed fan impatiently. "You could be describing the Duke."

"No. The Duke was here as well that night. We're also looking for a much younger man. Someone between the ages of twenty-five and forty-five."

Rebecca stared at her. "How, pray tell, do you know that?"

"Age is the most difficult thing to identify with an unsub. However, what was done to that girl—both in luring her out and the killer's brutality—shows a level of sophistication. It takes time for this type of killer to develop their fantasies, which means the unsub isn't too young. At the same time, the longer an unsub gets away with his aberrant behavior, the more confident he becomes. And the more disorganized he becomes. The Duke is an older man. I believe if he were responsible, this wouldn't be the first time you would have found a dead woman in the area. We're dealing with someone who is comfortable, but not complacent with his success. Besides . . ."

"Besides . . . what?"

"I can't imagine the Duke hurting anyone," she admitted, and laughed softly. "Which is the worst reason for ruling anyone out."

Rebecca smiled. "As I happen to know the Duke, I agree. He is one of the kindest men on earth." She glanced up at the portrait above the fireplace. "Did you know that his daughter was only a few years older than I? I've been told we were great playmates when we were infants. I do not remember her." She wandered over to the ornate globe that came up to her waist, spinning it with her fingertips. "My father and the Duke were schoolmates at Eton and later Cambridge. They maintained their friendship. The Duke's my godfather, which is why I've spent so much time here at the castle."

"Are your parents dead?"

"My, you are blunt, aren't you?" Rebecca laughed. "No. My parents are touring my father's sugar plantations in Barbados. The Duke—or rather, the countess—was kind enough to invite me to her house party. She has one every year at the end of the Season."

"I see. And Alec—the marquess' parents?"

Rebecca's gaze sharpened, but she answered readily enough. "Both have passed. His mother was an Italian countess, Alexandria—a diamond of the first water. I heard Sutcliffe's father, Edward, fell in love with her at first sight while on his grand tour. *His* father—Duke's—was not happy when his youngest son brought home an Italian bride, no matter how fine her pedigree or how full her family coffers. Alexandria was beautiful, but she was not English."

"You knew her?"

"No. She died before I was born. But I have seen portraits of her, and heard the tales, which are rather legendary. She had a fiery temperament and had rows against the Duke—not the current Duke, but his father."

"I get it."

"Pardon?"

"I mean, I understand. How'd she die?"

"A carriage accident. I've been told the marquis was inconsolable. And Alec, too."

"I'm sure it wasn't good for Gabriel, either." She thought of Alec's brother, and wondered if that was at the root of his drinking, his anger issues.

Rebecca lifted her brows. "Oh, Alexandria wasn't Gabriel's mother. A year or so after she died, the marquis remarried. Emily Telford. Very English. Very proper." Rebecca made a face. "A high stickler if there ever was one. She was the youngest daughter of a viscount. I'm certain the Duke was ecstatic when his son married her, but he died less than a year later of some sort of fit. Then Sutcliffe's father died three years after siring Gabriel. Naturally, as the eldest son, Alec inherited the title and all the estates that were entailed. The marchioness and Gabriel had a town house in London, and Alec, I daresay, gave them a generous allowance in addition to what Lady Emily had from her own inheritance."

Past tense. "The marchioness is no longer alive?"

"She passed away from consumption six years ago."

"Is that when Gabriel started drinking?"

Rebecca's mouth tightened. "You *do* ask personal questions."

"They may get even more personal."

Rebecca stared at her for a moment, then shook her head. "I don't know what to make of you, Miss Donovan." She sighed. "Gabriel's behavior is not that unusual for a young buck sowing his wild oats, you know."

"Maybe, but he seems to be sowing more than wild oats. He seems to have some major issues."

Rebecca's brow puckered. "Lady Emily was not an easy woman to be around. Alec . . . I remember she made his life miserable, as well, but he was away at Eton, then Cambridge. Gabriel was not so fortunate. I can't say I blame him for letting loose now."

"What about Dalton?"

Rebecca frowned. "Mr. Dalton? I don't know very much about him other than he comes from good stock in Manchester. His father was a doctor. Mr. Dalton was an army surgeon until he inherited Halstead Hall, one of the neighboring estates."

"He's not married?"

"Well . . ." She hesitated, giving Kendra an uncertain look.

"What?"

"'Tis nothing. Old gossip."

"It could be important."

"Mr. Dalton was married once. The *on dit* is his wife died after she fled the country with another man." Rebecca saw the expression in Kendra's eyes and hurried on. "I know what you're thinking, Miss Donovan, but, as I said, that gossip is ancient history. Surely you cannot believe Mr. Dalton's tragedy has any bearing on this poor unfortunate girl's demise?"

"Ancient history is usually where a psychosis begins. The unsub has a problem with women."

Rebecca looked uneasy. "Mr. Dalton isn't the only man who has had a runaway wife. The whole of England knows how shabbily Lady Caroline has treated her husband by publicizing her passion for Lord Byron."

It still shook Kendra to have historical names thrown out so casually, a reminder that this wasn't a dream, that those long-dead figures were alive at this very moment. *Christ, I can't think about it.*

"Dalton fits the profile. We need to find out more about his past. What about Morland?"

"Mr. Morland? His family has lived on the neighboring estate for generations—Tinley Park."

"I need more information than that. Does he have family? Brothers? Sisters? Is he married? Ever been married?"

"Those are a lot of questions," Rebecca murmured, moving to the sideboard. She poured a glass of claret, then cocked her head at Kendra. "Would you like a drink?"

"No, thank you. Do you have answers to the questions?"

Rebecca eyed her over the rim of her wineglass. "For a maid, you are an imperious sort, aren't you?" Before Kendra could reply to that, she hurried on. "His grandfather passed a few years back. He was the Earl of Whilmont. His mother is still alive, but has become a recluse. He has no brothers or sisters, and to the best of my knowledge he has never been caught in the parson's mousetrap."

"No scandal or skeletons in the closet?"

"I didn't say that." Rebecca sipped her wine. "I don't know how this can be relevant since it happened so many years ago, but Lady Anne—Morland's mother—eloped with his father, who was an infantry man. The old earl was furious."

"Why? Because she eloped?"

"The elopement was disgraceful enough, but she married an *infantry man,* Miss Donovan. No title. Undoubtedly penniless. Most earls would have been displeased by the match. Do you really not understand that?"

"Okay. I get it."

"The earl had a tyrannical reputation. He quite terrified me when I was a child and chanced upon him while visiting the Duke." She gave a mock shudder. "They say he fetched Lady Anne home and dispatched her husband to India. As a member of Parliament, he had connections with the War Department. The poor man died over there without ever setting eyes on his son. It really is quite tragic when you think on it."

"I wonder how Morland felt about never knowing his father because his grandfather sent him away?"

"I've no idea, but the earl quite doted on his grandson. Of course, it didn't hurt that Morland took after his grandfather in looks, which undoubtedly appealed to the old earl's vanity," Rebecca remarked cynically. "Nothing like seeing the family line continue on with your male heirs, while your daughters and granddaughters can wither on the vine. If, that is, you cannot use them to expand one's empire!

"'Tis a *man's* world, Miss Donovan," she added, scowling. She was silent for a moment, then huffed out a sigh. "But that's neither here nor there. There was no estrangement between Morland and his grandfather when the earl was alive. Sadly, the earldom couldn't be passed to Mr. Morland, but rather went to a distant male cousin. However, Morland was fortunate in the fact that Tinley Park was not entailed."

"Why didn't Lady Anne follow her husband to India?"

"I don't know the details. I suspect she discovered that she was increasing, which would have made traveling to India out of the question. I daresay by the time it was a possibility, it was too late. Her husband had already expired. Sad how life works out sometimes, isn't it?"

"You never know what life will throw at you, I'll give you that." She joined Rebecca at the slate board. "Who else do you know that fits the profile?"

"I don't—"

"Yes, you do."

Rebecca lifted her brows. "Are all maids as dictatorial as you are in America, Miss Donovan?"

Kendra frowned. "The Duke came up with eight men that fit the profile. I'd like your input."

"And what then, Miss Donovan? What do *you* expect to do?"

"Interview the suspects, find out where they were on the night of the murder. We can eliminate everyone who has an alibi."

"I see." Rebecca gave her a strange look. "And you will do this . . . how? You—a maid—expect to quiz your betters?"

Kendra stared at her in consternation. How in God's name was she going to conduct this investigation if she wasn't allowed to interview the suspects?

Lady Rebecca looked amused. "You seem to forget your station in life, Miss Donovan. What is done, and what is *not* done."

"I'm sure the Duke will assist me."

Rebecca raised her brows. A Duke required assistance from a servant; not the other way around. She smiled suddenly, tapping her chin with her fan as she circled Kendra. "Hmm. I don't require a lady's maid. My maid, Mary, is most exceptional."

Kendra eyed her warily. "Good, because I pretty much sucked at being a lady's maid."

"Sucked?" Diverted, Rebecca laughed. "You Americans have such *colorful* expressions. However . . . I've never had a companion."

"Companion?"

"A lady's companion."

"Lady Rebecca, are you by any chance asking me to be your companion?"

"Yes, I believe I am. 'Tis most unusual, but . . . you, my dear Miss Donovan, have just bettered yourself."

23

From her bedroom window, April Duprey watched the Bow Street Runner make his way carefully down the cobblestone street that gleamed black from the thin drizzle falling from the evening sky. When he stopped abruptly, glancing back toward the house, his eyes seeming to angle straight toward her window, her heart jolted and her fingers, on the lace drapery, tensed. She forced herself to let go of the material and step away.

She wondered uneasily if he knew that she'd lied to him. She was very good at lying—it was a necessity for being a good whore.

She smiled, a cynical twist to her painted lips, thinking of the rogues she'd serviced over the years. They'd never wanted the truth. Nay, they'd wanted to be cooed over and coddled, and complimented on how virile and handsome they were even if they were on the far side of seventy. They all had their fantasies. And every fantasy began with a lie.

April Duprey wasn't even her given name. She barely remembered the name she'd been christened or the chit she'd been before her drunken sod of a father had bartered her to a whoremaster in exchange for the bill he'd owed. She'd been eleven at the time.

That had been a long time ago, of course. April knew a cool satisfaction over surviving those early days. After that brutal first year, she'd put aside girlish dreams she no longer remembered and ruthlessly applied herself to becoming a skillful courtesan. She had the looks and the wits to become more than a streetwalker, although she'd done her share of back alley tumbles with drunken rakes. She'd been clever enough to do it for a coin or two, not a tipple of gin. She'd ended up in an academy for a time, until she'd craftily seduced one of the coves into setting her up in her own house.

It had been a lovely time, that. Of course, she'd never been so foolish as to believe it would last. In her world, nothing lasted. She'd hoarded her coins and jewels, worked on her speech and manners. When her protector had found a younger mistress and given her *congé*, she'd bought the house on Bacon Street and acquired a small selection of girls. It had taken her years, but she'd built her business as brothel keeper. She might not offer the most exclusive demimondaines at her academy, but she'd carved out a solid reputation by catering to a broad range of tastes.

Now as she spun away from the window, she caught her reflection in the beveled glass mirror across the room. For a brief moment, she saw a pale, golden-haired Cyprian in a diaphanous blue empire-waisted gown. The candlelight helped weave an illusion of youth and beauty. She knew the truth.

One lied to the clientele; one never lied to oneself.

At thirty-five, she had long since parted ways with youth. If she looked closely into the mirror, she'd see that the years had caught up with her, leaving a web of fine lines around her eyes and forehead. Her figure was still good, lush and round, but she could no longer conceal a certain hardness in her countenance or the shrewdness in her eyes as she was tallying up a business transaction.

It was just as well that she'd given up the role of prostitute to be an abbess. She preferred it, if truth be told, although she wasn't above servicing the occasional request. She believed in keeping the customers happy. That's why she'd loaned out Lydia.

When the chit hadn't returned, she'd assumed the worst, that the little bitch had sunk her claws into one of the bucks to become a *chère-amie*. April had to confess that she was surprised to learn that the girl was dead. Surprised, but not necessarily shocked. Such things happened; some games, she knew, went too far. Yet the way she saw it, she was owed reparation.

She moved to the table where she kept the decanters. Pouring a splash of scotch into a glass—she allowed herself just two drinks a day, her father having cured her of any desire to use spirits to sink into oblivion—she took a quick sip, the taste strong and sharp on her tongue, as she considered the matter.

It would involve some delicacy. But surely the gent would see the inconvenience he'd given her? Replacing Lydia would require some diligence on her part. Not to mention the expense of dressing a new whore. *And* she had to lie to a Runner. Silence didn't come cheap.

Taking another swallow of scotch, April sat down at her desk. She wasn't dealing with some thief down the street. There were proprieties to be observed with the fancy. Best to send him a note outlining her dilemma. She reached for a foolscap and quill pen. Her eyes gleamed in the candlelight. Odd how life worked, she mused with a thin smile. Lydia's unfortunate demise might actually turn out to be her most profitable transaction yet.

24

It was probably something of a world record, to be demoted from lady's maid to downstairs maid, and then promoted to lady's companion within a five-day time span. It certainly caused a stir below stairs, as everyone regarded Kendra with shock and a new sense of mistrust when she made her way to Mrs. Danbury's office.

"This is highly irregular, Miss Donovan," the housekeeper said, staring at her from across the shiny expanse of her desk. She then murmured, as though trying to explain to herself what motivated Lady Rebecca's unprecedented behavior, "Though Lady Rebecca has always been charitable, even as a child."

Maids, Kendra deduced, did *not* become hired companions. Ever. That, apparently, was reserved for women of rank who'd fallen on hard times. Sort of like a nineteenth-century welfare system for the privileged.

The housekeeper shook herself out of her reverie, straightening her narrow shoulders. Her lips tightened. "Nevertheless, if Lady

Rebecca has indeed taken you on as her companion, arrangements will need to be made."

"What kind of arrangements?" Kendra asked warily.

Mrs. Danbury lifted a heavy leather-bound book off the side shelf. "Sleeping arrangements, for one." She opened the ledger, studying the pages with a critical eye. "All the castle's spare rooms are occupied with either guests or their servants for the duration of the house party. However—"

"I don't need to move out of the room that I'm in."

The housekeeper lifted her brows. "Miss Donovan, you are no longer a servant . . . precisely. It wouldn't be proper to sleep in the same room as a servant, especially a tweeny."

"Says who?"

"Those are the *rules*, Miss Donovan."

Fuck the rules, Kendra wanted to say. She wondered what the housekeeper's reaction to that would be. Probably she'd faint dead away. "I'd prefer to stay where I am."

"It's not up to *you*! Lady Rebecca will decide, as you are now her responsibility."

Frustration knotted Kendra's stomach. "I'm my own responsibility!"

"The minute you set foot in Aldridge Castle, you were someone else's responsibility, Miss Donovan," the other woman corrected with a look of cold dislike. "As a maid, you were entirely dependent on the Duke's largesse. And now you shall be answerable to Lady Rebecca. While you've managed to better yourself in a most extraordinary manner, I'd strongly advise you *not* to forget yourself, Miss Donovan. This is not America, where ill-mannered commoners pretend to be their betters. In England, we have a system, and you must learn your place in that system."

Hell, no, Kendra thought, but clamped down on her rising irritation. Instead, she forced a smile as she stood. "I'm sure Lady Rebecca will agree that there's no reason for me to change rooms. I'll talk to her about it."

She went to the door.

"Miss Donovan?"

Kendra paused. "Yes?"

"Why in heaven's name do you insist on sharing a bedchamber with a tweeny?" Mrs. Danbury sounded genuinely baffled.

Kendra stared at her, momentarily at a loss. "Because it's my choice, Mrs. Danbury," she finally said. "It's *my* choice."

"You want to share a room with a chambermaid?" Lady Rebecca paused in the act of pouring tea.

"She's a tweeny. And, yes, I see no reason to sleep anywhere else." Kendra was beginning to feel slightly foolish for digging in her heels on this particular matter. After all, why did she care where she slept, as long as she eventually slept somewhere in the twenty-first century? *That* should be her main priority.

But, as she told Mrs. Danbury, it was her choice to sleep where she goddamned pleased. She was tired of everything being out of her control. *This*, at least, she could control.

Now she looked at Lady Rebecca, ready to argue, but the other woman simply shrugged and continued pouring tea. "As you wish. How do you take your tea—white or black?"

She found herself deflating. "Black. One sugar."

Rebecca suppressed a smile as she added the lump of sugar, and thought how utterly absurd it was that she was serving tea to her companion, not the other way around. And yet Kendra appeared to find nothing abnormal about the tableau. The American was a puzzle. She understood why both the Duke and Alec were intrigued by her.

"You shall need a new wardrobe, of course." She lifted the teacup and saucer and handed them to Kendra. "I have taken the liberty of sending for the local modiste, but Mary shall begin by taking your measurements."

They were sitting at a small table positioned in front of a window in Lady Rebecca's bedroom, a generously appointed space with ivory silk walls, rich mahogany furnishings, and an enormous velvet canopied bed done in the colors of ancient amber. It suited her, Kendra thought as she glanced at the other woman. Despite her disfiguring scars, Lady Rebecca presented a quaint, old-fashioned picture, pouring tea from the dainty porcelain pot, wearing her high-waisted, blue-sprigged muslin gown with her auburn hair swept into a charming topknot.

"What exactly does a companion do?"

Rebecca smiled. "You don't have paid companions in America? How very primitive."

So are chamber pots, Kendra thought. "Primitive is a relative term."

"Indeed. Well, a Lady usually hires a companion to see to her needs. Fetching one's shawl or fan. Providing amusing company. Don't fret, Miss Donovan. We both know that I didn't offer you this position so you could entertain me. As you are no longer a servant, you will be allowed to attend the evening festivities. It will give you a chance to converse with people." She paused. "Although I suggest you adopt a demure disposition tonight at dinner. Lady Atwood was *not* pleased with my unorthodox decision to elevate your status."

"Did she give you a hard time?"

"She warned me that I'd be setting tongues to wag in the Polite World. As I care naught for the so-called Polite World, her argument fell flat. Lady Atwood's a bit high in the instep but she is a good woman. Thankfully, the Duke supports my decision."

She set down her teacup and saucer and rose from the table. "I shall ring for Mary before Mrs. Griffith arrives."

Rebecca's lady's maid was a small bird-like woman that Kendra recognized from her first breakfast in the upper staff dining room, before her demotion. She gave Kendra a look, sharp with distrust.

"Please take off your clothes," Rebecca ordered Kendra.

"I'm usually offered dinner before that request."

"Pardon?"

"Never mind," Kendra sighed, and began to strip. She couldn't hide her scars, and knew the instant the two women saw them. Rebecca gasped.

Suspicion flared in Mary's dark eyes. "Looks like ye've been shot, miss."

"Yes," Kendra said simply.

"How—never mind," Rebecca said abruptly. "Forgive us. I understand all too well what it's like to be stared at." She turned to Mary, who began unrolling her measuring tape. "What is the gossip below stairs, Mary?"

"Everyone's all aflutter at how ye hired the miss here to be yer companion." The woman shot Kendra another narrow-eyed look as she looped the tape around her waist. "Miss Beckett says the countess was apoplectic."

Rebecca waved her hand airily. "I am well aware of the countess' objections."

"Are ye certain ye know what ye're about, milady?" Mary fitted the tape snugly beneath Kendra's armpits, intersecting across her bosom.

"The countess may wish me to Jericho, but I know what I am doing."

"This is about the gel in the lake, ain't it? Talk is *she* be mixed up in that business, too."

"I didn't ask to be here," Kendra muttered beneath her breath.

"Why'd ye come, then?"

Why, indeed? "I'm still working that one out."

"Hush, Mary. Miss Donovan is not the enemy."

"They think she's queer in the attic. Hold still, miss." She knelt down, measuring from waist to hem. "They may give ye the cut for supporting the likes of her, milady."

"They wouldn't dare. Not with the Duke of Aldridge lending his support. At least not a *direct* cut. You'll need slippers, Miss

Donovan. You can hardly wear those dreadful boots to dinner. And, oh, we really must do something with your hair. Mary, suggestions?"

"Why ever did ye cut it so short?" Mary gave Kendra an accusatory look.

"Some ladies have cut their hair . . . but this style *is* rather unusual, Miss Donovan." Rebecca circled Kendra, tapping her chin critically. "I've never seen anything like it."

"Maybe I'll start a new trend."

Mary sniffed. "Not bloody likely."

"I'm not so certain," Rebecca said. "It is odd, but rather becoming. Still, we shall have to be creative, Mary. Miss Donovan is an Original."

"What exactly is an Original?" Kendra asked.

"Someone who is unique, one-of-a-kind. You most certainly are that. Mary, we must make the most of it."

The maid muttered, "We're doomed."

Rebecca rolled her eyes, but before she could respond to that dire prediction, Mrs. Griffith, the local modiste, arrived. She wasn't alone. She was accompanied by two young women and five large trunks, which the footmen brought in. As Kendra watched in amazement, Rebecca's bedroom was transformed into a dressmaking atelier. The five trunks sprung open to reveal countless bolts of fabric, trimmings, and fashion plates.

This was, Kendra thought with a sinking heart, way before the time of ready-to-wear, before women could buy an entire wardrobe in about twenty minutes at Macy's or Walmart, or, better yet, order it online. Here, it was painfully obvious to Kendra that each item would have to be individually designed, cut, and stitched by hand. *How long will this take?*

Rebecca performed introductions. "We shall need morning dresses, walking dresses, underclothes, and several evening gowns," she explained. "I would like most of it done and delivered in a week. Is *that* possible?"

"Certainly, your Ladyship."

"We shall need you to alter one of my evening gowns for this evening. Mary has Miss Donovan's measurements. And I must insist on a gown or two to be delivered tomorrow. An afternoon dress and an evening gown. Is that possible?"

Mrs. Griffon hesitated only briefly. Then she nodded. "Yes. We must begin work immediately, your Ladyship."

It was funny what could bring on a panic attack, Kendra thought fifteen minutes later. Silks and satins shouldn't do it. But as the women scurried around the room, pulling out the bolts of material, Kendra had the choking sensation of being trapped. In that instant, she saw her future stretched out before her in paisley and pinstripes; in the cottons, wools, and muslins used in walking and afternoon dresses, and the lighter-than-air organza, silks, and heavier velvets to be cut into evening gowns; in the endless array of styles and silhouettes that would take her months—*years*—to wear.

Rebecca handed her a silk robe, oblivious to her inner turmoil. "Put this on, Miss Donovan. While Mary and Mrs. Griffon become organized, we shall sit down and drink our tea and I will explain to you what you ought to expect this evening."

Kendra tried to shake off the strange, panicky feeling squeezing her chest. "I don't suppose you have something stronger than tea?"

25

"You have no appetite, Miss Donovan?"

Kendra pulled her gaze from the steaming bowl in front of her to glance at the man seated on her left: Mr. Harris, the local vicar. Although, he didn't look like a man of the cloth. Early thirties and attractive, he wore the same sort of uniform—cravat, shirt, waistcoat, topcoat, and pantaloons—as most of the other men at the table. He also carried himself with the same air of self-importance.

"Monsieur Anton's turtle soup is nonpareil."

She glanced at the chunks of meat poking out of the creamy base. "I prefer my turtles in an aquarium."

He gave her an odd look. "What, pray tell, is an aquarium?"

They don't have aquariums? She reached for her glass of wine, taking a hasty swallow. "It's sort of a zoo, for aquatic animals and plants . . . never mind."

The evening was turning out to be more nerve-wracking than she'd anticipated. The countess had put her as far away from the

Duke and Lady Rebecca as she could, while still having Kendra in the same room. She was at the end of the long, elegant table, wedged between the arrogant vicar and Major Edwards, who was eighty if he was a day. The best thing about the old military man was he didn't seem inclined to conversation, content to slurp away the evening with his soup.

The seating arrangements could've been a retaliation of sorts, but Kendra suspected it was more a matter of rank, the Duke being the highest ranking person and she being the lowest. It was, Kendra realized with a flash of humor, a mirror image of how the dining room for the upper staff operated.

She knew she was under scrutiny from the rest of the guests. The women had eyed her carefully. Rebecca had been right about them not wishing to risk the Duke's displeasure by ignoring her completely—which, she was told, was the cut-direct. Instead, this treatment, Rebecca told her, was the cut-indirect—acknowledgment *before* being ignored. Georgina and Sarah had observed her with astonishment, retreating behind their fans to whisper.

The men had viewed her change in status with more amusement. At least, she thought she saw amusement in their eyes. More often their gaze was directed lower, since the rose gown that Mrs. Griffith had altered for her showed off her cleavage in abundance.

"You have turtle zoos in America?" That came from the woman on the other side of Harris. Kendra glanced over at her. It was difficult to believe that the insipid blonde was the vicar's wife. Despite the bright canary yellow striped gown she wore, she appeared to want to shrink into herself. Except for introductions, this was the first sentence Kendra had heard her utter all evening.

"Don't be ridiculous, Mrs. Harris." Her husband's lips thinned. "Miss Donovan is obviously telling us a Banbury tale."

His wife gave him a nervous look, flushing miserably.

Kendra picked up her wineglass and twirled it thoughtfully. "Actually, the Sumerians raised fish simply for decoration in artificial ponds more than four thousand years ago. The ancient Romans also stocked their own ponds for entertainment purposes. Sort of a fish zoo." She smiled. "The way I look at it, if you can have fish zoos, there's no reason you can't have turtle zoos."

Harris's eyes narrowed. "How utterly . . . eccentric."

She'd say this for her nineteenth-century counterparts: they were polite even when they were accusing you of being full of crap.

"Turtle zoos!" Next to her, Major Edwards seemed to rouse himself. "That would be a devilishly odd undertaking."

"Miss Donovan is having sport with us, I think," Harris said coldly.

"I say. Why would she do that?"

"I am not certain. American humor, mayhap?" The vicar gave a small shrug, turning back to his soup as though he couldn't be bothered to figure it out.

Kendra surveyed him. Harris hadn't been on the list of suspects that the Duke had come up with.

"Have you always lived in the area, Mr. Harris?"

"No. The Duke graciously appointed me to the vicarage here five years ago." He put down his spoon and arched a brow. "And you, Miss Donovan? You are new to the castle, are you not? I haven't seen you in the village."

"I haven't been here very long." She paused while the footmen cleared the table of the first course.

Harding brought forth a fresh bottle of wine, which the Duke inspected. Once approved, several bottles of the same vintage were uncorked, and new glasses were filled in anticipation of the second course—stuffed lobster shells.

"You've been very fortunate, haven't you?" Harris murmured, sliding her a look.

"That depends on whether you're a glass half empty or half full kind of person." She picked up the slim, two-tined lobster fork to sample the delicacy.

Harris frowned. "I do not comprehend."

She reached for the new wineglass. "You've no doubt heard about the young girl who was killed and found in the lake."

Mrs. Harris fingered the ruffle at her throat. "The gossip is that she was savagely murdered. Dear heaven." She shivered, glancing at her husband. "I thought we were well away from that sort of thing, Mr. Harris."

Kendra eyed her. "You've been involved in a murder before?"

"Don't be preposterous." Harris's mouth tightened. "My wife and I lived in London for a brief time. Dreadful, dangerous place. A maid-of-all-work who lived down the street from where we had rooms was killed by a footpad. Not an uncommon thing to happen."

"Aye. Terrible place, London," the Major muttered into his wineglass. "Rife with cutthroats and rogues."

"We were ever so grateful for his Duke's patronage to escape the lowbrow atmosphere of Sutton Street," Mrs. Harris agreed, darting an uncertain glance at her husband.

"The dinner table is not the place to discuss such a subject," Harris said abruptly, giving Kendra a reproving look. The Voice of Authority.

Kendra toyed with her wineglass. Early nineteenth-century London had no official police force, and she was reasonably certain that the crime rate was pretty high. It wouldn't be unheard of to encounter a homicide if you lived there, as the Harrises had done. It could be a coincidence. But she'd never been a big fan of coincidences.

Catching the vicar's eye, she smiled. And she thought it wouldn't be a bad idea to get word to the Bow Street Runner to check out the lowbrow atmosphere of Sutton Street.

Kendra was still turning that over in her mind an hour and a half—and ten courses—later, as she followed the glittering parade of women to the drawing room, while the men lingered with their port at the table. Rebecca approached, carrying two small glasses filled with Madeira. Kendra eyed the dark amber liquid in the cut crystal. *Jesus.* These people knew how to *drink.* She'd probably sampled at least a half dozen different wines at dinner, meant to complement each course. She felt a little buzzed, but no one else seemed affected.

"What do you suppose the men do when the women are gone?" Kendra wondered when Rebecca handed her the glass.

Rebecca grinned. "Most likely habits that are frowned upon in a Lady's presence—blowing a cloud or taking snuff. Cursing freely. Discussing business. Especially now that the war with Boney and the colonies are finally at an end. Oh. Forgive me, Miss Donovan. Does it trouble you overmuch—the war between our two countries?"

"No. Why should it? We won." T*wo hundred years ago.*

"Yes, well. 'Twas a stupid war. Not the one against the French. Napoleon's a mad tyrant. I pray he stays on St. Helena."

Kendra drew in a deep breath and let it out slowly. *I'm standing in a drawing room discussing Napoleon Bonaparte. Who is alive.* That made her head spin more than the wine.

"Tell me about Harris," she said. "He doesn't strike me as a preacher."

Rebecca made a face. "The Duke appointed Mr. Harris to the local vicarage as a favor to the Earl of Clarendale."

"He mentioned that. Who is the Earl of Clarendale?"

"Mr. Harris is the youngest son of the Earl of Clarendale. The family has been punting on the River Tick for years, although Mr. Harris did manage to catch himself an heiress."

"Really?" Kendra glanced in surprise in the direction of Mrs. Harris, who was sitting on the end of the gold damask sofa, trying to look inconspicuous, as if her yellow dress could merge with the gold damask and she could disappear altogether. "His wife's rich?"

"Her father's a wealthy wool merchant. He wanted entry into the world of the Ton. The estates are entailed, but the Clarendale family can trace their lineage back to King William."

"In other words, her father sold her."

Rebecca cocked her head and studied Kendra. "Is it any different in America? You may not have titled aristocracy, but I daresay there's no shortage of ambition—parents willing to use their daughters' looks to trade up in the world or flaunt their sons' pedigrees to make a good match with an heiress."

Kendra thought of America, past and present. No, she couldn't deny that it wasn't any different. How else could you explain every sixty-year-old rock star marrying a nineteen-year-old supermodel with the blessing of her parents?

"You're right. Dynasties have been and will continue to be made one marriage at a time. But I think Mrs. Harris got the bad end of that deal."

Across the room, one of the young ladies sat down at the harpsichord and began to play Johann Sebastian Bach's *Prelude in C major.* This, Kendra realized, was what people did before TV and the Internet: played cards and the piano, talked. Maybe that's why they drank so much.

"Why do you ask about Mr. Harris?" Rebecca asked.

Kendra shrugged. "He's the right age, lives in the area, and, if he has access to his wife's money, he has the means."

"The moment he married his wife, he had access to her dowry," Rebecca remarked dryly. "Still, Mr. Harris *is* married. Surely, he couldn't have committed such atrocities."

"You think a marriage license stops a man from being a sociopath?"

"I think a wife would know if her husband was such a fiend."

"You'd be surprised at the lengths wives will go to delude themselves, or to rationalize what may be occurring right under their nose." She thought of all the cases where loved ones had lived under the same roof as the serial killer. Many were shell-shocked by the revelation; most refused to believe it until the evidence piled up. And even then, a few still needed a confession before they accepted the facts.

She glanced at Mrs. Harris, who sipped her wine quietly on the sofa and looked like she wanted to be anywhere but there.

"I can't imagine such willful ignorance," Rebecca said, shaking her head.

The door opened, and the men came into the room. Their presence was like a jolt of electricity, energizing the women. Fans began fluttering. A few moved forward to intercept the new arrivals. A beautiful blonde—Lady Dover, Kendra remembered—glided over to Alec.

The Duke came toward them, although he was forced to stop here and there to politely converse with those who demanded his attention. When he finally managed to reach them, he smiled at Kendra.

"Miss Donovan, I hadn't the opportunity to speak with you earlier, but may I say now that you are in exceptional looks this evening. Lady Rebecca had the right notion, hiring you as her companion. This suits you."

Kendra had to smile. "I don't think anyone here would agree with you."

"'Tis a pity, but such is the way for those who are different, Miss Donovan. And you, most delightedly, are different. To quote Voltaire, 'Our wretched species is so made that those who walk on the well-trodden path always throw stones at those who are showing a new road.'"

"If it's all the same to you, I'd rather avoid any stone-throwing. Especially if I'm the recipient of said stone-throwing."

He laughed. "We'll try to make sure that does not happen."

Try? Kendra thought. She changed the subject. "Is there any way you can get word to the Bow Street Runner to check on a murder that happened in London five years ago?"

The Duke's smile disappeared. "What's this about?"

"Mrs. Harris mentioned a maid who was murdered nearby when they lived in London, on Sutton Street."

Rebecca frowned. "You can't possibly think there might be a correlation to that crime and the girl in the lake? London is notorious for its criminal element."

"That may be, but I'd still like to know the specifics of that crime, and if anyone was caught." And since she couldn't pick up a phone or check out the Internet databases, she had to do it this way. The killer wasn't a novice; he'd been practicing somewhere.

The Duke regarded her steadily for several moments. "I tend to agree with Lady Rebecca, that it would seem an unlikely connection. Still, if you feel it necessary, I shall send word to Mr. Kelly."

"Thanks."

"Bertie." Lady Atwood approached like an elegant yacht in full sail. Kendra's eyes were drawn to the enormous black ostrich feather that jutted out from the dark purple turban the woman wore. The countess hooked her arm through her brother's before giving Kendra and Rebecca a chilly nod. "Lady Rebecca . . . Miss Donovan." She said that, Kendra thought, like she was coughing up a hair ball. "I need to borrow my brother for a game of whist."

"Oh. I . . ." Aldridge shot a longing glance at the cloudless night sky beyond the open French doors, clearly intent on quietly escaping to observe the celestial heavens.

"One game, Bertie," his sister insisted, and before he could protest again, she dragged him off to a card table.

They brushed past Alec, who was heading toward Kendra and Rebecca. He'd ditched the blonde, Kendra saw; the woman in question now stood alone, and not looking too happy about it.

Alec greeted Rebecca with an easy smile, then cocked a brow at Kendra. "I see you've changed your status yet again, Miss Donovan. One can only wonder what tomorrow will bring."

"It was my decision to hire Miss Donovan." Rebecca rapped him with her fan. "At least now she'll be able to mingle in polite society without raising eyebrows."

"One has the impression that eyebrows are permanently raised when it comes to Miss Donovan," he murmured. Still, he grinned at Rebecca, flicking her nose affectionately. "Hiring a maid to be your companion is simply not done, minx. As well you know."

"The Ton has an amazingly short attention span, as well *you* know. And it helps having influential friends like the Duke . . . and you." She smiled at him, and picked a minuscule piece of lint off his dark green velvet sleeve. "No one shall dare give myself or Miss Donovan the cut-direct with your patronage, Sutcliffe."

Kendra was surprised to find herself growing annoyed. "You know, I'm not a complete idiot. I didn't drink out of the finger bowl at dinner, did I?"

Alec suppressed a grin as he flicked her a look. "Yes, I noticed. Your table manners were very pretty."

"Gee, thanks."

The tone was so sharp that he had to laugh. He looked at Rebecca. "Even so, I'd like to know the reason behind this unorthodox promotion."

Rebecca tilted her chin. "'Tis simple. The man responsible for the atrocity allegedly walks among our class. I've made it possible for Miss Donovan to be in a position to converse with whomever necessary. The Duke is in agreement."

Alec shifted his gaze back to Kendra, no longer smiling. "You shan't win any friends in your endeavor, Miss Donovan. You may even make enemies. This could become very dangerous."

"It's already dangerous. One girl is dead," Kendra reminded him flatly.

"And you believe you are the one to stop him?"

His tone was just incredulous enough to put her back up. "I'm the best chance you've got. I know what I'm doing. If you can't accept that . . ."

"What?"

"Then there won't be enough water in all of England to wash the blood off your hands, because more girls are going to die."

26

The victim was decomposing.

Kendra had known that the girl couldn't be kept in the ice-house forever, but she still felt uneasy watching the simple pine box being lowered into the grave by thick ropes and four burly workmen. There was nothing more she could do, she reminded herself. The body wouldn't yield more evidence.

Kendra turned her attention to the meager gathering of mourners at the village cemetery: Alec, Rebecca, the Duke, the vicar and his wife, the constable, Morland, Dalton, Alec's brother Gabriel, and his friend, Captain Harcourt. The last two looked like they'd gone on a bender last night, given their bloodshot eyes and pasty complexions. The only thing that brought them out this morning was curiosity.

Maybe. Sometimes murderers attended their victim's funeral; inserted themselves into investigations. It was something to consider.

Across the open grave, Mr. Harris read his bible passage. The breeze carried a hint of rain, fluttering the pages of the book in his hand and ruffling his dark hair. She'd heard that he'd objected to burying the victim in the village cemetery, given the suspicion that she was a prostitute. But the Duke had overruled him.

Mr. Harris finished reading and immediately turned to the Duke to exchange a few words. Beside him, Mrs. Harris bowed her head and waited.

She looked like a timid crow, Kendra thought, dressed in unrelenting black, from her veiled bonnet to her ebony shoes. As the vicar's wife, she probably had clothes set aside for funerals. Rebecca had explained earlier that she hadn't brought any mourning colors to the house party, and there was no time to dye dresses for the event. She wore her long brown velvet coat and a matching bonnet over a navy pinstriped frock, and loaned Kendra a cape of deep forest green and a lighter, apple green bonnet decorated with yellow silk roses, bows, and ribbons.

"We don't even know the name of the poor girl," Rebecca murmured as everyone began walking through the ancient cemetery. "How can a soul be at peace without a name?"

"If there's such a thing as a soul, I'd think it would be more interested in justice. After all, the dead already know their names."

Rebecca blinked at her. "You don't believe in eternal life, Miss Donovan?"

Kendra thought about the question. In truth, she'd never spent any time on what she'd considered to be a theological debate. Her entire focus had been on becoming an FBI agent and, afterward, on proving herself capable of handling whatever task was thrown her way. *Show no weakness.* That had become her own personal motto as she climbed the ranks, accomplished her goals. And in the field, when she'd dealt with death and its aftermath, there'd simply been no time to waste wondering if the victims were now in a better place. It had always been a race to capture the unsub before there were more victims.

Aware that Rebecca was staring at her, she shrugged. "I guess it always seemed pointless to speculate about something you can't prove or disprove."

"I disagree. I find such speculation fascinating," Rebecca began. She looked as though she wanted to continue the discussion, but broke off with a smile when Simon Dalton skirted several tombstones to approach them.

"Ladies." He had his hat in his hands, and the wind teased his ash blond hair around his head as he smiled. "I'm delighted to see you, of course, although I would ask for a less solemn occasion."

"Graciously said, Mr. Dalton. I had wondered if our company had begun to pall, as you were not at dinner last evening." Rebecca gave him an arched look as they began walking again.

"Not at all, Lady Rebecca. The countess invited me, but I had a bit of trouble in the stables. A mare was foaling, and it was breech."

"Oh, no. Is everything all right?"

"Yes. Both are doing well, thank you. You must come and see for yourself. Already he promises to be a champion Arabian like his sire. Strong legs, great hindquarters."

"Is your plan to race him, sir?"

Kendra listened with half an ear as the two traded horse information. Horses weren't her thing. What she knew of racing came from meeting Sid the Greek, one of her informants, who spent most of his time at the racetrack—it seemed like a lifetime ago. Or a lifetime from now. God, time travel really screwed with one's syntax.

"I think we're boring Miss Donovan," Dalton said suddenly, smiling at Kendra.

"Oh. Sorry, my mind was elsewhere."

His expression turned somber. "Have you heard any news from the Runner?"

She met his gaze. Simple curiosity? Or something more? "We're following a couple of leads."

"I see. Well, I pray that the thief-taker uncovers the identity of the madman. If I can assist in any way, you must let me know."

That, Kendra decided, was as good an opening as any. "Actually, you can. We're questioning men in the area. Where were you on Sunday night and early Monday morning?"

He stopped walking and stared at her. If she'd stripped naked and sang "Yankee Doodle," she doubted if she could've surprised him more. "Me? Are you . . . are you, perchance, asking me if *I* killed that girl, Miss Donovan?"

"Please don't take offense, Mr. Dalton," Rebecca said hurriedly. "As Miss Donovan stated, 'tis a question we'll be asking everyone."

He blinked, then shook his head. "I am not certain that lessens the insult, my Lady." He was quiet for a moment, glancing down at the hat in his hands. "I attended Lady Atwood's dinner party, if you recall. It was the first evening of the house party."

"What time did you leave the castle?" Kendra asked.

"I don't know whether to be amused or insulted by this line of inquiry, Miss Donovan."

"Try to be understanding. We just buried that girl over there. Questions need to be asked."

His eyes darkened. "I saw what was done to that girl, Miss Donovan. I conducted the postmortem. I don't know if I can be so indulgent when you clearly think I am capable of that atrocity."

"That's one way to look at it. Or you might try looking at it from a different angle—we're trying to eliminate you from being suspected of that atrocity. It would help matters if you had an alibi for the time in question."

He frowned. "I cannot accommodate you. I returned home and retired for the evening to my bedchamber. I was asleep when the wh . . . that Unfortunate Woman was being viciously murdered."

"You don't have anyone to verify your whereabouts?"

"No."

"What about your valet?" asked Rebecca. "He must have assisted you before you retired."

He flicked her a glance. "As I was uncertain when I'd return, I told Roberts not to wait for me. I spent many years in the army, your Ladyship. Unlike the gentlemen of the Ton, I am not as reliant on the services of a valet. Now, I must take my leave. Lady Rebecca, Miss Donovan." He gave a slight bow, before walking quickly away.

Kendra watched him for a minute, then looked at Rebecca. "How unusual is it for a gentleman to tell his valet not to wait up for him?"

"It's not unreasonable to be considerate of one's servants, Miss Donovan. And he explained that his years in the army have given him a different sort of disposition."

"Yes. He did, didn't he? Without any nudging, too."

Rebecca frowned at her. "You make it sound as though he did something wrong. Mayhap Mr. Dalton was simply being helpful."

"Hmm."

Rebecca gave her an exasperated look. "Would you prefer that he be evasive and unhelpful?"

"I prefer he had an alibi."

Kendra liked Simon Dalton. That didn't mean he wasn't a murderer.

Some of the most notorious serial killers had been well-liked until their crimes had been uncovered. Ted Bundy, handsome, charming, who even worked on a suicide-crisis hotline, had been the model of decency. A mother, Kendra was sure, would've been thrilled if her daughter had brought him home to dinner, would never have suspected that he had killed more than thirty women and young girls. John Wayne Gacy, not so handsome but equally popular in his neighborhood, had been a successful entrepreneur who entertained sick children by dressing up as a clown—until he was caught and convicted of murdering thirty-three teenage boys and men. More than one unsub, even on cases Kendra had been involved in herself, had turned out to be the grandfatherly figure down the street, the helpful neighbor, the good-looking doctor.

Whoever had said that appearances were deceiving was only partially right; they could also be deadly.

For a second, the image of Terry Landon blowing off Daniel Sheppard's head flashed through her mind. She'd worked beside him for eight months and hadn't realized he was a traitor, she reminded herself bitterly. And she hadn't really even liked him. Dalton she liked, but damned if she was going to trust him.

Despite the castle's enormous size, Kendra felt stifled after returning. The overcast skies and cold temperature of the day brought everyone indoors. The ladies were in the drawing room, embroidering and gossiping. Kendra had no desire to join them, and suspected they had no desire for her company either. Rebecca was spending the afternoon painting in the conservatory. The men were in another room playing cards, with the exception of the Duke, who was in his laboratory.

Kendra went to the study, but instead of reviewing her notes, she found herself pacing restlessly. She was in a weird no-man's-land. Her promotion had catapulted her above the servants, so she was no longer allowed below stairs. They regarded her with varying degrees of distrust. Rose was the only one who hadn't changed. Then again, it was hard to be distant with someone with whom you shared a chamber pot.

Deciding some fresh air would clear her head, Kendra headed out of the castle. She forgot to grab the cape she'd worn earlier, and regretted that when the chilly wind speared right through the thin muslin of her walking dress. Still, she hurried on, up the hill and into the forest, which was even more mottled beneath the slate gray skies.

She again walked the lake where the body had been found, then followed the river to where the stone hut stood. Smoke, slightly darker than the sky, curled out of the stone chimney, she noticed as she approached. The small patch of ground near the building resembled a junkyard. Wooden crates were stacked on top of each other, chest high. Glass jars, some broken, some just cracked, were tossed to the side. Earthenware bowls, jugs, and tin cans were jumbled in random piles. An iron tripod over a circle made out of stones, its interior covered with cold gray ash, indicated Thomas the Hermit cooked at least some of his meals outside. Clearly, Thomas wasn't a neat freak.

She'd encountered people who lived like this in her own time line. Some had fallen on hard times or gotten involved with drugs. Some liked living off the grid. Others had mental illnesses. But this guy was a professional—he got *paid* to live like this.

From inside, she thought she heard a shuffling movement. It was either Thomas, or he had some really big rats. She couldn't rule out the latter. She stepped up to the door and knocked. Sudden silence. Not a rat.

"Thomas? It's Kendra Donovan. I want to talk to you." She waited and banged again on the door. "I know you're in there!"

It still took several more minutes before the door cracked open an inch. The smell hit her first, strong enough to knock her back a step. The hermit peered out from the gloom.

"What'dya want?"

"I told you. To talk."

She didn't wait for an invitation, drawing in a deep breath and pushing her way into the small building. A stone fireplace took up one wall. A small fire was crackling in the hearth. There was a single cot, the wool blankets balled up on top of a straw mattress. Dozens of canvases were stacked against another wall, half covered by coarse blankets. A small table was littered with unlit candles and pots of dried paint and paintbrushes; a wooden cupboard held a dented, bronze teakettle, iron pots, and utensils. A trunk was wedged between the bed and the cupboard. A crude easel had been set up next to that. On it was a canvas that had been painted blue except for the beginnings of a featureless, ghostly shape lying horizontal in the center.

The shape, though, was decidedly female.

The single window was shuttered, leaving the interior in premature twilight. A lit oil lamp was in the middle of the dirt floor. Kendra's gaze shifted to the tools next to the lamp, including the bamboo pipe that was fitted to a clay cup: a primitive bong. Well, that explained the glazed look to his eyes, and the sweetish scent that cruised above the primordial smells of earth, sweat, linseed oil, and grime. *Opium.*

"Not your day to terrorize ladies, Thomas?" she asked casually, toeing aside the drug paraphernalia to stand before the easel.

He frowned. "I do what I'm hired to do."

"You should ask for a raise."

"Eh?" Bafflement.

"Never mind." She turned to face him. "I wanted to ask you again about the girl who was killed. Did you see anybody or hear anything unusual Sunday night, early Monday morning?"

Instead of answering, he dropped down in the middle of the floor, near the opium pipe. He regarded her sullenly. "I already told you—I don't know nothin'."

There wasn't much space in which to move around. Four steps to the cupboards. Two steps to the easel. She moved in the direction of the blue canvas. She studied it for a long moment, letting the silence pool, before glancing back at him. "You see, Thomas, there's a problem with that. I don't believe you."

Absently, she picked up a paintbrush. Like everything in this time line, it was homemade, just a thin stick of wood that had twine and wire wrapped around the base to keep the bristles in place. Thumbing the soft dark hairs, she glanced back at the hermit. "Nothing to say to that, Thomas? No denial?"

He was staring at her as though mesmerized.

Christ. *Higher than a kite*, she realized.

"You get paid to be a hermit. To run around the forest. To watch for people. Like the other day when you saw me."

He was silent.

Impatiently, she tossed the paintbrush on the counter, moved around the easel, and squatted down so she could look him in the eye. "You're not in trouble, Thomas. I just want to know if you've ever seen anybody down by the river. One of the gentry."

"Nay."

"Maybe you want to think about that for oh, I don't know, a second or two longer."

The glazed look became a glare. "I don't know nothin'!"

"I'm not asking you what you know. I'm asking if you *saw* anyone."

"Nay."

She still didn't believe him, but she eased back, tried another tactic. "Okay, Thomas. I'd appreciate it if you kept an eye out, let me know if you see anyone hanging out by the river or the lake. Gentry. Do you understand?"

He just stared at her.

"The Duke will give you a coin or two for your help." Kendra wasn't entirely sure about that, but bribery, in her experience, usually worked with the indigent in the twenty-first century. She saw no reason that it wouldn't work just as well here.

She regarded him closely, and thought she saw a flicker of interest in his eyes. Or it might've been a trick of light inside the shadowy hut. She got to her feet. Thomas stayed exactly where he was.

It had been impulse to approach the hermit. Her gut told her that he was hiding something, that he knew more than he was saying. Still, it couldn't hurt to encourage him to keep a look out.

It wouldn't be the first time a murderer returned to the scene, even if it was to make sure he hadn't left anything behind.

She let herself out, grateful for the fresh air after the putrid stench of the hut. Surveying the ominous gray clouds gathering overheard, she began walking fast. And hoped she'd make it back to the castle before it began to rain.

Alec stared out at the distorted view of the gardens and green hills as the rain struck the arched windows, rattling the glass and running down the panes in silvery streams. In contrast, the small drawing room he was standing in was warm, with a cheery fire crackling in the hearth. Candles had been lit, their glow playing over the Sheraton tables, tufted settees and sofa, the rosewood chimneypiece. A perfectly normal day in the English countryside.

Except that morning he'd attended the funeral of an unidentified dead girl who'd most likely been a whore, who most likely had been murdered. And, if Kendra Donovan were to be believed, she'd been murdered by somebody he knew. It was madness.

He frowned, his mind shifting to the American. She was an enigma. She wasn't a Lady, although her table manners, as he'd observed last night, were flawless. He'd made a point of observing. She'd known which spoon and fork to use for each dish. She'd known, as she'd told him pertly, not to drink from the finger bowl.

Of course, that could mean she'd been around people of a higher station, knew how to ape their manners. He could almost convince himself that was the answer to the mystery of Kendra Donovan. Except her table manners had come so damn naturally to her. Not once had she hesitated, or surreptitiously studied her fellow diners in order to follow their lead.

And her hands were that of a Lady—or, at the very least, someone not used to manual labor. Maybe she was the daughter of a wealthy American merchant or plantation owner. America was an odd place, where the mercantile class ruled. He'd visited Charleston briefly, five years before the war. Yet he couldn't recollect any of the women he'd met behaving as brazenly as Kendra. In fact, the American ladies seemed to be remarkably like their British counterparts.

And if she'd been high-born in America, how had she come to work as a servant in England? The Duke had said she'd been trapped by the war. It happened. But the war was over. Why didn't she return home? Even if she'd been stranded with no money, surely she recognized that his uncle was charmed by her. Alec was certain he'd either loan or give her the blunt to book passage back to America.

Yet she hadn't approached the Duke. She evaded questions about her background. They didn't even know how she'd made a living in England during the last four years, before she'd arrived at Aldridge Castle.

It was damn perplexing. In a strange way, Kendra Donovan seemed to be an amalgam of *all* the classes. Educated and ladylike in certain areas, and yet she spoke in such a casual way that he didn't think she was aware that she'd taken the Lord's name in vain at least half a dozen times since he'd met her. And her knowledge of man's baser instincts was startling, sometimes embarrassing, like her comment about the handcuffs. Becca had been quite rightly bewildered, innocent of such play. But Kendra Donovan's knowledge had been obvious. *What kind of a woman was she?*

The door opened behind him, interrupting his speculation. He turned as his brother stepped into the room. Gabriel stopped abruptly, and Alec saw his eyes spark with hot resentment, before hardening. It was, he knew, sheer, bloody-minded stubbornness that propelled Gabriel across the room, to the rosewood sideboard, which held a silver tray and a glittering assortment of decanters and glasses.

"It's a little early for that, isn't it?" he remarked idly, as Gabriel poured two fingers of scotch into a glass.

Gabriel's lip curled. "For what?"

"To become foxed."

Defiantly, Gabriel tossed back the drink, immediately pouring another. "But it's so pleasurable."

Alec stared at him. When had his brother become a sodding drunk? They'd never been close, but when had they become enemies? "What the devil is wrong with you?"

Gabriel laughed. It was an ugly sound. "Don't pretend you finally care, Sutcliffe."

"You're my brother—"

"*Half*-brother," Gabriel corrected. He stared at his empty glass blankly, as though uncertain how it had become that way. Then despite Alec's disapproval—or maybe because of it—he poured more whiskey into the tumbler. "Don't forget that. Don't ever forget that. You're the prince, Sutcliffe."

Alec lifted a brow at the sneering tone. "Jealous, Gabe? Seems petty of you, considering you receive a rather sizable allowance from me—not to mention the income you inherited from your mother and her family."

"Goddamn you, this isn't about *money*!" Gabriel slammed down his glass on the sideboard with such force Alec was surprised it didn't shatter.

Alec's own temper rose. "You'll have to explain to me what it is about then. As I recall, *you* were the little prince. My father wasn't even cold in his grave before your mother packed me off to boarding school. I didn't even get a reprieve during the holidays. Not until the Duke began inviting me here. No doubt Emily wished I'd gotten the plague. Bitter disappointment for both of you when I did not."

"Don't talk about my mother."

"Yes, she always did keep you on leading strings, if I recall."

"Silence!"

"Come now, Gabe. Emily was—"

"—a manipulative bitch!" Gabriel snapped, and didn't know who was more stunned that he said it, himself or Alec. For just a moment, memories slammed into him. Then he forced them back. He didn't need to remember, didn't *want* to remember. She was dead. That was all that mattered.

"Gabe—"

"Let it alone." Savagely, he shoved himself away from the sideboard, away from his brother. *Half*-brother. He swung toward the door and stopped abruptly, an unpleasant smile twisting his lips as his gaze fell on Kendra hovering in the doorway. His eyes burned as they took in the wet hair and damp dress. "Well, well, well. If it ain't the little maid. Or companion now. You're a saucy bit of baggage, aren't you? Bettering yourself through Lady Rebecca. You should have come to me, Miss Donovan. I'm certain I would've found a position for you, one more enticing than being required to fetch a Lady's handkerchief."

"Gabriel." Alec's tone was a low warning.

"When you are finished with her, of course, Sutcliffe," he tossed back viciously. "I daresay I couldn't take anything away from you even if I tried."

Kendra took a small step to the side as Gabriel, his face flushed with anger and alcohol, brushed past her. Thoughtfully, she stared after him until he disappeared around the corner. Then she glanced back at Alec. Unlike the younger man, his face was set in hard, impassive lines. The only thing that suggested temper was the way he held himself, and the glittery light in his green eyes.

"What was that about?"

"You look like a drowned rat, Miss Donovan. Go change before you catch a chill."

"Your brother seems to have a problem."

"Apparently my brother's problem is me."

Kendra frowned. "It seems more than that."

He glared at her. "My brother had nothing to do with that girl. He was here at the castle the night that she was murdered."

"Are you certain?"

"Stop. Stop stirring up trouble, Miss Donovan." He shot her an angry look before he, too, brushed past her, following in his brother's footsteps.

Alone, Kendra shivered, becoming aware of the damp fabric clinging to her skin. Alec was right; she needed to change into dry clothes. But he was wrong about her making trouble.

Trouble was already here.

27

No one wanted to think that one of his friends could be a murderer. That went double for relatives.

Alec and Gabriel had a combative relationship. Even so, the marquis had made it clear that he wasn't receptive to regarding his brother as a possible suspect. Too bad Kendra couldn't accommodate him.

She bided her time through another long dinner, and the even more tedious after-dinner small talk in the drawing room. When the men finally filed in, several ladies gathered at the harpsichord to show off their musical talent in an impromptu concert.

Surveillance and patience, Kendra knew, went hand in glove. She was rewarded when she watched her quarry slip out the French doors. After a moment, she followed.

He was slouched against the stone balustrade, his back to her, staring out into the dark gardens. As she watched, he lifted his arm and she caught the metallic glimmer in the moonlight as he lifted his flask to his lips.

"It stopped raining," she commented.

Gabriel froze, and then he slowly lowered the flask. His eyes gleamed at her over his shoulder; his grin, a wicked slash of white in the darkness. "Ah . . . the little maid. No . . . the companion—pretty, improper Miss Donovan."

"These dinners tend to go on, don't they?"

He gave her a mocking smile that reminded her of Alec. "Better to attend the dinner than clean up after, eh?"

So much for being polite. "I'd like to ask you a couple of questions, Gabriel."

"The correct form of address is Lord Gabriel Morgan. Or Lord Gabriel. Or simply my Lord."

"Lord Gabriel, then."

"'Course if you're really nice to me, I might let your familiarity stand." He gave her an insolent once-over, lingering on her chest before slanting back up to meet her gaze.

She ignored the innuendo. "Where were you last Sunday evening?"

"Is this about the whore's death?"

"That whore was a person. A child, really."

Something dark and ugly flickered behind his eyes. "She was a woman who used her body to entice men, manipulate them for her own greed."

"That's pretty harsh. Sounds like you don't like women much."

"Oh, I like women. In their place." He lifted his flask again to take another swallow. Kendra noticed his hands were shaking. "You don't know your place, do you, Miss Donovan?"

"You haven't answered the question."

He glared at her. "Why the devil should I? What gives you the right to quiz me like I am a common criminal?"

"Why don't you just answer the question? Got something to hide?"

"I have nothing to hide." Yet he looked away.

"Really? Because I had the strangest feeling that maybe you recognized the victim." She watched him closely, and observed the slight jerk his body gave before he shot her a furious look.

"That's ridiculous! Why would I know the dead harlot?"

"You tell me."

"I have nothing to tell."

"How about where you were last Sunday? Did you leave the castle?"

He remained silent.

"You know, it would be easy enough to find out, I suppose," she mused. "I doubt if you walked. So someone from the stables must have seen you. Maybe even helped you."

His mouth tightened. "What has this to do with you?"

"I'm assisting the Duke in this matter of the girl's death," she said in her most neutral tone. "So tell me . . . why did you leave the castle that night? Where did you go?"

"Who said I left?"

"You're working too hard for it to be otherwise. Where did you go?"

He stared at her, saying nothing.

Kendra sighed. "Do you want the Duke to ask you these questions? It might be easier if you told me the truth, my Lord."

He scowled. "To the village, if you must know. Harcourt and I went to the cockfight at the King's Head."

"Captain Harcourt left the castle as well?"

"I just said so, didn't I?"

"You were together all night?"

Gabriel's gaze slid past her, darkening. She didn't have to turn around to know that Alec had joined them on the veranda.

"Gabriel." Alec eyed his brother coldly. "You and Miss Donovan have been out here long enough. People have begun to talk."

Gabriel stiffened. "I didn't know you were so bloody concerned with propriety," he sneered, slanting his gaze back to Kendra. "Miss Donovan isn't. Miss Donovan has no sense whatsoever."

"Go inside, Gabe. Go to your room. You're disguised. Sleep it off."

"Devil take it! Stop talking to me like that, like I'm some sort of half-wit." Gabriel glared at his brother, but pivoted for the French doors. His gait was only slightly unsteady as he stalked through them.

Kendra's mouth tightened as she looked at Alec. "You might not like it, but your brother fits the profile. You can't ignore the evidence."

Alec said nothing, just looked at her.

"He left the castle on the night of the murder," she told him flatly. "He and Captain Harcourt. They went to a cockfight in the village."

"Then they alibi each other."

"Maybe. It has to be checked out."

"I shall take care of my brother, Miss Donovan."

"Dammit, you can't look the other way."

"You need to worry less about my brother's actions and more about your own. You should never have come outside alone with a man who is not a relative. Have you no thought to your reputation at all?"

"Oh, please. I've been out here five minutes, tops."

His expression was grim as he grabbed her upper arm to steer her back into the drawing room. "My dear, that is five minutes too long."

28

Alec passed a sleepless night, which he blamed mostly on Kendra Donovan. Who the devil was she? And how dare she question his brother's behavior?

You can't ignore the evidence. You can't look the other way.

Hell and damnation. At dawn, he gave up chasing sleep, and dressed himself in riding clothes. There was no sense wakening Ramsey, his valet. The castle was silent, with most everyone still abed as he slipped through the corridors and out the door, walking the path to the stables. There, a sleepy boy woke to saddle his Arabian, Chance. Alec spent the next two hours exercising the beast, galloping through meadows still slick with morning dew, while his mind circled the puzzle that was Kendra Donovan, as well as Gabriel's erratic behavior.

By the time he returned to the stables, he was no closer to having any answers, but he felt clearheaded. With a determined stride, he went to his brother's bedchamber and rapped on the door.

It opened, and Finch, Gabriel's valet, stared out, dark-eyed and haughty. The haughtiness vanished as soon as he recognized Alec.

"My Lord. Good morning." His voice was low and dignified. "I must inform you that Lord Gabriel has yet to awaken."

"Not to worry, Finch." He shouldered his way past the startled manservant into the darkened room. "I shall wake him."

Alec glanced at his brother, who was sprawled on his stomach diagonally across the bed, his tousled dark head turned toward the wall. He crossed the room to the windows, and began removing the wooden shutters that kept the morning sun at bay.

"Get up, Gabriel. 'Tis already nine."

Behind him, Gabriel shifted, burrowing into the pillows. Alec thought he heard a muffled groan.

"My Lord, perhaps if I'd—"

"Go have your breakfast, Finch. I'd like to speak with my brother."

"Oh, ah . . ." The valet's protest died on his lips as he caught the marquis' set expression. He bowed. "As you wish, my Lord. If you or Lord Gabriel should need anything . . ."

"I shall send for you." He followed the valet to the door, and closed it behind him. Turning, he crossed his arms in front of his chest and viewed the only thing visible to him—his brother's back. "We need to talk, Gabriel."

"Bugger off," Gabriel muttered from beneath the pillows.

Mouth tightening, he moved forward and yanked the pillow off Gabriel's head, tossing it across the room where it landed with a soft thud. "I am not in the mood for your insubordination today!"

Gabriel opened bloodshot eyes, glaring. "Damn you! I'm not one of your toadeaters! Leave me alone! *God*. My head is pounding!"

"You'll not get any sympathy from me." Yet Alec felt a thrill of alarm as he eyed his brother's ashen complexion. Christ, was he actually ill?

"Did I seek it?" Gabriel muttered angrily, rolling onto his back and scrubbing a hand over his unshaven face. He pushed himself into a sitting position then, groaning, he leaned forward to put his throbbing head in his hands. "Hell's teeth. You smell of horse." When the insult didn't elicit any response, he asked sullenly, "What do you want, Sutcliffe?"

Alec spied several empty bottles on the nearby table. "You're drinking yourself into an early grave. For God's sake, why? *Why* are you doing this to yourself?"

"'Tis none of your damn business what I do."

"It is if you hurt that girl."

Gabriel's head came up and he stared at Alec for two seconds before his gaze slid away.

Alec's nerves tightened, aware that his brother didn't issue a denial. "Miss Donovan said you and Harcourt left the castle last Sunday for the King's Head. You went to Hawkings's cockfight."

"What of it?"

"You and Harcourt were at the cockfight until you returned to the castle?"

"I don't answer to you, Sutcliffe."

"You bloody well will answer to someone. I want to know if you and Harcourt were in each other's company all night."

"I'm not Harcourt's keeper," Gabriel muttered.

"So you were *not* with Harcourt all evening?"

"Devil take it, stop quizzing me!" Gathering the sheet around his hips, Gabriel surged to his feet. He was trembling. Their eyes met briefly, and again Alec felt a whisper of dread at what he saw in his brother's gaze. Anger, yes. But also fear. Then Gabriel looked away. Frustration knotted Alec's stomach. Again he wondered when Gabriel had begun to regard him as the enemy. What had happened to him? What had Emily done?

"Leave me alone, Sutcliffe."

"Just tell me if you stayed at the cockfight."

"I don't have to tell you anything," Gabriel shot back. Holding on to the sheet, he moved toward the dressing room.

"God help you, Gabriel," Alec said, as his brother opened the door. "God help you if you had anything to do with that girl's death!"

For just a second, Gabriel stilled. Then without a backward glance, he stumbled forward, shutting the door behind him with a snap.

Alec stared at the wooden panel as anger and fear rose up inside him. What the hell was going on? He wanted to follow his brother, to demand an answer to that question—to shake some bloody sense into him.

Tension bunched the muscles along his shoulders as he stood in indecision. He reached for the doorknob of the dressing room's door, but at the last moment, he dropped his arm and pivoted toward the other door.

Coward, he thought and shook his head in self-disgust. He'd leave Gabriel alone for now. There were other ways of getting to the truth. *If* he wanted the truth. And that, he realized, was the problem. He wasn't entirely sure that he did.

Gabriel heard the outer door click shut. The relief that coursed through him had him sagging against the wall. He hadn't been entirely certain that Sutcliffe wouldn't force his way into the dressing room to hound him.

He couldn't handle it. Not now. Not when his stomach burned like acid and his head pounded so hard it felt as though it would split in two. Passing a shaking hand over his face, he stumbled to the chaise lounge in the corner of the room, collapsing onto the cushions.

Who the hell was Sutcliffe, anyway, to come into his room and treat him in such a way? Sutcliffe, who had left and never looked back, who never once wondered about *Gabriel's* life, *Gabriel's* happiness. Anger and self-pity welled up inside him.

God help you, Gabriel, if you had anything to do with that girl's death.

Alec's words echoed in his mind, sending shudders through him. He put his throbbing head in his hands and squeezed his eyes shut to block it out.

Pretty brown eyes, dark hair tumbling down her back. *Alive.*

He jerked upright, opening his eyes. The vision was his imagination, nothing more. He wiped a trembling hand against his mouth. He needed a drink. That would ease his suffering.

God help you, Gabriel, if you had anything to do with that girl's death.

"It's too late, Sutcliffe," he whispered. God, he knew, had abandoned him years ago. There would be no hope in that quarter. He put his head in his hands again, and wept.

29

Kendra was with Rebecca when they got word that Sam Kelly had returned.

"Do you think he has learned the name of the fiend?" Rebecca wondered with some excitement as they hurried down the halls.

"I don't know," Kendra admitted.

The Bow Street Runner was telling the Duke and Alec something, but broke off when they entered the study. Kendra felt the full impact of his gaze as he flicked her a look, hard enough to make the back of her neck tingle.

"Good morning, ladies," Aldridge greeted. "Mr. Kelly has only just arrived. I suggest we sit down to hear his report. Would you like anything to drink?" He gestured to a side table that was laden with elegant silver pots, a creamer, and a sugar bowl. "I ordered tea, chocolate, and coffee."

Some things here aren't so bad, Kendra decided. At least this was a lot nicer than the thousands of Styrofoam cups filled with bad cop coffee that she'd consumed over the years.

Sitting down, she surveyed Sam. He looked like he'd spent the last four days sleeping in his clothes—or, rather, *not* sleeping in them, judging by the bags under his eyes. His cravat and shirt seemed more gray than white, only a few shades lighter than his dove-gray topcoat. This, along with the black waistcoat and breeches, was wrinkled and dirty. A film of dust coated his scuffed Hessian boots. His eyes held the same flat, watchful expression that she remembered from their previous meeting, so at odds with his elfin features.

After everyone had the beverage of their choice, the Duke settled behind his desk and nodded to the Runner. "Now, we shall begin. Mr. Kelly. Pray tell, have you discovered anything of significance?"

"First, I'd like ter say that several of me men made inquiries on the rattlers that go between here and London Town. There's not many, so it made the job a good bit easier."

"Rattlers?" asked Kendra.

"Beggin' yer pardon, miss—I mean ter say, coach."

"Perhaps if you'd limit your cant, Mr. Kelly. Miss Donovan is an American and is unfamiliar with some of our English vocabulary," Aldridge put in.

"Aye, sir." Again, the detective's eyes were hard with suspicion as he flicked another look in Kendra's direction. He continued, "I asked a friend ter copy the likeness of the young lass from Lady Rebecca's sketch. It ain't as good as yours, milady."

"You are too gallant, Mr. Kelly," Rebecca said mildly.

"Excellent notion." The Duke stirred his tea. "I should have thought of it myself."

"Even so, no whip—er, coachman—remembered her as a passenger. Not in the last month, that is. And she's pretty enough ter draw somebody's peepers."

"You don't think she came by public coach then?"

"Hard ter say, sir. She could've worn a bonnet and veil. As no one recalled seeing anyone wearing that either, I wouldn't wager on it."

"Then somebody brought her here in a private carriage," the Duke mused.

"Aye. Most likely."

No one said anything for a moment, but Kendra knew they were considering the implications. A private carriage added weight to her theory that they were dealing with a member of their own class.

She asked, "Any luck with the brothels?"

"Depends on what you mean by luck, miss." He paused, then put down his teacup with a sigh. Reaching into his inside breast pocket, he pulled out a small wedge of paper, which he carefully unfolded, increasing its size to reveal Rebecca's original pastel sketch of the victim. The paper was now smudged and creased from being repeatedly folded and unfolded, and passed around.

"This is why I came back," he said slowly. "There was naught that knew this lass."

"Oh, what a shame," Rebecca said, her face falling in disappointment.

"You can hardly have gone to every academy in London," the Duke said.

"Nay, sir. I told you that me and me men would stick ter the mid-range bawd houses."

"It was only conjecture on our part that this girl was from London. In point of fact, it's only conjecture that we're dealing with a madman who has killed before and will kill again." Alec shot a veiled look at Kendra. "Mayhap we need to review this entire affair. Miss Donovan could be wrong."

Kendra stiffened, but the Bow Street Runner was already shaking his head. "Nay. I do not believe Miss Donovan is wrong."

Everyone looked at him.

Rebecca frowned in confusion. "You said that no one knew the girl."

"Aye. No one claimed ter know *this* lass. But in the course of our inquiries, we found something peculiar."

"What, Mr. Kelly?" asked the Duke.

Sam drew in a deep breath. "We found other lasses who've gone missing, sir."

"Well, it *is* London . . ." Rebecca began uncertainly.

"They looked like this lass. Looked enough like this lass ter be her kin." Sam picked up the sketch, studied it. "Young. Pretty. Brown eyes. Dark brown or black hair. Small in stature."

There was a moment of silence. He glanced up, and shrugged. "Seems a wee bit of a coincidence ter have so many lasses missing who could've been sisters, if you take my meaning."

"He has a type." Kendra set down her coffee cup and stood up. She went over to the slate board. "He's not picking these girls at random. He saw these girls; he wanted *them*."

"But . . . why?" the Duke asked, perplexed. "I don't understand."

Kendra admitted, "I don't know. It could be anything—something in his past, a real or perceived injustice by a woman who looked like our victim—victims."

Alec shook his head. "You're assuming these other women are dead. They're Birds of Paradise—fickle creatures, at best. They may have left their academy. They may have found a protector or a more generous abbess. They may have wanted to become a brothel-keeper themselves. Or, devil take it, they may have married the bloody butcher down the street! Any number of things could've happened other than murder."

"Beggin' yer pardon, milord, but these bits o' muslin didn't just leave," Sam argued. "They went *missing*. Not a one gave their notice or talked about finding a protector. Cartes blanches offered by buckfitches are usually brokered by the abbess, so she can get her cut.

"No, sir. These lasses haven't been seen hide nor hair of since the day they disappeared from their bawd house."

Rebecca shivered. "How many, Mr. Kelly? How many girls have disappeared?"

Sam hesitated, and the look in his eyes had Kendra holding her breath.

"Eleven, Lady Rebecca. Eleven lasses have simply . . . vanished."

30

Numbers had power. One dead hooker versus almost a dozen girls who'd vanished without a trace—though the first was a certainty, Kendra didn't have to ask which number carried more weight. She saw it in the shock that registered on the faces of Rebecca and the Duke. Alec hid it better, but even he appeared nonplussed by the information, frowning darkly into the coffee cup he held.

In the silence that followed, Kendra picked up a piece of slate, and added under the *Victimology* column: "*Missing London Prostitutes; dark brown/black hair; brown eyes; petite . . .*" She glanced at Sam Kelly, who was studying the board with a frown. "How young, Mr. Kelly? What's the estimated age range?"

"Fifteen to eighteen, or thereabouts."

"Similar to our victim." She nodded, and wrote the additional information on the board. "What was the time frame that the girls went missing?"

"The first bit o' muslin went missing four years ago. The most recent was two months ago."

"What months?"

Sam stared at her. "Why would that matter, if you don't mind me askin'?"

"Details, Mr. Kelly. Every detail is important. It could move us closer to identifying the unsub or at least—"

"What's an unsub?" the detective interrupted, perplexed.

The Duke answered. "Unknown subject. Is that not correct, Miss Donovan?"

"Yes." She had to smile. There was no denying the Duke's intelligence. "As I was saying, gathering details about the victims will help us establish the killer's patterns. Eleven girls in four years—does that mean three girls a year? How long between disappearances?" Kendra scanned her audience. It wasn't just Aldridge; they were all intelligent. But how much to say? How much would they accept?

"It's typical of this type of killer to have a cooling-off period," she said finally. "They've satisfied their need . . . but it's temporary."

There was a short, stark silence as they absorbed that implication.

Sam lifted his brows. "You mean ter say that after the villain has killed, he takes his time before he kills again?"

"Yes. And he *will* kill again. He has to."

"Why?" he asked suspiciously.

"There are many theories." *Too many,* she thought. "Suffice to say that we could argue endlessly as to why he does what he does. Point of fact is that he does it. We need to stop him before he can do it again."

"Patterns," murmured Aldridge. "If determining his pattern will assist us in stopping this monster, we are obliged to do so. Proceed, Mr. Kelly."

"Aye, sir." He drew out a sheaf of papers from the pocket of his overcoat, unfolding them across his lap.

"Yvette—I doubt that's her real name, mind you—was the first lass ter go missing, in—let's see—February 1812," he read, and his eyes narrowed. "She was fifteen. Then Sofia, also fifteen, in June of that year—Saturday, the thirteenth. Mary, seventeen, disappeared in October, around the sixteenth. In 1813, Clara, eighteen, vanished in February—Friday, the twelfth; Elizabeth, fifteen, June the thirteenth; Matilda, seventeen, on October eighth. Not another chit until the next February—Saturday, the twelfth, and . . . by God . . ."

He scanned the papers he held and then lifted his gaze to Kendra. "They're all in those months. Every disappearance. February, June, and October. What does it mean?"

"Patterns," Aldridge repeated softly.

"The madman is taking a girl every four months!" Rebecca's eyes darkened with horror.

Alec scowled, crossing his arms in front of his chest as he regarded them. "Wait a bloody moment. I think everyone needs to remember that this is still conjecture. We can't be certain these girls are dead, or that they didn't leave by their own accord, despite their apparently rather abrupt departures."

Aldridge shook his head. "No, Alec. The odds suggest the disappearances of these women are related."

"Mr. Kelly admitted that he didn't go to every brothel. There could be even more missing girls in the same months or different months than the ones we know about," Kendra conceded with a frown.

"We covered a lot of ground, miss, including a few of the lower establishments. Not every academy had missing lasses. Just them here." Sam lifted the sheaf of papers he held.

"If this pattern is correct," Alec began, and by the tone of his voice, he wasn't buying it completely, "then the assailant broke it with this girl, as the month is August—not October."

Cold dread shivered up Kendra's spine. "You're right. His cooling-off period just became shorter."

"Whatever does that mean?" Rebecca asked, frowning.

"Three girls per year aren't enough anymore. He's escalating."

31

Kendra wrote down each missing girl's name, accompanied with the pertinent information of their ages, and the month they'd gone missing. Afterward she stood back and surveyed the slate board. She might not have each girl's photograph pinned up on a murder board, but the names, filling one entire column, were eerie reminders that lives most likely had been lost.

Everyone seemed to feel the same. For several minutes, no one said anything.

Then Kendra looked to the Duke. "Could we get a map of London? I'd like to identify the location of the brothel where each of these girls worked."

"That can be arranged. I assume you are looking again for patterns?"

Cluster analysis, she thought wistfully. In the twenty-first century, sophisticated computerized models would replace paper maps and pushpins. But nothing was stopping her from using the old-fashioned approach.

"If a pattern emerges, we could learn his comfort zone." She shrugged. Every bit helped. She shifted her gaze to Sam. "Did you find out anything about the maid killed on Sutton Street five years ago?"

"Five years is a long time, Miss Donovan. And London is fair ter burstin' with cutthroats. I had one of me men talk ter the local watch, but . . ." He shook his head. "Nobody much recalled the maid who died."

It had been a long shot, she knew. Since there was no official police force, there'd be no official police files. She sighed, pinching the bridge of her nose as she thought about the next step. She knew what it was. She also knew no one would like it.

"The Duke and I have compiled a list of men fitting the profile who live within a ten-mile radius," she finally said. "It's a starting point—"

"Pardon, miss, but why?" Sam interrupted. "Why ten miles? She got caught in the river's current. She could've floated a long way."

Kendra shook her head. "Jane Doe had sustained considerable damage, but I believe it would've been much greater if the body had traveled farther downstream. In fact, I don't even think the body floated ten miles. I decided to err on the side of caution when I developed that parameter. I think we're actually looking at a fairly tight parameter, probably much closer to where Jane Doe ended up in the lake."

She waited for Sam to object. But the detective nodded. "Aye. That's sound thinking, miss."

She continued, "As I said, we considered men that fit the general profile—affluent, between twenty-five and forty-five. That's when this type of killer hits their prime. The Duke and I then eliminated anyone who is not a landowner or doesn't have access to property. We further narrowed the field by removing all the locals who never or rarely visited London. Finally, we crossed off any men who aren't currently in residence because they're traveling abroad. That leaves us with eight possibilities within the ten-mile radius. We need to find out where they were on the night of the murder."

"'Tis a process of elimination—a logical approach." The Duke nodded in approval.

Sam gave Kendra a thoughtful look. "'Tis an approach that's worked well for the Runners."

"Since Mr. Dalton has no alibi for the time in question, I assume he must remain on your list of suspects," Rebecca commented, earning a surprised glance from Sam.

"You actually asked the guv— er, the gent where he was on the night of the murder?"

"No. Miss Donovan made the inquiry. I fear he was displeased."

"Imagine that," Alec murmured.

Kendra ignored the sarcasm. "I'd like to check into Mr. Dalton's background. His wife left him for another man—I'd like to learn more about that, and about what she looked like."

Sam eyed her curiously. "You think she may resemble the lasses?"

"May have, past tense. Mr. Dalton's wife died—another thing to be explored. How'd she die? And when?"

"I'll have one of me men look at Mr. Dalton's background," Sam agreed.

"His family is from Manchester," the Duke told him.

"Thank you, sir. I'll send someone up north ter make inquiries." Sam rubbed his nose. "I can return ter London Town ter continue my inquiries at the brothels, but I'd just as soon stay here ter help with the investigation. If you're interviewing the gents, I can talk ter the servants and like."

"You might want to start at the King's Head," Alec said abruptly.

Kendra stared at him in surprise. She hadn't expected him to volunteer that information.

His gaze was cool as he met hers. "I don't believe my brother committed these atrocities, Miss Donovan, and I intend to prove it by having his alibi confirmed. I won't have his reputation besmirched by the vile suspicion that he is a killer."

Aldridge leaned forward, looking at both of them. "Gabriel? What does he have to do with this business, pray tell?"

"He and Captain Harcourt left the castle after the dinner on Sunday evening to attend Hawkings's cockfight," Alec told his uncle. "If you recall, the publican has a cockpit behind his tavern."

"Yes. I had not realized they left the castle that night. But surely you don't think Gabriel—"

Kendra cut him off sharply. "No one can be ruled out unless they have a verifiable alibi." She was afraid, she realized, very afraid that they'd let their personal bias dictate the investigation. She couldn't let that happen.

Aldridge frowned at her. "It is entirely plausible that Gabriel is telling the truth, my dear. I am not an admirer of the blood sport of cockfighting. 'Tis gruesome business to watch an animal literally peck the eyes out of another. But I understand it is a lucrative venture for Hawkings. Many attend. There is no reason to think Gabriel did not."

"I'm not thinking anything. That's my point. We must approach this rationally rather than subjectively."

"What about being presumed innocent until proven guilty, as Sir William Garrow so eloquently argued?" Rebecca asked. "Should we not give Lord Gabriel the benefit of the doubt?"

"He's not on trial. We're . . ." Kendra didn't know what to say. *Law enforcement*? Only she and Sam Kelly belonged to that group. And she still wasn't entirely sure about Sam Kelly's position. He seemed to understand basic police procedure, but Bow Street Runners were paid by their clients, not the citizenry of the town they were sworn to serve and protect. At the moment, he was being paid by Aldridge. Because of that, he might not be entirely objective when he dealt with the Duke's nephew.

"I'm feelin' a might thirsty for a good English ale," Sam declared suddenly, and stood up, effectively ending the argument. "I think I'll go ter the King's Head."

"Very good, Mr. Kelly." After the Runner left, Aldridge searched his desk until he found the list of names tucked in the ledger. "Now we must go over the names again. Mayhap Alec and Rebecca will have suggestions . . ." He spread the foolscap in front of him. "Then we will divide up the names between us, and conduct the interviews. Does that meet with your approval, Miss Donovan?"

It would have to.

32

The coach was luxurious. April Duprey had to admire that, her sharp eyes automatically calculating the cost of the plush, red-velvet interior, and the seat cushions and pillows that were gold trimmed, tufted, and tasseled. And she couldn't help but appreciate the carriage's excellent springs. She'd noticed the smoothness of the ride in London, automatically comparing it to the cheaper hackneys and carriages that she used. No doubt about it, she was dealing with Quality.

After nearly four hours of traveling, however, she was no longer impressed. Even the coach's excellent springs couldn't disguise the roughness of the country roads, and the swaying and jolting of the coach left her feeling slightly queasy. She pressed a gloved hand to her stomach, and prayed that it wouldn't be much longer before she reached her destination.

As though in answer to her prayer, the coach began to slow, then turn. She stifled a groan when the coach lurched forward again, the ride increasingly bumpy as the wheels hit rocks and ruts, forcing her to grip one of the brass handrails near the door.

Her patience worn thin, she silently cursed the gentry, who issued orders with no thought to the comfort of the likes of her. Initially, she'd been delighted when she'd received such a prompt response to her letter, and had obeyed the contents of that letter without argument. He'd send for her, he said. A private carriage, he said, to take her into the country, where they could meet.

He'd asked that she keep the drapes closed during the journey. It was an odd request, but she'd shrugged it off. After all, she'd made a career out of servicing the odd requests from gentlemen. Still, she'd disliked staying in the gloomy carriage when they'd made their one stop at the mail-coach inn to feed and water the horses, and she'd resented the silent coachman as he went about his business without once opening the door to see about *her* needs or to acknowledge *her* company. It was one thing to be ignored by Quality; it was another to be ignored by her own class.

After that, her mood had turned sour. Once, she'd defiantly flipped open the heavy velvet drapes to look outside. Not that there was much to look at: forests and rolling green hills dotted by the occasional thatched house. She'd eyed the open countryside with the discomfort only a born and bred Londoner could feel, preferring the congested streets and familiar grime-coated buildings of Town.

Now she became aware of a change. Again, the horses were slowing. She twitched the curtains to peer outside. On the other side of the paned glass, the dense trees that crowded alongside the lane, the dark branches and green leaves stretching across the road in a canopy effect, seemed closer. As though when she wasn't looking, the woods had crept nearer, hemming her in. She shivered and dropped the curtain, half-remembered stories of evil wood elves, sprites, and mischievous fairies flitting through her mind.

The carriage rattled to a stop. She straightened, shrugging away the silly superstitions, her attention already shifting to the business at hand. Self-consciously, she tidied her hair, listening as the coachman scrabbled off his perch, rocking the carriage. A moment later, the door opened, and the coachman folded down the three steps. He lifted a hand to help her down.

She accepted the assistance, her gaze sweeping the wooded area with growing consternation. She'd expected some form of civilization, a cottage or inn, at the very least, in which to do their business, not this desolate stretch of forest. Again, though she wore an ankle-skimming wool pelisse over the bright pink, cotton walking gown that she'd chosen for this meeting, she shivered.

Movement drew her eye. A rider and horse emerged from the shadowy trees. The rider didn't dismount, drawing the beast to a halt about ten yards away. Knowing it was expected of her, she began walking, making sure she rolled her hips in a well-practiced move. Behind her, the servant climbed onto the coach and moved off down the lane.

"Did you tell anyone about our meeting today?" the rider asked abruptly.

So that's how it was going to be, she thought. No coy flirtations to smooth the way of their dealings. "No, sir. As you wrote, this is a private affair." She paused, and when he was silent, she arched a brow. "Shall we get down to business, then?"

For the first time, he smiled. But it wasn't a pleasant smile, and April felt a whisper of disquiet that had nothing to do with the forest and everything to do with the man.

He leaned forward. "I prefer pleasure before business."

"Pleasure?" Mayhap she'd misjudged him. If he wanted a tumble before they got down to business, well, she'd simply add the cost of whoring to the bill that she'd worked out to pay for Lydia's untimely demise. Not that she didn't expect to do a little negotiating. Catching the gleam in his eye, she smiled and lifted her gloved hand to stroke his thigh with practiced familiarity. "I'm not adverse to pleasure. What do you have in mind, sir?"

His voice was low and throaty. "I want you to . . ."

She tilted her head and smiled encouragingly. "Yes? You want me to . . . ?"

"Run."

April stilled, uncertain that she heard him correctly. "I beg your pardon?"

"I want you to run." As she stared at him, trying to comprehend the unusual request, he extracted a large knife from the folds of his caped redingote. She only had a moment of surprise, to observe the blade that gleamed wickedly in the gloomy light of the forest, before he slashed it down, splicing open the back of her gloved hand, still resting on his thigh.

The action was so sudden, so unexpected, that it took a moment to feel the sting. Then she fell back with a gasp, snatching her hand away and watching in disbelief as blood welled up, soaking the kid glove crimson. Clutching the wounded hand to her chest, she met the man's eyes. A chill raced through her at what she read in his gaze.

"*Run,*" he whispered.

April Duprey ran.

33

Sam Kelly stepped into the King's Head. As he headed toward the bar, he did a quick scan of the shadowy interior. There was a low-timbered ceiling, and whitewashed walls tinged gray from the oil lamps, the customers' clouds of smoke, and probably from the fireplace, too. But today, the kindling in the hearth was yet unlit.

The tavern was only one-third occupied, a fact that Sam attributed to it still being early enough in the day. Still, he deliberately chose a corner spot at the bar, where he could keep his back to the wall and an eye on everyone else. The clientele veered toward farmers, mill workers, blacksmiths, not the rogues he was used to dealing with in the rookeries and flash houses of London. Yet it was never a good idea to let down one's guard, which was why he kept his back to the wall, and his Sheffield four-inch blade in his boot.

A big man with bushy red hair and mustache approached. "W'ot can Oi get fer ye, guv'ner?"

Sam produced two shillings. "A pint . . . and some information."

The man's blue eyes narrowed. "W'ot kinda information?"

"Heard tell you had a cockfight last Sunday."

"Aye." Hawkings eyed him warily. "Every Sunday, after sundown. Doesn't stop folks from goin' ter church."

"I'm not concerned with anyone's salvation. I wanna know if Captain Harcourt and Lord Gabriel attended the fight."

"'Oo are ye ter be askin'?"

Sam reached into the deep pocket of his coat and brought out the baton with its infamous gilt crown. He saw Hawkings's eyes widen as he recognized it.

"Ye're the thief-taker 'is Grace 'ired." He licked his lips nervously. "Lemme get yer drink."

Sam watched the publican shuffle over to the bar pull, filling a pewter tankard until it overflowed and foam ran down the side. He returned with the mug, slid it toward Sam. The two shillings disappeared beneath the man's beefy paw.

"This 'as ter do with the 'ore in the lake?"

Casually, Sam dropped a couple more shillings onto the bar. In his experience, three things loosened a man's tongue—women, ale, and money. He picked up the tankard, admired the head before taking a swallow. "I want ter know about your cockfight that night."

"Hmm." Hawkings eyed the shillings, rubbing his chin. "'Twas a bang-up night. We h'ad more'n two 'undred blokes wagerin'. Mr. Dorin' brung 'is bird—a bloomin' big bastard. Undefeatable, 'e is. 'Tis a problem, that. No one wants ter bet against 'im."

"Aye, I can see how that would be a problem. But I'm not interested in the outcome, Mr. Hawkings. I want ter know if Lord Gabriel and Captain Harcourt was there."

"Lemme think. Seems ter me that both gents came in. Oi think I saw 'em for the first fight." He rolled his massive shoulders. "Don't remember 'em after that."

"What time did the first fight start?"

"'Alf past nine. Starts the same time every Sunday, Tuesday, and Thursday."

"How long have you been in Aldridge Village, Mr. Hawkings?"

"Since Oi got caught in the parson's mousetrap—nigh on fifteen years ago, Mr. Kelly."

"Ever hear of any lasses gone missing or cockin' up their toes like the one in the lake?"

Uneasiness flashed across the publican's face. "Nay, not like thata one, Mr. Kelly."

Sam pushed the extra shillings toward Hawkings. "Thank you, sir. I'd appreciate it if you kept an eye and ear out for any gossip pertaining ter Lord Gabriel and Captain Harcourt."

"Aye, guv." Again he scooped up the coins with thick fingers, and began turning away. He hesitated, then pivoted back, leaning in close. "Oi dunno nothing about Lord Gabriel, but the Cap'n . . . 'e's under the 'atches."

"How'dya know that, Mr. Hawkings? He's from London Town."

"Aye, but 'e's got a huntin' lodge about these parts. 'E comes in 'ere frequent-like. 'E's tryin' ter keep 'is circumstances quiet, but 'e needs to pay cash. No credit."

"Afraid he'd leave you hanging, eh?"

"Oi'm more 'fraid of what me wife would do if 'e did!" Hawkings laughed heartily and moved away.

Sam slowly sipped his beer. Captain Harcourt being in dun territory was an interesting tidbit. That didn't mean he couldn't have lured the whore—the way he saw it, the *appearance* of wealth was the key. Sam had been a Runner long enough to know that many of the Ton lived on credit. Like Brummel. That lad had dined with royalty until he'd had his falling out with the Prince Regent. He still moved in high circles, but if the whispers on the street were true—and Sam suspected they were—the dandy was quite penniless.

As far as Sam was concerned, Captain Harcourt still fit Miss Donovan's profile, and neither he nor Lord Gabriel had a firm alibi for last Sunday night. Sam pondered that for a bit before his mind shifted to another puzzle: the American. Who was she?

He'd heard the gossip. She'd been a lady's maid before suffering a demotion to below stairs maid, and then an unprecedented elevation to Lady Rebecca's companion. 'Twas damned unusual, much like the lass. In fact, if he hadn't known any better, he'd think she was one of the fancy. Except for her peculiar knowledge of murder. He didn't know *who* she was, but knew *what* she was: Kendra Donovan was a liar.

34

The Duke's carriage rattled down the dirt country roads toward Morland's home of Tinley Park. Only four miles separated the two holdings, but the rural landscape seemed to stretch endlessly. *The world really has gotten much smaller during my time,* Kendra thought.

She reached for the brass rail to hold when the carriage turned down the lane and into the park. Glancing out the window, Kendra was surprised by her first glimpse of the manor. It looked like the White House, with its fluted columns, portico, and classic triangle pediment. The stones hadn't been painted white, but left in their natural state, the color a warm honey that seemed to glow in the sun's rays.

Then she remembered that in *this* era, there was no White House. The British had burned that structure down a year ago.

"It's quite a sight, isn't it?" the Duke said, misinterpreting her expression.

"Ah. Yeah. Yes, it is."

"Mr. Morland's grandfather, Henry Richford, the Earl of Whilmont, had an excess of passion for ancient civilizations,

Greece, in particular. When he bought Tinley Park, he tore down the previous manor and built what you see now."

"It's not something you expect to see in the English countryside."

Something in the silence that followed had her shifting her attention from the window to Aldridge. He was eyeing her oddly.

Panic flared. *What did I say?* she wondered. It took her a moment, then she remembered that England had a Greek Revival movement that had begun in the eighteenth century. Tinley Park wasn't so unusual after all. Damn, and double damn.

"I meant to say, it doesn't seem very *English*," she amended. That sounded lame, even to her own ears. She felt her face heat at the Duke's scrutiny.

"Well, the earl preferred ancient Greece over anything English, including its legends. We had many discussions on the subject, although I must confess my interest lies more in the Greek civilization and contributions to natural philosophy than in its myths. What of you, Miss Donovan? Do you have any interest in Greek mythology?"

"Not particularly, no."

The carriage rolled to a jerky stop in front of the manor and the coachman jumped down. Kendra made a scooting move toward the door, but the Duke held up his hand, his expression amused.

"We may be here to conduct our inquiries, but we still must observe the social necessities." He produced a slim silver case from his inside coat pocket. Opening it, he extracted what looked to Kendra to be a business card, which he handed to his coachman. "My calling card," he explained.

Kendra sat back, frowning. "Now what?"

"Now we wait to see whether Mr. Morland is at home to us."

"We couldn't have just knocked on the door to find that out?"

Aldridge's lips twitched. "Only if we are uncouth—which we are not. No need to fret, my dear. If the gentleman is at home, he won't decline to see us. That would be foolish."

"I see. Is anyone *not* at home to someone who has a title?"

"That would depend on whether the person one calling upon has a more elevated title." He gave her a quizzical look. "Surely it is the same in America—if not with titles, then with people of consequence?"

Kendra didn't know what to say to that. She didn't know too much about societal etiquette in nineteenth-century America. Her calling card had been her FBI badge, now as out of touch as the moon. Just thinking about it depressed her.

The servant returned with the expected response—Mr. Morland was at home. Morland's butler met them in the enormous foyer, a cavern of icy-gray-veined marble floors and columns, and fixtures trimmed in gilt. A fresco had been painted across the vaulted ceiling, depicting a toga-clad man showing off his physical prowess by shooting an arrow into a tree, splitting it as another man leapt out from its shattered core toward a woman in flowing white. The Duke hadn't been kidding when he'd said that the late earl had been enamored with Greek mythology.

He followed her eyes to the ceiling as they ascended the circular stairs. "'Tis striking, is it not?"

"It should be in a museum." Then again, *everything* here should be in a museum, she thought.

The butler led them to a drawing room painted in airy pastels. The Greek influence extended to the silk-covered furnishings, classically carved cabinets, and scrolling volutes atop Ionic pilasters. Another fresco dominated the ceiling, this one of a regal couple seated on thrones in the middle of big, billowing clouds.

Zeus and Hera, Kendra identified, the chief god and goddess of Greek mythology.

"Mr. Morland shall be in shortly," the servant told them. "Please be seated. May I offer you a drink? A sherry or brandy, mayhap? Or tea?"

"A cup of tea, thank you," the Duke smiled. "Miss Donovan?"

"Oh . . . sure. Yes. Thank you."

"I shall bring a tray at once, Your Grace." The butler bowed and departed.

Clasping her hands behind her back, Kendra circled the room. On the far wall were several paintings, mostly portraits, and a few landscapes. The middle portrait was the largest, roughly sixty inches by forty-eight, featuring a woman in a flowing, toga-like white dress. Her dark hair was unbound, tumbling past her shoulders. She was leaning against a stone pillar, her dark eyes pensive. Dark clouds boiled in the background. Kendra was in the process of trying to figure out which goddess or demigoddess she represented when the Duke came up beside her.

"Lady Anne," he said.

"Excuse me?"

He nodded toward the painting. "'Tis Morland's mother, Lady Anne. Of course, this painting was commissioned at least twenty-five years ago."

Kendra studied the figure more closely. "She's beautiful." She slanted a glance at the Duke, and wondered if he realized that the woman bore a striking resemblance to Jane Doe.

"Your Grace . . . Miss Donovan." They turned as Morland strode into the room. He sent Kendra an enigmatic glance, probably wondering what the hell a paid companion was doing with the Duke. "Welcome. This is a rare pleasure."

"Your home is very impressive," Kendra said.

A wry look crossed Morland's face as he lifted his gaze to the painted ceiling. "I'm afraid that I am less interested in Greek legends than my grandfather or mother. I've considered refurbishing, but I fear it would upset Mother."

"How is Lady Anne?" asked Aldridge. "Will she be joining us?"

Morland looked down at his hands, his expression tightening. "No. I fear my mother is unwell."

"Oh, my dear boy, I am distressed to hear this. If you have need of any remedies, we have an excellent stillroom maid at the castle."

"You are most kind, sir." His gaze flickered up, then away. "However, I fear there is no remedy for what ails my mother."

Behind them the door opened and the butler entered, followed by a maid carrying the tea service.

"Ah, excellent." Morland seemed relieved at the interruption. "Let us sit, shall we?"

The maid set down the tray on a nearby table, curtsied, and left. The butler stayed behind to pour.

"How do you take your tea, sir?"

"Two sugars. Cream."

"Miss?"

"Black. One sugar."

The butler doctored the tea, passed around the cups. He obviously knew Morland's preferences, handing him a cup and saucer without inquiring.

"Will that be all, sir?"

"Yes. You may go, Adams." As the butler closed the door behind him, Morland raised his brows. "Is this visit about the soiled dove? Has the Bow Street Runner returned?"

Aldridge's expression pulled into grave lines. "As a matter of fact, he has."

"Has he learned the identity of the chit?"

Kendra watched him closely, but couldn't detect anything other than curiosity in his gaze. "No, but he uncovered something significant. Prostitutes similar to the girl found in the lake have vanished from London over the last four years."

"Vanished? I don't understand. If they were not found murdered, pray tell, how can you make the correlation between those prostitutes and the dead girl in the lake?"

The Duke answered. "It's difficult to explain. However, based on the evidence, I am confident that there is a connection."

Kendra looked at Morland. "Where were you Sunday night, Mr. Morland? I understand that you were at Lady Atwood's dinner party, but where did you go after?"

For a moment, he simply stared at her. As though he hadn't heard her correctly. Then his gaze swiveled to the Duke. "What does my whereabouts have to do with this, Your Grace?"

Aldridge sighed. "I apologize for our impertinence. Miss Donovan has convinced me that this line of inquiry is necessary."

"Miss Donovan has persuaded you to believe I am capable of this—this barbarism?"

"We're questioning several people, Mr. Morland," she stated calmly. "It's procedure."

"Procedure? *What* procedure? I'm the bloody magistrate!"

"Think of it as your civic duty."

"My—" A muscle worked in his jaw. "This is absurd!"

The Duke sighed again. "I truly was hoping you would not take insult. Nevertheless, I'd like an answer."

His tone was mild, but Kendra recognized the steel beneath it. She was reminded again of the power the Duke wielded in this world. *Better than a badge.*

Morland put his teacup down and surged to his feet. Spine rigid, he stalked to the window. When he answered, his voice was abrupt. "I returned home from the dinner party. After Monsieur Anton's most excellent dinner, I took a turn around the garden. Then I read in the library before retiring to my bedchamber."

"Can anyone verify your whereabouts?"

He flicked her a hard look. "It was late. Mayhap the servants observed my nocturnal activity. Mayhap they did not."

"What about your valet?" Kendra asked, remembering Rebecca's question to Dalton. "Wouldn't he have helped you get ready for bed?"

"He assisted me before I occupied myself reading in the library. I did not need his assistance later."

"What book did you read?"

He frowned, puzzled. "What does my reading material have to do with anything?"

"I realize this is confusing, but I'd appreciate an answer."

He continued to frown at her for several more seconds as though trying to figure out the reason behind the question, then shrugged. "*Tom Jones*. Have you read it, Miss Donovan?"

"Yes. It's an old book." Even in this time period.

Morland said nothing.

Kendra continued, "You are familiar with London, my Lord?"

"Of course. I have a town house that I make use of, especially during the season. As does most of the Ton, including His Grace."

Aldridge acknowledged that point with a nod. "It's been many years since I made use of my townhome, but my sisters and their families often use it for their sojourns to Town."

For the first time since they'd begun the interview, Morland's eyes glinted with amusement. "If, by your query, you are wondering about my escapades in London, Miss Donovan, I shall admit to sowing my wild oats. But that was when I was a young buck. And if being a rascal is now a crime then the entire aristocracy is at risk of deportation or the gallows. With the exception, of course, of the Duke of Aldridge."

"But you go back and forth between your home here and London?"

He gave a shrug. "I suppose. No more or less than anyone else though, including Lord Sutcliffe and his brother, Lord Gabriel."

"Thank you for answering our questions, Mr. Morland."

He raised a brow, surprised. "We are at the end of the interrogation?"

"I prefer to call it an interview."

"I suppose that depends on who is asking the questions, does it not?"

Taking that as a signal, Aldridge set aside his teacup and stood up. "Again, I apologize for any inconvenience, Mr. Morland. My sister has orchestrated a dinner and dance tonight. I hope this will not influence your decision to attend?"

"Not at all, Your Grace." The magistrate was back to being affable, even managing a smile as he opened the door and ushered them out into the hall. "'Tis not easy to be quizzed about a harlot's murder, but one must make allowances. I certainly want this villain caught."

"That is what we all want, I daresay," the Duke agreed.

As they stepped out in the hall, Kendra caught the flurry of movement out of the corner of her eye. Turning, she felt a jolt of surprise as a creature right out of a horror movie raced toward them. The woman's skin so pale that it glowed as luminescent as the moon, yet was almost fleshless against the sharp bones of her face. The only color in that bloodless countenance was the dark half-moons beneath her sunken eyes, and the eyes themselves, glittering like black agates. Her hair was the color of dull ash, falling in a tangled disarray down her back. She wore what appeared to be a shapeless white gown, yards of fabric fluttering around her skinny legs as she ran. Her slender feet, Kendra noticed, were bare and dirty.

Kendra heard the Duke's swift intake of breath, then the woman was throwing herself into Morland's arms, oblivious to everyone else.

"Oh, Adonis! Where have you been? The harpy is here!"

Morland brought his hands up to grip the woman's upper arms, trying to disengage himself from her clutching fingers, but she wrapped herself around him like lichen. "Mama, where is Mrs. Marks?"

Shocked, Kendra thought of the portrait in the drawing room. There was no resemblance between that beautiful girl and this old crone.

"My God," Aldridge breathed.

Morland shot him an anguished look.

"He mustn't find us," Lady Anne whispered. "We must flee before it's too late."

"Hush, Mama. You should not be out of your rooms. You are unwell."

She began to pat his face with veined, speckled hands. "Adonis. My Adonis," she crooned. "We shall flee to Mount Olympus. He shall never know."

Morland grasped her wrists. "Mama, you must return to your rooms. 'Tis not safe for you to wander about."

"Oh, sir!" A woman built like a fire station and wearing a maid's uniform came trotting down the hall. "I'm most dreadfully sorry. She got away from me!"

Morland glared at her. "Obviously. We shall speak of this later, Mrs. Marks. Now, please take my mother back to her rooms."

"Oh, aye, Mr. Morland."

Lady Anne glanced around, her eyes widening in fear. "No! No!" She clutched at Morland. "She's a harpy. Please, Adonis—"

Mrs. Marks's beefy hands came down on the old woman's frail shoulders, pulling her away from her son. "Ma'am, we mustn't disturb Mr. Morland," she said in a surprisingly gentle voice. "Come along, dearie. Let's get you back to your rooms."

The black eyes blinked in confusion. Her face went slack as she stared at her son. "Who are you?" she whispered.

"Mama—"

"No! *NO!* You are not my Adonis!" Terror rippled across Lady Anne's face, and she shrank away from Morland. "No! No! Do not touch me!" She began to sob.

Mrs. Marks hauled the old woman to her side. "There now, ma'am. Would you like a nice cuppa chocolate?" She herded her down the hall, casting one anxious glance back at Morland. "We'll sit by the fire, you and me, and drink our chocolate."

"He's not my Adonis! Where is Adonis?" the old woman whimpered against the servant. They turned a corner and eventually Lady Anne's sobs faded, leaving a stark silence in its wake.

They stood frozen, locked into place by a myriad of emotions. Kendra exchanged a glance with the Duke, and saw horror and pity in his gaze.

"I apologize, Your Grace, for that scene," Morland said stiffly. He looked so dazed that Kendra actually felt sorry for him. "My mother, as I said, is ill."

"I had no idea," the Duke murmured. "I haven't seen Lady Anne since . . . well, since your grandfather died."

"Yes. It happened shortly after. She began to forget things. There were days she had to be told to eat or dress. Sometimes . . ." He swallowed hard, and stared unseeingly down the corridor where his mother had disappeared. "Sometimes she mistakes me for my father. Or her reality becomes blended with mythology. Mrs. Marks takes care of her, watches her." His lips twisted. "Or tries to. Despite my mother's failing mental capacity, she's canny enough to escape the woman."

"My deepest sympathies, my boy. I remember Lady Anne . . ." Aldridge paused and then sighed. "That is neither here nor there. We shall leave you in peace, Mr. Morland. Forgive our intrusion."

Morland nodded with an air of distraction, accompanying them down the stairs to the foyer. "I would prefer it if you would be . . . discreet about my mother, sir. I would not wish her name bandied about."

"Quite understandable." Aldridge hesitated. "If you should require any assistance . . ."

"Thank you, sir. I have brought in mad-doctors from London, but they say there is nothing to be done. I won't put her in a lunatic asylum."

"No, certainly not."

They stood in an awkward silence until the carriage arrived. Aldridge waited until the coachman flicked his whip, and the horses began trotting down the drive. The afternoon was sliding fast into evening and there was a chill in the air, but Kendra thought they were dealing with another chill that came from horror.

"My God," the Duke breathed. "I had no idea. Lady Anne is quite mad."

35

The sun was sinking rapidly to the horizon when they gathered again in the study. As Alec poured drinks, two footmen arrived to silently bring in wood and light a fire in the hearth, as well as lighting the candles and wall sconces.

Rebecca waited until the servants had departed before she revealed, "Harris was not at home."

Kendra accepted a glass of claret from Alec. "Not at home, literally? Or not at home to you?"

Rebecca gave her an astonished look. "My dear Miss Donovan, Sutcliffe is a *marquis*. I am the daughter of an earl. Mr. Harris is the youngest son of an earl. A *vicar*. He would hardly have *not* been at home to us if he *were* at home!"

Aldridge chuckled as he took a sip of his brandy. "I believe Miss Donovan is jesting, my dear. I explained to her the calling card etiquette during our visit to Tinley Park."

The aristocrat raised her brows. "You do not have calling cards in America?"

Again Kendra thought of her FBI badge. "My calling card was a little different. Where was Mr. Harris?"

"Out in the woods riding. Mr. Kelly, would you like a glass of claret, brandy, or whiskey?" Alec glanced at the Runner.

"Oh. Whiskey, thank you, sir."

"We shall have to interview him another time," Alec continued, passing a stout glass with a generous four fingers to Sam. "However, I am happy to report that we can eliminate Squire Wilding from our hunt."

"Yes." Rebecca sipped her claret. "The poor man is suffering most dreadfully from the unwalkable disease. Podagra," she added when she saw Kendra frown.

"Podagra? Foot pain?" Kendra translated the Greek phrase.

"Gout, Miss Donovan," the Duke added. "The disease of kings. The good Squire has a prodigious fondness for food—red meat in particular, if I recall. Which, I have been told, exasperates the illness."

"His big toe has swelled up almost to the size of a cricket ball," Rebecca informed everyone. "It's quite remarkable. He was in a chair with his foot raised on a stool with pillows. He can scarcely stand upright without two servants to carry him about."

"The Squire's misfortune is fortunate for us, then," Aldridge glanced at Sam. "What of you, Mr. Kelly? Do you have similarly good news to report?"

"Regrettably, no. Mr. Hawkings saw Lord Gabriel and Captain Harcourt at the beginning of the first cockfight, but couldn't swear they were around after. It was a crush, with more than two hundred men. They could've left."

Alec's mouth tightened. "I shall speak to my brother again."

Kendra shook her head. "I don't think that would be wise."

"He is *my* brother, Miss Donovan."

"Which is precisely why you shouldn't speak to him. You're too emotionally invested. You don't want him to be guilty. You may hear only what you want to hear."

"Don't be stupid. I am not deaf, woman."

"No, you're human," she snapped.

Aldridge raised his hand to curtail any argument. "Miss Donovan and I will speak with Gabriel tomorrow, Alec."

Kendra could see that Alec didn't like that idea, but he said nothing. After a moment, Sam cleared his throat. "I also learned that Lord Gabriel's companion, Captain Harcourt, has a hunting lodge in the area, and he's in dun territory."

That surprised the Duke. "I knew he had a hunting lodge hereabouts, but I had no idea about his financial situation. My sister must be unaware of it, as well. She is not in the habit of inviting fortune hunters to her soirees."

Rebecca looked thoughtful. "Mary told me that he was on the pursuit for a wife. Now I realize he must be looking for an heiress."

"Mayhap you should ask your maid who killed the girl," Alec muttered. "'Twould save us all time."

Rebecca ignored him, looking at Kendra and the Duke. "And what of your inquiry? Were you able to eliminate Morland from the list of suspects?"

Aldridge frowned down into his brandy glass. "Alas, no. Morland was very reasonably in bed during the night of the murder. However, we did discover something distressing. Lady Anne is quite ill. Her mind has shattered."

Rebecca's eyes widened. "Good heavens."

"We shall not speak of it beyond this room," Aldridge instructed. "We may be forced to inquire into these gentlemen's lives, but we must be circumspect in the information that we uncover. They deserve that much consideration."

"Though dementia has taken its toll on her, Lady Anne bore an uncanny resemblance to our victims when she was younger," Kendra pointed out.

"Yes, she does, but such coloring is hardly rare," the Duke said slowly. His eyes lifted to the portrait above the fireplace. "My wife and daughter had similar coloring—as you do yourself, Miss Donovan. Lady Anne's physical attributes may simply be a coincidence."

"Maybe. Either way, it's something to take into account. We also learned something else. You were surprised to see Lady Anne's mental deterioration."

Aldridge frowned. "Yes. She has become a recluse, but I had no idea that she was ill. Still, it is not something one would want known."

"Probably not, but people tend to talk. It's how Lady Rebecca's maid knew that Captain Harcourt was looking for a wife. Mr. Morland and his household are remarkably tight-lipped. They know how to keep a secret. I have to wonder what other secrets they might be keeping."

Everyone was silent as they considered that. Then Sam finished off his whiskey, eyeing the empty glass somewhat mournfully before he pushed himself to his feet. "A couple of me men arrived earlier ter help with inquiries. Unless you have other instructions, Your Grace, I'll be joining them. Tomorrow night, Hawkings'll have another cockfight. As it'll most likely draw the same crowd, I'll go and see if any of the blokes remember seeing Lord Gabriel or Captain Harcourt last Sunday."

"Very good, Mr. Kelly."

After the Bow Street Runner left, Aldridge stood up. "Tomorrow we'll continue this business. But tonight let us put aside these grim musings. Caro has arranged a dance to follow dinner. Mayhap we can enjoy the rest of the evening, eh?"

Kendra doubted whether she'd enjoy the evening. But if she had any inkling of what was about to happen, she would've come up with any excuse to stay behind.

36

A chill of déjà vu raced up Kendra's arms as she hovered on the sidelines of the grand ballroom. Six days ago, she'd stood in this very spot, watching Sir Jeremy Greene drink champagne beneath a blazing chandelier.

Now Sir Jeremy was dead, and the candles weren't cleverly designed bulbs, but real candles. The people around her were not playing roles in history—they *were* history, living, breathing history.

"I see Duke persuaded Rebecca to take a turn on the dance floor." Alec smiled as he came up beside her, looking outrageously handsome in his bottle-green cutaway coat, creamy cravat, and pantaloons.

She followed his line of sight to where Aldridge and Rebecca were doing some sort of robust dance that involved trotting high steps and multiple partners, their movements timed to the rich flute, piano, and violin notes played by the local musicians Lady Atwood had hired. Among the dancers, Kendra caught sight of Mr. Morland paired with Lady Dover, and Mr. Dalton with Sarah Rawlins. Harris and his wife were not in attendance.

"Would you care to dance, Miss Donovan?"

"God, no."

He laughed. "You crush me."

She gave him a look. "I doubt it. I don't know how to dance." *Like that,* she silently amended. In fact, she couldn't remember the last time she'd gone dancing—probably when she was fifteen and in college, and she'd felt awkward and out of place then. Younger than her college peers. *A freak.* Another moment of déjà vu.

Alec snagged two champagne flutes from a passing footman, offering her one. Silently, they viewed the dancers spinning by.

"What do you think of my aunt's little soiree?"

"Colorful." Kendra smiled slightly. She sipped the champagne as she watched the Duke and Rebecca clasp their hands high in the air, their bodies twisting in an intricate maneuver. "It reminds me of Jane Austen."

"Jane Austen?"

"Yes. You know . . . *Pride and Prejudice, Emma, Persuasion.*"

There was something in his silence that made her glance at him. His eyes were fixed on her. Kendra's smile faded and her mouth grew dry. What if she hadn't slipped back in time after all, but sideways, into a different dimension? String theory proposed the universe was made up with different membranes or planes of existence, alternate worlds. Maybe Jane Austen had never existed, or she'd existed but had never become a writer. That was the problem with time travel—there was more than one theory, more than one possibility.

She licked her lips. "Maybe . . . maybe I'm wrong about that . . ."

"*Pride and Prejudice* was quite well received, as I recall," Alec said slowly. "Rebecca is an admirer of that novel, as well as *Sense and Sensibility*. You have read them?"

Something was wrong, Kendra knew. But what? If Jane Austen existed in this time line, why was he behaving so oddly?

She swallowed some champagne, trying to think. "Yes." That seemed a safe enough answer. Except Alec's green eyes had taken on an intensity that made her palms sweat.

"Do you know the authoress?"

Alarm bells were now ringing. "Why do you ask?"

"'Tis a simple query, Miss Donovan. Do you know the authoress of the novels?"

"No."

He said nothing. Instead, he turned his head to watch the dancers as they whirled by. He didn't look like he was seeing the dancing; he looked like he was thinking hard about something.

"What's wrong?" she felt compelled to ask.

He glanced at her with a frown. Then he appeared to come to a decision, reaching out to grasp her elbow. "I would like you to come with me, Miss Donovan."

"Come with you? Where? Why?"

"To end this farce." His hand tightened briefly when she resisted him trying to maneuver her toward the door. After a moment, he dropped his hand and presented her with his arm. To all outward appearances, it would seem like a courtly gesture. But she knew it was a challenge.

"What are you talking about?" she demanded. Her heart was thrumming uncomfortably.

"Come with me and you shall find out."

Still, she hesitated.

"Don't be a coward, Miss Donovan."

Kendra shot him an angry glance. Although she suspected he was trying to goad her, she laid her hand on his arm, aware of the contrast of his coat's soft velvet and the hard muscles beneath her fingertips. As they walked to the open doors, Kendra realized they probably looked like any other couple strolling around the ballroom, the tension between them hidden beneath the ballroom's gaiety. Only the footmen seemed to be aware of it when they left the ballroom. Kendra could feel their curious eyes on them as they walked out in the hall.

Alec didn't speak, and Kendra found that she couldn't, her throat closing almost painfully. The music and murmur of conversation, punctuated with laughter, faded as they continued down the hall. Soon, the only sound was the whisper of silk from the evening gown she wore, their footsteps muffled on the carpeting and their own light breathing.

"Where are we going?" She forced herself to ask the question, needing to break the oppressive silence between them.

Alec didn't answer, ushering her around another corner. Kendra began to withdraw her hand from his arm, ready to have it out right here in the hall, but their journey came to an end in front of a pair of wide double doors. Alec opened them, and stepped into the shadowy room.

Like any animal scenting danger, Kendra kept to the threshold. Alec found some flint and lit nearby candles. Kendra didn't need the minuscule light to reveal the bookshelves and enormous paintings above. She hadn't spent any time here, but she knew this was the library.

"Please come in, Miss Donovan." Alec wasn't looking at her. He'd taken a candle and was now perusing the bookshelves on the right.

Shivering—the room was drafty, although Kendra wasn't entirely sure that was the cause of her goose bumps—she took three steps into the room. The nasty feeling in the pit of her stomach intensified. She was still holding her champagne glass, and now downed the remaining contents with one swallow. "Why'd you bring me here?"

He ignored her, continuing his search.

Her mind raced, and she tried to think what she'd said to provoke this reaction. Something about Jane Austen obviously. Jane Austen existed in this time line, and she'd written the books that remained popular in Kendra's own era. What could be wrong?

"Ah." Alec let out a sigh of satisfaction as he pulled a book out of the shelf. "I was certain it was here." He turned and came toward Kendra. "Now I have a question," he said softly. "Who the devil are you, Kendra Donovan?"

37

"I don't understand." Mouth dry, Kendra stared at the book in his hand like it was a ticking time bomb.

"'Tis a simple question." He kept his gaze fixed on hers, watching every flicker of emotion that crossed her face. "Shall we begin with this: Where were you employed before you arrived at the castle last week?"

She stared at him.

His mouth tightened. "Shall we take this from another angle, then? You told the Duke that you arrived in London in the month of May 1812. Yet your name does not appear on any ship manifest during that month."

"How do you—?" She remembered the suspicious look Sam had given her earlier. "Mr. Kelly. You had him investigate me when he was in London."

"Actually, it was the Duke who had the Runner send his men around to check on your tale."

"He never said anything." She turned away to set the empty champagne flute down on a nearby table. Her hand, she noticed, wasn't quite steady.

"My uncle is a most unusual man. He admires your intelligence, Miss Donovan. He has affection for you. He was hoping you'd come to him, trust him enough to tell him the truth."

She felt sick. "This has nothing to do with trust."

Alec lifted a brow. "Then what does it have to do with, pray tell?"

"You wouldn't understand."

"Not unless you confide in me."

"I can't."

"Why the devil not?"

"Because you wouldn't believe me."

"Who are you to decide what I would or would not believe?"

She pressed a hand to her churning stomach and simply shook her head.

"Are you an American spy?"

That made her blink. "What? No. That's ridiculous."

"A spy for the Irish rebels?"

"No!"

"Working for the French?"

"Oh, for God's sakes, no. No, I'm not working for any government." Not any longer. She'd left the FBI. Gone rogue—more than two hundred years in the future.

"Then I do not comprehend the secrecy."

She doubted he'd comprehend time travel any more.

"What are you hiding?" he asked softly.

Kendra had nothing to say to that. What the hell *could* she say? The truth? He would think she was crazy. She shuddered to think where she'd end up—a nineteenth-century mental hospital, probably. She had visions of screaming patients chained to beds, locked in deplorable conditions. She couldn't risk it.

The silence between them lengthened. Alec looked frustrated. Then he moved forward, handing her the book.

Kendra frowned, automatically taking it. Glancing down, she saw the title. *Pride and Prejudice*. Puzzlement mixed with the nerves that were leaping in her belly.

"Jane Austen. That is what you said, is it not? The authoress of that book?"

"Yes." Once again she was baffled by the intensity of his gaze.

"How did you come to know the authoress' identity?"

"What? Well, because . . ." Kendra's fingers trembled as she studied the hardcover, which was in pristine condition. Completely natural, she realized, for a book only a few years old.

Pride and Prejudice was engraved in gold letters on the red leather. Below that was inscribed: *By A Lady.*

Even though she knew what she'd find, she opened the book and scanned the inside page.

> Pride and Prejudice
> A Novel
> In Three Volumes
> By The Author of "Sense and Sensibility"

Nowhere on the cover or in the book was the name of the author.

Lies had a way of catching up with people, she knew. In the FBI, she'd always counted on it. Still, she'd never figured it would be something as innocuous as Jane Austen that would be the thing to trip her up. She lifted her gaze to Alec's eyes. "I can't explain."

"Cannot . . . or will not?"

She sighed and looked away. His hands came down on her shoulders, surprising her into swinging her gaze back to his.

Too close, was all she could think.

His green eyes bored into hers. "Do you fear someone, Miss Donovan? Are you in hiding?"

He was giving her a way out. She only wished that she could take it, spin a believable tale, but her mind was blank.

"My uncle shall protect you, Miss Donovan. *I* shall protect you."

"You thought I was a thief and a liar."

He frowned. "'Twould appear I was correct in half of that assumption."

Kendra realized that she had no right to feel insulted at his words. Or hurt. But she did.

"I will not judge you, Miss Donovan."

You say that now, Kendra thought. Regretfully, she shook her head and handed him back the book. "I'm sorry . . ."

He drew in a sharp breath. "You ask us to trust you with your unorthodox theories, and yet you cannot extend us the same courtesy."

"It's not the same."

"I do not agree with you, Miss Donovan. I believe it is very much the same."

The silence pooled between them again. He looked at her, and then his eyes dropped to her mouth. When he lifted his gaze, her heart was thumping with an awareness she didn't want to have. Deliberately, she took a step back.

"I should go to the study. Review my notes again."

"Escaping?"

"I need to work," she said, but they both knew it was a lie. Still, he didn't try to stop her as she walked to the door. She didn't run, even though she wanted to. It probably took five seconds for her to leave the library, but it felt like an empire could've risen and fallen in the time that it took her to reach the hallway.

She was half afraid that he'd come after her. Her heart raced. It continued to race when she reached the study alone. Her hand shook as she went about the task of lighting candles. She finally had to stop and do a couple of deep-breathing exercises to calm down. She had to focus. She didn't know how she'd come here—vortex, wormhole, whatever. But she'd begun to believe in the *why.* She was here to catch a killer. This was her purpose.

Catch the killer. Go home. The two had become firmly interwoven in her mind. She couldn't afford a distraction like the Marquis of Sutcliffe.

38

"W'ot's wrong, miss?"

Kendra was sitting on the bed, allowing Rose to practice her hairdressing skills by pinning up her hair. But her mind was replaying what had transpired the night before when Alec had neatly trapped her through her own words, and revealed that the Duke was aware that she'd lied to him. Odd how that bothered her the most.

He was hoping you'd come to him, trust him enough to tell him the truth.

Kendra recalled Alec's words, and felt the same stirring of dismay, guilt, and defiance that she had then. The last time she'd truly trusted anyone was when she'd told her parents that she wanted a say in her own future. And look at how well that had turned out. They hadn't even argued with her. They'd simply abandoned her.

She thought of the Duke's gentle blue-gray eyes. He wouldn't abandon her, she knew. But he might help her all the way into an insane asylum.

"Miss?"

"I'm sorry, Rose. I'm a little distracted."

"You seem a bit blue-deviled—" Rose broke off when the door flew open and Molly came running in. The tweeny was flushed, her eyes bright as she came to a halt, clutching the door.

"Lud! W'otever are you doin', Molly Danvers?" Rose exclaimed. "I could've skewed miss 'ere with the 'airpins if I 'and't been done!"

"Where's the fire, Molly?" Kendra echoed.

Molly's face went blank in confusion. "Oi dunno anythin' about a fire . . . but 'is Grace asked me to fetch ye!"

Kendra went still. Alec must have told the Duke about her deception, and Aldridge had finally decided to put an end to the charade. What, she wondered, could she possibly tell him?

"All right." She stood up slowly, and wiped her suddenly clammy palms on her skirt. "I'll meet the Duke in his study. I just need a moment—"

"Nay. Not the study, miss. The woods. That's where the Lady is." Molly's eyes were wide as she gave an exaggerated shiver. "She's *dead,* miss! Dead in a most 'orrible way!"

The woman was most definitely dead; Molly had been right about that. And how the woman had gotten into that state had indeed been horrible. She lay sprawled, faceup, eyes open, across one of the narrow paths, just inside the cool dappled green of the forest. A handful of men dressed in rough tweeds stood five steps away, staring down at the body. As Kendra approached with Alec and the Duke of Aldridge, the men doffed their hats—a courtesy that Kendra wasn't entirely sure was directed at her, or at the men.

"Did anyone touch anything? Move her?" Kendra demanded sharply, as she hurried to squat down beside the victim. This close, the grisly scent of death blended with the loamy earth odors. In a few hours, once temperatures climbed and morning slid into afternoon, she knew from experience that the smell would have reached her from at least a yard away. The body was relatively fresh.

The boy who'd reported the body and ushered them to the area answered. "Aye, well, me pa and Mr. Black over there, they turned 'er over, ma'am." His Adam's apple bobbed up and down in his throat as his eyes were drawn back to the dead woman. "We didn't know she'd stuck 'er spoon in the wall until then. Me pa told me to fetch 'elp."

"We thought she mighta been bosky, and fell down and 'urt 'erself," one of the older men offered. "We 'ad Martin 'urry ter the castle to tell ye, Yer Grace."

"You didn't carry her here?"

"Nay, miss."

Kendra frowned as she scanned the body. The woman appeared to be in her early to mid-thirties. Her head was tilted to the side, her face—it had been very pretty at one time—now mottled and marred with nasty scratches, dirt, and dried blood. Her eyes were blue, cloudy with the milky film associated with corneal opacity after death. The sunlight streaming through the canopy of oak leaves touched the hair tangled around her face, turning it into a nimbus of gold. She was wearing a long wool coat, flung open to reveal the brown silk inner lining and gown that had been candy-pink. The lower skirt was torn and soiled, and from the hips to the edge of the bodice, the fabric was stiff, stained nearly black with dried blood.

Absently, Kendra swatted at the flies buzzing around and crawling across the corpse. The blowflies had already begun their cycle of life and death, dropping their eggs to produce the maggots that fed on the decaying flesh. "She wasn't killed here. Looks like she was stabbed in the torso, near the heart, but there's no blood on the ground. She bled out somewhere else. She also appears to be missing a shoe. Anyone find a shoe?"

There was a chorus of negatives.

"I need to make notes, look around the area before we move the body," Kendra said, looking at the Duke. Perhaps it was because he was a scientist and understood the importance of documentation that he nodded.

He turned to the kid. "Martin, is it? Go and fetch Miss Donovan foolscap and writing implements from the castle."

"A tweezers and magnifying glass would also be helpful," she added.

Martin glanced at the Duke, who nodded his permission. The boy sprinted off.

"If she wasn't killed here, why do we need to worry about the area?" Alec wondered.

Kendra met his eyes. Last night was still fresh in her mind, but the dead woman lying at their feet trumped any feelings of discomfort. "You never know what you may find. I'd at least like the chance to find it before we trample all over it. Speaking of trampled . . ." She looked down the path. "This isn't the route to the lake, but it's obviously used."

"Yes. 'Tis often used by those who live in the surrounding area but work on the castle grounds," Alec replied.

"So he wanted her to be found," Kendra said softly.

"I believe you are correct, Miss Donovan," Aldridge said slowly, puzzlement in his blue eyes. "But why?"

Kendra had a few ideas. And because none of them were good, she simply shook her head. "Not here. Later."

The Duke crouched down next to the victim. "It looks as though the poor girl ran through the forest."

"Ran and fell down at least once, maybe more. The skirt around the knees is heavily soiled. She lost a shoe, but obviously kept running."

Terrorized, Kendra thought. The tights covering her foot were so shredded and caked with dirt and blood that it was impossible to determine their original color. "She can't have been out here that long. We've got flies and maggots, but no beetles or spiders. The animals haven't done too much damage either. The ears suffered the most. Soft tissue. Something's gnawed on the lobes. What time did you find the body?"

"A bit after seven," one man said.

Kendra did the calculations in her head. It was now eight-thirty. Ten minutes to the castle to report the crime. A little longer back since the boy had to wait for them. Even though they'd set off at a brisk pace, they hadn't been jogging. "What's your name?" she asked.

The man turned his hat in his hands. "Bobby, miss. Bobby Black."

"Does anybody know when the path might have been last used?"

Bobby Black darted a nervous glance at the Duke. "Oi can't speak fer anyone else, miss. But me and Reggie Carter came through 'ere last evenin', about eleven or so. We used it coming 'ome from the stables. The chit wasn't 'ere then."

"You're sure of the time?"

"Aye."

"And you're sure she wasn't here? It was dark. You could've overlooked her."

"Nay. We would've tripped right over 'er!"

Kendra looked at the Duke. "We'll need to interview the rest of the servants. Find out if anyone else used the path after Mr. Black and his friend went through. It will give us a window for when the victim was dumped here."

Aldridge nodded. His expression, as he scrutinized the corpse, was grim. "You were right, Miss Donovan. You predicted the madman would kill again, and he has."

"Yes, but . . ." Kendra frowned, her own gaze dropping to study the body again. "This isn't right. This is all wrong."

"I do not comprehend."

"Our killer has a type. It's his signature. It means something deeply personal to him, and he won't change it. It's not a whim that he targets young girls with the dark eye and hair color. This woman doesn't fit the victimology. She's opposite in every way—blonde, statuesque, and much older. She wasn't even killed in the same method as our Jane Doe. Look—no strangulation."

The Duke raised his brows. "I recognize the anomaly in appearance and even manner of death, Miss Donovan, but I refuse to believe we're dealing with two separate killers. The mathematical odds of that would be staggering. We're not in a large metropolis."

Alec reached over and threaded his fingers through the victim's tangled hair. It was easy to see that several sections had been hacked off. "This remains the same."

The sound of approaching feet—more than one pair—had everyone turning. Martin was trotting down the path, carrying the requested items, followed by several more workmen, and Sam and Rebecca.

Flies, Kendra knew, weren't the only thing drawn to death. There were always gawkers around crime scenes. That's why yellow tape was rolled out and a perimeter established.

Beside her, Alec sighed. "Becca, you shouldn't be here."

"Oh, stuff and nonsense, Sutcliffe! Mary told me another woman had been discovered . . ." She paled a bit as she stepped near to study the dead woman. "'Tis true, I see. Dear heaven . . ."

Kendra asked, "Does anyone recognize her?"

"Nay, miss," said one of the men. "She be a stranger."

She wasn't really surprised by that answer. Clothing often determined a person's socioeconomic status, especially in this era. Even damaged, she could see that the woman's coat and gown weren't that of a servant or someone in the lower classes.

"She's unfamiliar to me as well," Aldridge murmured.

"I can identify her," Sam spoke up.

"What?" Startled, Kendra turned to look at the Bow Street Runner. "You know who she is?"

"Aye. She was a cagey one—all bawds are. But I didn't know—didn't suspect—she was telling me a Banbury tale. I interviewed her during the course of my inquiries about the lass in the lake.

Her name is—was—April Duprey. She owns an academy on Bacon Street."

Alec frowned. "You showed her the sketch?"

"Aye. She claimed not ter recognize the lass."

The Duke said, "It would seem she lied to you, Mr. Kelly."

"Aye." He let out a sigh. "She lied."

Kendra caught his eyes, and knew what he was thinking: April Duprey had lied, and it had cost her everything.

Kendra did what she could. She walked the area. She studied the path. She made copious notes and a rough sketch of the perimeter and the body within it. Twenty yards, she judged, to the edge of the forest and open glen. Even though she didn't think it would mean a tinker's damn, she dropped to her knees and went over the dead woman with the magnifying glass and tweezers, carefully plucking some of the tiny twigs and leaves from her hair and placing them on the sheet of foolscap, which she folded into an improvised envelope.

"There's a slash through the glove on the back of her right hand, and what looks like blood," she observed, frowning. She slid the tweezers into the gap and pried off the leather, stiff now with dried blood, to view the cold, bluish-gray flesh beneath. "Hmm. It appears to be only one laceration. Odd."

"Why is that odd?"

She twisted her head to look at Alec. She'd forgotten she had an audience. Her eyes traveled to the dozens of curious eyes circling her. Remembering how quickly gossip had flowed through the castle with the last victim, Kendra shook her head, sat back on her heels, and sighed, "There's nothing more I can do here. We might as well move the body."

"To the icehouse?" Rebecca glanced between Kendra and the Duke.

Kendra shrugged. "There's a vacancy."

39

The woman was laid on the same wooden table as the first victim. The Duke's normally soft blue eyes were shadowed in the lamp-lit room, his expression forbiddingly grim.

Kendra looked at him. "Dalton can't do this autopsy."

"Yes," he agreed. "I see where that would pose a problem."

Sam cleared his throat. "Ah, Your Grace, I may be of assistance. I know a London sawbones that the Watch uses on occasion. Dr. Munroe—he was actually trained as a doctor before he studied in Edinburgh ter be a sawbones. He opened an anatomy school in Covent Garden two years ago. I can vouch for his character."

"Very good, Mr. Kelly. If you give me his address, I shall post a letter immediately."

"Well, as ter that, sir, I feel I should go back ter Town, show the sketch again ter the other light-skirts at the brothel. 'Tis clear Miss Duprey misled me the first time."

"I'd like to go with you," said Kendra.

Four pairs of eyes swiveled around to stare at her in shock.

Alec was the first to recover, shaking his head. "Impossible, Miss Donovan. You cannot venture into a brothel and consort with prostitutes. Your reputation would be damaged beyond repair."

Kendra raised her eyebrows and gestured to the body lying in front of her. "But it's all right for me to consort with dead prostitutes?"

Despite the grisly atmosphere, Aldridge's mouth twitched. "I rather think society would frown upon this, as well, but allowances have been made. Don't fret, my dear. I'm confident Mr. Kelly will be able to conduct this inquiry without your assistance. Now, I suggest we return to the castle. Nothing more can be done here until Mr. Kelly's man arrives to conduct the postmortem."

As they gathered in the study around the breakfast that the Duke had ordered, it occurred to Kendra that for all this era's finely tuned sensibilities, no one's appetite had evaporated. Then again, it was still a time when public hangings were viewed as date nights.

"Miss Duprey clearly saw an opportunity to extort money from the killer," Alec said, as he forked eggs and sausage onto his plate from a silver platter.

Kendra stared at them, suddenly feeling queasy. "It's my fault. I'm the one who thought to do a sketch of the victim and send it around to brothels for identification. If she hadn't seen that, she'd never have tried to blackmail the murderer."

Another thought struck her. Who was April Duprey? Yes, she was a bawd, but who was she in *history*? What if she'd been the great-great grandmother of someone important, like Francis Crick, one of the Nobel Prize–winning scientists who had helped map DNA? Would she return to her own time and find out that everything had changed because of this one incident? That DNA, so vital to police work in the future, might not even exist?

"It is not your fault, Miss Donovan," Aldridge said firmly, probably noticing how pale she knew she'd become. "The sketch was an inspired idea, but we would have sent out a verbal description to the London brothels. I daresay the woman would have recognized one of her own birds, particularly since she'd recently gone missing. Everything would have transpired exactly as it has. 'Tis the thread of fate."

Kendra began to breathe again. She wasn't entirely sure she believed in the thread of fate, but maybe she hadn't begun unraveling the fabric of time after all. Or did she only want to believe what the Duke was saying because the alternative was too awful to contemplate?

The Duke eyed her as he cut his sausage. "Something else troubles you. What is it, my dear?"

Kendra hesitated. She drank her coffee, and then gave a sigh as she set the cup down. "Blackmail is why April Duprey was killed," she finally said, "but it doesn't explain why she was killed *here*."

Rebecca frowned. "I do not comprehend. You've gone to great lengths to convince us that the madman lives in the area. He most likely has been luring Unfortunate Women here for the last four years. Naturally, he would kill Miss Duprey here. 'Tis part of his pattern, as you have said yourself."

"No. First of all, April Duprey is not part of his pattern. She looks nothing like his victims. She lived in London and he could have killed her there, probably without raising any alarm. Or why not kill her somewhere else in the country? Why *here*, specifically?" Kendra picked up her own knife and fork, concentrating on the meal as she let the words sink in.

"He killed her because she was attempting to blackmail him," Rebecca said, bewildered. "We agreed that it explains the anomaly of her appearance and age."

Kendra shook her head. "The unsub killed her because of the blackmail, but she wasn't someone he deliberately chose. In that sense, she wasn't a victim like the other girls." She paused, searching for the right word. "She was a liability. He could have eliminated her quietly. But he didn't."

"He didn't choose her, but he chose this area," Aldridge realized. "The fiend *chose* to put her body on a public path where he knew she'd be found. Why?"

Alec slowly put down his knife and fork. "He's trying to elicit a reaction."

"Yes." Kendra nodded. "That's what I believe. And that tells us something. He's watching and listening. You remember when I told you that he's escalating?"

Aldridge said, "His—what did you call it? His cooling-off period was becoming shorter."

"This is another form of escalation. He didn't expect our Jane Doe to be discovered. That was unexpected. Unplanned. But I think . . . it excited him.

"April Duprey doesn't fit his pattern," she added softly, "but he took the opportunity to use her to engage us."

Rebecca looked appalled. "*Us*? What are you saying, Miss Donovan? Are we in danger from this madman?"

"No," Kendra answered quickly—too quickly. She had to pause and consider that. Could she be so certain with her conclusion? "At least not yet," she amended carefully. "In my opinion, he'll become more unpredictable as the situation becomes unpredictable. As I said, control is important to him. He won't like it when things slip outside his control."

"Like the bawd being identified," Alec surmised.

"Yes. Exactly. He views this as *his* game, with *his* rules. He wanted April Duprey found. But identified? No. We've changed the rules on him; he just doesn't know it yet."

"And when he does?" Rebecca asked.

Kendra sipped her coffee, and frowned. "I don't know."

Alec looked across the table at her. "In the woods, you mentioned that the cut on the back of Miss Duprey's hand was odd. What did you mean by that?"

"It was, as far as I could tell, one laceration, through the glove, fairly shallow. Attacks using a knife follow a fairly predictable pattern. Either you're dealing with someone in a frenzy—multiple stab wounds—or you're dealing with someone who is controlled. They'll deliver one or two blows, but those tend to be mortal—in the thorax region, for example, aiming for the heart. I believe that's how April Duprey eventually died. Or the attacker goes for the throat, slicing open the jugular. Death is almost instantaneous."

"So the monster broke pattern in this regard as well," the Duke commented.

"And she didn't put up her hand to protect herself," Kendra said. "That would've been on the palm of the hand."

"He did it to get her attention," Alec said.

She nodded. "That's what I think, too. He wanted her fear. And *that* fits his pattern."

They fell silent, contemplating April Duprey's last moments on earth. She hadn't been tortured like Jane Doe, but she'd felt terror, hunted down like a wild animal.

Rebecca shivered, and pushed away her half empty plate. "Pray God that Mr. Kelly will get the name of the madman from the Unfortunate Women at the academy."

The Duke picked up his teacup and gave Kendra a curious look. "Miss Donovan, you said something else earlier about beetles and spiders helping you determine how long the poor creature was left in the woods. I would like an explanation."

Kendra had forgotten her comment, and now felt the weight of history pressing against her again. What to say? What not to say?

"Miss Donovan?" he prodded gently when she remained silent.

"There was actually a case in China—the thirteenth century," she finally said. That, at least, seemed safe to share. "When a villager was found in his field stabbed to death, the authorities determined the murder weapon was a sickle. They confiscated all the sickles from the victim's neighbors and observed how blowflies were attracted to one particular sickle. Even though the killer had wiped the blade, microscopic bits of blood and soft tissue were still on it—enough to attract blowflies."

"Why, how terribly clever!" Rebecca exclaimed.

"I am familiar with Francesco Redi's experiments, which proved that insects are attracted to decomposing flesh, as opposed to the Aristotelian abiogenesis theory, which purported spontaneous birth of maggots in decaying meat." The Duke nodded, and gave her a look. "I am not familiar, however, that Redi's experiments ever determined *time* of death."

Kendra stifled a sigh. Sometimes she wished the Duke wasn't so damn shrewd. Did she give them information that shouldn't be around for another forty years, when a French physician began using insect life cycles to determine time of death? Could *that* screw up the whole space-time continuum?

She pinched the bridge of her nose, and sighed again. *Fuck it.* "No one can give you the exact time of death. But as a general rule of thumb, beetles will arrive after twenty-four hours. Spiders later, since they feed on other insects. She was still in full rigor mortis and hadn't suffered too much discoloration yet—although that's the most imprecise measurement to determine time of death."

"I see. And as there were no beetles or spiders . . ."

"She was killed some time yesterday. And since we have a witness who says the path was clear last night around eleven o'clock, I'd say she was killed, stashed somewhere, and then dumped later. It gives us a window of time. We have our list of suspects. Now we have a new question to ask—where were they yesterday afternoon? I hope you have more calling cards, Your Grace. We're going to need them."

40

Unlike yesterday, Morland wasn't smiling when he came into the drawing room. His expression was shuttered, his eyes wary. "Good afternoon, Your Grace. Miss Donovan. Is this a social call, or another inquisition?"

Kendra suspected there'd be no offer of tea this time, either. "There's been another murder," she told him bluntly.

He raised his eyebrows. "Another light-skirt in the lake?"

"No. This woman was found in the forest, along a public path. She wasn't murdered there, but was dumped sometime after eleven last night and before seven this morning."

"How the devil can you deduce that?"

Kendra ignored the question. "Where were you during those hours, my Lord?"

Morland's mouth tightened. He was over the shock of being questioned, but not the insult. "I was in bed. Alone."

"What about during the day?"

"I seem to remember that you came to call," he said dryly.

"We arrived after two. Tell us where you were before that—and after we left."

Morland looked at the Duke. "Really, sir, must we go through this again?"

"I apologize, but it is necessary."

"Very well." Morland gave a put-upon sigh. "I spent most of the morning in my study, attending to correspondence that I'd been putting off. After my noon meal, I went riding. I viewed several of my tenant properties. I certainly was not out murdering a bawd, Miss Donovan."

Kendra decided to overlook the sarcasm. "Did you meet anyone? Or see anyone?"

"No one. I returned home, then you arrived. After you departed, I . . ." Here, he fumbled slightly. "I spent some time calming my mother. I spent the rest of the afternoon in my study, with my land steward. As you know, I attended the countess' ball last evening."

"I am aware." The Duke nodded.

"Did you know an April Duprey?" She watched him carefully. If he knew the name, she couldn't tell by his expression, which remained coldly hostile.

"No. Who is she?"

"Someone who misjudged a situation."

"That is a rather enigmatic answer, Miss Donovan."

"It's all I can give you right now. Can you give us a list of the tenants you visited yesterday during your ride?"

"I told you that I saw no one."

"Yes. But someone could've seen you."

He hesitated, then sighed, crossing the room to a table. It took a moment of dipping quill in ink, scribbling the names down, and sanding the paper. He handed the list to the Duke, but looked at Kendra when he spoke. His eyes were hard.

"I would not want my tenants harassed, Miss Donovan."

"I'll keep that in mind."

Dalton's home, Halstead Hall, was pure British Georgian: weathered red brick, white trim cornice, and sash windows, boxes, and lintels were an advertisement for stately elegance mired in tradition. The lawn, trees, and courtyard were ruthlessly neat and utterly symmetrical. Kendra wondered what that said about Dalton, if it said anything at all. He'd inherited the estate, so the order and control reflected in the mansion and its grounds may have more to do with past occupants than the present one.

As the carriage crunched to a halt, the white-paneled front door swung open, revealing the butler and a footman. For an era that had no satellite technology or surveillance cameras, no cell phone cameras to record a person's every move, Kendra was impressed at how little seemed to get past the servants' eyes.

Servants were vital strands woven into the fabric of this time. The grand manor houses and their corresponding grounds would cease to function without the chambermaids who emptied the chamber pots, the scullery maids who scrubbed the dishes and oiled the stoves, the footmen who carried in the kindling for the fireplaces and lit the candles, the gardeners who tended the grounds. In the English textile factories, the Industrial Revolution was just beginning, but it would be another hundred years before this particular workforce would find itself diminished and made obsolete by machines. Despite how heavily the upper class relied on the lower classes, Kendra knew it was the lowly worker who worried most about losing their job. She wondered if someone had observed the murderer, either leaving or returning. And if they had, would they risk their livelihood by talking?

They went through the calling card ritual. The footman returned with official word that Dalton was "at home."

He was waiting for them in a drawing room, looking like he'd just stepped inside himself. His dark, ash-blond hair was windblown, his cravat slightly mussed. The brown tweed jacket, darker brown breeches, and well-worn Hessian boots gave him the look of a proper English country gentleman. Faint circles shadowed his eyes, though, and Dalton flicked Kendra a guarded look, obviously still remembering their last encounter.

"Your Grace, Miss Donovan, I was out in the stables when I got word of your arrival. Checking the foal." He summoned a smile. "Would you like refreshments?"

"No, thank you," the Duke declined. "This isn't a social call."

"This is about the girl in the lake?"

"No. I'm afraid another woman has been found on my lands. Murdered."

"My God. I shall gather my tools for the postmortem—"

"No, that will not be necessary this time. I've sent for a London surgeon."

"I see." Something flickered in his gaze, but was gone so quickly that Kendra could only wonder at the emotion. "I appreciate you coming here to deliver the news yourself, sir."

Aldridge kept his eyes on the younger man. "Pray do not take offense, Mr. Dalton, but we must ask you a few questions."

Dalton nodded slowly. "I see," he said again. "Please, won't you be seated?" Once they had settled on the sofa, he said, "Miss Donovan has already quizzed me as to my whereabouts last Sunday. I suppose this visit will be in the same vein?"

"It would help if you have an alibi for yesterday," she admitted.

He said nothing for a long moment. "I cannot help but dislike the implication that I could have committed these crimes."

"We're not accusing you," she emphasized. "This is standard procedure."

His brow puckered in confusion. There was nothing standard about having a paid companion accompany a duke to question him about a murder, after all. But he spoke. "Very well. I spent yesterday morning in the stables, with the foal. My head groom and several stable hands can vouch for me. In the afternoon, my housekeeper packed a basket of food and I went fishing along the river, where I spent the remainder of the day."

"Alone?"

"Yes. 'Tis one of the many benefits of living in the country, Miss Donovan."

"Did you catch anything?"

"No."

"I thought the point of fishing was to catch something to eat."

He gave her a cool look. "Not necessarily. Fishing relaxes me."

"And nobody saw you?"

"Not that I am aware."

"What about last night, after, say, eleven?"

"I retired for the evening at that time."

"Alone?"

He flushed. "Of course."

"Do you know a woman by the name of April Duprey?"

He frowned. "I do not recall the name."

"Are you sure?"

"Quite certain."

"Can you tell me what happened to your wife, Mr. Dalton?"

He gaped at her. "I beg your pardon?"

"I know you were married before you came here. Now you are not. What happened to your wife?"

"My wife is dead, Miss Donovan." Dalton surged to his feet. Kendra thought she saw his hands tremble before he clenched them. "Sir, this is beyond the pale," he appealed to the Duke. "My wife is an unhappy memory, one best left in the past."

"I sympathize, my dear boy. However, given the unusual circumstance we're dealing with here . . ." Aldridge lifted his hands, then left them fall. "I'm afraid you must forgive our impudence."

Kendra suspected that Dalton would've loved to toss them both out on their asses, and the only thing preventing him was the Duke's social status. He stood silent for a long moment.

"I do not know how Marianne died," he said finally.

Kendra lifted her brows. "What do you mean, you don't know? How could you not know?"

He tossed her an angry look, then shifted his gaze to the Duke. "How much do you know of my family history, sir?"

"I am aware that your grandmother was Lady Ellen—and her father was the Marquis of Grafton. She married Mr. Peter Morse, did she not? His family was involved in the river navigation around Manchester."

"Yes. My grandfather's family worked with the Duke of Bridgewater to build the Bridgewater canal."

"A brilliant piece of engineering." The Duke smiled. "My father invested in the canal mania that followed. It was a lucrative venture."

Dalton seemed to relax a little. "Quite. My mother received a sizeable settlement when she married my father, who was a doctor in Manchester. Marianne's family lived in the house next door. She was eight years my junior. A pretty thing, but still a child when I left for university and later medical school in Glasgow."

"You followed in your father's footsteps," Aldridge commented.

"Not quite. He wished me to become a doctor. I was more fascinated by the surgeon's role. It caused . . . disagreements. I joined the military as a sawbones. When my father passed away, I returned home, and discovered that Marianne was no longer a child, but a beautiful woman." He shrugged. "Quite frankly, I was bedazzled. She seemed to feel the same. We married a month later, before I was required to return to my post."

He fell into a brooding silence. When he finally spoke again, his voice was carefully modulated. "We married with the blessing of both our families, but it proved to be a mistake. We moved to Dover, and I returned to my post overseas."

"You were involved in the Peninsular War, were you not?"

"You are well informed, sir. Yes. I was sent to Spain. It was a difficult time. So many men . . ." His voice trailed away. He shook his head and continued, "Naturally, because of the danger involved, I couldn't bring Marianne with me. She disliked being left alone. She disliked being the wife of an army surgeon.

"Marianne was beautiful, vivacious, and willful. She became enamored with a military officer stationed near our home in Dover, who, I believe, seduced her." His mouth tightened. "Of course, I knew nothing until she wrote a letter explaining how she wished to petition for a divorce. Naturally, I returned home to salvage the marriage, but it was too late. She'd already left with the man."

"My God . . . what of the scandal?" Aldridge wondered. "Did she care nothing of her reputation, much less your own?"

"As I said, she was willful. She and her lover fled to Geneva. I returned to my post and agreed not to fight the divorce. Marianne died before the petition went through. Her family sent me a letter to inform me of her death."

"You never asked what happened?" Kendra pressed.

"No. What would be the point? 'Twas too late."

She studied him. "When did she die?"

"Five, almost six years ago. But we'd been estranged for almost a year prior to her death."

"How long were you married until you separated?"

"Two years." He looked at the Duke. "Really, sir, I have nothing more to say regarding my late wife. You, of all people, should understand how painful these memories can be."

"Yes, Mr. Dalton. I am keenly aware of how painful memories can be," Aldridge acknowledged, and exchanged a look with Kendra. "Are we finished, Miss Donovan?"

"Yes. Thank you for your time, Mr. Dalton." She stood up. "I apologize for bringing up painful memories. It's not personal."

"Odd. It feels very personal to me."

He escorted them to their carriage and stood watching as the coachman flicked the reins, and the carriage started down the drive.

Kendra looked across at the Duke. "When did Mr. Dalton inherit Halstead Hall?"

"Five years ago."

"Hmm. The timing is interesting. He came here right around the time of his wife's death. Right before the prostitutes began disappearing." She glanced at Aldridge. "Do you believe that he doesn't know how his wife died?"

"No. But there are many reasons why a man would lie about a runaway wife."

That was probably true, Kendra reflected. Still, she wasn't convinced that was why Dalton was lying, though. She went onto something else that troubled her. "He never asked who April Duprey was."

"I'm cognizant of that fact, my dear. However, he knew a woman was found this morning. Most likely he made the connection."

"Maybe."

They lapsed into a thoughtful silence. Aldridge was the first to break it. "You appear to feel that the death of Mr. Dalton's wife could have transformed him into this fiend who kills prostitutes for pleasure."

"Not transformed. The unsub was . . . warped a long time ago. He had dark fantasies. As a child, he probably tortured and killed animals. Maybe even set fires. He was destructive. And then something set him off, a trigger of some kind that pushed him into making his terrible fantasies real."

The Duke gazed at her, troubled. "How, Miss Donovan? How does a man become a monster?"

"I don't know," she whispered. And she didn't. Were serial killers born that way, or did they become that way? Scientists had uncovered the Monoamine oxidase Agene on the X chromosome—also known as the "Warrior Gene"—which was believed to predispose men toward violence. But not everyone who had the defective gene exhibited violence. There were also plenty of examples of serial killers who'd been abused, physically and mentally, during their formative years, yet not all children who suffered horrific abuse turned into serial killers. It was quite a conundrum.

"If Mr. Dalton is the fiend we seek, wouldn't his wife's infidelity and abandonment actually have been the thing that pushed him? Why would he wait two years until her death to become a monster?"

Kendra felt a shivery sensation, like the brush of a bony finger against her nape. "There's another possibility," she said slowly. "Mr. Dalton was in the army. He said he lived in Dover. We need to check with authorities there to see if any young girls went missing. If Dalton is our killer, London might not have been his only hunting ground."

41

"Is this about the harlot in the forest?"

Kendra exchanged a glance with the Duke, before giving Harris her full attention. Moments before, the butler had escorted them into Harris's darkly paneled study. The vicar had greeted Aldridge enthusiastically and offered the usual refreshments. The Duke had declined, explaining that they were not making a social call, which had prompted Harris to ask the question.

"Who told you about the woman in the forest?" Kendra asked carefully.

He'd been ignoring her presence, but now the vicar gave her a condescending look. "Why, everyone is talking about it. 'Tis the news around the village."

"What exactly are they saying?"

"That another whore has been slain." He shrugged. "And the Bow Street Runner is investigating, although he has returned to Town."

Aldridge shifted in his seat. "Miss Donovan and I are assisting Mr. Kelly in his investigation."

"Indeed? How so, sir?"

"Please don't take offense, Mr. Harris, but we need to ask you about your whereabouts yesterday—and last Sunday evening."

"I do not comprehend, sir . . ." Harris's jaw loosened, and he regarded the Duke in astonishment. It was, Kendra thought, becoming a familiar look. "Are you, perchance, trying to connect *me* to the death of these whores, sir?"

"We're not making any connection. We are conducting an investigation," Kendra corrected. "It's standard procedure to question anyone who may have had the means to commit the crime."

Kendra remembered Harris's stare—like she was a peculiar creature that had crawled out from beneath a rock—from the first dinner she'd attended with the gentry. "That is very insulting, Miss Donovan," he said.

"It isn't meant to be."

"Why on earth would I do such a thing? Murder a whore?"

Kendra didn't like how he kept calling the victim a whore. It might simply be the manner of speech particular to this era, but there was an undertone of contempt, like she'd been less than human. Though prostitutes, regardless of era, didn't generate a lot of respect from their fellow citizens.

"You haven't answered our question," she pointed out. "Where were you yesterday?"

He looked down his nose at her. "I was writing my sermons, Miss Donovan. And I returned correspondence with my father. He is the Earl of Clarendale, you know."

It was a reminder. He wasn't a lowly vicar. He had *connections.*

"You were not at home when my nephew and Lady Rebecca came to call yesterday afternoon," Aldridge put in, drawing the other man's gaze.

Harris frowned. "No. They called in the afternoon. I was out riding. I often ride in the afternoon."

"But not this afternoon?"

"No. I had other matters to attend to."

Kendra asked the standard questions: Where did you go? What did you do? Did you meet anyone? See anyone?

No. No. No . . . *Yes* . . .

"I saw your hermit, Your Grace," he drawled. "I forget his name."

Kendra leaned forward. "You saw Thomas?"

Harris shrugged, as if he couldn't be bothered with such details. "He was in the woods. We didn't cross paths. I don't know if he saw me."

It wasn't really an alibi, Kendra thought. Even if Thomas could corroborate seeing the vicar, it only meant Harris had been out riding. But there was also the possibility that the vicar wasn't the only one Thomas had seen in the woods. She made a mental note to visit the hermit again.

"What about last night and last Sunday evening?"

"Last Sunday evening, my wife and I were at the castle. 'Twas the first night of Lady Atwood's house party."

"What time did you leave?"

"When the other guests departed—half past nine, I believe."

"What did you do after you left the party?"

"We returned home. And retired for the evening."

"Your wife can verify that?" asked Kendra.

"My wife sleeps in her own bedchamber as I do mine," he said stiffly.

She'd forgotten about the upper class custom of this era to sleep in separate bedrooms. "What about last night?"

He gave her a cold look. "We did not deviate from the norm, if that is what you are asking, Miss Donovan."

She switched subjects. "How often do you go to London?"

He looked puzzled by the question, but shrugged. "Rarely. I find the city vulgar."

"Do you know a woman named April Duprey?"

"No. Is she the whore found in the forest this morning?"

"She's the woman found murdered and dumped in the forest this morning."

His eyes were expressionless as he stared at Kendra. "I did not realize she had been identified."

"Yes, Mr. Kelly recognized her. That's a bit of good news, isn't it?" The Duke's smile didn't reach his eyes, which remained watchful. "It's only a matter of time before we identify the killer."

Harris picked an infinitesimal piece of lint off his sleeve, looking bored. Either he was a damn good actor or he was innocent.

"Good," he drawled. "Then we ought to be able to put this disturbing incident behind us."

42

"So much for the idea of the kindhearted vicar," Kendra remarked sarcastically. They had settled in the carriage for the short ride home, but she couldn't contain her anger any longer.

"Pardon?"

"What's *up* with that guy? He's . . ." *An asshole,* she wanted to say. "He's not exactly empathetic, is he?" she said instead. "He's a pastor. Women have *died*. Where's his compassion?"

Aldridge frowned. "He is not a vicar by choice, Miss Donovan, but by circumstance. There are very little acceptable employment options open to younger sons of the aristocracy. It's either the military or the clergy. His father, the Earl of Clarendale, asked me to appoint him to the vicarage here, not wanting him involved in the conflict with Boney. I saw no reason to deny him, although I fear you are correct about his lack of compassion for these Unfortunate Women. 'Tis troubling."

It would be even more troubling if Harris was responsible for their murders, Kendra thought. The Duke must have been thinking the same thing, because his expression turned dark, almost forbidding further discussion. They lapsed into an uneasy silence until the carriage came to a halt outside the steps of the castle.

The Duke of Aldridge chose one of the smaller drawing rooms in which to conduct the interviews with Captain Harcourt and Gabriel. It was comfortable rather than imposing, done in warm burgundy and muted grays. The footmen had been in to light the wall sconces, candles, and fireplace, which cast the entire room in a rosy glow.

Captain Harcourt was the first interview, and he came in with an expression that was polite but quizzical. Being summoned to privately meet with the Duke was both a privilege and a puzzle.

"You wished to speak with me, Your Grace?"

"Yes. I hope you are enjoying my sister's house party?"

"It would be impossible not to enjoy the festivities. Lady Atwood is a highly skilled hostess."

"Having two dead women murdered in the vicinity probably casts a pall on the revelries," Kendra said dryly.

Harcourt hesitated, shooting her a wary look, but nodded. "Yes. 'Tis dreadful."

Aldridge said, "Please sit down, Captain. Would you like something to drink?"

"A whiskey, thank you, sir."

The Duke poured a glass, and brought it over to the young man. "Miss Donovan? Do you wish anything?"

"No, thank you."

Aldridge settled himself into the wingback chair near Harcourt, and fixed his gaze on the man. "I'm certain you are aware that we are investigating the death of those two women."

"Yes, sir. I heard talk."

"Then you are also aware that the investigation forces us to ask awkward questions. I must ask you where you were last Sunday evening, and again yesterday afternoon and evening?"

"Yesterday I was in the grouse-hunting party," the captain answered promptly. He showed none of the insult that the other gentlemen had at being viewed as a possible murderer. But his social position was the lowest. Kendra suspected that made him more forthcoming, eager to cooperate.

"Major Edwards and Mr. Smythe can attest to the fact that I was with them," he continued. "Last evening . . . I was here, of course. I did not leave the castle."

"Thank you, Captain Harcourt. I understand that you and my nephew went to Hawkings's cockfight last Sunday after the dinner here at the castle. Yet we cannot verify whether or not you stayed the entire evening."

"Yes. Last Sunday was a terrible crush."

Kendra asked, "So you stayed the length of the cockfight?"

Something flickered in Harcourt's gaze. "Yes."

He's lying. Kendra's eyes narrowed. "And you were with Lord Gabriel the entire time?"

He frowned, dropping his gaze to the drink in his hand.

"That answer really shouldn't require that much thought. A simple yes or no."

He looked up at her. "Not the entire time, no. As I said, it was a crush. 'Tis easy to become separated."

"Did my nephew join the grouse-hunting yesterday?"

Harcourt shifted his attention to the Duke. "We rode out together, but he did not feel quite the thing. He returned to the castle."

"Alone?" Kendra wondered.

"Yes."

"So you don't know if he actually returned to the castle?"

"I had no reason to doubt him. He did not look well."

Kendra nodded. Leaning back, she gave the Duke a look, then said, "Thank you for your time, Captain Harcourt. I hope we did not inconvenience you too terribly."

"I may go?"

"Unless you have something else to add?"

"No." Harcourt got to his feet, gulped down the whiskey, and set the glass on a nearby side table. "Thank you, sir." He glanced at Kendra. "Miss."

Once alone, Aldridge said, "It will not be difficult to ascertain whether the captain remained with the grouse-hunting party yesterday. I found his manner about Sunday evening, however, evasive."

"I agree. There's something he's hiding about that night. Maybe Lord Gabriel will shed some light on it." Kendra was actually eager to interview Alec's younger brother. He possessed the most volatile temperament, which meant he'd be the most susceptible to pressure. If she applied just the right amount, she might even get some answers.

Harcourt was right: Gabriel did not look well. His complexion had a pale gray cast, his eyes sunken and bloodshot. As he entered the drawing room, he shot Kendra a sullen look, as though blaming her for his uncle's summons. Then he ignored her.

"Sir? You wished to speak with me?"

"Miss Donovan and I shall need to ask you a few questions. Please sit down, my boy."

Kendra watched as Gabriel flicked a hungry glance at the decanters on the side table. Then he swallowed hard and obeyed the command by slouching on the sofa opposite Kendra and the Duke.

"Where were you yesterday afternoon?" she asked abruptly.

He gave her a baleful look. "Who are *you* to question your betters, Miss Donovan?"

"*I* am giving Miss Donovan the authority to conduct these interviews, Gabriel," Aldridge said sharply.

"I apologize, Your Grace. But this is quite preposterous! Do you really believe I am responsible for the dead whores? That is what this is about, is it not? 'Tis madness!"

Kendra eyed him. "Why don't you want to answer the question?"

"Because it is none of your damn business!"

"Gabriel!"

Gabriel surged to his feet. He stuffed his hands into his pockets and began to pace. Kendra recognized nervous energy mixed with anger. And something else. *Desperation.*

"I went grouse hunting," he said.

"We were told you left the hunt early."

He glared at Kendra. "I was unwell."

"You returned to the castle?"

"Yes."

"What time?"

"I did not observe the time."

"Early afternoon? Late afternoon?"

"Bloody hell, I don't know. Late afternoon, I suppose."

"Did you leave the hunt and come immediately back to the castle?" Gabriel's sudden stillness had Kendra narrowing her eyes at him. "Don't lie. We'll find out the truth."

He scowled. Then gave a jerky shrug. "I did not return immediately. I went to the lake."

"Why?"

"Why not?"

The Duke gave a sigh. "Gabe, what did you do at the lake?"

Gabriel raked a hand through his hair, leaving it even more disheveled. He shot Kendra another dirty look as he paced. "Not a bloody thing! 'Tis a pleasant spot for reflection."

That pleasant spot was a crime scene a week ago, Kendra thought. She regarded him for a moment, then, coming to a decision, she stood. "What about the previous Sunday night when you said you went to the cockfight. Where did you really go?"

"I went to the cockfight!"

She moved in closer, until she was only a foot away from him, her eyes trained on his. He crossed his arms, an instinctive gesture, Kendra knew, against her invading his space. It was a technique favored by law enforcement during interrogations. It gave the interviewer the upper hand, a position of dominance, and it put the suspect on edge, made him more likely to talk.

She shook her head, and inched in closer. "No. I don't think so." She could see the sweat filming his brow. "You may have gone there, but you didn't stay there. Where did you go?"

He backed up, bumped against a cabinet. His chin jutted out belligerently, and he glared at her. "I didn't kill that whore!"

"Then tell us where you went."

"How dare you speak to me like this?"

"Gabe—" the Duke tried.

"Tell me where you went that night," Kendra persisted, crowding Gabriel.

He said nothing, only looked at her with glittery eyes.

"You don't like women very much, do you, Gabriel?"

He kept silent.

"What's that about anyway?" she goaded. "Something to do with your mother probably? You have mommy issues, Gabriel?"

His reaction was instantaneous. He turned bright red; his eyes bugged out of his head. "How dare you!"

Hot button, she thought, satisfied. Kendra leaned in, intentionally provocative. "I guess that's a yes. What, did she not love you enough? Or did she love you too much? Was she too controlling? You said it yourself. Women have their place."

"You—"

"My dear . . ." the Duke said uncertainly.

She ignored him, pressing, "Your mother controlled your life, didn't she? That's it. I'll bet she had you on a strict schedule. When to wake up—"

"Shut up!"

"—when to eat, when to sleep. I'll bet she even chose what clothes you wore."

"Shut up!"

"Gabriel!"

Out of the corner of her eye, Kendra saw the Duke rise, but she kept her attention fixed on Gabriel. "You're looking a little red, Gabriel. You know what I think? I think you don't want anyone to know the truth—that you actually hated her."

His breath was coming out in furious puffs. His mouth twisted with rage. His hands, now down at his side, were clenching and unclenching.

"What did she do to you?" Kendra kept up the pressure. "Did she punish you when you didn't do exactly what she said?"

"Damn you! Shut up! *Shut up!*"

"Gabriel—" That was from Aldridge, a low warning.

"Was that why you called her a manipulative bitch? Do you hate women, Gabriel? Do you hate women like you hated your mother?"

"No!"

Something seemed to snap inside him. She saw it in his face, in his burning eyes. Belatedly, a warning bell rang inside her head and she took a hasty step back, but it was already too late. He launched himself at her, his hands finding her neck.

"Shut up! Shut up!"

Kendra stumbled backward, completely unprepared for the attack. The back of her knees hit the sofa, and she fell down, with Gabriel crashing on top of her, his hands like a vise at her throat, squeezing. She bucked and twisted, her fingers trying to pry his hands away, her nails scoring bloody grooves into his flesh. Through the loud buzzing in her ears, she thought she heard the Duke shout. Above her, Gabriel's face loomed red and sweaty.

Monstrous.

Lungs burning, she abandoned her attempt to peel away his hands. Instead, she brought her own hands up to his face, positioning her thumbs against his eyes and digging down viciously.

He howled and reared back, releasing her and rolling onto the floor. He pressed his palms to his eyes, momentarily blinded.

"Jesus Christ!" Kendra gasped for air, her chest heaving. She caught sight of the Duke standing, his face pale, his blue eyes

pinpricks of shock. He was holding a beautiful old vase like a club. One more second and she suspected Gabriel would've been nursing a headache in addition to gouged eyes. Holding a hand to her throat, she got shakily to her feet. Her chest felt as tight as if she'd run a marathon.

"My God!" the Duke whispered, his gaze moving from her throat—which was already showing bruises—to Gabriel. *"My God . . ."*

Kendra bent over at the waist, hands on her knees, drawing in great gulps of air.

"Miss Donovan, are you—?"

"Yeah. I'm fine. Just give me a second. A minute. Maybe a *year.*"

She looked across at Gabriel. He was curled up on the floor, his hands against his eyes. Blood oozed from the scratches she'd inflicted.

As she stared, he slowly began to lower his hands. Sanity, she could see, was returning. His eyes were demonic red, the white cornea obliterated from burst blood vessels.

"I didn't . . . oh, my God, I . . . didn't mean to . . ." Horror filled his face. He looked at Aldridge. "Your Grace . . . *Duke,* I do not . . . I do not know what came over me! I *swear!"*

The Duke stared at him with matching horror. Carefully, he set the vase he held on a nearby table. His hands, Kendra noticed, were shaking, almost as much as hers. He looked at her. "Miss Donovan, are you all right?"

"Yeah . . . no lasting damage." Her voice was only a little hoarse.

His gaze fell to her throat. Fury sharpened his features and he wheeled around to confront his nephew, who was getting to his feet. "Dear God in Heaven, Gabriel! You nearly killed her! What kind of monster are you?"

The flush had receded, leaving Gabriel's face ashen. In contrast, his red eyes stood out, looking even more fiendish.

"I-I beg of you . . . I did not intend harm!"

"You put your hands on her throat! You throttled her! And you have the utter audacity, the bloody *gall*, to tell me that you *did not intend harm!*" Aldridge yelled, staring at his nephew as if he'd never seen him before. "Dear God, Gabriel, did you kill those women?"

Gabriel looked like he was going to cry. "No. I . . . I . . . *no!*"

"How can I believe that? You *attacked* Miss Donovan!"

"I don't know . . . I didn't intend . . ." He shook his head miserably. His fingers trembled as he ran them through his hair.

Kendra felt nauseous. She laid a hand on the Duke's arm. "Enough. Let him go."

The Duke shot her an astonished look. "I'm thinking of calling the bailiff!"

Panic crossed Gabriel's face. "I swear to you—"

"Let him go," she repeated. "I'm fine."

She didn't know who looked more stunned at the dismissal—Gabriel or the Duke.

"Miss Donovan—"

"Please."

Aldridge frowned. "I am not certain—"

"Please."

He sighed. "Very well, Miss Donovan. But only because you insist. Gabriel—leave. Go to your room. And stay there."

Gabriel hesitated only for a second, then he moved toward the door, his gait like that of an old man, measured but unsteady. The aftereffects of an adrenaline rush, she knew—she was feeling the same jittery nerves.

Gabriel opened the door and paused, glancing back at them. He looked as though he wanted to say something, his face twisting, but in the end he simply shook his head and left the room.

The silence was profound.

Aldridge sank down on the sofa as though his legs could no longer support him.

Kendra glanced over at the decanters that Gabriel had been coveting earlier. "I think I could use a drink. Do you want one?"

Aldridge stared at her like she was crazy. "Gabriel attacked you, Miss Donovan!"

"Yeah. I was there." Screw the sherry, she thought, and selected the more hard-core scotch. She splashed the amber liquid in two glasses, surveyed it in the soft light of the room, then added some more—what the hell? She brought a glass to the Duke.

"Cheers," she said, taking a hearty swallow. The alcohol burned its way down her tender throat and lit a merry fire in her belly.

"How can you be so calm about this?"

"I'm not calm." She sat facing the Duke, and lifted one hand. It was trembling violently. "Adrenaline's a bitch."

He stared at her for a full minute, then shook his head. "Miss Donovan, I don't know what to make of you."

When she said nothing, he lifted the glass to his lips and tossed back a healthy portion of the scotch. "God. Gabriel . . . I cannot believe it. I simply cannot believe that he attacked you!"

"I deliberately pushed him."

"There's no excuse for what he did!"

"No. He's definitely got problems. I didn't anticipate his reaction to become so . . . physical."

"Miss Donovan, this is not amusing! He most likely killed those women! He most certainly would have killed you. I still believe I should send for Mr. Hilliard. Alec . . . Alec will be devastated."

She took another swallow of scotch. "Gabriel isn't our killer."

He stared at her, bewildered. "You are now sitting there with bruises on your throat because he tried to *throttle* you!"

"I told you. I pushed his buttons, and he lost control. The unsub wouldn't have lost control so easily. I would've had to apply a lot more pressure than I did just now."

"You do not believe Gabriel killed those women?"

"I believe if Gabriel *had* killed those women, it would have been in a frenzy. That's not what we're dealing with." She thought of the calculated cutting of the torso.

Aldridge rubbed a shaking hand over his face. "Dear God. This is incredible."

"I don't think he's responsible for the murders, but I think he's hiding something."

"What?"

"I don't know." She frowned. "I'd like to find out."

"You truly do not believe he's responsible for the murders?"

"No. I do not."

"Gabriel just tried to kill you, yet here you are, professing his innocence."

"Not his innocence," she stated carefully. "I just don't think he's our killer."

"You are one hundred percent certain of your hypothesis?"

Kendra considered that. "Not one hundred percent," she conceded finally. "I'm ninety-nine percent certain. That's pretty good odds."

"And the other one percent?"

"I could be wrong."

43

Because she needed to think, Kendra went up to the battlements on the central tower. She welcomed the cool night air against her skin. Above her, the moon was a waxing gibbous. Without the artificial backsplash of a city to mute them, the stars were a billion brilliant speckles scattered across the night sky. The heavens were, she knew, brighter now, the planets and stars closer to earth. Two centuries closer in the expanding universe. She understood why Aldridge had set up his enormous telescope here on the roof.

Absently she massaged her bruised throat. She could still feel Gabriel's hands on her, squeezing, could still see his face contorted above her in mindless rage. She was more than a little annoyed with herself for not having anticipated the attack. She'd known Gabriel was unstable. She'd pushed and pushed until he'd lost control.

Still, she believed what she'd told Aldridge. Gabriel had lost it. And if both women had been viciously and uncontrollably stabbed, he'd be her main suspect. But they were dealing with a killer with ice water running through his veins, a killer who actually felt in control enough to taunt the investigators by deliberately positioning April Duprey's body across a public path.

The vast majority of serial killers existed in the darkest seams of humanity. They didn't want notoriety. They never sought to bring attention to themselves or what they considered to be their work. They went about their gruesome business, leading dual lives, as noiselessly, as unobtrusively, as possible.

Yet there were a few who made a game out of it. They enjoyed stirring up the media, provoking the police. *I'm smarter than you.* It was, Kendra knew, another form of control. Dennis Rader, the brutal killer in Wichita, Kansas, had even created his own sobriquet by using BTK—Bind, Torture, Kill—in his public correspondence. He'd taken special joy out of offering up detailed descriptions of his murders. And David Berkowitz, who had identified himself as the Son of Sam, had sent notes to the press and police, labeling himself a monster.

You couldn't be afraid of the monster under the bed if you didn't know he was there. With April Duprey's body, the monster had let them know he was there. And he wanted to play.

She rubbed her arms, mentally reviewing the interviews that they'd conducted. Harcourt's alibi for yesterday held up—the Duke had questioned the men in the hunting party; they'd insisted the captain had been with them the entire time. But she wondered what he was hiding from the previous Sunday night. It didn't really matter, she supposed, except for being a loose thread—and she hated loose threads.

Except for Gabriel, who'd gone off like a rocket, the rest of the men had exhibited remarkably similar behavior during the interview process, voicing insult, anger, outrage. They'd also cooperated. Or appeared to cooperate.

Something tickled at the back of her mind. She frowned. Mentally, she flipped through the interviews. Someone had said something that was just a little bit off. *What was it?* But it remained elusive, as bothersome as an itch she couldn't scratch.

Then another sensation assailed her, a cold prickle at the back of her neck. This time she could pinpoint the source: she knew that she was no longer alone on the roof.

Slowly, she pivoted to peer into the thick shadows below. As she watched, one shadow detached itself, solidifying into the silhouette of a man. She tensed when the silvery rays of the moon fell across Alec's chiseled features.

As he walked toward her, she moved to the short flight of stairs that led off the battlements to the roof. He met her halfway, lifting his hand for assistance. She hesitated briefly, then placed her hand in his, feeling the warmth of his palm against her chilly fingers. His gaze flicked to the marks circling her throat, and his hand tightened around hers. The green eyes were colorless in the moonlight. Kendra tried to identify the emotion flaring in them. Anger, yes. And, she thought, remorse.

"Gabriel did this to you?" He lifted his other hand, fingertips grazing the discolorations. His touch was featherlight, but her skin tingled from the contact. "You warned me. This is my fault."

"No."

"He's my brother."

"You're not your brother's keeper."

"By God, he needs a keeper!" He frowned, puzzled. "Duke said you don't believe he killed those prostitutes."

"Did he tell you what I base my conclusions on?"

"He lacks control, or some other such nonsense."

It probably did sound like nonsense to them. "We're looking for a very specific sort of individual," she told him. "I deliberately gave your brother a great deal of stress to see how he'd react. I knew that he was . . . sensitive about his mother. I used that against him. Do you understand?"

"I understand Gabriel tried to strangle you, Miss Donovan. The first girl *was* strangled."

"It's not the same." She folded her arms in front of her chest. "Someday, someone will push him and he'll have a weapon in his hand, or he'll strangle someone who can't fight back. But it'll be an impulsive act. Hot-blooded."

Alec gave her a somber look. "I do not know what to do with him."

"Intense psychotherapy maybe."

"Pardon?"

She sighed. "Maybe you should just try talking to him?"

"Don't you think I haven't tried?" he began, and then paused, shaking his head. He was silent for a long moment. When he spoke again, it wasn't about his brother. "You're shivering, Miss Donovan."

She shrugged away his concern, but he was already taking off his jacket, dropping it over her shoulders. His hands stayed there, his eyes darkening as he stared at her.

She was intensely aware of him, every detail, from his lean strength, the warmth of his body, the smell of his skin, the way his dark hair fell against his forehead. The tingle she'd felt earlier became a hum. She knew he was going to kiss her. She just didn't know how she felt about it.

Still, she didn't step back when he slid his fingers into her hair to cradle the back of her head. The action nudged her closer. She hesitated rather than resisted, her mind spinning with all the reasons why this was a bad idea. *Too many reasons.*

"Kendra," he whispered.

It was, she realized with a jolt, the first time he'd ever said her name. In this era, where the formal address was used even between husbands and wives, it seemed intensely intimate. How would she feel when he actually kissed her?

She had only a half a second to wonder before he *was* kissing her, his lips pressing against hers, softly at first, then more deeply, with growing passion. Her brain seemed to short-circuit, overwhelmed by the sheer physical pleasure of his stroking tongue, his slanting mouth. Hazily, she was aware of his hands moving up and down her back. She pressed closer, the jacket sliding off her shoulders as she wrapped her arms around his neck, her fingers tunneling through his thick hair, giving as good as she got.

She was shivering again, but this time it was from excitement. And a deep hot need.

He pulled back slightly to give her a look, eyes gleaming black in the moonlight. Then he tightened his arms, and bent for another long, savoring kiss that was as earth-shattering as the one before. Kendra didn't know how long it went on—the guy could kiss—before she pulled back. "Wait. *Wow.*"

Deprived of her mouth, Alec nibbled a sizzling path across a high cheekbone to her ear. She was out of breath. It made her instantly wary. She'd known there was an attraction—and how tepid that word sounded. *Attraction* she could handle, that slightly warm undercurrent, the glow. The buzz. But this was somehow . . . *more.* It was too intense, too intimate. She felt as though her skin was on fire, her bones melting against the hard length of his body. As his mouth found a sensitive spot below her ear, she clutched at his shoulders and arched against him.

I don't belong here.

Blood pounded in her ears. "We can't do this."

"I believe we can," he murmured, and brought his mouth back to hers.

She was again breathless by the time they finally eased away from each other. With more than a little satisfaction, she noticed that he was breathing heavily as well.

Then he blinked. He looked like he was coming out of a dream, and entering into something unpleasant. "Good God, what am I doing?"

"I assume that's a rhetorical question."

He dropped his hands and stepped away from her. "Forgive me, Miss Donovan."

Miss Donovan again.

"It was just a kiss." A really *good* kiss, a freaking *fabulous* kiss. But still.

He gave her a strange look. "My actions are inexcusable. I am no better than my brother."

"You didn't try to strangle me."

"I took advantage of you! It could be said that I compromised you."

They were alone, and they'd kissed. In this era, that was enough to force the issue of marriage. No wonder he looked so freaked out. *Men*, she thought. Regardless of century, they always believed they were the center of a woman's world.

Although, she had to concede, in this era, that assumption was understandable. Women had few resources outside of marriage available to them, and with Alec's good looks, title, and fortune, he'd probably spent most of his life dodging women whose biggest ambition was to drag him up the aisle.

"*I* won't be saying that." Her irritation increased when she recognized the wariness and skepticism in his gaze. He looked like an animal that had just realized it was sitting in the middle of a trap. "You're safe, Lord Sutcliffe. I'm not interested in marrying you, or anyone else."

"You have no wish to wed?"

"Don't sound so shocked. I've got more things on my mind than marriage, my Lord." Like finding a murderer. And going home.

April Duprey.

They knew her name. The Bow Street Runner had gone to the establishment on Bacon Street to ferret out more information.

He'd been careful, he reminded himself. His only dealings had been with the bawd and her little whore. Still, what if they'd confided in another strumpet? Would he get another note? Another extortion attempt? Or would they whisper his name to the thief-taker?

The thought sent panic skittering through him, followed by a molten rage.

It's the bitch's fault!

Kendra Donovan.

He stood in front of the window, staring into the night, and thought of yesterday with the whore. The memory exhilarated him. He remembered the utter power that had flooded him when she'd looked at him with shock after he'd cut her. When she *knew*.

She'd stumbled back, then. And ran.

Her golden hair had come undone, catching in branches as she'd plunged heedlessly through the forest. It must have caused her pain, but she never once stopped. Sometimes, she had tripped. Yet she'd scampered to her feet quickly, looking back at him, her face white with terror. She hadn't known that he'd kept his horse reined in so as not to trample on her and finish the game too quickly.

Closing his eyes, he smiled, recalling how the whore had fallen the last time. It was as though she'd known it was the end. She'd been crying, her face streaked with dirt and tears, and she'd begun pleading with him, bargaining, offering herself, offering her other whores.

He'd smelled her fear.

She'd tried to crawl away. He'd straddled her. She'd been mesmerized by the blade as he deliberately raised it above her, then held it for a moment, before he'd thrust it into her chest.

The experience had been . . . pleasurable. But not satisfying, not like the others. She'd died too quickly. Not that he'd ever had any intention of playing with her as he had the others. To put his mark on her—the desire simply wasn't there.

This had been a different game entirely.

As he thought of the others, his skin tightened. The pressure built. He opened his eyes, staring at his own reflection in the glass windowpanes. This time, when he thought of Kendra Donovan, he felt calmer. He was in control. An idea began to take shape, and he smiled. He would teach the bitch a lesson.

Soon.

44

If Finch was surprised to find Alec knocking on Gabriel's door at half past eight in the morning, he didn't show it. He cast a hasty glance into the room behind him, then departed without a word. Alec closed the door, frowning at his brother, who was soaking in a copper tub, a rag over his eyes. With a glass of whiskey on the floor.

The sight infuriated Alec. "'Tis morning, Gabe."

"What are you, the bloody Watch now, Sutcliffe?" Gabriel muttered, and pulled the rag away from his face so he could squint up at Alec.

Even though he'd been expecting it, Alec was startled by his brother's appearance. The violet shadows beneath his eyes looked like someone had given him two shiners. The eyes themselves were such a burning red that it almost hurt to look at him.

"I see Miss Donovan left her mark on you, as you did her."

Gabriel's face darkened. "Bugger off!"

"No. Hell and damnation, you attacked her, Gabriel!"

Gabriel let his head fall back against the rim of the tub, closing his eyes with a grimace. "I didn't intend to . . . it was her fault. She kept nattering away. I told her to shut it. She didn't listen."

"And you think that gives you the right to lay hands on her, to attempt to strangle her? Christ, Gabriel."

"Goddamnit!" Abruptly Gabriel sat up, the water sloshing over the rim of the tub. Glaring, he gestured to his eyes. "Look at what she did to *me*! She nearly blinded *me*!"

Alec stared at his brother in disgust. "Kendra only defended herself."

"She's a bitch."

Alec's hands curled into fists. It took all his effort to keep calm, to not give in to the desire to haul the younger man out of the water and plant a facer on him. "Have you no remorse for your actions?"

Gabriel dropped his gaze, studying his knees poking out of the water, and said nothing.

"Oddly enough, Miss Donovan no longer believes that you had anything to do with the death of those girls." Alec watched Gabriel's face closely, and saw the jolt of surprise. He pressed his advantage. "Where did you go on the first night of the house party?"

Gabriel scowled.

"Dammit, Gabe—"

"What does it matter, if you say Miss Donovan no longer believes I killed the whores?"

"You lied about your whereabouts. You did not stay the evening at Hawkings's cockfight. Why?"

"'Twas a private affair."

"For God's sake, Gabriel, if you were sleeping with some chit or somebody's sodding wife, tell me now!"

Gabriel surged to his feet, water dripping down his naked body. He reached for the folded towel that Finch had laid on a nearby chair and began rubbing himself dry. "I do not need to tell you a damn thing." He shot him a sullen look, stepping out of the tub. He wrapped the towel around his waist. "You and I may share a father, but we share nothing more. Do you hear me?"

Alec studied his brother. "I hear you. Now you hear me. If you lay another finger on Kendra Donovan, I'll break it and every goddamn finger in your hand, before I finish with the rest of your miserable body."

Gabriel absorbed the threat in silence, then curled his lip. "'Tisn't like you to become involved with the servants, Sutcliffe."

Alec tensed, once again surprised by the fury that rolled through him, the desire to beat the younger man into a bloody pulp. Keeping a tight rein on his temper, he turned and, with measured steps, went to the door. There, he paused and glanced back at his brother with a warning look. "Remember what I said, Gabe."

He waited, and when Gabriel said nothing, he let himself out of the bedchamber.

Alone, Gabriel bent down and snatched the whiskey glass off the floor. For a long moment, he stared down into the amber liquid. Kendra Donovan no longer believed him to be the monster responsible for killing the harlots. But instead of relief, he felt confusion. How could she be so certain when he couldn't be absolutely certain himself?

Sam Kelly and the London medical examiner, Dr. Munroe, arrived at nine A.M., which must have meant they'd been on the road at dawn. Certainly, the Bow Street Runner's elfin features looked even more drawn. He'd washed his face, wetted down his curly hair, but he hadn't bothered to shave since yesterday. The result was like an elf who had gone on a bender. His golden-brown eyes were red, but, unlike Gabriel, it wasn't from whiskey—or her thumbs—but lack of sleep.

Kendra turned her attention to Dr. Munroe. He was a big man who looked to be in his early fifties, with black brows that contrasted sharply with a thick silvery mane he'd brushed back from his square face and tied into a ponytail, a style that had been popular in the eighteenth century and would become popular again among aging Hollywood producers, fashion designers, and artist-types in a few centuries. His dark gray eyes were piercing behind Harry Potter–type gold spectacles, pinched into place on the bridge of his hawk-like nose.

Aldridge was in the process of introducing the coroner when the door was flung open and Rebecca came flying into the room. She halted, her eyes automatically going to Kendra's throat. Her lips tightened. "How are you feeling this morning, Miss Donovan? The damage looks even worse today than yesterday."

Aware of everyone staring at her, Kendra gave an embarrassed shrug. "I'm fine." She wished that she could cover up the contusions somehow, but none of the dozens of gowns Rebecca had bought for her had high necklines. And she could hardly run out to a corner drugstore to buy a bottle of Maybelline cover-up. Her only consolation was that Gabriel would have a bigger problem concealing his bloodshot eyes.

"I have apprised Mr. Kelly and Dr. Munroe of Gabriel's shocking outburst," said the Duke, "as well as your opinion that he is not responsible for these monstrous acts."

Sam gave her a curious look. "How can you be certain, if you don't mind me askin', miss? His violence seems ter fit your pattern."

Because there was a pot of coffee (as well as pots of tea and chocolate) on the side table, Kendra walked over to pour herself a cup. "No, that's my point. Lord Gabriel reacted emotionally when I pressed him. The man responsible for these murders wouldn't have been so rash."

Sam didn't look entirely convinced, but was distracted when the door opened again, and Alec came strolling in. Aldridge quickly made introductions.

"When will you do the postmortem, sir?" Rebecca asked Munroe, her forthright manner earning a surprised look from the doctor.

Alec sighed. "Dr. Munroe, do not be put off by this hoyden's blunt manner."

Rebecca sniffed. "I would think, given Dr. Munroe's profession, that it would take more than my blunt manner to put him off."

Munroe smiled. "I shall begin my work shortly. First, though, I have a few questions. I have been informed that Miss Donovan has a rather unusual expertise in this area, but my topic of discussion may be rather gruesome. I would protect your delicate sensibilities, your Ladyship. Perhaps you ought to retire from the room until it is concluded?"

Kendra hid a smile as she watched Rebecca's eyes narrow.

"I do not see why I ought to do any such thing. I have been involved in these proceedings much longer than you have, my good man!"

Munroe lifted a dark brow.

"Lady Rebecca is progressive in nature—as are we all," Aldridge remarked mildly.

"Does that offend *your* sensibilities, Dr. Munroe?" Rebecca inquired pertly.

"Many of my colleagues are advocates of Aristotle's theory of human development," Munroe replied, "which purports that women's energies are concentrated in their reproductive organs rather than their brains."

Rebecca gave the doctor a stony stare. "You ought to find better colleagues, Doctor."

He grinned suddenly. "Aye. I agree with you, your Ladyship. Sadly, too many of my esteemed colleagues are stuck in the past. We are living in a dynamic time. New discoveries are made daily. To move forward, I believe, one must keep an open mind."

"Excellent. Now that that's settled, I suggest we get down to business." Aldridge sat down behind his desk, turning his gaze to the Bow Street Runner. "I have not had the chance to ask Mr. Kelly what transpired in Town."

Sam grimaced, and shook his head. "None of the birds at the academy could identify the devil. But I did get a name for the lass in the lake. Lydia Benoit. Not her true Christian name, I suspect."

"Ah, yes," Munroe said. "A nom de guerre. Lady birds enjoy a touch of the exotic. They believe it enhances their appeal. In this case, terribly ironic."

Rebecca glanced at him. "How so, Dr. Munroe?"

"'Benoit' means blessed."

A grim silence settled over the company. Then Sam cleared his throat. "She'd worked at the brothel for a year. The other birds liked her well enough. Seemed proper shocked that she'd cocked up her toes. They remembered that the bawd—Miss Duprey—had hired her out, which was a rare thing. Miss Duprey tended ter be cheeseparing with the lasses, so whoever it was had ter be plump enough in the pockets ter get the bawd ter agree."

"But they have no idea as to his identity?"

"Nay."

Kendra frowned as she sipped her coffee. The niggling sensation was back. Something . . . something . . . what was it? It brushed at her consciousness with fragile butterfly wings, before fluttering away. She had to let it go.

"April Duprey had to contact the killer somehow. Is there any way to track that?"

"I don't see how," Sam said. "She had her footman post the letter—an unusual enough occurrence for him ter take note. But as he can't read, he had no way of knowing who was on the receiving end."

Kendra let out a frustrated sigh. Would every lead turn into a dead end? She set her coffee cup down, and walked over to the slate board. Picking up a piece of slate, she crossed off the name of Jane Doe, and wrote Lydia Benoit. It didn't matter that it probably wasn't the name that the girl had been born with. Anything was better than the anonymous Jane Doe. Maybe Rebecca was right; it was important for a soul to be identified.

"Captain Harcourt has an alibi for the time April Duprey was killed," she said. "I don't think he and Gabriel are telling the truth about their whereabouts on the night Lydia was killed, but for the reasons I've already stated, I think we can cross them off the list and focus elsewhere."

Munroe joined her at the slate board. "'Tis an unusual assortment of observations you have written here, Miss Donovan. Yet I have to ask: are these facts, or conjecture?"

Kendra considered that for a moment. "You could say it's conjecture based on facts."

"I see."

"It is most unusual, but Miss Donovan takes a scientific approach to crime," said Aldridge. "One that involves deductive reasoning."

"That is unusual, sir."

Kendra couldn't tell if the doctor believed in the process, but she wasn't going to try to convince him. She had the Duke's support, and that was all that mattered.

She looked at Sam. "Did you find out anything about Dalton's late wife?"

He gave her an incredulous look. "I only dispatched a man ter ride up north ter make inquiries. 'Tis several days' ride. Me men in the area here are still questioning servants. Maybe someone'll have something ter say."

No matter how complex an investigation, it always boiled down to the basics, Kendra thought. Canvassing the neighborhood, questioning colleagues, friends, family, neighbors. The techniques changed, but the approach remained timeless. There was something comforting in that.

Munroe set aside his teacup. "'Tis time for me to meet April Duprey. God willing, she will have something to say as well."

45

Dead men could tell tales, Kendra knew. So could dead women. In the future, science would give voices to the dead with such discoveries as chromatography at the turn of the century, and then luminol and the scanning electron microscope in the 1930s. And, of course, the most valuable tool of her time, DNA typing, which law enforcement would begin to make use of in the mid-1980s—more than a century from now.

What tales could April Duprey possibly tell, she wondered, with such primitive tools at their disposal?

They gathered around the body. Everyone except Rebecca, who, despite her protests and the gentlemen's proclamations for being progressive thinkers, couldn't bridge this era's gap between the sexes. Nor the class system, Kendra suspected. Rebecca was a *Lady*. And ladies had more delicate sensibilities than a woman from the lower classes.

They had yet to determine where Kendra belonged. Even though Munroe had seen her "handiwork" on the slate board, he gave her a critical look over April Duprey's body. "Do you understand what is involved in a postmortem, Miss Donovan?"

"Yes."

"I shan't catch you if you swoon."

"I'll keep that in mind."

He was silent for a moment, then shrugged. "As you wish. I shall begin with an external examination."

Dr. Munroe discarded his jacket and cravat, rolled up his sleeves, and put on something that reminded Kendra, a bit ghoulishly, of a butcher's apron. He leaned over the body. "If someone could assist me by holding the lantern to give me better light?"

Kendra picked up one of the lanterns that had been brought into the gloomy room, angling it so the amber light fell directly on the woman's pale face.

"Thank you, Miss Donovan."

With interest, she watched Munroe slide several sheets of foolscap beneath the head, then begin to work a comb through the tangled hair. "Looks to be mostly twigs, leaves . . ." He dumped the debris into the glass vials he'd lined up on the table behind him.

"Lacerations on the face, varying sizes. Looks to be from branches." He moved down the body. "She appears to have been cut on the back of the hand."

"From a knife, and only once," Kendra pointed out.

"Yes. I can see that." He did what she had, taking a tweezers and magnifying glass for the initial inspection. "I shall need to remove the glove."

He attempted to remove it manually, but dried blood and moisture and internal gases that bloated the dead woman's hand had effectively glued the leather to the skin beneath. Abandoning the effort, the doctor cut off the glove and then scrutinized the hand.

"Shallow knife wound," he observed.

"It's not a defensive wound," Kendra felt compelled to add. How much did he understand about forensic pathology? How much did anyone in this century?

Munroe regarded her through his Harry Potter glasses. "I am aware of defensive wounds, Miss Donovan."

"Oh."

He turned back to the body. "In fact, there appear to be no defensive wounds. The attacker clearly surprised her, and she ran. The palms of her gloves are heavily soiled, indicating that she fell several times during her ordeal. Her palms are abraded. This corresponds with the area of the glove that is most heavily soiled."

Kendra had to admit that she was impressed by the doctor's thoroughness in his visual examination. He used the tweezers to pick off more debris from the bodice and skirt, and carefully inspected the foot with the missing shoe. With the help of Alec and Sam, he turned the body over to make the same detailed journey from that angle.

"There appears to be some sort of discoloration across the upper part of her pelisse, spanning the right shoulder blade." He examined it through the magnifying glass, asking Kendra to move the lantern closer. "Dark gray in coloration. It does not appear to be a soil stain, though. I must examine the fabric under a microscope to reach any sort of conclusion."

"You are welcome to use my laboratory, Dr. Munroe."

"Ah. Thank you, Your Grace. Now I shall need assistance in disrobing the woman." He slanted a glance at Kendra. "Miss Donovan, you may wish to depart if you feel your sensibilities will be affected by the next phase of my examination."

"I know what a naked woman looks like, Doctor." She set down the lantern. "I'll help you."

The pelisse was easy enough to strip off, as were the stockings. They were forced to cut away the rest of the clothes, which Kendra folded carefully and placed on the wooden table after Munroe matched the wounds on the body with the corresponding tears and slices in the fabric.

"Miss Duprey was fully clothed when she was killed."

Aldridge arched a brow at the doctor. "Was there any doubt?"

Kendra said, "The killer could've dressed her afterward."

Munroe nodded approvingly. "Quite right, Miss Donovan. There can be no doubt—now—that she was fully clothed when she was killed. In my work, I've found it is best not to make assumptions regarding what may seem obvious."

They returned to their inspection of the dead woman. Her knees were black and blue, and swollen from the impact of falling. Her right ankle was also distended, and, Munroe determined, broken. Kendra suspected the injury had come at the end. She imagined April Duprey had fallen one last time.

"Miss Duprey died as the result of a single knife wound. The blade entered her chest cavity, most likely piercing her heart. There's bruising surrounding the injury, consistent with marks made by the hilt of a knife." Munroe meticulously measured the entrance wound. "The blade appears to have been one-inch in width, but an internal examination will better determine the width, as well as the length. Again, Miss Donovan, I will ask you—"

"I'm staying."

"Very well."

Kendra had attended countless autopsies before, and this one—despite the lack of electrical saws, high-tech tools, stainless steel, and overall sterile atmosphere prevalent in her own time—was surprisingly similar, beginning with the standard Y-shaped incision curved beneath the breasts toward the breast bone, bisecting the body to the pubic bone. Familiar, too, was the stench of decay and blood and internal gases that wafted up from the cadaver.

Despite the cool temperature of the room, a fine film of sweat gathered on Munroe's brow as he worked to open the woman's rib cage with pruning shears, allowing him access to the internal organs. Once again Kendra was surprised and impressed by the doctor's painstaking approach. She'd known medical examiners in the twenty-first century who were less thorough.

"The blade was approximately five inches long. Double-edged. Most likely a hunting knife or dagger of some kind," he said, carefully inspecting the organs with measuring instruments. "The attacker thrust the knife into the chest, angling the weapon in an upward motion, which punctured the victim's heart. She died of cardiac tamponade."

The Duke crowded closer to examine the organ. "I am unfamiliar with the term. What exactly is cardiac tamponade, Doctor?"

"It is the process where blood fills the pericardium—the membrane surrounding the heart. 'Tis what prevented her heart from pumping."

"Fascinating."

Kendra said, "I don't know who was luckier—the killer or April Duprey." When the men stared at her, she shrugged. "It's actually not that easy to kill someone with a knife. The fact that it was only one knife wound suggests the killer got lucky. One thrust, and April Duprey was a goner. On the other hand, her death was relatively quick, probably within minutes. If she hadn't died immediately, I don't think the killer would've stopped stabbing her."

Munroe raised his brows. "An interesting hypothesis, Miss Donovan. You appear to be an expert on the heart."

Kendra stiffened, immediately on the defensive. "The only thing I know about the heart is that it beats approximately one hundred thousand times daily. And it doesn't like pointy things stuck in it."

The doctor's eyes behind the round glasses gleamed with amusement. "I wasn't criticizing you, Miss Donovan. You are quite correct in saying many people survive stab wounds. Then again, Julius Caesar was stabbed twenty-three times by his assassins, but the physician Suetonius proved that it was only one wound—the second one near his heart—that was mortal." He smiled, and returned to his examination.

It became apparent that April Duprey had not bled out so much as bled internally. The sac around her heart wasn't the only thing filled with her blood; so too was her lungs and stomach.

"My conclusion is that Miss Duprey was a healthy, middle-aged woman . . . except for the knife wound that killed her," Munroe said as he finished his inspection, and began the process of sewing her back up.

Middle-aged? That gave Kendra a jolt. Though, given the average life span for women during this era, she supposed thirty-five *would* be about middle-aged. It made her a little queasy, and she nearly laughed at the absurdity. She had no trouble watching an M.E. disembowel another human being, nearly up to his elbows in blood and gore, but the idea that someone in their thirties would be considered middle-aged left her weak in the knees.

Munroe made use of the bucket of water someone had brought in earlier to scrub the blood off his hands. He glanced over at Kendra. "I must say that I had reservations about allowing a woman to view a postmortem, Miss Donovan. You, however, have been a pleasant surprise."

The doctor, Kendra realized suddenly, wasn't the only one who'd been hampered by prejudices. If she were honest, she'd thought little of her nineteenth-century counterparts. She'd judged them and, because they were different, had found them wanting. It shamed her. These people might not have the sophisticated tools of her era, but they were all intelligent. She might not be able to trust them with her time-traveling secret, but she could trust them in this quest for truth and justice.

She smiled. "Right back at you, doc."

46

Having two women turn up dead didn't hamper the house party's festivities, although Kendra noticed that the outdoor nuncheon Lady Atwood had planned for that day was set close to the castle, in the east garden. The garden was walled off, deep green lawn bordered by trees and topiaries that had been trimmed into fantastical geometric shapes. Pretty flagstone footpaths wound around flower beds exploding with a rainbow of color. Tables had already been set up around the lawn, but most of the couples were strolling the walkways rather than sitting.

Kendra watched the ladies with their absurdly small parasols. It took her a minute, but she finally figured out that it was meant more for flirtation than a protection from the sun. That was the root of this entire affair: the house party, the nineteenth century's version of Match.com.

"Lady Dover has already sunk her claws into Sutcliffe, I see," Rebecca observed dryly from beside her.

Kendra's gaze traveled to where Alec stood with the Lady. They made a striking couple, she had to admit. Alec's dark good looks were the perfect foil for Lady Dover's golden beauty. She was twirling a tiny lavender parasol that both matched her gown and brought out the violet flecks in her lovely blue eyes. The gown in question clung to Lady Dover's exquisite figure like a long-lost lover, her alabaster skin—and there was an indecent amount showing, Kendra thought critically—luminous.

"Lord Sutcliffe doesn't appear to mind," Kendra said, and hated how snippy she sounded. It was none of her business who Alec was sleeping with, she reminded herself.

"He will if he loses that arm," Rebecca muttered. "The way she is holding on to it, it's liable to pop right off."

Despite her own irritation, Kendra had to laugh. "You don't like her very much, do you?"

"I loathe her. She is a coldhearted shrew."

Kendra watched as the woman pressed herself against Alec. Whatever she murmured in his ear caused him to laugh. "I don't know about her heart, but the rest of her should be cold, wearing a dress like that." She fingered the ruffled fichu around her throat—a concoction, like a modern day dickey, that Mary had whipped up to tuck into her gown in order to hide the bruises around her throat. "How long have they been involved?" She hadn't meant to ask that, but once it was out, she couldn't take it back.

Rebecca didn't pretend to misunderstand. "According to gossip, since the Season began."

The Season, Kendra had learned, was the London social calendar that began with the opening of Parliament in January. Seven months, then. "I'm guessing there isn't a Lord Dover."

"He expired five years ago, and she's been having a grand time ever since. I only pray that Sutcliffe is not stupid enough to get himself caught in the parson's mousetrap. She'd love to land a marquis, especially someone with his prospects."

Kendra was reminded of her own thoughts last night, that Alec had more than his share of women throwing themselves at him. "You mean because he's rich."

"Rich as Croesus. *And* the Duke's heir. That's heady enough to turn any maid's head—not that that creature needs any incentive. Come along, Miss Donovan. I see the Duke and Dr. Munroe."

Kendra put Alec and Lady Dover out of her mind—or tried to—and allowed Rebecca to drag her across the lawn to where the two men stood by one of the tables. After the postmortem, they'd locked themselves in the Duke's laboratory with April Duprey's clothes and the evidence that Munroe had scraped from her body. Kendra was eager to talk to them about their findings.

"My dear Duke . . . Dr. Munroe," Rebecca greeted. Then, in her usual brisk way, she asked, "Did you discover anything of significance in your laboratory, sir?"

Aldridge shot a quick glance around, then held out his arm. "Shall we walk . . . away from listening ears?"

They paired up, with Kendra escorted by the Duke, and Rebecca walking with the doctor. Like the other couples, they meandered seemingly at random along the flagstone paths. Unlike everyone else, they spoke of death.

Munroe began, "I am not a botanist. However, His Grace kindly assisted me in identifying the debris we found embedded in Miss Duprey's shoe, stockings, and clothing. To wit, we discovered crushed bits of *Campanula glomerata*—purple bell flowers—acorn seeds, pine needles, twigs from the live oak tree, all of which are common in the area."

Aldridge nodded. "Unfortunately, there is no way to pinpoint Miss Duprey's location based on that. Yet we found one discrepancy. The stain on Miss Duprey's pelisse was potash."

Kendra frowned. "Potash? That's some sort of fertilizer, isn't it?"

"That is its main use, yes. Certainly here in the countryside, its most common use would be as such, or as a supplement for stock feed."

"I don't understand. If it's so common, what's the discrepancy?"

"'Tis more a matter of where it was on her person, and where it was not," Munroe answered. "As you may recall, the potash was located on the upper back of Miss Duprey's pelisse—not on the garment's hem. Nor did she have any traces of the compound on her lower skirt, or stockings, or the sole of the shoe that she still had on. In other words, she did not run through fields or gardens fertilized with potash."

"Then she probably picked up the trace evidence wherever she was stored until the killer could dump her on the path," Kendra said slowly.

"Exactly my thought," Dr. Munroe agreed.

"Of course, there's another possibility."

The Harry Potter glasses glinted in the sunshine as he looked at her. "What, pray tell, would that be, Miss Donovan?"

"She could've had the stain on her coat *before* she met the killer," she pointed out. "We're assuming it happened here."

Aldridge beamed at her. "Excellent point, my dear! *Post hoc ergo propter hoc.* I told you, Dr. Munroe, that Miss Donovan has a keen and discerning mind. We cannot jump to a false conclusion based on a coincidental correlation."

Munroe smiled. "Very true, sir. Alas, I cannot determine when Miss Duprey's coat was contaminated, only that it *is* contaminated." He shook his head. "'Tis a most fascinating case, I confess. I have worked many times with the London Watch and Bow Street Runners like Mr. Kelly. I am familiar with the more unsavory elements of humanity. The criminal element." He gave Kendra a thoughtful look. "I must say, your hypothesis that a man of good birth is responsible for these despicable acts is disturbing, Miss Donovan."

"That's another fallacy, Doctor—that evil is limited to the lower classes."

"You are correct, of course. Still, I have encountered more crime in the bowels of London than in a privileged environment like Aldridge Castle."

"I'm not talking about crime brought on by desperation and poverty. I'm talking about evil. *That* has no class. In the fifteenth century, Countess Elizabeth Báthory of Hungary was convicted of torturing and murdering more than eighty young girls. She confessed to killing more than six hundred. She was an aristocrat."

"Dear heaven," Rebecca breathed.

Munroe eyed Kendra curiously. "I am aware of the account. However, as you noted, it was the *fifteenth* century. As I recall, the countess was under the belief that virgin blood would enhance her beauty and make her immortal. People of that era believed that witches and wood sprites brought about disease."

"Superstitious nonsense," the Duke sniffed.

"Times have changed, Miss Donovan. Mankind has evolved. We are more enlightened thinkers than our ancestors."

"I've heard that before."

He raised his brows. "You don't believe we are evolving as a species?"

She thought of her earlier epiphany, that she wasn't superior to her nineteenth-century compatriots. And she thought of the countless murder boards she'd stood before, centuries from now, detailing man's depravity toward man, and shook her head. "We might be becoming more civilized as a whole—and I'm not even sure about that—but I don't think mankind ever really changes. We're not smarter, better, kinder people, Doctor." She paused, grim. "We're just inventing better technology."

Aldridge gave her a puzzled look. "Technology? You mean, techniques?"

Dammit. "Or tools. We have better tools. They've improved and will continue to improve. But human beings?" The sun was shining, but she felt cold. "I think people like Sam Kelly and you, Dr. Munroe, will always have work. Because there will always be monsters."

47

The sun was sinking behind the green and gold fields, casting long skinny shadows over the landscape, by the time Sam returned to Aldridge Castle. He'd spent the entire day riding over the sodding countryside, trying to chat up the snooty servants in the neighboring households. It always amazed him how they adopted the airs of their betters, looking down their noses at the likes of him, even when he brought out his Bow Street Runner baton. He much preferred outdoor servants, the stable hands, and gamekeepers, down-to-earth folk whose tongues could be loosened with a dram of whiskey.

Unfortunately, even the free use of his flask hadn't elicited much information, he reflected ruefully.

Fifteen minutes later, a footman escorted him to the Duke of Aldridge's study. Entering, Sam saw that everyone was gathered around a table, studying the map of London that had been spread across it. Someone—Kendra Donovan, he guessed—had marked it with red and blue dots, using Lady Rebecca's colored sticks.

"Ah, Mr. Kelly." The Duke glanced at him, straightening. "Good evening. We are attempting to determine whether or not there is a pattern to where the girls vanished. Would you like a refreshment?"

Music to his ears. "Whiskey, thank you, sir."

Alec took it upon himself to stroll over to the side table that held the selection of crystal decanters. He poured a generous three fingers into a stout glass, and brought it over to the Bow Street Runner.

"Have you found a pattern?" Sam asked curiously as he took the glass from the marquis.

"Not really," Kendra answered. "There's a heavier concentration of brothels near Sutton Street where Harris once lived."

"Which may be attributed to Sutton Street's location in a less desirable area in Town," Munroe pointed out.

Aldridge picked his pipe off the desk, and lit it. "And you, Mr. Kelly?" he asked. "Have you learned anything of value?"

"The vicar's household ain't enamored of Mr. Harris."

Rebecca gave a sniff. "That, my good man, *I* could have told you."

"Aye, ma'am." He grinned and took a sip of whiskey, appreciating the superior quality compared to the stuff he usually could afford. "'Tis a small household—a butler, the cook, a valet, and a maid-of-all-work. The cook does not live in. The butler, valet, and maid have rooms near the kitchen, on the other side of the vicarage from the family's rooms."

Kendra shot him a look. "Basically you're telling us that only Mrs. Harris would know if her husband left in the middle of the night. And I doubt if she'd say anything."

"Aye, miss." Sam eyed the American. "Mrs. Harris ain't one ter preach . . . er, ter share personal information about her husband."

"What of the other households, Mr. Kelly?" Aldridge asked.

"As they are much larger than the vicarage, me and me men didn't speak with everyone." He hesitated. "Mr. Morland's mum, Lady Anne, had an episode earlier this morning. He went ter London ter fetch a mad-doctor. The servants are a closed-mouth bunch, but I was told she wandered into the stable yard, demanding a horse and calling herself a lass named Myrna or Mina."

Rebecca put a hand to her throat. "Good heavens. Is there nothing that can be done for the poor woman?"

Munroe shook his head. "I've heard of this kind of madness before. There is no cure, my Lady."

"Most likely Lady Anne was calling herself Myrrha. The other day, she called Mr. Morland Adonis. Myrrha is the mother of Adonis." Aldridge sighed heavily. "It makes a dreadful sort of sense, doesn't it? Lady Anne spent her life with her father's passion for ancient Greek mythology. Now she can no longer distinguish reality from the myths she studied as a child."

"I cannot imagine a worse fate," Rebecca said softly.

Kendra remembered how she thought she'd had a psychotic break on her first day in this time period, and had to suppress a shiver. "Neither can I."

Another heavy silence descended. Sam cleared his throat. "Aye, well. We checked the list of tenants that you gave us. No one remembers seeing Mr. Morland riding the other day."

"He also said that he did not see any of his tenants," Aldridge reminded him. "What of Mr. Dalton?"

"Mr. Dalton has gone ter Barking for a cattle auction, so it was easy enough ter conduct the interviews. Much of the staff at Halstead Hall served his aunt. The general opinion is that he is a likeable enough fellow, but they're suspicious that he was a sawbones, especially when his pa was a doctor, and he has ties ter the gentry. Why lower himself in such a way?"

Kendra assumed the question was rhetorical, so she asked instead, "Did they say anything about Dalton's late wife?"

"They never made her acquaintance. But Lady Halstead referred ter her as a flighty piece of baggage."

Alec said with a slight smile, "Lady Halstead was never one to mince words."

Kendra stared at the map of London spread before her, and shook her head. "He has to have a hidey-hole."

"A hidey-hole?"

"A place that he's taking the girls. Somewhere private. Somewhere away from the servants' watching eyes."

"There are a few abandoned cottages in the area," Aldridge said. "Derelict buildings and barns. We even have old monastery ruins in these parts."

"And caves," Rebecca added. "This entire vicinity is riddled with caverns. When I was a little girl, I often went about exploring them, searching for fossils. It was quite a passion of mine. Remember, Duke? There were rumors that some caves were even used as priest holes for local Catholic landowners when Queen Elizabeth attempted to obliterate all ties to the papacy."

Alec scowled. "Bloody hell. If the fiend is hiding in one of the caves, finding him will be like searching for a needle in a bottle of hay. Duke's property alone is more than fifteen thousand acres. A search would take weeks, perhaps months."

"Well, there's a happy thought," Kendra muttered.

There was a small knock at the door, and Harding came into the room. Aldridge lifted his brows slightly, having expected the footmen to light the wall sconces.

The butler hesitated, a dark uneasiness shifting beneath the man's normally impassive face. "I apologize for disturbing you, sir. Mrs. Danbury asked me to speak to you . . . ah, there's been a bit of a worry below stairs, you see."

"If this is about Monsieur Anton—"

"No, sir. It is about . . . well, a maid seems to have gone missing, sir."

Kendra swung around to look at the butler. "What? What do you mean? Gone missing?"

Harding glanced at her, and then back at the Duke. "A tweeny. Rose. Cook said . . ." He gave a helpless shrug. "We can't find her, sir."

Cold dread gripped Kendra. "Rose?" she echoed.

"Yes, miss."

She barely heard him. Her heart began to pound as she spun to face the slate board. Her gaze became transfixed on the victimology column. The words seemed to dance in front of her eyes, taunting her. *Pretty. Petite. Dark hair. Dark eyes. Young* . . .

Oh, dear God . . . *Rose.*

48

Kendra felt sick—ice cold and sick.

"No," she whispered, and her knees began to buckle. Her vision wavered. There was a flurry of movement, then arms went around her. The next thing she knew, she was sitting on the sofa and Alec was pressing a glass of brandy into her hand.

"Drink it," he ordered tersely.

"No . . ." She tried to shove it away, but couldn't seem to catch her breath. The air had evaporated from her lungs. She was getting dizzy. Leaning forward, she put her head between her knees and concentrated on breathing. *In. Out.*

Rose.

"Doctor, can you do something?" Rebecca cried, and rushed to sit next to Kendra, putting her arms around her. She frowned when she felt the American trembling. "She's going to be ill! Does anyone have any smelling salts?"

Kendra straightened, pushed aside the helpless terror gripping her. "No, I'm fine."

"You are not fine—"

"I'm fine," she snapped at Rebecca. "It's Rose who needs help now. When was she last seen?"

The butler spread his hands, looking as helpless as she felt. "Sometime this morning, I believe. We were busy preparing for the nuncheon in the garden."

Rebecca shook her head. "But she could not have been taken by the madman. She is not a prostitute. She is a tweeny. She does not fit your pattern, Miss Donovan."

"She fits in every way except one." A knot was forming in the pit of Kendra's stomach. "We know that he's escalating. We know that he wants to engage us. The only reason the unsub chose prostitutes was because they were expendable to society."

"A servant in my household is *not* expendable." There was a note of raw fury that Kendra had never heard before in Aldridge's voice. His eyes were no longer gentle, but a burning blue. "This madman, whoever he is, must realize that I shall use all my resources to hunt him down."

Kendra crossed her arms in front of her, trying not to shiver. But she was cold. *So cold.* "He is aware of your power and influence, Your Grace. He already believes that you're using all your resources to find him—and yet, haven't found him. Don't you see? He believes he's smarter than you. He believes he's smarter than all of us!"

And maybe he is . . .

She rubbed her palms against her face. She needed to *think.* But the horror was welling up inside her, choking her.

"We don't know if the madman has the girl," Alec said.

Yes, I do, Kendra thought. *I know.* "It makes sense," she whispered. "He's taunting us. He's showing us that he can come here and snatch one of our own."

"We must organize a search," Alec said.

"But where?" asked Rebecca.

"Everywhere!" Kendra said. "Goddamn it! He's taking them somewhere!"

"I'll gather me men to help," Sam volunteered.

With an effort, Kendra pushed herself to her feet. It took even more of an effort to keep her voice steady. "I need to interview the staff, get a time line together. And then we need to go see Morland, Dalton, and Harris. *Immediately.*"

Sam stared at her. "Harris was in the village when we questioned his household, but he was the only one who was nearby. I told you that Mr. Morland and Mr. Dalton were both gone."

"Or so they'd have everyone believe."

The Duke was already moving toward the bellpull. "I'll have the carriage brought around."

Alec touched Kendra's shoulder. "We shall find the maid."

His gentleness was almost her undoing. Her throat tightened, and she could feel the surge of hot tears pressing behind her eyes.

"I would also like to lend my assistance," Munroe said.

The lines in Aldridge's face deepened. "Thank you, Doctor. Your assistance would be appreciated."

Kendra bit her lip until she tasted blood. But dear God, she needed to keep her emotions in check, because she knew that the Duke wasn't only thanking him for searching for Rose. He was talking about the possibility of needing Munroe's assistance if they should find her.

The kitchen was its normal iron-melting temperature, but Kendra felt ice-cold as she and Alec stood in front of more than a dozen servants. Her head was throbbing. The general cacophony of the kitchens didn't help, as the remaining staff scurried back and forth in a mad dash to prepare the evening's dinner.

Cook was among the servants, her arms around Molly, who was pressing her face into her apron to stifle her gut-wrenching sobs. "Hush now," she whispered, but her anxious gaze was fixed on Kendra. "Mayhap the lass ran off, like Jenny."

"Has Rose ever run off before? Disappeared for a while before?"

"Nay. Nay!" Molly lifted swollen eyes to Kendra. "The monster's got 'er!"

"W'ot we goin' ter do?" Another maid began to weep.

Kendra's head throbbed harder. Everyone was staring at her like she had the power to save Rose. And all she could do was offer them basic police procedure.

She drew in a breath, tried to steady her heartbeat and stave off the horror. "Okay, we need to establish a time line." She lifted the pad of paper and pencil she'd procured from the Duke's study. "When was the last time you saw Rose?"

That unleashed a flood of comments. "One at a time," she ordered, and pointed the pencil at a maid named Tess. "You. When did you see Rose last?"

"Oi saw 'er this morning, 'elpin' with the polishing upstairs."

"What time?"

"After nine. Mebbe 'alf past."

A freckle-faced maid added, "Oi saw 'er around ten. She was fetchin' vegetables from the garden."

"She was back in the kitchens after that. Oi know, cause Oi saw 'er with the 'ermit."

"The hermit? Thomas was here?"

"Aye. 'E came fer some bread an' cheese."

"What time was that?"

The girl—Mildred, Kendra remembered—frowned. "'Twas before 'er Ladyship's nuncheon. Eleven, Oi think. Mebbe 'alf past."

"S-she was s-supposed ter 'elp me with the l-linens upstairs." Molly wiped at the tears running down her face. "But she never came up. Oi was angry at 'er. Oi thought mebbe she'd snuck off."

Kendra heard the guilt in the tweeny's voice, but there was nothing she could do about it now. "What time was this, Molly?"

"Oi dunno. One. Mebbe a little later. Oi don't remember!"

"It's all right. You're doing fine."

"'Ow is this gonna 'elp us find the lass?" demanded one of the footmen. "We don't need to know where she was this mornin'—we need to know where she is *now*!"

Alec stepped forward. "We are organizing a search party of the grounds, outbuildings, woods." His voice was firm as he looked at the servants. "Let's not jump to false conclusions. The girl may have fallen and hurt herself. There may be a rational explanation as to why she is now missing that has nothing to do with the other unpleasantness."

"'Oi'd like ter volunteer, sir," a chubby-faced footman offered.

"Aye. Me, too—"

Several other footmen crowded around, offering their help.

"Que faites-vous? Au boulot!" Monsieur Anton's voice rose above the chorus of volunteers. The little man pushed his way through the knot of footmen. He held a bunch of carrots that he'd brought in from the garden himself. Now he shook them beneath several footmen's noses, spraying dirt. *"Vite! Vite!"*

Cook surged forward until she was toe-to-toe with the Frenchman. "Go tend ter ye ducks yerself, ye blasted Frenchie! Can't ye see we're busy here?!"

"Comment osez-vous?! J'essaie de créer mon chef-d'oeuvre—"

"Why don't ye go back ter yer froggy—"

"Je ne peux travailler avec si peu d'égard! Je suis un artiste! Je—"

Kendra's head was ready to explode. *"Ça suffit ! Taisez-vous!"* she shouted. *"Cher Dieu, une femme est disparue! Elle peut être morte! Ayez un peu de compassion!"*

Monsieur Anton swung around, gaping at her. *"Vous parlez très bien français!"*

She was aware everyone was staring at her with the same shocked expression. She massaged her aching temples. "Goddamnit. I don't have time for this."

Alec put his hand on her shoulder. Kendra wasn't sure if it was meant to comfort or restrain.

It was obvious that Monsieur Anton hadn't recognized Alec until that moment. His dark eyes rounded and he blanched. *"Pardonnez-moi, Monseigneur! Je ne vous ai pas vu!"*

"Je comprends, Monsieur Anton. Ne vous inquiétez pas." In fluent French, Alec dismissed the apology and turned back to the footmen, ordering them to gather the volunteers and meet him in the stable yard.

Alec glanced at Kendra. "You continue to surprise, Miss Donovan."

Kendra said nothing. Alec shook his head, then followed the departing footmen out the back door. Several maids surged forward.

"W'ot can we do ter 'elp, miss?" one of them asked Kendra.

"Miss Donovan!" Mrs. Danbury's voice sliced across the noise of the kitchen. "Please come here."

Kendra hesitated, glancing at the anxious faces around her. "Keep thinking about the last time you saw Rose—if you saw her with anyone, or if you noticed any strangers around the castle," she told them, and then broke away to join the housekeeper at the door.

"The carriage is ready," Mrs. Danbury said quietly.

Kendra nodded, but when she tried to move past her, the housekeeper caught her arm.

"You will find the girl, won't you?" For once there was no suspicion or contempt or dislike in the other woman's gaze. There was only fear, and a terrible need. Like the others, Mrs. Danbury seemed to think she could actually do something.

"I'm . . . I'm going to try."

Mrs. Danbury nodded. "Then, go. Please, go find her before it's too late."

Kendra managed a nod, but there was an icy lump in her throat. The last time anyone had seen Rose was eleven that morning.

It might already be too late.

49

Time was the enemy in every missing person case, every kidnapping, every homicide. There was always a phantom clock ticking in the background, counting every second.

Darkness had fallen, and Kendra was reminded again of how much she took for granted in her era. Something as simple as street lighting would be a blessing. Here, they relied on the moon—and thank God there was a moon that night—and the carriage's brass lanterns, which were, she supposed, a precursor to headlights.

As the carriage made its now familiar lurch forward, she clenched her hands on her lap in an attempt to alleviate the unbearable tension twisting in her gut.

"'Tis hazardous to travel at night," Aldridge said mildly, recognizing her anxiety. "London recently acquired gas lighting on its streets, but the countryside is a far different matter. We must proceed more cautiously."

She'd already figured that out, but she nodded anyway. They lapsed into a grim silence that was only broken by the clatter of horses' hooves, the rhythmic turn of the carriage's wheels and the crunch of gravel, the occasional squeak of leather. Kendra tried to clear her mind, to compartmentalize her thoughts, but horrifying images of Rose kept intruding, expanding the icy ball of terror that had become permanently lodged in the pit of her stomach.

Is Rose alive? Or were they racing around like rats in a maze for a hopeless cause?

The ride felt like hours, but it was actually only fifteen minutes before the vehicle swayed to a stop outside the vicarage. The Duke dispensed with the calling card ritual, opening the carriage door himself and jumping down. He waited only to assist Kendra, then hurried up the flagstone path to bang on the door.

"We need to speak with your master, my good man!" he said when the butler opened it.

The servant gaped at him, completely taken aback by someone as important as the Duke of Aldridge appearing on the doorstep with no announcement. "S-sir? Your Grace. Mr. Harris and Mrs. Harris only sat down to dine. I shall inform them of your presence at once!"

"No need." Aldridge shouldered his way past the man, moving down the long, skinny hall to the stairs. "I know where the dining room is."

Kendra followed.

"Sir!" The butler finally had enough presence of mind to race after them, but by the time he caught up, Aldridge was already opening the door to the dining room at the top of the stairs. Kendra caught the gleam of dark mahogany paneling, and the warm, buttery glow cast from wall sconces, the fireplace, and a scattering of candles on the table. Harris was sitting at one end of a long table, his hand poised to spear a boiled potato from the serving dish that a maid was holding in front of him; Mrs. Harris sat primly at the other end.

The vicar glanced in their direction, frowning at the unexpected intrusion.

"What the devil—?" Seeing the Duke, Harris's eyebrows hiked and he dropped the fork, rising to his feet.

"The Duke of Aldridge," the butler announced belatedly behind them.

The Duke strode forward. "I beg your pardon for interrupting your meal, Mr. Harris, ma'am." He gave a nod at Mrs. Harris. "We've come on a matter of great urgency. One of my maids has gone missing."

Harris frowned. "I don't understand, sir. Your maid is missing, and you are under the impression that she is here?"

Kendra studied him closely, couldn't see anything beyond his confusion—or the *appearance* of confusion. Serial killers were chameleons. They adapted to whatever the situation called for, and lied without batting an eyelash.

"Where were you today, Mr. Harris?" she demanded bluntly. She'd be damned if she'd waste time being polite. *Time*. They were running out of it.

Harris flicked her a haughty look. "Are you accusing me now of murdering your maid, Miss Donovan? It wasn't enough for you to insult me yesterday by suggesting that I went about murdering whores?"

"I want to know where you were today. I'm not too concerned if that insults you or not."

Red tinged his cheekbones. "Your Grace, surely—"

Aldridge cut him off, his tone sharp. "I shall apologize for any insult, but please answer the question, Mr. Harris. Time is a factor here."

The vicar gave a put-upon sigh and shrugged. He wouldn't challenge Aldridge, Kendra knew. "I worked in my study in the early morning hours, and then rode over to the King's Head, where I indulged in a pint. Mr. Hawkings can attest to my whereabouts if my word isn't good enough for you." He let that hang for a moment, but when no one contradicted him, he continued, his tone becoming even more brittle. "I returned home, had my midday meal. Later, I went riding."

"You rode yesterday."

Harris gave her a look that suggested she was an idiot. "What of it? That does not preclude me riding today, Miss Donovan. I recall pointing out to you yesterday that I ride most afternoons. This afternoon was quite typical, I assure you."

"Did anyone see you or did you see anyone while you were riding?"

"I have no idea."

"You don't know if you saw anyone? What, were you struck by temporary blindness?"

His face tightened at her sarcasm. "You are being impertinent, Miss Donovan, and I do not appreciate it. I did not see anyone. Therefore, I have no idea if anyone observed me."

"Where did you go riding?"

"The woods, the same as yesterday."

"What time did you leave the King's Head?"

"Eleven. Mayhap half past."

Rose had last been seen around eleven o'clock. "And you came right home?"

"Yes."

Kendra swung around to face Mrs. Harris, who was watching wide-eyed. "Is that true?"

She gave a frightened squeak. "P-pardon?"

"When did your husband return home today?" Kendra demanded impatiently.

"I shall not have you intimidate my wife, Miss Donovan!" Harris protested.

"I'm only asking her a question. I'll leave the intimidation to you." Kendra approached the woman, made sure to shift her body to block the woman's view of her husband. "Mrs. Harris, what time did your husband return home? Was it eleven or eleven-thi—half past eleven? I need you to be specific."

"I-I . . . think . . . half past," she said faintly. "Yes. Yes, it must have been."

"You need to tell me the truth, Mrs. Harris."

"How dare you!" the vicar declared.

Mrs. Harris looked on the verge of tears. "B-but I am. I am not lying, I swear!"

"Miss Donovan, I believe we have what we came for," the Duke said quietly. Kendra threw him a desperate glance. "Come, my dear." He approached, took her arm, and steered her toward the door.

Kendra looked back at Harris, and thought she saw triumph in his eyes. "I am sorry I could not be of more assistance, sir."

Asshole, she thought. But that didn't make him a killer.

Aldridge gave her a concerned look as soon as they were settled once more in the carriage. "A half an hour is not much time to abduct the maid, Miss Donovan," Aldridge pointed out gently.

"How far is the tavern from the vicarage?"

"By horse, a few minutes."

"If it's so close, why'd he take a horse? Why not walk?"

The Duke frowned and shrugged. "'Tis not unheard of, Miss Donovan."

She supposed he was right. Hell, she'd known people who drove their car across the street rather than walk. Maybe Harris was like that. Or maybe he had another reason.

"And the tavern to the castle?"

"It would depend on the pace you set. Five minutes perhaps. Less than ten. As I said, scarcely enough time to snatch the maid."

Kendra thought of the abduction cases she'd been involved in. A mother takes her eyes off her child for a minute in a crowded mall, and the child is gone. A teenager leaves a neighbor's house to walk down the street and disappears. Minutes. *Seconds.*

She shook her head. "You'd be surprised how little time it takes to change a person's life forever."

❖

Like Harris's servant, Dalton's butler was dumbfounded to open the door to the Duke of Aldridge.

"I need to speak with Mr. Dalton," said the Duke. "Immediately!"

"He . . . he is not at home, Your Grace."

Aldridge lifted his brows, every inch the aristocrat. "To *me*, Farstaff?"

The butler looked like he was going to faint. "No, sir! I meant, Mr. Dalton is actually *not at home*. He left for Barking to attend the estate auction at the Avery farm."

"We are aware of Mr. Dalton's journey to Barking. However, I am surprised he has not returned. When do you expect him?"

"I am not privy to Mr. Dalton's plans for the evening. He may stay the night if he is too fatigued to travel home."

"Does he do that often?" Kendra asked.

Farstaff had recovered his poise, and now gave her that slightly suspicious, slightly standoffish look she often got from the upstairs servants at Aldridge Castle. "Sometimes," he said.

"What the hell does that mean?" she snapped angrily, taking a step toward him. The Duke grabbed her arm, even as the butler took a step back, offended.

"Miss Donovan—"

"We don't have *time* for this. He needs to answer the goddamn question!"

Aldridge shifted his eyes to the butler. "Well?"

"Mr. Dalton is attempting to transform Halstead Hall into a stud farm. He often travels overnight or several days on business in that quest, sir."

"Did he travel alone?" Kendra struggled to get her voice under control.

"Yes, miss."

"Is that unusual?"

"No, miss."

She stared hard at the butler. "A young girl has vanished from Aldridge Castle. She may be in danger. Could you tell Mr. Dalton that we need to speak to him as soon as he returns?"

"Yes, miss."

Kendra didn't like that Dalton wasn't home. It was too damn convenient. But there was nothing she could do about it.

As they turned to leave, somewhere in the manor, a clock began chiming eight o'clock. Sweat dampened her palms, and her heart pounded. Rose had been missing for nine hours.

Tick, tock.

They went to Tinley Park, where the butler told them Morland hadn't returned from London.

"Why did he go to London?" Kendra demanded, wanting to see if he'd repeat the story that Sam had told them, or if he would come up with something else.

The butler looked uncomfortable. "I-I'm afraid that I cannot say, miss."

Aldridge said, "I would not want you to gossip about your betters, Adams, but I must insist that you tell Miss Donovan and me the truth."

"I . . ." The servant cleared his throat. "Lady Anne is ill, sir. She had an . . . episode earlier this morning. Mr. Morland went to London to fetch a mad-doctor."

"Did he take a coach?" Kendra asked. A coach would mean a coachman, and therefore an alibi.

"No, miss. 'Tis faster to go on horseback."

"When did he leave?"

"Ten, I believe."

"That's ten hours ago." Two hours to London, two hours back. Four hours travel time, which would leave six in London, she calculated. "Isn't it odd that he hasn't returned?"

"I can't say, miss."

Aldridge asked, "Is Lady Anne better?"

"Much better, thank you, sir. Mrs. Marks calmed Her Ladyship. Unfortunately, Mr. Morland had already departed."

"What set her off?" Kendra asked.

The butler frowned. "I do not know, miss. Mr. Morland was visiting his mother, and she became agitated. Mr. Morland was upset by the incident. He left for London shortly thereafter."

There was nothing to do except ask the butler to give Morland a message to come to the castle when he returned. In the carriage, Kendra pressed a hand to her stomach, which was knotted in anxiety.

"I know this is difficult for you, Miss Donovan," the Duke said. "But all is not lost. We must have faith that the girl is still alive. We must pray for that."

Kendra bit her lip and said nothing. She remembered the rape and butchery that Lydia had endured before she died. *I want Rose to be alive.* She just wasn't sure that was the kindest thing to pray for.

50

As they approached Aldridge Castle, Kendra saw what seemed like one hundred specks of light, flickering like fireflies in the darkness along the sloping hills and in the woods.

"They are still searching," the Duke observed quietly. "There is still hope, Miss Donovan."

Kendra didn't know what to say to that, didn't know what to think. Was there still hope? A dark seed had taken root inside her, strangling any confidence that she might have over Rose's fate. It left her feeling sick and shaken.

The coach clattered to a stop in the stable yard. Kendra didn't wait for the footman to lower the steps, but threw open the door and hopped down onto the gravel. At least twenty men with lanterns milled around the area. She spotted Alec immediately in the center of the throng, his figure distinguished by his finer clothing—a sharp contrast from the roughly dressed men around him—and his air of authority.

As she watched, she had an eerie feeling of familiarity. *This is the same.* Not the clothing and hairstyles, of course. And there were no powerful LED flashlights, no dizzying strobes from nearby police cars, no thumping of blades from sleek helicopters as they circled the sky, their lights piercing the ground in an aerial search. There were no television crews or reporters covering the search, peppering her with impatient questions from behind the barricades.

But she saw the same terrible fear etched on the faces of the crowd; the same pungent odor of desperation and urgency; the same dread filling their gazes as they worried about what they might find at the end of their search. The accouterments of humanity may change, but its heartbeat remained the same.

Before Kendra had set out, Rebecca had insisted that she don what was called a spencer—basically, a jacket with a high neckline and long sleeves. The design reminded her a little of a modern-day shrug, because the material ended just below the breastbone, leaving the skirt of her gown exposed. Yet the jacket was no match for the chill of the night air, which easily penetrated the woven cotton and wafted up her skirt. She had to clench her jaw to prevent her teeth from chattering.

Alec spotted them. He finished giving instructions, then he and Sam shouldered their way through the crowd. Alec's eyes were fixed on Kendra, intense.

"Did you learn anything?" he asked as soon as the two pairs met.

"No," Aldridge answered. "The vicar was in the vicinity. Miss Donovan believes he had enough time to snatch the maid. I, however, am not so certain."

"What of Morland and Dalton?"

Aldridge shook his head. "Neither were home."

"We will need to have their whereabouts verified," Kendra said, crossing her arms in front of her chest in an attempt to retain her body heat. "What's happening here?"

"We have sent out the hunting dogs, hoping to pick up the maid's scent. And Mr. Kelly and I rode out personally to nearby hunting lodges. There was no sign of the girl. No sign of any recent occupation."

"The lass seems ter have vanished."

The lass. The girl. The maid.

"She has a name," Kendra snapped, turning on the Bow Street Runner. Her anger was irrational, she knew, but it filled her like helium expanding a balloon. "She has an *identity.* She's not Jane Doe. Rose. Her name is *Rose.* She wants to be a lady's maid someday. She . . . she . . ." Her breath hitched. Appalled, Kendra could feel hot tears surge into her throat. She pressed her face into her hands, as taken by surprise by the unexpected emotion as the men staring at her.

Alec made a low sound, and moved forward. Kendra stiffened for just a second when he took her into his arms, but didn't move away, trembling so hard she might shatter.

"We know," he murmured. "We shall find her, I promise you."

But will she be alive? Kendra wanted to ask. But she doubted if she'd be able to formulate a sentence at the moment, and that shook her even more. She wasn't the kind of person who lost control like this.

That reminder had her straightening, pulling away, already ashamed at her weakness—though she missed Alec's warmth. Without it, her body temperature seemed to drop ten degrees.

"I still need to interview Thomas. He's the last person to have seen Rose . . ." *Alive.* The word was on the tip of her tongue. "Before she disappeared," she said.

"Thomas ain't around," Sam told her. "He's helping with the search. He said that the lass . . . that *Rose* gave him some bread and cheese when he came ter the kitchen earlier."

"You spoke to him?"

"Aye. He didn't see anything."

"I still want to interview him."

"Not tonight," Aldridge said firmly. "I have no intention of letting you freeze to death out here in the stable yard, Miss Donovan."

"Mr. Kelly and I will continue the search," Alec said.

Aldridge nodded, "Very good. Come along, Miss Donovan. We must find Rebecca."

As Alec and Sam melted back into the crowd, Aldridge took Kendra's elbow, escorting her down the path that led to the kitchens.

For once Kendra appreciated the room's sweltering temperature. She could feel her frozen muscles and tendons warming, loosening. The room was ablaze with light. Every candle, from the wall sconces to the chandeliers, was burning, and there was a strong scent of tea and coffee and baking bread in the air. The dinner had been served, Kendra realized, and at this hour, the staff would normally be in the process of cleaning up. But tonight, the dirty dishes and platters had been left stacked on the counters, pushed out of the way. Like the stable yard, the kitchens were teeming with activity. An informal assembly line had been formed, where the women made sandwiches and served hot beverages to the men who'd recently returned from the search.

Kendra wondered where Lady Atwood had taken her guests. Probably to one of the drawing rooms, laughing and drinking, oblivious to the fact that a young girl, a girl responsible for keeping their rooms clean, who helped prepare the food they ate, was at this moment suffering at the hands of a madman.

The thought made her angry, but she forced herself to put it aside. Anger was a distraction she couldn't afford.

"Lady Rebecca!" Aldridge exclaimed. Surprised, Kendra glanced at one of the workstations where Rebecca, wearing an apron, was slicing slabs of ham off the bone.

"Duke." Rebecca handed the knife to the maid standing next to her, and came around the counter, wiping her hands on the apron. Her gaze was anxious. "Have you learned anything new?"

"What are you doing here?"

"I could not attend dinner and listen to everyone prattle on about their nonsensical lives! And I would go mad if I sat alone and waited for you. At least here, I could be of assistance. Have you learned anything?"

"No," Kendra answered.

The cornflower blue eyes were earnest as she reached over and placed a warm hand on Kendra's arm. "We must not give up hope, Miss Donovan."

Kendra wondered how often she'd hear that.

"Let's go to the study." Aldridge turned to the butler, who was hovering nearby. "Harding, please send up pots of tea and coffee."

"At once, sir."

Aldridge hesitated, then turned to address the room, which fell silent. "We are doing everything in our power to find Rose. If anyone should remember anything, any detail, regardless of how small, do not hesitate to tell me or Miss Donovan. Is that understood?"

There was a general murmuring of agreement. Rebecca took off the apron, and they moved out into the hallway. Kendra thought she heard the faint strains of the pianoforte, the soft tinkle of laughter.

In the study, embers glowed demonic red in the fireplace grate, the only light in the dark room. Normally, a footman would've been on hand to light the sconces and candles, and get the fire going again. But all available footmen had volunteered for the search.

Aldridge dropped down to one knee to put more logs into the grate and coax the fire back to life. Rebecca and Kendra took over the task of lighting candles. Afterward, Aldridge poured three glasses of brandy. "The tea and coffee will allow us a clear head, but this ought to take the chill away."

Rebecca accepted a glass and sat down. "Tell me what transpired on your calls."

As the Duke shared their journey, Kendra peeled off her spencer. She picked up a piece of slate. On the board, she began to create a time line.

"Rose was seen upstairs either at nine or nine-thirty. Around ten, she was asked to bring in vegetables from the garden. At eleven, she gave bread and cheese to Thomas." She underlined that time. "Unless someone else comes forward, that's the last time she was seen. Molly said she was supposed to help with the linens at one o'clock, but never showed. That's a two hour window for her to disappear."

Rebecca frowned. "The girl must have been taken right here in the castle. How the devil is that possible? Surely someone would have seen one of our suspects loitering about? The servants know Mr. Morland, Mr. Dalton, and the vicar. They would have seen them!"

"It's more possible than you realize." Ted Bundy had kidnapped women in the middle of busy parks and crowded beaches. No one expected a predator to be in their midst, especially if a predator so fully blended into his surroundings.

"I, too, am finding it difficult to believe," Aldridge admitted.

Kendra asked, "Did you notice Lord Sutcliffe when we arrived in the stable yard?"

He raised his brows. "Of course."

"Why?"

"Why? I'd recognize my own nephew, Miss Donovan!"

"Would you recognize him if he was dressed as the gardener? We were in the kitchens for a few minutes before you realized Lady Rebecca was there. We see what we expect to see. There's a lot of extra help around, and some of the guests brought their own servants. If the unsub dressed the part, he may have gone unnoticed."

How many serial killers did exactly that by wearing a uniform? A repairman, a postal worker . . . a policeman.

"Yes. I recognize what you are saying, Miss Donovan," Aldridge said slowly. "And you are quite right. 'Tis a technique employed successfully by spies during war, to infiltrate enemy territory. Of course, not without considerable risk. He is bold."

"Yes, he's confident," Kendra agreed, "and we may use that to our advantage, because confidence breeds arrogance. And an unsub who becomes arrogant tends to slip up."

And he *would* slip up, she was certain. But would it be in time to save Rose?

Kendra had never felt so helpless. In all the investigations she'd been involved in, she'd been an outsider, brought in to review the evidence with a cool head and an even colder eye. She hadn't been emotionless. She'd felt pity for the victim, for the victim's family and friends. It was impossible to be part of something like that and not be touched by the fear and grief. But the source of her personal terror had always come from not doing her job properly, from missing a vital piece of evidence that could lead them to the victim—or, after the victim was found, to the killer.

For the first time ever, she was fully invested. Her fear was twofold: the gnawing anxiety that she was missing something, and for Rose herself. She could imagine all too well what the girl was going through. She'd seen the killer's work with Lydia. She paced the room, made notes, circled back to reevaluate the old notes.

Despite the pots of coffee she had consumed, Kendra could feel exhaustion creeping in. Rebecca had tried to persuade her to go to bed, but had finally given up. After Rebecca had left, the Duke had added his voice. "You need to sleep, Miss Donovan. You can do nothing more here. You will make yourself ill."

But it wasn't until around two in the morning, when the words blurred on the slate board, that Kendra conceded. She needed sleep. She would start fresh in the morning.

The castle's corridors were silent as she walked down them. The silence pressed heavily against her chest. She carried her own candle to light the way up the backstairs to the bedchamber. Inside that shadowy room, she simply stood and stared at Rose's empty bed.

Her eyes burned with tears. She set the candle down and pressed the heels of her hands against her eyelids. Jesus. She was so damn tired.

Why the hell am I here? If I can't even save Rose, why the fuck am I here?

She began undressing, her movements robotic. Shoes first, then the tights. The dress was another matter. The buttons were down the back. She could reach some of them, but not all. It was why she and Rose had always helped each other.

After a moment of consideration, she finally unpinned the fichu, unfastened the buttons she could reach, and then pulled the dress over her head. It took some wriggling. There was no spandex in this era. Without that stretch, Kendra could feel the seams strain, and half expected them to rip apart. She finally managed to pull herself free of the gown, which she tossed on the floor. Next, she rid herself of the shift and chemise, and slipped into the shapeless white nightgown that had been part of the wardrobe Rebecca had ordered for her. The gyrations loosened her hair. She removed the pins, and used her fingers to comb the thick mass before climbing into bed. Blowing out the candle, she yanked up the thin blankets.

Despite her fatigue, she found herself studying the shadows and moonbeams that dueled across the slanted ceiling. Nighttime noises in the overall quiet screamed at her: a light wind rattling the windowpanes, the faint creaks and low groans as the ancient fortress settled. But she was keenly aware of the absence of sounds that she'd grown accustomed, Rose's light breathing from the narrow bed next to her and the rustle of blankets as the tweeny shifted in sleep.

Kendra's throat tightened, and tears began to trickle hotly down her cheeks. With a moan, she curled into a ball beneath the covers, and thought of the irony of crying for a girl who'd already died more than two hundred years before she'd been born.

51

Kendra didn't think she'd be able to sleep, but the next thing she knew, she was opening her eyes to the misty light of dawn. She glanced at the small clock on the bedside table. *Six forty-five.* She'd slept about four hours.

For a moment, she just lay there, staring at the ceiling. Her head had that dull ache brought on by too much adrenaline and too little sleep. Her eyes were gritty from the tears she'd shed last night. She felt drained and disheartened. She didn't want to think about the day that stretched out before her, or wonder what it might bring.

She forced herself to roll out of bed and used the chamber pot. Afterward, she poured water in the ceramic bowl and gave herself a quick sponge bath. She was rubbing baking soda against her teeth when there was a knock at the door, and Molly poked her head in.

"Oi wasn't certain ye'd be awake, miss." Her eyes, Kendra noticed, were red and puffy.

"I'm awake. Come in." Kendra rinsed out her mouth, and then surveyed her throat in the mirror. The bruises were still noticeable.

"The villagers 'ave begun to arrive for another search, but . . ." Molly faltered. In the mirror, Kendra saw how Molly's eyes cut to Rose's bed, and noted the sheen of tears over her eyes. "Oh, miss, everyone is frettin' that it's 'opeless!"

Kendra wished that she could give her some reassurance that Rose would be found, that she would be all right. But she couldn't. She couldn't even reassure herself.

When Kendra remained silent, Molly stifled a sob and bent down to pick up the gown that Kendra had discarded last night. Smoothing it over her arm with an aura of melancholy, she walked back to the wardrobe to hang it up.

Rose did that, Kendra remembered suddenly. Rose was always so careful with clothes, picking up what Kendra treated so carelessly, making sure everything was put away properly. It was the behavior of someone who valued clothing because it wasn't plentiful. This was not the disposable society that Kendra was familiar with.

"W'ot do ye wish ter wear today, miss?" Molly asked as she studied the gowns in the wardrobe.

"I don't care. You choose."

She pulled out a blue-and-yellow paisley muslin. "'Ow about this?"

"Sure." Really, who cared?

Molly helped Kendra into the dress. "Oi can pin up yer 'air," Molly said after she'd finished fastening the buttons.

Kendra was about to tell her that there was no point, but caught the look in Molly's eyes. Routine, she realized. It was something Molly needed. A bit of normalcy in a world suddenly tainted by tragedy.

She understood that need. It was what drove her to the study fifteen minutes later. Again, she stared at the names she'd written down. Morland. Dalton. Harris. They each fit her profile.

She circled the room, and tried to come at it from a different angle. The unsub had established a pattern of taking girls in the months of February, June, and October. But this year, with Lydia, he'd broken his pattern. *Why?*

If that kind of acceleration in behavior was usually connected to a stressor in the unsub's life, then they all might have a reason. Morland was the most obvious, because Lady Anne was suffering from dementia, an illness that would add stress to anyone's life. Morland's father had also been absent in his childhood—a common denominator among serial killers. But he'd had a father figure, an authoritarian: his grandfather. If he'd been abusive, Morland might've come to resent, even hate, his mother for allowing the cruelty. That kind of pattern was disconcertingly familiar. But by all accounts, the late earl had doted on his grandson.

Kendra rubbed her temples, tried to ease the dull ache that she suspected would turn into a full-blown headache in the next couple of hours. She shifted her focus to Dalton. A likeable guy, trying to build a horse farm. It couldn't be easy, she mused. There were always a lot of stressors when you started a business. Maybe he'd had a financial setback.

She considered his background: affluent family, father a doctor. A doctor was more prestigious in this era than a surgeon. For the first time, Kendra wondered what was behind Dalton's decision to become a sawbones rather than a physician. Some sort of rebellion against the father?

She remembered the small cuts on Lydia's torso. Fifty-three in total, four different knives. A surgeon was familiar with knives. Was it a taunt against a society that thought less of him because of his profession?

Then there was Dalton's wife, who'd left him for another man. Kendra didn't believe for a second that Dalton didn't know how his wife had died. So why lie about it? Unless he'd killed her. She could've been the first victim, triggering the killings that followed. The timing was right.

Kendra moved on to Harris. He was the least likeable of the bunch, the one who openly expressed his contempt for prostitutes. And beneath that, a disdain for all women. *Arrogant asshole.*

Like Dalton, Kendra didn't know much about the vicar's background other than the fact that his father was an earl who'd fallen on hard times. What had Rebecca said? *Punting on the River Tick.* That had to be a blow to Harris's ego. He'd been forced to marry a woman he considered his inferior, to take a job that, although respectable for younger sons of the aristocracy, was not one he'd have chosen.

That time line was also interesting. He'd married his unwanted heiress a year or so before the prostitutes began vanishing. And a young maid had been murdered in a similarly brutal manner down the street from where he and his wife had lived in London. Was the maid the first victim? An impulsive act, to release the pressure building inside because of his unwanted marriage? And then, perhaps, he'd found that he'd liked it? It was possible.

And that was the problem. Each scenario was possible, each suspect viable.

Kendra studied the slate board, and again felt that whispery sensation at the back of her neck. Someone had said something . . . *what?* She couldn't get a handle on it; the thought remained as elusive as ever.

Fresh air. That's what she needed. And she might as well get it on the walk to Thomas's shack, as she still needed to interview him about yesterday. He'd been the last person to see Rose. Maybe he'd seen someone lurking nearby.

As she reached the door, it swung open and Alec entered. He raised his brows when he saw her. "Miss Donovan. I had hoped you were still in bed. Did you sleep at all?"

"Long enough. How about you?"

"A few hours. We plan to resume the search in the next hour."

She nodded. "Good. I'm going to talk to Thomas about yesterday."

Alec grabbed her arm, glaring at her. "Are you mad? Have you no *sense*? I am not about to let you go traipsing through the woods alone with a murderer on the loose!"

"I can take care of myself."

"Bloody hell. You look like the victims, Miss Donovan! Do you not realize that?"

On some level, she had. But she shrugged, "In size and coloring, yes. But I'm older. I don't fit the pattern."

"He already broke his pattern!"

"I'm not a helpless fifteen-year-old. I can protect myself!"

Alec's grip tightened, as though he wanted to shake her. "You would not be able to protect yourself against a lead ball."

"Guns aren't his style. He wants his hands around his victim's throat. He wants to see her panic, her terror. He wants to watch the life go out in her eyes."

"If this is your attempt to ease my concern, you are doing a bloody awful job of it!"

"I'm going to talk to the hermit. If you want to, you can come with me."

"I shall." He dropped his hand. "You might want to fetch your spencer, Miss Donovan. There's a chill in the air."

The hermit opened the door in answer to Alec's knock. His eyes locked on the marquis, and Kendra thought she detected a gleam of fear.

"Your Lordship." He licked his lips nervously. "Er, what do you want?"

Kendra said, "We need to talk to you, Thomas."

His gaze swung back to her. "I helped search for the maid last night."

"Yes. I heard. Can we come in?"

He hesitated, but they knew he wouldn't deny her request. Not with the Marquis of Sutcliffe standing right there.

As Thomas stepped back, Kendra's eyes scanned the dim interior. It was as she remembered, except the shutters from the window had been removed, though the window was so greasy with dirt that it barely allowed the gray light of the overcast day inside. She saw that the drug paraphernalia was no longer on the floor, but crammed on the table with dirty dishes and paint supplies. The odor was the same, a mixture of sweat, turpentine, and paint, mingling with the smoke from the fireplace.

Alec hung back in the doorway, his expression filled with distaste. She couldn't really blame him; the air was fresher back there.

"You haven't done much painting," Kendra observed. She moved forward to stand in front of the easel. The canvas was still blue. The white female form in the center had taken on flesh tones, with more dimension, but it was otherwise faceless.

"Art requires sacrifice," he mumbled, his eyes skating away from hers.

"Sure it does." She moved around the easel. The space was so tight that her hip hit one of the cabinets, rattling the paint supplies strewn across the grimy surface. She put a hand up to steady them. "We need to talk to you about Rose. She made a sandwich for you yesterday."

"I don't know nothin'."

"You went into the kitchens. Who did you speak to?"

He frowned. "The cook. I asked for somethin' to eat. She told the little maid to give me some bread and cheese."

"Did you wait in the kitchens while she prepared it?"

"Nay. I waited outside."

"So Rose came outside to give you the sandwich?"

"Aye."

"Did you talk?"

"She said the countess was havin' a nuncheon out in the gardens. She had to help with that."

"While you were talking, did you notice anyone around?"

"Who?"

"Anyone. People."

Thomas shrugged. "A couple of gardeners."

"How did you know they were gardeners? Did you recognize them?"

"Nay. I . . . I dunno. They could've been stable hands, I suppose."

"Were they standing in a group, or were they separate from each other?"

"I don't remember."

"Thomas, I want you to think about the girl who gave you bread and cheese yesterday. She needs help."

"I dunno nothin'."

"You might know more than you realize. That's why I want you to think about it." Kendra paused, then asked, "Were you in the woods last Sunday? The vicar said he saw you."

He stiffened. "I'm often in the woods."

"Did you see the vicar?"

"Nay."

"He was riding. You didn't see someone on horseback?"

"Nay."

Was he telling the truth? Kendra's gut said no. But if he was lying, for what purpose? She let that go, and circled back to Rose. "After Rose gave you the sandwich and you talked, what happened?"

"Nothin' happened."

"After you talked, did you see where Rose went? Back into the kitchen? To the gardens? *Think* Thomas. This could be important."

"I dunno. I left."

"You're not *thinking*!"

"Miss Donovan."

She swung around, and glared at Alec.

"He does not know anything," Alec said gently.

Anger and frustration rose inside of her. And fear, terrible fear.

"Miss Donovan, Thomas does not know where Rose is," Alec said, even more gently.

She let out a sigh, and stepped back. "I want you to keep thinking, Thomas. If you remember something, *anything*, you will let us know."

He looked at her like a dumb animal. She wanted to hit him. Instead, she turned on her heel, and walked out the door.

Though she walked fast, Alec easily fell into step beside her. He wisely kept silent.

They'd entered the forest when Kendra finally spoke. "I still think he's hiding something. Or not telling the truth."

"Maybe he was poaching in the woods. 'Tis a serious crime, punishable by transportation, even hanging. The Duke does not adhere to those harsh penalties, but Thomas may err on the side of caution."

Kendra rubbed her hands against her arms, suppressing a shiver as she considered hanging for such a simple transgression. *I don't belong here.*

Neither one spoke as they retraced their footsteps through the woods. As they emerged from the forest, Alec suddenly grasped her arm. His touch brought her out of her dark reverie.

She saw what he had seen: a large crowd walking along the path that led to the front courtyard. Her first thought was that Aldridge had organized another search party. He was walking with Sam and Dr. Munroe. But then she saw the black bag Munroe was carrying, and her stomach knotted.

"No." She shook off Alec's hand, picked up her skirts and ran. Her heart was thundering in her chest by the time she caught up to the Duke. She stood transfixed, but she knew. Dear God, she *knew.*

Aldridge met her eyes. "Yes," he answered her unspoken question. "The maid's been found."

52

In a distant corner of her mind, Kendra was glad that she hadn't eaten breakfast yet, because she knew that her stomach would've revolted. As it was, the sour taste of bile surged up the back of her throat, making her want to gag. She pressed a hand to her stomach, as if she had the power to keep the churning acids contained by her touch.

"Where?" She didn't ask whether Rose was alive. She knew that she was not.

"Near the lake, where the first girl was found."

Just a short distance from the hermit's hut. Had the tweeny been dumped there while they'd been talking to Thomas? Had they just missed the murderer?

"We searched the area yesterday." Alec came up behind Kendra, and laid a warm hand on her shoulder.

"He knew," Sam said, looking angry. "The bastard's been watching us."

"Rebecca is waiting for you inside the castle, Miss Donovan," Aldridge began.

"I have to go to Rose," she said sharply. "I need to see the body."

Alec's hand tightened on her shoulder. "Is that truly necessary?" He was furious suddenly. "Hell and damnation, why put yourself through that?"

"I have to go! It's why I'm here!" she shouted. But was that true? Why was she here if she couldn't save anybody? If she couldn't save Rose?

Alec frowned, puzzled. Before he could question her, Aldridge lifted a weary hand. "I will allow you to accompany us, Miss Donovan. But you shall not attend the girl's postmortem. Is that understood?"

Kendra shifted her gaze to the Duke. "Yes," she whispered.

"Then come." The Duke's expression was bleak, but fiercely determined. "Whatever has been done, has been done. 'Tis time to bring the poor girl home."

Someone had covered Rose's naked body up with a coarse wool coat. Two men stood as sentries next to the body, tears shimmering in their eyes. This wasn't like Lydia or April Duprey—Rose was one of their own. They probably knew her family, had watched her grow up.

She was only fifteen.

Kendra had looked down at other fifteen-year-olds who'd suffered the butchery of a serial killer, and had felt pity. Now she also felt a sorrow so heavy that it made her heart ache.

"You do not need to subject yourself to this, Miss Donovan," repeated Alec, his voice low. "Why are you punishing yourself this way?"

Am I punishing myself? Self-flagellation for not protecting Rose? She didn't know.

"Let Dr. Munroe take care of her," he persisted softly, so close that she could feel his body heat.

Kendra was tempted to do as he suggested, to take the coward's way out. No one here would think less of her—but she'd hate herself for it.

Straightening her shoulders, she shook her head. "I need to see this through." She turned to look at the circle of faces. "Who found the . . . who found her?"

A tall, gangly youth whose ears stuck out almost sideways from his close-cropped sandy hair shuffled forward. "That would be me, ma'am. Me and Gerald." His pallor was a sickly green, his face tear-streaked. His freckles looked like they'd been drawn on with a Magic Marker. Ridiculously young. He stood before her nervously, twisting a knit cap with his hands. It struck her that all the men around her had taken off their hats. Not a courtesy to her, but as a sign of respect for the dead girl at their feet. A lump formed in her throat.

"What's your name?"

"Colin, ma'am."

"When did you find her?"

"Er . . . 'alf hour. No more."

Kendra scanned the area. Rose had been placed near the grassy knoll where they'd had the nuncheon, about ten yards from the lake. Unlike the path upon which April had been dumped, this was isolated enough. The area, as the Duke said, had been searched the previous evening. There was no reason to search it again. Rose could've lain here for days before anyone found her.

"What made you and Gerald come to this area, Colin?"

"Nothin' really." His gaze fell to the cap he was twisting. "Me and Gerald . . . we just wanted ter talk a bit."

Kendra looked over at Gerald. Same age as Colin, but smaller in stature with flaxen hair and baby blue eyes. The boys were still at that developmental stage in their life, probably eager to slip away to share their horror in private, away from adult ears. Too bad for them, then, that they'd encountered a fresh horror.

"It's significant that the killer didn't dump . . . the body in the lake." *The body. The victim.* It was easier for her to think of Rose in more impersonal terms. "He wanted her to be discovered, but it would've been too risky for him to put her on a more public path. Too many people searching, too many possible witnesses. When, exactly, was this area searched yesterday?"

Someone spoke up from the back of the crowd. "We went through 'ere at about 'alf past ten."

"It was dark. Could you have missed her?"

"Nay, ma'am. We 'ad lanterns. We would've spotted 'er."

"Aye. Or one of the dogs would've found 'er."

"Okay. If everyone would step back, please . . ." She gave a nod to Dr. Munroe. He'd been waiting, and now squatted down beside the shrouded form. He opened up his black bag and withdrew a magnifying glass.

Kendra's heart lurched when he slid the coat down to reveal Rose's face. Her eyes were open. There was a dark bruise on her right temple, which Kendra pointed out.

"That's new." Even to her ears, her voice sounded strained. "It's not part of his ritual."

"It could be how he abducted her from the castle grounds," Aldridge murmured. "Mayhap he knocked her unconscious."

Munroe peered closer. "Hmm. The skin appears intact. He most likely used a blunt object of some kind."

She found herself praying that Rose had never regained consciousness.

"Her hair has been cut," observed the Duke.

Kendra forced herself to watch as the doctor dragged the wool coat away, exposing her. The crowd shifted, moving farther back. It was human nature to gawk, and Kendra was certain that if this girl had been a stranger, they'd have edged in closer to get a better look.

"She's been throttled," said Munroe, even as Kendra's gaze flicked to the deep bruising around the throat.

How many times? She felt sick. How many goddamn times before the son of a bitch had exerted too much pressure, killing her?

"One bite mark," the doctor pointed out, and lifted his gaze to Kendra's. "'Tis as you wrote on the slate board."

"Yes. It's the killer's signature."

He returned to his examination. "It appears she was restrained."

Kendra's heart sank as she looked at the deep contusions around the wrists. There would've been no need to restrain her if she'd been unconscious. And the way the skin was cut suggested that she hadn't been passive. She'd struggled in panic. In pain.

Unwillingly, Kendra slid her eyes to the dark slashes marring the marble-white torso. Something was off. She frowned, trying to understand, but her head began to spin with unexpected vertigo. Someone was breathing heavily. Kendra could hear it. Ragged pants, in and out. With a tiny shock, she realized that she was the one making the harsh sound.

"Good God . . ." the Duke breathed, his voice weighted with sorrow.

Kendra barely heard him. She stumbled back, pushing through the onlookers as her stomach quivered and heaved. She managed four steps before dropping to her knees and vomiting.

53

The Duke of Aldridge pressed a teacup and saucer into Kendra's trembling hand. "Drink this, Miss Donovan."

They'd returned to the study, where a fire had been lit. But while Kendra sat near the crackling flames, they couldn't penetrate her frozen state.

Rose had been transported to the icehouse, where Dr. Munroe and Sam Kelly were conducting the postmortem. Kendra didn't need to view the slice and dice to know how Rose had spent her last hours on earth. They'd been filled with unimaginable pain, unimaginable terror.

And I'm responsible.

The teacup rattled in her hand. How was that possible? How was *any* of this possible? How could she be responsible for the death of a girl who'd died before she was born?

It wasn't the grandfather paradox, a theory many quantum physicists often dusted off to illustrate that time travel into the past was impossible. A person could *not* go back into the past and kill his own grandfather before his own mother or father was conceived, they argued. That would negate his existence in the first place, which in turn would make it impossible to kill his own grandfather. The ultimate Catch-22. An endless loop of impossibilities.

But could someone go back in time and inadvertently cause the death of someone who had nothing to do with her own future existence? Rose wouldn't affect Kendra's own time line, unless the tweeny was the great-great grandmother of someone who would eventually affect her future. Kendra felt like her head was going to explode.

"Mayhap Miss Donovan requires something stronger than tea," Rebecca suggested.

"No. I'm . . . this is fine." More because it was expected of her than out of any real desire, she took a swallow of tea. Then she set the cup and saucer down.

Aldridge said firmly, "You are not to blame for the maid's death."

"I knew he was escalating. He deliberately placed April Duprey where he did because he wanted to engage us. I should have seen this coming!"

"You are not omniscient, Miss Donovan," snapped Alec.

A knock at the door startled them. Harding's face looked graver than usual as he stood on the threshold. "I beg your pardon, Your Grace. Mr. Morland has arrived. He is wondering if you are at home. What shall I tell him?"

Aldridge looked at Kendra. "Do you wish to see him?"

Kendra straightened. "Yes."

"Very well. Tell Mr. Morland that I am at home. Put him in the Chinese drawing room. Miss Donovan and I will be there shortly."

Morland stood in front of the Palladian windows overlooking the flower gardens, but turned as soon as the Duke and Kendra entered.

"I heard that you visited Tinley Park last evening, Your Grace . . . and about the tragedy that has befallen your household. May I offer my condolences and any assistance that you may require?"

"That is very good of you. Won't you sit down?"

"You can assist us by answering questions," Kendra said bluntly, taking the seat opposite him.

He frowned. "As you know, I was not in residence when your maid went missing. I was in London. In fact, I only returned a couple of hours ago."

"So you say."

He stiffened. "I understand you are in distress. Nevertheless, I find your implication offensive. I would like to point out that I came as soon as I heard the news—you did not need to seek me out."

She eyed him. It could be neighborly consideration that brought him here. But sometimes cold-blooded killers enjoyed getting close to the victim's family, watching the devastating aftermath caused by their crime. Like demonic parasites, they fed off the grief.

"We appreciate your concern, Mr. Morland," Aldridge interjected smoothly. "And my sympathies in regards to Lady Anne. I understand she had some sort of seizure yesterday?"

Morland lowered his gaze to his hands. "Yes. As you saw yourself, my mother is not well. When I visited her yesterday morning, she . . . she had a fit." He drew in a deep breath. "She was quite out of control. I left immediately to ride to London."

"Why you?" Kendra asked. "Why didn't you send a servant to bring back a doctor?"

"Of course I considered that, but . . ." He shrugged, lips twisting. "I confess, I wanted to escape. 'Tis not a noble thing to admit, but I simply did not wish to deal with my mother's current reality. Have you ever had to watch a family member slowly go mad, Miss Donovan?"

"No."

"Then you cannot possibly understand the state of mind I was in yesterday."

"You left yesterday morning. Yet you didn't return until a few hours ago. I'd have thought you'd be more eager to bring help back for your mother."

His mouth compressed as he looked at her. "I sought out the mad-doctor that had treated my mother previously. He was not in Town. I spent several hours searching for another doctor. When I finished my quest, night had fallen. 'Tis not safe to travel the country roads alone. There are highwaymen lying in wait. I chose to put up at my town house for the night."

"Sadly, robberies are too common an occurrence on our highways," agreed Aldridge.

Kendra didn't take her eyes off of Morland. "Your staff at your town house should be able to confirm your whereabouts."

"I do not keep a staff at my town house when I am not officially in residence."

"Did you go to your club?" asked the Duke.

"No. I went to a nearby pub. Anyone there can confirm my presence, I'd assume."

"And everyone you spoke to in your search for a doctor," Kendra added.

Morland inclined his head. "Naturally. I spoke with servants, nurses at Bedlam in search of Dr. West. As he was not in Town, I was directed toward other hospitals, but it proved a fruitless search."

"Regardless, we'll need a list of everyone you spoke to."

He gave her a look of annoyance. "I am not used to having my word challenged in this way." He paused, then sighed. "Dr. West is on staff at Bethlem Royal Hospital. When I discovered he was not in residence, I continued my inquiries at St. John's Hospital, and then St. Luke's."

"And they didn't have any doctors who could help you?" Kendra wondered.

He shrugged. "When I was at St. Luke's, I realized that I had been hasty in my journey to London. I did not wish to further upset my mother by inflicting upon her a strange doctor. Again, I do not expect you to understand the emotional duress which motivated my desire to go to Town."

It would be easy enough to send someone to London to follow up. After all, how often could the gentry go searching for a mad-doctor? Then again, it could happen every damn day, for all Kendra knew.

"Are you certain your maid was murdered by the fiend who killed the other women?" Morland asked, shifting his attention to Aldridge.

"We can't go into details," Kendra interrupted.

He glanced back at her. "Why ever not?"

"It's an ongoing investigation."

He looked incredulous. "You will not tell me if the madman is now targeting servant girls? Pray tell, should I be concerned for the safety of my own household?"

"Tell all the women on your staff not to go anywhere alone. They shouldn't trust any man. No matter who he is."

Morland glared at her. He stood up. "I shall relay your message to my staff, but I will emphasize yet again that I am an innocent man."

Kendra met his eye. "I've never met a guilty man who doesn't say the exact same thing."

54

By the time Kendra and the Duke returned to the study, Dr. Munroe and Sam had appeared, having apparently completed the postmortem. Munroe eyed Kendra with concern over the cup of tea he'd poured for himself. "Are you quite certain you wish to hear this, Miss Donovan?"

No, she didn't want to hear it. But she had to. "Yes. Give us your report, Doctor."

Dr. Munroe shot a glance at Rebecca. "And you, your Ladyship? I am aware of your progressive nature, but what I have to report is not pleasant."

"Thank you for considering my tender sensibilities, sir. However I am made of sterner stuff."

"Very well, madam." He drew in a breath, like a diver before plunging deep beneath the ocean waves. "The maid was strangled like your first victim. Likewise, the perpetrator used four different knives, primarily in the rectus abdominis."

Kendra tried to block out a mental image of Rose as he talked.

"The number of lacerations, however, are different from Lydia Benoit."

Surprised, Kendra asked, "More or less?"

"More. I counted sixty-five."

Aldridge glanced at Kendra, frowning. "What does that mean?"

"I'm not sure," she admitted slowly. "It could mean that the number of incisions are not significant."

"Or the perpetrator is becoming more unstable," said Munroe.

Aldridge looked at him. "Why do you say that, Doctor?"

"You must understand that since I did not conduct the first postmortem, I only have Miss Donovan's notes as a guide. Still, I've found those notes to be remarkably detailed, and have no cause to doubt their veracity." He offered Kendra a slight smile. "You wrote that the incisions were slashes or deliberate cuts. Half of the lacerations on this victim followed a similar pattern. Varying degrees of length and depth, but still deliberate incisions. However, more than a dozen were consistent with stabbing rather than slashing. The wounds were deeper, longer, wider, and more jagged."

Kendra remembered her sense that something was off when she'd looked at the wounds. Subconsciously, she'd recognized the difference. "Which were made first, Doctor?"

He shook his head. "I have no way of determining that, Miss Donovan. If I were to surmise . . . I believe the more deliberate incisions came first, followed by the stabbing."

"I see. That's why you think the unsub is becoming more unstable."

"Yes. Comparing the two types of wounds, there appears to be more of a frenzy to the stabbing lacerations. I cannot determine whether those wounds were inflicted postmortem or before."

Kendra raised her brows. "Why do you think those wounds would be postmortem?"

"Because, Miss Donovan, I believe the girl died before the perpetrator could do his work."

"I don't understand."

"She died from trauma to the brain."

There was a moment of stunned silence.

Alec broke it. "She didn't die from strangulation like the first victim?"

"She was strangled repeatedly like the first victim. She was also sexually assaulted. The rest you know from your own visual examination—the bite mark to the left breast and abrasions on her wrists indicating she was restrained." He stood up, clasping his hands behind his back as he addressed the room. "However, this victim received a head injury. Possibly from a rock, or a cudgel of some kind, although I found no wood slivers or particles in the wound.

"The blow fractured the girl's skull, causing epidural hemorrhaging," continued Munroe. "The blood clotted, putting immense pressure on her brain. She would have lived for several hours after the blow, but the head injury is the cause of death."

"A rock suggests that this was a crime of opportunity," Kendra said. "She wasn't targeted, per se. Not like the other girls."

Kendra turned to study the slate board, although the words were now burned into her brain. "Control is important to the unsub. But he's been losing that control ever since the first victim was found. Part of his need to engage us is to reassert his control. If . . . if Rose . . ." the name lodged in her throat. "If she died prematurely, he would have been enraged. That would explain the postmortem stabbing frenzy."

"Like a child having a temper tantrum," Rebecca said softly, and shivered.

Munroe said, "One more thing of note. I discovered small wool fibers on the body, embedded in the wounds. With the aid of the Duke's microscope, I've determined that the source of those fibers come from a coarse wool blanket, rug, or sack."

Rebecca gave him a look. "How can you be so precise in your determination, sir?"

"'Tis simple, my Lady. The fibers lack what is known as crimp. The more crimp a wool fiber has, the finer the material it is spun into. Conversely, the less crimp in the wool fiber, the more coarse the material."

"Someone—one of the boys who found her—put a wool coat over her," Kendra reminded him.

"The skin would have to come in close contact with the material—the body *wrapped* in the wool coat, for instance—to get the degree of contamination that I observed."

Aldridge frowned. "It would make sense for the fiend to have transported her away from the castle in a sack."

"He's bold and quick," Sam said.

"And now he's frustrated," Kendra said quietly. "His fantasy was disrupted." They stared at her, and she added, "You might want to speak to your sister about ending the house party early, Duke. There's no predicting what the unsub will do."

55

The Duke followed her suggestion, and spoke to Lady Atwood about ending the house party early. The guests' planned departures for the next day resulted in a flurry of preparation—clothes and linens had to be laundered, pressed, and packed into trunks—but it couldn't dispel the somber mood that had invaded the castle.

By evening, the ancient fortress had settled into a calm. Dinner was a simple affair, followed by cards rather than dancing. Unable to go through the pretense, Kendra stole a bottle of brandy and a glass from the Duke's study and crept up to the roof.

The night air chilled her skin, but by her third glass, she didn't notice. The alcohol ensured she didn't feel the cold as she sat huddled halfway up the stairs that led to the battlements. Above her, the clouds of the day had thinned to reveal a handful of stars and the moon, which spilled icy light across the roof.

"I thought I'd find you here."

Kendra stiffened, glancing down as Alec materialized out of the shadows. She lifted her glass. "You should be a detective."

He frowned. "You missed dinner."

"I brought my own."

He watched her toss back the brandy in one gulp. "You are abusing good brandy, Miss Donovan," he said gently. "'Tis meant to be sipped, not swilled."

"Well, thank you, Miss Manners. If you're going to criticize, go find your own party. I didn't invite you."

Sighing, he removed his coat. "You are not only foxed, Miss Donovan, you must be frozen."

"Actually, I'm quite warm, thank you very much." Still, she didn't protest when he climbed the steps to drop his coat around her shoulders. "And I'm not drunk. Yet."

"Getting drunk will not help you."

She poured more brandy into the glass. "Right now, it's not hurting either."

He was silent for a moment. Then he said softly, "It is not your fault, Miss Donovan."

"Then why am I *here*?" she wondered bleakly, staring into the glass. "If I can't save anyone, why am I here?"

"I do not understand you, Miss Donovan."

She laughed, but the sound was bitter. "Yeah, I'll bet you don't."

"How would your presence here stop fate?"

"There has to be a reason," she muttered into her glass.

"I do not know why you bother with using a glass at this rate."

She gave him a crooked smile. "You're right. It's probably an unnecessary step."

"Miss Donovan."

"Lord Sutcliffe."

He sighed heavily, and sank down on the step beside her. "You are following the same path as Gabriel."

She was silent, feeling sorry for herself. "I just want to forget about everything for one damn night. Is that too much to ask?"

"That," he pointed at the bottle, "will not make your pain go away. It will be waiting for you tomorrow. Along with a headache."

"I don't need a lecture." She leaned forward and pressed the cool glass to her hot forehead. "God. I just want to go home. I want to go where I belong. I don't belong here. I'm making things worse."

"Miss Donovan—"

"April Duprey died because of me."

"No."

"Rose is dead because of me."

"No. You cannot blame yourself."

"Yes, I damn well can! *I'm* the reason the killer turned his attention to the castle! If I hadn't been here to tell you that you had a fucking serial killer on your hands, you'd have thought Lydia had tripped and drowned while bathing!"

He regarded her steadily, disturbed by the profanity and her pain. "Do you think we are so stupid that we would not have recognized that Lydia Benoit had been strangled? That we would not have known we were dealing with murder?"

The rage left her as suddenly as it had taken hold. She slumped against the stones. "I don't know," she whispered.

"Is crime detection so much more sophisticated in America?"

She couldn't stop herself. She began to laugh helplessly. "*My* America, yes. In *my* world, yes!"

"You forget, Miss Donovan, I've been to America—"

"No. No, you haven't." She suddenly knew what she was going to do. What she *had* to do. She was going to take a chance, a leap of faith, her courage helped along by the bottle of brandy. "My America is the world's superpower."

"America may have won the war, but your country is hardly that powerful—"

"*Superpower*—one word. It refers to global dominance." Her hand trembled as she splashed more brandy into the glass. "The term was coined around World War Two."

"World War Two?"

"In the 1940s."

"I . . . see."

"I can't seem to remember the exact date. And I have an excellent memory."

"Why don't you give me the brandy?" He reached over to extract the brandy bottle, but she yanked it away, hugging it close to her chest. He sighed. "Miss Donovan . . . Kendra, the brandy has addled your wits."

"No, it hasn't. In my world, the United States of America is a superpower." She tossed back the contents of her glass and ignored the little voice in her head that was yelling, *Shut up!* "This . . . all of this . . ." She waved the empty glass around. "It's not my world, Alec."

"I see."

"Ha!" She leaned back and wagged her finger at him. "I *told* you that you wouldn't believe me!"

"Believe you about *what?* You are not making any sense."

"You're not *listening.*" She shifted and nearly toppled over. Alec caught her, but she barely noticed. She leaned against him. "This is not my world."

"You are talking as though you are from another planet."

She frowned, considering that. "I'm from this *planet,* but not this *time.* Do you understand?"

"I understand that you have drunk half a bottle of brandy."

"I'm being serious! Alec . . . I'm different."

"I cannot dispute that." He reached again for the bottle of brandy, and this time she relinquished it.

"Dammit, Alec. Have you listened to what I'm saying?"

"Yes. You are saying that you are from the future, the 1940s."

That made her laugh again. "Oh God, no. That was *way* before I was born." Her laughter faded when she caught his gaze. "I can't prove anything I've told you. I don't have any device from the future to show you, no time travel machine. I only have my knowledge . . . and it might not be wise to share too much of that with you."

"Why not?"

She shrugged helplessly. "Because it could change the future. Look, you can send Sam Kelly all around England, and he's not going to find my name on any ship manifests or in any place of employment. Ever. Don't you see? I don't exist in this time."

"You may have used another name. Or Kendra Donovan may not be your real name."

"Why do you have to be so damned logical? I know how insane this sounds, but I'm telling you the truth. I went into the secret passage in the twenty-first century, and when . . . when I came out, I was here."

He stared at her uneasily. "This is inconceivable."

"It takes a little getting used to."

"Let's say I believe you. How did it happen?"

"I don't know. It was outside of my control." She shivered as the memory came flooding back to her, the suffocating darkness, the terrifying sensation of being ripped apart and then knit back together. "My best guess is that it was some sort of vortex or wormhole."

"A *worm*hole?" He sounded skeptical.

"Basically a shortcut between dimensions or through space and time—if space and time folded in on itself." She sighed. "It's complicated. At first I thought it was a random event. Horrible and strange, but still random." She stared unseeingly out into the darkness, talking softly, almost to herself. "But then Lydia's body was found."

"What does that have to do with . . . your tale?"

She roused herself, looking at him. "Because I knew Lydia had been murdered, and her murderer was a serial killer. And in my time line, that's my job. I hunt serial killers."

"You *hunt* killers?"

"*Serial* killers. Otherwise known as stranger killings. I'm a special agent in the FBI. I study this type of killer, determining his patterns and predict what he might do next."

"But you are a woman!"

She glared at him. "So? You think nothing is going to change in two hundred years for women? Let me tell you something, buddy . . . Oh, God, what am I doing?" She shook her head and pinched the bridge of her nose, tried to focus. "I'm getting off track. Let me just say that women will accomplish great things.

"And I am good at my job. Or I used to think I was." She was silent as a wave of remorse hit her. "I never even considered that Rose would be in danger. I didn't anticipate that." She rubbed a hand across her face, feeling suddenly weary. "I screwed up. What good am I here if I screw up? What's the *point*?"

She put her head in her hands. Alec watched her, saying nothing. Eventually, he prompted, "FBI?"

"Federal Bureau of Investigation," she mumbled, then jerked her head up to look at him. "Do you believe me?"

"I shall need time to consider it," was all he said. He stood up, grabbing her hands and hauling her to her feet.

The world swirled, and Kendra found herself clutching at his arm. "I think I may have drank too much."

"I *know* that you have drunk too much."

She peered up at him. "That doesn't mean I'm lying. Or inebriated. I'm not seeing pink elephants."

"You say the damnedest things." He hauled her to his side, practically carrying her down the remaining steps.

"Are you going to tell the Duke about what I've told you?"

"Do you want me to tell him?"

She bit her lip. "I don't know."

"If anyone would be open-minded about such a fantastical subject, it would be the Duke."

"I'll think about it."

Alec took her by surprise when he skimmed a finger across the blunt bangs. "Your hairstyle . . . is this typical of women in the future?"

Kendra had to think about that for a moment. "It's not *a*typical. We have trends, but there's a lot more variety in hairstyles and fashions during my time."

Alec shook his head. "I cannot believe I am having this conversation. 'Tis outrageous."

"Welcome to my world, Lord Sutcliffe."

Alec was silent again. Then he laughed softly. "Actually, Miss Donovan, if what you are saying is true, it is I who should be welcoming you to *mine*."

An hour later, Alec dismissed his valet and sat before the fire in his bedchambers, contemplating the glass of brandy in his hand. He wondered yet again in less than a fortnight if Kendra Donovan was mad, or if he was mad to listen to her. Her story of vortexes and wormholes—devil take it, of being from the *future*—it was ridiculous. Utterly preposterous.

And yet his mind continued to flash back to the first night, after she'd stumbled through the passage. He remembered how she'd stared at the candles like she'd never seen such a thing before. And the Ming vases.

Two hundred years old—more like over five hundred years old!

He thought of how she'd subdued the hermit with those odd moves. She was a special agent for the Federal Bureau of Investigation; she hunted serial killers. Dear Christ, what kind of woman did that? Although, if she could be believed, women's role in society would shift significantly. Becca, at least, would be ecstatic to hear that.

He shook his head, unable to figure out his own emotions. Did he believe her? Who could invent such a tale if it weren't true?

She'd spoken so blithely about Jane Austen, the authoress of *Pride and Prejudice.* He'd thought she must have some connection to the writer, and had immediately posted a note to the publisher. He had yet to receive a reply, and now wondered how he'd feel if the answer seemed to confirm Kendra's wild tale.

He couldn't bring himself to believe that these were the ravings of a lunatic. But she'd been foxed. Could he convince himself that it was a story spun by someone who'd imbibed too much strong drink? Perhaps.

Alec was torn between disbelief, denial, and a strange sort of wonder. Slowly, he finished the brandy and set the glass aside. He moved to the bed, shrugging out of his banyan. He blew out the candle and, in the darkness, he slid beneath the crisp sheets and bedding. Stacking his hands beneath his head, he contemplated the light and shadows that danced across the painted ceiling from the glow of the fireplace.

The Duke would be interested in hearing Kendra Donovan's story, as peculiar as it was. But he'd promised to keep quiet, and he intended to keep that promise. A time traveler deserved a little consideration, he supposed.

56

She'd told Alec that she was from the future.

The memory came flooding back in horrifying clarity as soon as Kendra opened her eyes the next morning. She'd drank a lot—could still feel the aftereffects of the brandy, the way her head swam just a bit woozily as she pushed herself to a sitting position—but she knew she hadn't imagined her conversation with Alec.

What would he do? She suppressed a panicky shiver, and considered all the angles. If he told Aldridge, the Duke would . . . what? He'd always been surprisingly accepting of what he undoubtedly regarded as her eccentricities, but there was a big difference between thinking someone odd, and thinking them *certifiable.* Really, Aldridge had known her less than two weeks. If the positions were reversed, she knew she'd be calling for a psych evaluation. Could she blame him if he called in a shrink—a *mad*-doctor? Even the name made her shudder. Like the insane asylums of this period, it conjured up primitive, torturous conditions and ignorance. She'd never survive it.

But what recourse was open to her? Here, she was a servant. Although she wasn't familiar with this era's laws regarding mental disorders, she knew her voice would never be heard over the powerful Duke of Aldridge's.

Of course, there was another possibility. He might actually believe her. Could she get that lucky?

She thought of her life so far: involuntarily sucked through a vortex, stuck in the nineteenth century, her one friend murdered. No one would consider her lucky. But everyone's luck had to change sometime.

She didn't know how long she sat there, fighting panic and waves of nausea, until a soft knock at the door roused her. She glanced up as Molly poked her head in. Her eyes, Kendra noticed, were still red and puffy.

"Oi came ter see if ye need 'elp dressin', Miss. Are ye ill?"

"I don't feel so hot."

"Aye. There's a chill in the air."

"No, I mean—forget it." Kendra slid out of bed, then hesitated, a lump forming in her throat. "I'm sorry, Molly. About . . . about Rose."

New tears shone in the maid's eyes. "'Tisn't yer fault, miss. It's the bastard 'oo done that to 'er. We'll catch 'im and 'e'll 'ang from the gallows. And Oi 'ope 'e rots in 'ell!" She sniffed, and bent down to pluck the dress and spencer that Kendra had discarded on the floor the night before, tossing both on the bed. "The gentry are leavin' terday," she said in a quieter tone.

"Yes. I know." Kendra hastily donned her underwear.

"A funeral needs ter be planned." The tweeny dashed the tears from her eyes as she opened the wardrobe. "Do ye 'ave a preference for w'ot ye be wearing terday?"

"No."

Molly brought over a pale lavender gown, and helped Kendra into it. "Oi'll pin up yer 'air, miss."

Kendra nearly groaned out loud. Her head ached without having heavy pins stuck in it. "That's not necessary."

"'Tis no trouble, miss."

"Honestly, I don't—"

"Oi'd like ter do it. For Rose, miss."

Put like that, Kendra couldn't deny the tweeny. She sat down on the bed as Molly retrieved the brush and pins.

"She wo'nted ter be a lady's maid, ye know," Molly said softly.

"I know." As the tweeny brushed her hair, her mind flashed to the question Alec had asked last night. *Your hairstyle . . . is this typical of women in the future?*

"Rose taught me ter do this." Molly twisted Kendra's hair into a low coil, and then pushed the long hairpins in place to anchor it. She took a step back to admire her handiwork. "Ye look right proper, miss."

"Rose would be proud of you, Molly."

"Thank you, miss." Blinking back tears, Molly retreated to the other bed, picking up the gown and spencer. She started toward the wardrobe, but paused. "Oh. Ye're dress 'as got a stain. Oi'll take it down ter Mrs. Beeton ter scrub it out. Ye've picked up a bit of dirt on yere spencer, too. W'ot were ye doing yesterday—?" she broke off, her expression stricken as she remembered what everybody had been doing.

"It's my laundry," Kendra said, walking toward her. "You shouldn't have to do extra work, Molly. I'll take it to Mrs. Beeton." She lifted the jacket out of Molly's hands.

"'Tisn't any trouble, miss. 'Tis good to work." The tweeny was reaching for the clothes, but stopped when she noticed Kendra's expression. "W'ot is it, miss?"

Kendra's eyes were on the brownish gray stains. "I'm not sure." Was she imagining the similarities?

"Miss?" Molly asked uncertainly when the silence lengthened.

Heart pounding, Kendra carefully inspected the smears running across both the gown and the spencer. They looked the same, but it didn't make sense. "Have I been mistaken?" she wondered, frowning.

"Mistaken 'bout w'ot?"

Kendra came to a decision. She thrust the bundle of material back into Molly's arms as a sense of urgency came over her. "Do me a favor, Molly. Take these clothes to the Duke and Dr. Munroe. Tell them to compare the stains to the one on April Duprey's coat."

The tweeny eyed the smudges dubiously. "W'ot is it?"

Kendra hurriedly slipped on her shoes. "I'm not sure, that's why I need the Duke to look at it under his microscope. But I think it might be potash."

"W'ot does that mean?"

Kendra paused at the door as she met the maid's confused gaze. "It means that I've been wrong, Molly. Wrong about everything."

57

No smoke was curling out of the chimney of the hermit's hut today. Of course, the abandoned feel of the place meant nothing; the appearance was easily deceptive. *And Thomas may have already deceived me,* she thought as she approached the door.

Kendra paused to listen intently, but heard nothing but birds trilling from nearby trees and the soft whisper of leaves and grass, stirred by the breeze.

She pounded on the door. "Thomas? Thomas, I need to speak to you!"

Silence.

She pounded again. "C'mon! Open up!"

Nothing.

She tried the door. She hadn't noticed any lock when she'd been in the place earlier, so she wasn't surprised when the door swung inward easily.

The room was empty. The shutters were still open, the sunshine seeping weakly through the greasy panes, limning the clutter inside. If possible, the stench seemed even worse than before.

Look around, then get out, she decided. Although she wasn't entirely sure what she was looking for. She spotted the cupboard that she'd bumped into yesterday. Jars, pottery, and paint-brushes still littered the surface. Her hands, she noticed, were smeared with grayish dirt about two seconds after coming in contact with the containers. Was it potash? Or plain dirt? *How the hell am I to know?*

Without a fire in the hearth, the room was as cold as a tomb. Kendra shivered slightly as she rifled through the cupboards. There was no way Thomas had used this place for torture, but he could've stashed April Duprey here before he dumped the body on the path. And Rose . . . yes, he could've kept her here too, as everyone searched—as *he* searched. Who better to know when they had finished searching the area near the lake than a volunteer in the search party?

She paused, tension prickling along the back of her spine. Was that a noise? A scrape and shuffle outside? She held her breath and listened. No, nothing. Except for the thudding of her heart.

Trying to shrug off her tension, she resumed her search. Her hands were filthy as she opened jars and containers. She would need a bath afterward, even if it meant hauling up the buckets of water herself.

Her eyes narrowed on the top shelf of the cabinet, noticing the wooden container. It wasn't dust-free, but it seemed less grimy than everything else in Thomas's shack. It also struck her as too ornate for the hermit. She reached up, bringing the container down. It was eight inches high, six inches wide, and about ten inches in length. The wood looked like mahogany, the lid hand-carved with a floral design. Balancing it in the crook of her arm, Kendra lifted the lid, and frowned as she saw skeins of yarn inside.

Puzzled, she reached in. Her fingertips had touched the soft filaments before she realized what it was. In revulsion, she gasped, lurching backward and falling hard against the cupboard. The box toppled out of her arms, hitting the dirt floor and splintering. The contents spilled out.

Not yarn . . . *hair.*

Human hair.

58

Gabriel wanted a drink badly. His hands shook with the wanting. He clenched them into fists and thrust them into his coat pockets. He gritted his teeth together. His head was pounding; his stomach twisted into knots. Though he'd had a bath that morning, he could smell his own sweat, a pungent odor that added to his misery.

He'd dismissed his valet earlier, not wanting anyone's eyes on him. He had to be alone as he fought against the demon whispering seductively in his ear, urging him to end the pain that was eating him alive. *Take a drink.*

God Almighty, he hadn't touched a drop since he'd heard the maid had disappeared from the castle, since he'd heard that she'd resembled the first whore. Even now, he remembered the gut-clenching horror that his madness might be spreading.

How many months had he woken up, unable to recall what he'd done the night before? The yawning black stretches in his memory frightened him more than anything, and he'd submerged his growing fear with more whiskey. It was only when the whore had been found in the lake that memory had floated up like bits of flotsam, disjointed images that had sent a thrill of horror through him: big brown eyes, Cupid's bow mouth—smiling and alive.

He'd tried desperately not to think of it. Kendra Donovan had pushed and pushed him, until he'd lost his temper. Jesus, he would have throttled her, if she hadn't fought back. The Duke was right; he was a monster.

Yet when the maid had went missing, he hadn't lost his memory. He'd been here, confined to his room since Kendra had nearly blinded him. A recluse. Yes, he'd been drinking, but not enough to forget. And to satisfy his own peace of mind, he'd asked Finch, who'd confirmed his presence in his bedchamber.

The maid's disappearance had galvanized the household. It had galvanized *him*. He'd spent the last forty-eight hours in agony—*sober* agony. As a search had gone out for the maid, he'd sweated and cast up his accounts until his stomach and throat were raw. When news came that the maid's body had been found in much the same condition as the whore in the lake, he'd been sober, and an emotion had seized him was one that he hadn't felt in a long time—*hope.*

59

Kendra stared in horror at the ropes of human hair at her feet. Some had been braided and tied off with twine, she saw now. Others had simply been tied off, like hair extensions used in high-priced salons. There were dozens of them, dark brown and black except for one that was golden blond—*April Duprey.*

Thomas had been collecting the girls' hair like scalps. As souvenirs?

Not exactly. The truth hit her like a punch to the gut, and she glanced at the paintbrushes scattered about. Slowly, she picked one up, staring at the soft bristles, and remembered how Thomas had appeared mesmerized as she'd thumbed the bristle. She attributed his behavior to his opium use. But now . . .

Shuddering, she dropped the paintbrush and stepped back.

Art requires sacrifice.

Kendra glanced at the canvases stacked against the far wall. Her skin crawling, she forced herself to move toward them, to drag off the dirty wool blankets. The first row was benign landscapes: the river, the forest; local scenes.

She flipped those back to reveal the second row, and these were far different from the pretty landscapes. There was nothing pretty about the ghastly images Thomas had painted, young girls shackled and screaming.

Art requires sacrifice.

She turned and ran outside, drawing in deep gulps of fresh air. Leaning over, she put her hands on her knees and tried to get a grip on the emotions swirling through her. Something flashed in her peripheral vision. She didn't even have time to turn before pain exploded in her head, driving her to her knees.

And into darkness.

60

"Is something on your mind, my boy?"

Alec glanced at the Duke, who was studying him over the rim of a teacup. Dr. Munroe was also eyeing him, apparently finding him more interesting than the carefully ironed newspaper in his hand.

"Pardon?" Alec replied.

"You seem a bit blue-deviled. What is troubling you?"

Alec was at loss for words. What could he say? *You have a woman living under your roof who is from the future—or, at least, believes that she is.* In truth, Alec wasn't entirely certain which he'd prefer. He was not a natural philosopher like his uncle. His own interests tended toward the pragmatic: business, finance, investments. Having Kendra Donovan claim she was from another time period was disturbing on a fundamental level. He damned well didn't like the idea of . . . what had she called them? *Wormholes.* After all, if she could unintentionally fall into one, what would stop anyone from following suit?

He glanced uneasily at the tapestry that hid the stairwell. How many times had he used the passageway in his lifetime, first as a boy, with a boy's natural curiosity, and later because it was the most expedient route to the Duke's laboratory? How many times had his uncle walked that same route? What if one day they went in and never came back out? It was too incredible even to contemplate.

But he couldn't bring himself to believe that Kendra Donovan was mad. Nor could he quite convince himself that she'd been foxed, her mind flooded with fantasy after drinking half a bottle of brandy.

"Alec?"

He became aware that he hadn't answered his uncle. "'Tis nothing, Duke. The maid's death has left a pall on the castle." That much was true. He needed to speak with Kendra again, before he spoke to the Duke about her unusual circumstance. If some madness had seized her mind, his uncle was in the best position to help.

A knock at the door interrupted his morose thoughts. Relieved at the interruption, he crossed the room, opening the door to a young maid, who stood uncertainly, clutching a bundle to her chest.

"Yes?"

The girl dropped into a hasty curtsey. "Yer Lordship. Oi . . . ah, miss asked me ter give this ter 'is Grace and the sawbones—er, Oi mean, the Doctor Munroe."

"What is it, pray tell?" Aldridge set down his teacup and came forward. They all watched as the maid shook out the material.

"That's the gown and spencer that Kendra—Miss Donovan wore yesterday," Alec identified with a frown.

"Aye." The maid gave him a nervous look. "Miss said ye were ter look at the stains. Said it mebbe potash, sir."

"Potash?" Munroe questioned, coming forward. He took the dress from the girl, scrutinizing the smears. "'Tis possible. They have a similar look. I would need your microscope, Your Grace, to be certain."

"Of course."

"Where is Miss Donovan?" Alec asked sharply.

"Oi dunno. She said she'd been wrong."

Icy fear had Alec grabbing the girl's arm. "Did she leave the castle?"

"Oi dunno, ye Lordship!"

"Alec, you're frightening the girl."

"Devil take it!" Alec glared at his uncle, but let go of the maid. "I told her not to go anywhere alone!"

Aldridge frowned, glancing at the maid. "You know nothing of Miss Donovan's whereabouts?"

"Nay, sir!"

"You may go." Once the maid had left, Aldridge turned to Alec. "Calm down. Miss Donovan is no fool."

Kendra's words came back to him in a terrifying rush. "Dammit. We need to find her!"

Aldridge moved to the bellpull. "I shall summon Rebecca. If Miss Donovan isn't with her, she most likely will know where she's gone."

I hunt serial killers.

But that was the thing about hunting a wild beast—desperation made them more dangerous. Kendra may *think* she was hunting the killer, but Alec knew, a chill deep in his gut, that the situation could easily be reversed. The fiend could be hunting *her.*

61

Kendra did not have a first conscious thought. She only felt pain. It radiated from the top of her skull all the way down to her toes. Slowly, she became aware of two other things: she was lying on her back, and her hands were pinioned above her head. She tried to move her arms, and felt the pinch of metal against her wrists.

Panic jolted through her like an electrical current. Visions of other wrists rubbed raw flooded her mind. She opened her eyes, barely noticing the shadowy ceiling above her as she thrashed around, rattling the chains. The sour taste of terror invaded her mouth.

She stopped her frantic movements, concentrating instead on subduing the blind panic. She closed her eyes. *Breathe in; breathe out.*

As the fear receded, her senses expanded. The air was cold and dank. She could smell beeswax and mildew. And something else that nearly broke her control again.

Blood.

It took every ounce of willpower to keep calm. She opened her eyes. Golden light flickered over stone walls—a building of some kind, or a basement . . . no, *a cave.* One in the network of caves that Rebecca had mentioned. Which also meant it would be impossible to find.

"You're awake."

The voice was close, startling her. She cut her eyes to the source, the movement causing greasy nausea to roll through her. Thomas was sitting in the corner of the room, staring at her. In the candlelight, his eyes glowed like a demon.

"What the fuck did you hit me with?" Her voice was unsteady.

He stood and came over to her. "You were where you didn't belong."

"Story of my life."

"You will be punished now." The hermit giggled.

Kendra squinted up at him. Even in the dim light, she could see the unnatural shine in his eyes. Madness or narcotics? Maybe both.

"He's coming," whispered Thomas. He was close enough for his stale breath to fan across her face.

She stared at him, trying to make sense out of his words. "Who? Who's coming?"

"My master. *He's coming for you.*"

62

"I have not the faintest idea where Miss Donovan is," Rebecca confessed. Her eyes darted between the Duke and Alec, her brow puckering. "Why? What has happened? Should I be concerned?"

Aldridge hesitated. "I am certain she is about. We simply need to locate her."

Rebecca wasn't fooled. "Do not treat me as though I have cotton for brains. She is my responsibility! I demand to know if something is amiss."

"My dear—" Aldridge began, but he broke off when the door to the stairwell opened, and Munroe stepped into the room. "Ah, Doctor, what have you learned?"

"Lady Rebecca." Munroe nodded by way of greeting. He looked at the Duke and Alec. "I have finished my examination, and can conclude that the discoloration on Miss Donovan's dress is indeed potash. I cannot determine whether it is the same substance that contaminated April Duprey's pelisse, you understand."

Rebecca frowned. "No, I do not understand. What is this about potash on Miss Donovan's dress?"

"It would seem Miss Donovan acquired potash on the dress she wore yesterday. The question is, where did she come into contact with the substance?"

Alec straightened suddenly. "We visited the hermit yesterday."

Aldridge's gaze shifted automatically to the slate board. "Thomas? But he does not fit Miss Donovan's profile at all."

"The maid said Kendra had been wrong," Alec reminded him, his expression grim.

"Potash . . . The hermit claims to be an artist, does he not?" Rebecca asked.

"'Twas one of the requisites that my sister wanted in an ornamental hermit. Why?"

She looked at the men. "Potash is used by artists. If you mix it with animal oils, it creates Prussian blue. 'Tis often used by those who do not have the coins to buy paint supplies commercially. I have mixed it myself when my supply has run low. Dear heaven." Rebecca put a hand to her throat, looking stricken. "When potash was mentioned before . . . it simply did not occur to me to mention this use. I had not thought of Thomas."

"Surely Miss Donovan would not be so unwise as to confront the hermit alone?" Munroe said.

Horror flooded Alec. *I hunt serial killers.*

"Yes, she would!" He spun on his heel, striding to the door.

"Alec, wait!"

The marquis glanced back at his uncle. "There is no time to wait, Duke. I must go to the hermit!"

"I know. I shall come with you." Aldridge went to his desk and opened the bottom drawer. Face grim, he withdrew a flat, square box. Setting it on the desk, he flipped open the lid to reveal two dueling pistols. "But we ought to go prepared."

63

Partners.

Kendra closed her eyes, furious with herself. She hadn't even considered the possibility. Names floated through her mind, nasty bits from history: Leopold and Loeb, who, in the 1920s, committed the murder of a young teen just to prove they could pull off the perfect crime; Angelo Buono and Kenneth Bianchi, cousins who became known in the media as the Hillside Stranglers.

Duos fed off each other's perverted fantasies and murderous impulses. There was usually a dominant partner and a submissive.

Thomas was clearly the submissive. He'd probably been the one to dispose of the bodies afterward.

She opened her eyes and forced herself to meet Thomas's burning gaze. "You fucked up, Thomas. You didn't expect Lydia to be found in the lake, did you?"

He looked puzzled. "I done it before. Threw the whores in the river. None were ever found."

"Careless," she insisted. "You kept April Duprey in your hut, didn't you? Stashed her there until you could dump her on the path. She got potash on her coat, you know. Just like I got on my clothes yesterday. That's how I knew you were involved. That's how the Duke will know you're involved."

He said nothing, simply stared at her.

"Your master is going to be angry with you, Thomas. You're the only thing connecting him to the murders. The Duke of Aldridge, Lord Sutcliffe . . . they all know about you now. Do you know what that means? You're a liability. *He'll* know you're a liability, Thomas. He will have to dispose of you. He'll *kill* you."

"Nay."

"I can help you, Thomas." She kept her voice low. Persuasive. "I can save you, if you release me. Unlock the handcuffs, Thomas. Let me help you."

"The siren's call that lures men into temptation."

Kendra nearly jumped out of her skin as the voice spoke from the doorway. She'd been so focused on Thomas that she hadn't heard anyone approach. Now she turned her head, and met the mocking gaze of Thomas's master.

"Good God." Aldridge stared in horror at the piles of hair lying near the broken box on the dirt floor.

Sam crossed the room to the paintings. Images, he thought, as horrifying as the tangle of hair on the floor.

Alec joined the Bow Street Runner, and felt the blood drain out of his face as he stared at the monstrosities depicted in oil. Dark-haired, dark-eyed girls, naked and bleeding.

"Jesus," he breathed, and felt as though he'd been punched low in the gut. He broke out into a cold sweat. "He's got Kendra. The bastard's got Kendra."

No one argued.

"But where?" Sam was the one to give voice to what was in all their minds. "Where did the fiend take her?"

Rebecca didn't know what to think as she hurried down the corridor, chaotic with departing guests. Thomas was the killer? How could that be possible? And now Kendra had disappeared, most likely gone to confront him. It was madness.

She skirted several trunks that had been packed and pushed out into the hall, awaiting footmen to load them onto carriages.

"Lady Rebecca!" Lady Atwood sailed toward her, looking irritable. "Have you seen the Duke? He should be here to see our guests off. 'Tis his duty."

"He rode out to the hermit's shack."

"Whatever for?"

Rebecca wondered what the countess would say if she told her that the ornamental hermit she'd hired was the murderer—probably swoon or go into hysterics. Either way, she couldn't deal with it now. "I haven't the faintest idea, your Ladyship," she lied. "If you'll excuse me . . ."

Aware that Lady Atwood was staring after her in astonishment, Rebecca continued to hurry down the hall. As she rounded a corner, she collided with Gabriel.

"Oh, my. I beg your pardon!" she began, stepping back. Her eyes widened as she took in his appearance. She hadn't seen him for days, not since his shocking attack on Miss Donovan, but she was stunned by the change in him. His skin was pale, stretched tight across his cheekbones, and a dark stubble roughened his jaw. Purplish shadows made his eyes look even more sunken.

Concerned, she exclaimed, "Good heavens, Gabriel. Are you all right?"

He hesitated. "I . . . I need to speak to His Grace."

"He's not here. He rode out with the others to see the hermit."

"Thomas? Why?"

"Because he . . ." Rebecca shocked herself by bursting into tears. "Oh, dear!" She groped in her pocket for a handkerchief. "I beg your pardon! I'm overwrought. Miss Donovan . . . she's gone missing."

"What?"

She dabbed at her eyes. "The hermit may have something to do with her disappearance. He may even be responsible for all the murders!"

"No." If possible, Gabriel seemed to pale even more. "No, Thomas is his manservant . . ."

Rebecca lowered her handkerchief and stared at Gabriel. "I beg your pardon?"

He raked a shaking hand over his hair, disheveling it even more. "God. I've been a fool. A bloody fool."

Rebecca was taken aback by the look in Gabriel's eyes: utter despair.

"If I had my wits about me, I might've saved the maid."

"What are you saying, Gabriel?"

His mouth twisted. "Thomas isn't the monster. But I know who the monster is."

Rebecca put a hand to her throat, felt her pulse leap beneath her fingertips. "*Who?*"

64

Kenneth Morland stepped into the room, and smiled at her. "You are not in your best looks, Miss Donovan."

Her heart was hammering so loudly that it was a dull roar in her ears as she regarded that handsome face above hers, unable to quell the horror as she thought of how he'd raped, tortured, and strangled the others. Her predecessors.

How can I die now? I haven't even been born yet! she thought wildly. She struggled for calm. "What happened to you, Morland?"

Her eyes followed him as he walked over to a table that held more than a dozen flickering candles. He lifted a fabric bundle, and unrolled it. Metal glimmered in the candlelight.

Knives.

Mouth dry, Kendra jerked her gaze away from the instruments. *Don't look at them. Don't think about it.* "Something to do with your mother," she continued. "All the girls resembled your mother when she was younger . . . you know, before she went nuts, and everything."

He turned to look at her, his expression more puzzled than angry. "You have such a peculiar way of speaking. I daresay it is because you are an American."

"Nuts, as in crazy. Mad. *Cuckoo.*" Her blood turned to ice as she watched him pick up one knife, inspect it carefully, and then set it down. Then he picked up another knife, a bigger one.

Panic broke loose inside her, splintering her control. Even though she knew it was hopeless, she strained against the handcuffs, tried to pull the chains from the wall.

Morland glanced at her, amused. "You won't be able to get loose, Miss Donovan. You may as well accept your fate."

Like hell. Still, she stopped moving, concentrating on her breathing, trying to work past the terror that was filling her lungs. She seemed to be drowning in it.

Her feet and legs weren't restrained. Briefly, she fantasized about using her legs to snap his neck, like the femme fatales did in the movies. Unfortunately, the movies rarely reflected reality, and that maneuver was damned near impossible to accomplish. He'd have to be in exactly the right position. And even then, she'd only be able to disable him temporarily, probably not kill him. But it could buy her some time . . .

A small sound caught her attention. *Shit.* She'd forgotten about Thomas. Even if she had a chance with Morland, Thomas would intercede and finish her off. On the positive side, though, Thomas would kill her a lot quicker than Morland would.

"So . . . what's your problem with your mother? You've been figuratively killing her for years. Do you blame her for your father not being around?"

Morland stilled. He came over to look down at her again. But he was still too far away for her to do any damage.

His dark blue eyes had gone eerily flat. "My father *was* around, Miss Donovan."

It was hard to keep her own eyes fixed on that soulless gaze. Shivers ran up and down her spine. "I thought your grandfather had him shipped off to India."

"A clever invention."

"But he . . ." Kendra drew in a sharp breath as an ugly possibility took shape. She closed her eyes, ashamed at all the details that she'd missed. Details right in front of her face. *"Adonis."* She opened her eyes again. "She called you Adonis. And she called herself Myrrha . . ."

Morland watched her with that unblinking gaze, shark-like.

"My father was quite taken with Greek mythology. As was my mother."

"Jesus Christ." Kendra remembered the painted mural on the foyer's ceiling at Tinley Park. It was, she realized, the story of Myrrha, who'd been turned into a myrrh-tree after having committed incest with her father, King Cinyras. Nine months later, Adonis had been born from the tree.

She sometimes mistakes me for my father. Morland had said that to explain his mother's confusion. Rebecca had talked about how the late earl had doted on him, enjoying their likeness.

"Your mother didn't elope with anyone. There was no infantryman."

"They were forced to devise the story when she got herself with child. The world would have ostracized them both had they known the truth." His lips twisted and the flatness of his gaze was replaced by a glow of rage. "Society, with all its bloody rules to force men to conform, to be something they are not."

"Why do you hate your mother?"

"I do not hate my mother. She taught me, as her father taught her."

"Taught you . . . ?" Something in his face alerted her, and she felt the bile rise up in her throat. Like abuse, incest could be a vicious cycle, replayed over and over again for each generation.

"You sick son of a bitch. You really never stood a chance, did you?"

"Do not blaspheme me, Miss Donovan!"

"You're not God."

"Oh, but I am. I am one of the gods. I am not blinded by the falsehoods of society. I understand power in its fullest sense, because I recognize no boundaries." Now the glow in his eyes struck Kendra not as rage, but as madness.

He straightened suddenly, and ordered, "Thomas, come here."

Thomas shuffled forward, eager to do Morland's bidding.

Morland smiled. "Thomas has been my most loyal manservant. We met during one of my hunting expeditions in London, before I had, shall we say, honed my craft. I was slitting the throat of a street whore when Thomas spotted me. We quickly discovered we had mutual interests. When Lady Atwood mentioned that she desired an ornamental hermit, I thought of my young friend here."

Kendra said nothing. As long as he was talking, he wasn't slitting *her* throat.

"His help has been immeasurable in securing harlots. I formed a little club, invited a select group of disillusioned young bucks to join. It has been . . . amusing. My private joke on the Ton." He laid a hand on the hermit's shoulder. "Except for April Duprey, Thomas has been my emissary with the bawds."

Bawds. It came to her then, that niggling sensation that had been bothering her for days.

"You knew," she said slowly.

He lifted his brows. "I beg your pardon?"

"You knew April Duprey was a bawd. When we interviewed you, you identified her as a bawd—not a harlot, or any of the other slang you might have used to describe the prostitutes."

Morland chuckled. "You are very clever, Miss Donovan. Of course, not clever enough or else you wouldn't be in this . . . *position*."

He was still chuckling, still smiling, when he took a step back. Then he was no longer chuckling or smiling. A look of determination settled on his handsome face, and he raised his hand. Kendra caught the glint of the knife, before he brought it down in a swift left-to-right movement. It took only a fraction of a second to sever Thomas's common carotid artery.

Kendra gasped, instinctively turning her head. She felt the warm spray of blood across her face. In her mind's eye, she saw Thomas's surprised expression. Then his knees buckled and he folded like a discarded puppet—which, she supposed, was exactly what he was.

She nearly choked on the raw meat smell of blood in the room. She turned her head to watch Morland approach.

"Alas, Thomas has outlived his usefulness," he said. "As you so adroitly pointed out, he is the only thing connecting me to the murders. And he had become so terribly careless." Morland smiled, clucking his tongue. "Yes, I was eavesdropping, Miss Donovan. I know, I know, very ill-bred of me."

Kendra was still stunned speechless by the unexpected display of violence when Morland lifted the knife that was dripping with Thomas's blood, and brought it plunging down toward her chest.

65

Gabriel leaned forward in the saddle, flicking the reins, riding hell for leather over the uneven terrain. The Arabian's hooves pounded against the ground, spitting up dirt. Each gallop felt like a spike was being driven into his skull. He wanted to vomit. He wanted a bloody *drink*.

He shuddered with relief when he entered the forest and was forced to pull on the reins, slowing the punishing pace as he got his bearings. His eyes darted around the thick copse with its ancient elm and oak, uncertain. He hadn't anticipated this. The times that he'd gone to the club, it had been dark and he'd already been well into his cups. And Thomas had guided them.

The horse shifted, impatient. Twigs snapped beneath the beast's hooves. Leaves rustled around him. Gabriel heard the sharp trill of a bird somewhere above him, answered from a neighboring branch. He touched his heels to the Arabian's flanks, moving slowly forward. He considered returning to the castle. Let Alec handle this situation. Who was he to play hero? But then he heard a faint noise in the other direction. *The stream.*

He remembered the stream.

The horse gave a snort as he tugged at the reins, and wheeled the animal around.

Alec had never felt this kind of icy terror. His stomach roiled at the thought of Kendra in Thomas's clutches, as they rode into the courtyard a minute later. They'd organize a search party. They now knew *who* they were looking for, but not the where. And every second the monster held Kendra brought her closer to death.

Alec thought of the torture the other women had endured. He thought of the search that had been organized to find the maid, and how that ended. *Christ Almighty.*

He brought his horse to a stop so abruptly that the poor beast reared up on his hind legs, then did a skittish sidestep. There was more activity than normal in the stable yard, with all the carriages being prepared for the departing guests. A stable boy rushed over to grab his reins as he swung down from the saddle.

The Duke and Sam rode into the stable yard as he pointed at one of the grooms. "You! Go and gather up men for another search! Thomas—"

"Alec!"

He broke off as Rebecca ran toward him. "Not now, Becca. Thomas has kidnapped Kendra! We need to find her!" He glared at the groom who was still standing, staring at him wide-eyed. "Goddamnit, I told you to gather the men! Move your arse!"

A murmur rippled across the stable yard. Several men began to approach.

"We need to organize another search party. Thomas is the fiend we've been looking for! He—"

"No!" Rebecca grasped his arm.

"Becca!"

"No! You don't understand! It isn't Thomas. It's Morland. *Morland is the monster!*" she shouted at him.

"You're mistaken, Becca. We've been to the hermit's shack. We've seen his madness!"

"He assisted Morland."

Aldridge and Sam jogged over. "How do you know this?" Aldridge asked.

Rebecca swung around to look at the Duke. "G-Gabriel. Gabriel told me."

Alec grabbed her by the shoulders. "Gabriel *knew*?"

"Yes. No. Oh, hell and damnation! There is no time to explain! He told me that Morland has a club, like the Hell Fire Club. There's a cave on Morland's property. Gabe has gone there now. He believes that's where Thomas may have brought Miss Donovan. Oh, dear God, Alec . . . you must save her!"

"Where is this cave?"

"I do not know! Captain Harcourt may be able to take you there. He and Gabriel attended the club together. That's where they were the first night of the house party."

Aldridge frowned. "Where is Harcourt now?"

Rebecca dashed anxious tears from her eyes. "Most likely preparing to leave."

Alec didn't wait. He ran toward the castle, nearly knocking down several servants who were in his way. "Harding!" he shouted when he saw the butler ahead of him, in conference with Mrs. Danbury.

"Sir?"

"Where is Captain Harcourt? What room is he in?"

"He shared a bedroom with Mr. Digby. In the east wing, second floor. I will send for—"

"Bloody hell. No time." He grabbed the startled butler's arm and shoved him forward. "Show me!"

66

Kendra closed her eyes and held her breath, expecting to feel the deadly kiss of the blade as it eviscerated her. Instead, she felt a tug, and then heard the ripping of cloth.

Another kind of horror seized her as cold air washed over her, pebbling her skin.

"You son of a bitch!" The chains rattled again as she jerked her arms in a primordial response. Yet no shot of adrenaline could give her the strength to break free of the shackles. The steel cut into her wrists, but she didn't care. Panic overwhelmed her. "You fucking bastard!"

Morland laughed. "Such language. You are not a Lady, Miss Donovan."

"I'm going to fucking kill you!"

"I rather doubt that, Miss Donovan."

He continued to work his way through the fabric, leaving her breasts exposed. Her skin crawled. Her breath came out in harsh pants. She wanted to scream, needed to release some of the horror building inside her. Above her head, her fingers curled helplessly into fists she had no chance of using.

She thought of Rose, of Lydia, of all the girls who'd endured this same gut-wrenching fear—the knowledge that before death, there would be rape and torture. Was there a worse nightmare for a woman?

As the knife whispered down her body, her earlier thought about using her legs to snap the bastard's neck came rushing back. If she could scissor her legs up, she might have a chance to incapacitate him. Maybe even make him a paraplegic. The odds were not in her favor, but she couldn't lay there without at least trying to fight back. She would have only one chance.

But even as she braced herself, Morland suddenly stopped, and cocked his head, his expression intent. Kendra watched, afraid to move, afraid to even breathe. After a moment, he shifted his gaze back to her. Her stomach clenched as his eyes ran over her exposed torso. He smiled. "If you will pardon me, my dear, I shall only be a moment . . ."

Stunned, Kendra watched Morland turn and walk out of the room. She had a brief moment of euphoria at the unexpected reprieve. But that vanished quickly. Unless a miracle happened, he'd be coming back. She couldn't count on a miracle.

Needing a better look at the shackles, she twisted her head. She yelped at a sharp pain at the back of her head. *Fucking hairpins!*

She didn't know whether to laugh or cry. Her head was already aching from the blow she'd received, and she was waiting for a serial killer to come back to torture her. *Now* she was being skewered from the damn hairpins, because Molly had insisted on putting her hair up that morning.

Then she felt the thrill of exhilaration all the way down to her toes—*the hairpins.*

67

Morland watched from the shadows as Gabriel bent down and picked up the gold chalice that he'd accidentally kicked against the cavern wall—that was the noise Morland had heard. He didn't understand why Gabriel was here, and he didn't like it. Anger heated his blood at this unexpected complication.

Today had been nothing but goddamn complications, beginning with Thomas abducting the American. That had not been part of his plan. At least, not yet. He'd wanted to watch first, to observe the weeping and wailing over the little maid's demise.

Thomas's stupidity infuriated him. He'd known for a while now that he'd have to kill the fool, though he hadn't planned to kill him so soon. But, in truth, that was the one unexpected development that would work in his favor. Yes, it would work out very well indeed.

In the future, of course, he would have to be more cautious. Sutcliffe or the Duke might even take it upon themselves to keep watch in London. Should whores go missing, it could mean a new investigation. He might consider buying a town house in Bath. Or Edinburgh—no one would care if Scottish whores began vanishing. Unfortunately, that would require him to actually spend time in that barbaric country.

Morland shook his head. That debate was for later. Now, he must take care of his unforeseen visitor.

He announced his presence, stepping out of the corridor into the larger cavern. "Lord Gabriel." The younger man gave a surprised start, swinging around to face him. Morland smiled, moving forward, closing the space between them. "We have no fête planned. To what do I owe this unexpected pleasure?"

"I . . . I came to find Miss Donovan." Gabriel swallowed nervously, his gaze bouncing around the cavern.

Morland laughed. "My dear boy, do you honestly believe I am having an assignation with Lady Rebecca's companion?"

"I . . . I beg your most humble apology, sir. I was actually hoping to find Thomas . . ." Gabriel's voice trailed away when his gaze fell on Morland's hands. He frowned.

Morland followed his gaze and let out a sigh. "Oh, dear. It would appear that I have Thomas's blood on me."

Gabriel stared at him in confusion. "Thomas's blood?"

He smiled. "Yes. But I suppose there really is no point in wiping it off . . ."

In the blink of an eye, Morland had the knife out of his pocket, and was thrusting the blade into Gabriel's gut, twisting, as he stared down into the younger man's shocked eyes.

"Really no point at all," Morland murmured.

Kendra scooted up the bed, pushing herself as far as she could into a half-sitting, half-reclining position. It was an awkward angle, straining her arms, but she managed to just graze the back of her head with her fingertips. She tried to relax her muscles as she maneuvered her body up another inch, grateful for the years of yoga practice. The iron manacles bit viciously into her wrists as she moved her hands, but she ignored the pain, and the warm blood that trickled down her arms. Her fingers felt swollen and numb, both from the pressure of the restraints and having her arms above her head.

Tilting her head down so that her chin pressed into her chest, she continued to twist her hands until her fingers dug into the soft coil at the base of her neck. Gritting her teeth, she rooted around and nearly wept with relief when her finger touched the top of one hairpin. She managed to pinch the top of it with her index finger and thumb, and slowly extracted it.

She couldn't see the handcuffs, although she knew from their size and weight that she wasn't dealing with a brand she was familiar with. Still, if there was a lock, she'd be able to pick it—she just needed time.

She closed her eyes in an attempt to block everything out. Slowly, she maneuvered the hairpin around until it struck the iron of the manacles, and she then began to tap blindly along the metal, learning its shape, trying to determine its mechanical structure.

She froze when the point of the pin suddenly snagged against the microscopic grain in the iron, bobbling. In reaction, her hand flexed, and she tried to squeeze her thumb and index finger around the pin's head. Her attempt to control the slender wire was clumsy. She could feel it sliding.

She let out a sob as the hairpin slithered out of her grasp, dropping soundlessly to the bed, out of reach.

68

Alec didn't bother to knock—he simply barged into Harcourt's room. The captain had been stuffing a shirt into his satchel, but now whirled around, eyes widening in alarm at the sudden intrusion.

"My Lord? What is amiss?"

"I need you to take me to where Morland holds his club!"

"I-I do not know—"

Furious, Alec shot forward, slamming the other man into the armoire. He pressed his arm into Harcourt's throat. *"Don't bloody lie to me, Harcourt!"*

"Alec!" The Duke and Sam rushed into the room.

Alec didn't take his eyes off Harcourt. "The bastard's got Kendra. We're wasting time!"

Harcourt made a strangled sound, his hands trying to push away the arm cutting off his air supply.

"I know you attended Morland's club, Harcourt." Alec eased back, allowing the other man to breathe again. "You will take me there. *Now.*"

❖

Gabriel crumpled to the ground, clutching his stomach. His waistcoat was already soaked crimson. Blood oozed from between his fingers.

The wound was mortal, Morland knew. He stared down at the young fool and felt the rage rise inside him again. He felt no remorse over killing the man, but was upset that circumstance—not desire—had forced him to take the action. He walked in circles, struggling to control his fury. By the third loop, his vision no longer misted red.

He'd have to get rid of Gabriel, of course. It shouldn't be too difficult. He wouldn't be careless like Thomas; there would be no mistakes. The thought calmed him. *I'm in control.*

"Please . . ." Gabriel moaned. He was shaking, his eyes glazed with pain and shock.

Morland flicked him a dispassionate look. He could finish him off by slitting his gullet, but that would be too easy a death for someone who'd caused him such annoyance. Saying nothing, he turned on his heel, retracing his footsteps down the rough-hewn corridor.

The pressure in his chest eased even more when he pushed open the door, his gaze fixing on Kendra. She was older than his preference, but she was the right size and coloring. Anticipation flooded him as he approached the bed.

"I apologize for the delay, my dear," he said, shrugging out of his coat. His hand went to his cravat, loosening it. "You and I are going to have a lovely time. I must say that I am quite looking forward to it."

His gaze slid hungrily over her partially exposed breasts, traveled up the slender column of white throat. He was annoyed that there were marks on it already. Bruises not caused by him.

Still, he smiled as he lifted his gaze to meet her dark eyes, expecting to see fear, the gleam of tears. They did hold a gleam. But it wasn't terror or tears—it was rage.

Her mouth twisted in a parody of a smile. "Fuck you, Morland."

She came up swinging.

69

Adrenaline sizzled through Kendra as she sprang from the bed, swinging the one-pound chain like a medieval flail. It struck Morland on the side of his face with a satisfying crack. His cheek split open, pouring blood. With a stunned howl of pain and rage, he stumbled back.

She swung the chain around again, but Morland's legs tangled with Thomas's body, and he was saved from another lash by falling on his ass.

The element of surprise was officially lost. Kendra launched herself at Morland, straddling him as she brought the chain up and around his throat. His face turned bright red, his eyes bulging, as he tried to loosen the yoke. Apparently realizing she had the advantage, he eventually let go and began punching her on the side of her head.

Once, twice, three times. Her ears rang from the blows and her vision blurred. She tried to twist away without letting go of the chain, her biceps trembling.

Kendra yelped as pain seared down her hip. Her eyes snapped down, and saw her dress turn crimson. Her gaze went to the knife Morland held. She'd forgotten about the damn knife.

Abruptly, she let go of the chain and rolled off him, staggering to her feet. Her side was a blaze of agony, but she never took her eyes off him. They were both breathing raggedly. The harsh sound filled the room along with the coppery scent of blood: Thomas's, Morland's, *hers*.

"Now who's not in their best looks?" she taunted even though the right side of her face felt swollen and sore from the beating. Her eyes darted to the table, which held the knives. They were closer to Morland. To get to them, she'd have to go through the bastard.

"I'm going to kill you!" Morland's voice was raspy from her attempt to crush his larynx. Bruises circled his throat. It gave her some satisfaction to know that she'd inflicted the same wounds on him that he'd given to countless women. She said nothing to his threat, conserving her energy.

Morland got to his feet, his gaze flat and cold. They eyed each other, two predators who understood the stakes. There could be only one victor—unless they killed each other.

Morland rushed forward, the knife held high in one hand. Kendra tensed, her attention focused on the blade. As he brought it arcing down toward her, she catapulted herself forward, grabbing his wrist and twisting sharply, the same classic policeman's maneuver that she'd used against Thomas in the forest.

Morland let out a cry and dropped the knife. But he was bigger, stronger, and smarter than Thomas. Instead of falling to his knees, he gave a punishing kick that knocked her sideways, loosening her grip. He twisted, striking her again, and they both fell in a tangled heap on the bed.

He rolled on top of her, pinioning her body beneath his. His eyes were wild as he brought his hands up to her throat, reversing their earlier position. Yellow dots swam in front of her eyes as his hands squeezed. But Kendra felt something sharp sticking into her side.

The hairpin.

Frantically, she swept the bed linens. It felt like forever, but it probably only took two seconds for her to find the slender wire and another second to grasp it. Then she brought her arm up and, with unerring accuracy fueled by desperation, she drove it into Morland's left eye.

He screamed, a high-pitched sound of agony, and let her go. His hands flew to his face. Kendra didn't wait; she brought her right hand up in a quick, powerful jab to the base of his eyebrows, and felt the gristle give way beneath the heel of her palm. She followed that with a one-two strike with her left hand, smashing his nose and punching upward, knowing that the bits of cartilage that she'd broke a second ago were now being forced up into his brain.

Morland made a strange gurgling sound. Kendra stared at the grotesque image above her. He hadn't managed to pull out the hairpin before her attack, and it now protruded horrifyingly from his blind eye. His entire face was covered in blood.

He swayed almost drunkenly. Then he toppled to the bed beside her.

Kendra's breath was coming out in such harsh gasps that she couldn't tell whether Morland was breathing or not. If he survived, he'd have brain damage, she was sure. He wouldn't be butchering any more women.

Slowly, painfully, she rolled away from him. She tried to stand, but her legs gave out, and she crumpled to the floor. She waited a minute, then managed to get to her hands and knees, shaking violently. She wondered if she could somehow crawl back to the castle, or if she'd die on the way.

70

The first thing that Alec saw when they ran into the cave was Gabriel's prone form. "My God, Gabriel . . ." He rushed over to his brother, and at first thought him dead. Then he realized that Gabriel's eyes were open, staring at him with awareness.

His gaze fell to Gabriel's bloody hands. His brother had balled up a handkerchief and was pressing it into his stomach, but the handkerchief was saturated, so dark it looked black.

"Morland . . ." Gabriel coughed lightly, and with a terrible sense of foreboding, Alec saw flecks of blood on his lips.

"Don't speak, Gabriel."

"Morland . . ."

"We know. We know he's the monster."

"T-thought I . . . thought I was the monster."

Alec glanced around, and saw his shock reflected in the faces of the Duke, Sam, and Harcourt. He turned back to his brother. "You are no monster."

"Morland . . . Miss Donovan . . . in t-the room . . ."

"Stay still, Gabe. We will help you." As the Duke and Sam hunched down, Alec pushed himself to his feet. In the dim light, he saw a cut in the cavernous wall. *A hallway.* Pulling out the dueling pistol, he hurried over to it. He lifted the pistol, and pushed through the door.

The stench of blood hit him first. His eyes swept the room. Thomas was dead on the floor, a gaping wound across his throat, staring sightlessly at the ceiling. Morland was lying on his back on a bed, his face dark with smeared blood, his nose flattened in an almost comical manner. And there was something . . . what the hell was sticking out of his eye?

"Jesus," he breathed, as his eyes fell on Kendra Donovan. She was on her hands and knees, shivering uncontrollably and equally bloody.

Shoving the pistol back into his pocket, he rushed forward and lifted her into his arms. She let out a cry of pain. Her face was bruised, one eye swollen shut. But she was alive.

"Morland . . ."

"I know. He's the monster."

She shook her head, and winced. "Is he . . . dead?"

Alec glanced over at the still figure on the bed. "I believe so. Good God. What the devil is in his eye?"

"Hairpin." She allowed herself to curl against Alec's body. "I always knew those things could be lethal."

71

Kendra woke sometime during the night, possibly the early hours of the morning. She wasn't sure; she'd lost track of time. Which was a hell of thing for a time traveler to admit, she supposed.

Vaguely she remembered being held and rocked. It had taken a couple of minutes for her to understand that she was being held in Alec's arms, on horseback. There were no ambulances or EMTs in the nineteenth century.

She'd passed out again, but came to as Dr. Munroe worked on her. She realized there were no anesthesiologists, either. When she'd moaned in pain, he'd spooned some liquid into her mouth that had knocked her out cold, which probably accounted for the vile taste in her mouth now. And the icepick headache—though that could've come from having the crap beaten out of her.

She opened her eyes. Or, rather, eye. The other was swollen shut. Her face felt monstrous, twice its normal size. Using only her good eye—and, Jesus, even that hurt—she took stock of where she was.

It was not, she realized, the bedchamber she'd shared with Rose. Above her was a shadowy canopy. Across from the bed was a Carrara marble fireplace. A low fire crackled in its hearth, a hazy glow. She could make out paintings, the gleam of wood, the dark shape of furniture. Her heart constricted in fear when one of those shapes rose. She let out a little moan of terror, her whole body tensing for attack.

"Sh-sh, sweetheart." She recognized Alec's voice. He approached the bed and touched her hand, a featherlight caress. "You are safe, Kendra. Morland is dead."

"It's over?"

"Yes. Go to sleep. You must rest."

Kendra closed her eye. She doubted whether she would sleep, but next time she awoke, it was morning. A maid was bent over a nearby table, her back to her.

"Molly." Her voice was so low and raspy that she was surprised that the tweeny even heard her.

Molly spun around and hurried over to the bed, where she burst into tears. "Oh, miss!" She attempted to mop up the flood with her apron. "Ye 'ad us ever so worried!"

"I'm fine. Just bruised . . ." She tried to sit up, and pain sizzled down her side. *Oh, yeah, and stabbed.*

"'Ere now, let me 'elp ye." Molly plumped up the pillows and gently placed them behind her so she was at least half-sitting. "Oi'm ter let 'is Grace know as soon as ye woke up."

She hurried out of the room. Ten minutes later, the door opened again, but it was Dr. Munroe who came in. He set his black bag on the bed, studying her gravely through his Harry Potter glasses. "Well, Miss Donovan. It's been a while since I've had a subject who was still breathing. You were fortunate. The knife missed vital organs. You shall have a scar." The dark eyes turned speculative. "Of course, it shan't trouble you any more than your others."

Kendra knew he was waiting for some sort of explanation. Since she couldn't give him one, she said nothing.

"You are an enigma, Miss Donovan."

"I guess I have you to thank that I'm an *alive* enigma."

He smiled. "Yes, well, let's make certain you stay that way. I need to inspect your wounds. We wouldn't want infection to set in."

Kendra shuddered. Even in the twenty-first century, infection was the predominant worry in hospitals. So-called superbugs could be more deadly than the illness that brought the person into the hospital. She didn't want to consider what could happen if she got an infection here.

Munroe might work as an M.E. but he knew how to deal with the living. He was both gentle and thorough in his examination.

Afterward Kendra sank back against the pillows, exhausted. "So what's the verdict, Doc?"

"I do believe you shall live, Miss Donovan."

He was putting his instruments into his bag when the door flew open and Rebecca ran into the room in a swirl of lemon-colored skirts. Ignoring the doctor, she rushed over to grab Kendra's hand, and like Molly, burst into tears.

"You're the second person who started crying after looking at my face. I'm going to get a complex."

"Pardon me!" Rebecca blotted her tears with a lacy handkerchief.

"Miss Donovan shall recover, your Ladyship."

"Yes. Thank you, Dr. Munroe. It is only . . . dear heaven, Miss Donovan. You look simply *awful*!"

"Wow. Thanks."

"Oh. You know what I *mean*."

"Never fear, Lady Rebecca," Munroe assured her. "The inflammation ought to subside in a few days. The bruising will take longer, though I shall have a poultice brought up to help with both matters. It should be applied three times a day." He gave Kendra a long look. "I shall return later, Miss Donovan. Do not exert yourself."

Rebecca sat on the bed. "Can I get you anything, Miss Donovan?"

"A glass of water?"

She popped off the bed, and hurried over to the table that held a glass and carafe. A moment later, she returned, handing Kendra the glass. "I simply cannot believe what has transpired," she admitted. "Mr. Morland was the monster . . . and Thomas. And poor Gabriel . . ."

"Gabriel?"

"Oh." Her eyes slid away. "I am uncertain—"

"Tell me what happened to Gabriel."

Rebecca's eyes filled with tears again. "He was a member of that horrid club Mr. Morland founded. A vile, blasphemous club in the cave where you were held, where he—Morland—brought the other girls." She shivered. "Gabriel had no notion—none of the men involved had any notion what Morland was about, you understand. 'Twas similar to Sir Francis Dashwood's secret society. Are you familiar with the Hell Fire Club? As an American—"

"I know of it. Benjamin Franklin was rumored to be a member."

Dashwood had created the Hell Fire Club to mock the Catholic Church, Kendra recalled. He'd even purchased a medieval abbey for the club's activities, but when that had become too well known, he'd moved his group to his West Wycombe estate, where he had utilized its network of caves. There, the club members were reputed to have been involved in all sorts of drunken debauchery with prostitutes. The debauchery supposedly extended beyond sex into Satanism.

"I'd forgotten," Rebecca murmured. "It caused quite a scandal at the time, and several gentlemen—including the baron—were ostracized from society. Morland thought to re-create this abomination, and lured bored young bucks to participate."

"Gabriel."

"Yes. Gabriel." Rebecca let out a sigh. "He was troubled. More than anyone suspected."

"Ripe for the picking."

"I do not understand the whole of it. He . . . apparently, he had difficulty remembering events, details—"

"Blackouts caused by his alcoholism."

"Yes, his drinking was to blame. He wasn't entirely certain if he'd murdered the first soiled dove." She frowned. "I do not understand what exactly made him realize that he had not murdered her, but he *did* realize it. When you went missing, he knew where the caves were and went to find Thomas." Rebecca shuddered suddenly. "Thomas and Mr. Morland—they were partners in this madness."

Yes and no, Kendra thought. Partners implied equality. She remembered how Morland had brutally slit Thomas's throat.

"Thomas was a puppet." She dropped her eyes to the glass of water she held. "My profile never included two men. I should have factored that in."

"Would it have mattered so very much if you had considered it? Would we have uncovered these madmen any quicker?"

"I don't know."

"Partner or puppet, Thomas was as much a monster as Mr. Morland." Rebecca gave another shudder. "Sutcliffe said that they found hair from the victims in his possession, and paintings of the young girls. Terrible paintings. *Evil.* The Duke ordered them burned."

Kendra considered that. The Duke could destroy the paintings, but she knew it wouldn't be the end of such evil. In another hundred years, in 1920s Germany, there'd be an artistic movement called *Lustmord*—sexual murder. Artists would be celebrated for painting female sexual mutilations and death. Thomas had simply been ahead of his time.

It was a depressing thought. "Gabriel was in the cave?" she asked, to move away from it.

"Yes. Morland wounded him. They brought h-him back to the castle." Rebecca looked down at her hands. "He . . . could not be saved."

Kendra was silent, remembering how Morland had left her. The interruption had given her enough time to pick the lock on the handcuffs.

"I think Gabriel saved my life," she whispered.

They stared at each other for a long moment.

"I believe Gabriel wanted redemption, Miss Donovan. Mayhap he got it." She cleared her throat. "Captain Harcourt was also a member of Morland's club. He and Gabriel went there the first night of the house party. He didn't want it known, as he's hunting for an heiress."

They fell silent again. A soft knock interrupted their reverie. Rebecca went to open it, letting in Aldridge, Alec, and Sam. A young maid followed. She brought a cloth sack over to Kendra.

"The doctor said ye were ter put this on yer face, miss."

Kendra eyed the sack. "What is it?"

"'Tis a poultice, miss."

Rebecca reached for it and gave it an experimental sniff. "It smells like castor oil and slippery elm. Excellent for inflammation and bruises."

Gingerly, Kendra pressed it against her face, but couldn't help thinking a bag of frozen peas would've worked better. But what the hell—when in Rome . . . or the nineteenth century.

The maid curtseyed and left the room.

Aldridge came over to the bed. "I apologize for invading your privacy, Miss Donovan, but I"—he glanced at Alec and Sam—"*we* were anxious to see you. How are you feeling?"

"I'm still breathing." She hesitated, then looked at Alec. "I'm sorry about Gabriel."

Pain flickered in his gaze. "Gabriel and I were estranged for years. Perhaps if I had reached out to him before, tried to understand what demons were driving him—"

"You cannot blame yourself, my boy," Aldridge cut in. "In fact, I bear an even greater responsibility. I should have done something, used my authority with Lady Emily."

There was an uncomfortable silence, weighed down by guilt and sorrow. Everyone was reviewing their choices, Kendra knew. Life's odd twists and turns. Wondering if they could've done some differently to change the outcome.

Would've. Could've. Should've.

Sam cleared his throat. "I won't be staying long, lass. I . . . I just wanted ter see how you're doin'. And ter say that you've got pluck ter the backbone. Female or not, you'd make a damn fine Bow Street Runner."

Kendra stared at him in surprise. "Why, thank you, Mr. Kelly."

"And I thought you'd want ter know that me man got back from the north. Mr. Dalton's wife looked nothin' like the other lasses. He also discovered a bit of gossip. Mr. Dalton's wife died giving birth ter her lover's child in Geneva."

Rebecca put a hand to her throat. "Oh, how dreadful. 'Tis little wonder that Mr. Dalton did not want to discuss what had happened to her."

Sam nodded. "I'll be taking Thomas's body back ter London for Dr. Munroe's anatomy school. He never can find enough specimens."

"'Tis that ridiculous law," the Duke muttered angrily. "To restrict surgeons to only criminals who have swung in the gallows is the height of stupidity. How else can they expect to refine their skills if they aren't given a broader selection?"

"Well, it won't be a problem with Thomas since he'd have hung at Newgate," Sam remarked cheerfully.

"I daresay Thomas will serve a better purpose for Dr. Munroe in death than he ever did in his miserable life," Rebecca added. When the men gaped at her, she lifted her brows haughtily. "What? I am not to offer my honest opinion?"

Kendra suppressed a smile. She wasn't the only female in the room that had pluck.

"What about Morland?" she asked. Something inside her tightened when she saw the men exchange glances.

Aldridge was the one who answered. "He will be buried in his family crypt at Tinley Park."

Kendra fixed her good eye on him. And *knew.* "No one will know the truth, will they? He'll be buried without anyone knowing that he was responsible for the death of those women. The death of *Rose.*"

"'Tis for the best."

"Whose best?" she wondered aloud, bitterly.

Aldridge spread his hands. "My dear . . . there are innocent people to consider. Lady Anne may not be in her right mind, but she does not deserve to live out the remainder of her days under a cloud of suspicion."

Kendra thought of Lady Anne. Had she ever been innocent? Morland had been born out of an incestuous relationship between Lady Anne and her father. Morland had implied that she'd been a willing participant and even continued the incest with the son, an abuse that had helped shape the monster that he'd become.

Yet could she believe anything that came out of the mouth of a psychopath? And even if Lady Anne wasn't innocent then, her mind was undoubtedly shattered now.

The Duke continued, "And the servants at Tinley Park do not deserve to have their characters spoiled by the scandal. Right or wrong, they would have a difficult time finding other employment if it became known that they had served such a villain."

Kendra wondered about that as well. Were they really ignorant of what had been going on at Tinley Park? Or had they turned a blind eye?

Aldridge's blue eyes were grave as he regarded her. "It has to be enough for us to know that the madness ends with Morland's death."

There was an irony here, Kendra reflected. The cover-up involving Sir Jeremy had brought her to England, to Aldridge Castle on that specific night, at that particular moment in time.

That had been the beginning of her journey. Was it chance? Or fate?

Gabriel had chosen the correct moment to come into the cave; the interruption had saved her life and cost him his. And Molly had unwittingly saved her life by insisting on pinning up her hair that morning. Without those hairpins, she'd never have been able to free herself.

Little twists and turns, she thought again.

Kendra became aware that everyone was waiting for her to say something. "I suppose there's no point in forcing the issue," she said slowly. "Morland's dead. That's what matters."

Aldridge's smile was tinged with relief. "Thank you, my dear. Now, we shall leave. You must rest."

"A moment, Duke," Alec said. "I need to speak with Miss Donovan."

Sam was already out the door, but Rebecca and Aldridge hesitated, their gazes speculative. Kendra could feel her cheeks heat, but doubted anyone would notice with the bruising.

"Do not tire the girl, Alec," the Duke admonished lightly, before taking Rebecca's arm. "Come, my dear."

Kendra put the poultice down and looked at Alec.

"Bloody hell," he breathed. "Are you certain you are all right?"

"Sure. Let's go dancing."

He shook his head. "I think I died a thousand times when I saw you in that room."

She didn't know what to say. The last time they'd been alone, she'd told him that she was a time traveler. She wasn't sure if that had worked out for her.

Alec let out a sigh, and looked away. After a moment, he brought a piece of paper out of his pocket. "I received this letter today. 'Tis a reply to the note I'd dispatched to Mr. John Murray. He is a bookseller in London. Specifically, he is the publisher of *Pride and Prejudice*."

"Oh." She knew where this was going now.

"He asks me how you came into possession of the identity of the authoress, as he'd taken great pains to keep Miss Austen's identity a secret. An even greater concern to him is how you could possibly be privy to Miss Austen's upcoming work. While Miss Austen has yet to complete the book, they've discussed titles. *Emma* is one they have considered. He has no knowledge of the other book you mentioned, *Persuasion*."

Little twists and turns.

"You are either a soothsayer, Miss Donovan, or you are indeed, as incredible as it sounds, from the future."

Kendra held her breath.

"I have never set great store in soothsaying," Alec said at last.

"How do you feel about time travel?"

"The same. But there is *this*." He lifted the letter in his hand. "And *you*. I am inclined to believe you. Although I do not understand it."

Kendra let out her breath. "That makes two of us."

"The Duke may give us some insight."

"I'm not sure that would be a good idea."

Alec eyed her carefully. "You cannot simply sail off to America."

"I'm stranded until the wormhole or vortex opens up again." *If it opens up again.* She refused to contemplate that. Not yet.

"First you must heal, Miss Donovan. You need to regain your strength." He touched the back of her hand. "You may be stranded, Kendra, but you are not alone. You are among friends."

Kendra said nothing. After he left, she sank back against the pillows and wondered how that statement could be both sweet, and still so terrifying.

72

Alec left to accompany Gabriel's body back to his family estate. He'd be gone a week. Kendra didn't like the odd pang that gave her. It made her realize how much she'd miss him—miss everyone, really, if she accomplished her goal and returned to the twenty-first century.

The emotions churning inside her left her confused. Morland's burial only added to her disquiet. She was still bitter over the cover-up, but the fact that no one attended his funeral except for the Duke and the vicar and his wife made her wonder. Morland's horrors may have been hidden, but whispers had a way of spreading.

Slowly she healed. The swelling subsided. The black and blue bruises would take longer to disappear. The scars—visible or not—would never disappear.

Despite her injuries, Kendra insisted on attending Rose's funeral. In contrast to Morland's lonely burial, the amount of people who showed up for the slain servant was staggering.

No one seemed to blame her for Rose's death, but Kendra couldn't help but wonder if she hadn't drawn Morland's attention, maybe she'd be alive.

Could've. Should've. Would've.

After the funeral, Rebecca suggested a walk in the garden. Kendra knew there was a purpose, but she kept silent, content to meander in the sunshine until Rebecca stopped and gave her a direct look.

"My parents will be returning from the Barbados next week. I shall be returning home."

Kendra held her breath. Technically, she was Rebecca's paid companion. If this were the normal course of events, she'd be going with her to her family estates. But this wasn't the normal course of events, and she knew she couldn't leave the castle. If she had any chance of returning to her time line, it would be here, in the stairwell that had brought her to the nineteenth century.

"You will not be accompanying me, will you, Miss Donovan?"

Kendra stared at her. "There are circumstances . . ."

"Is it Alec? Pray tell, do you have hopes in that direction? I have seen the way you look at each other."

Kendra didn't want to think about how she or Alec might look at each other. That was a complication neither one of them could afford. "No. I can't explain, but it has nothing to do with Alec."

Rebecca was silent for a long moment, then nodded. "I would not want you hurt, Miss Donovan. Alec is a marquis, and the Duke's heir. There are expectations, you understand? He must think of his lineage when he looks for a wife."

Kendra shifted uncomfortably at the sympathy she read in the other woman's cornflower blue eyes. This was a polite reminder, she supposed, that she was—how did they put it in this era?—beneath Alec's touch.

"I'm not in the market for a husband, so you don't have to worry. Really, my decision to stay has nothing to do with Lord Sutcliffe."

Another long look. Then Rebecca nodded again and sighed. "You know, I shall miss having you as my companion."

That made Kendra laugh, though it made her face ache. "I was a horrible companion."

"Now that I ponder it, you have never once fetched my shawl or inquired after my health." Rebecca smiled. "Yes, you *were* rather a wretched companion. Still, there was never a dull moment . . ." The smile faded. "Will you be returning to America?"

"I don't know." As much as she wanted to tell Rebecca the truth, the less people who knew about her situation, the better. She'd already decided to tell the Duke. She would need his permission to stay in the castle, to walk through the doorway at the given time . . .

Rebecca grabbed Kendra's hands, her cornflower blue eyes brightening with tears. "I shall not say good-bye to you as my companion, Miss Donovan. I shall say good-bye to you as my *friend*."

Alec's words came back to her. *You are not alone . . . you are among friends.*

She'd always been a loner, a freak. Maybe she still was a freak. But she was now a freak with friends—*real* friends. The knowledge brought the sting of unexpected tears to her eyes.

"Thank you." Kendra gave her an impulsive hug. "That means more to me than you know."

The Duke took it upon himself to put Morland's affairs in order. With no immediate family, distant relatives needed to be tracked down, assets redistributed. Because Tinley Park wasn't entailed, Aldridge planned to buy it. Lady Anne, with Mrs. Marks and a couple of caretakers, would be relocated to a smaller house. The rest of the staff would be given severance packages and letters of reference. Coming from the Duke of Aldridge, that would go a long way.

While Aldridge occupied himself with those weighty matters, Kendra concentrated on regaining her strength, walking around the gardens and doing simple yoga moves. It reminded her of the time in the hospital after the mission to get Balakirev had been blown to hell and back—minus the Terminator and the Pilates machines.

With Rebecca's departure, the servants once again didn't know how to treat her. She wasn't one of the staff. She wasn't gentry. She had no place in Aldridge Castle. *I don't belong here.*

Ten more days and it would be one month since she'd found herself in this time line. The serial killer had been caught; there would be a full moon. If there was any chance of returning to her own era, that would be it.

Two days after Rebecca left, Kendra entered the Duke's study. He glanced up from his paperwork, and smiled. He hadn't asked any questions about her staying behind. Just as he had when he'd found out that she'd lied to him about her arrival in England, he waited for her to come to him.

She was finally ready.

He pushed himself to his feet. "Good morning, my dear. How are you feeling?"

"Nervous," she admitted, and pressed a hand to her stomach. It was knotted with apprehension.

His brows lifted. "Oh? Why, pray tell?"

"I need to talk to you about why I'm still here at the castle—about how I came to be at the castle."

Aldridge's blue eyes sharpened with interest. "It is a story that I would very much like to hear."

Kendra drew in a deep breath, aware that what she told him would change everything. The last time she'd taken such a chance, she'd been fourteen and telling her parents that she wanted her independence. When they'd let her go without a fight, she'd felt betrayed. She had never entirely trusted anyone after that, certainly not with her emotional welfare—too risky. Now, she was going to take another huge risk, and one that, if it went wrong, could mean the madhouse.

But maybe it was time to trust in someone other than herself. "I'll tell you my story, Your Grace. But you might want to sit down for it."

73

Three days later, Kendra sat beneath an ancient oak on the hill overlooking Aldridge Castle. She remembered her first view of the mammoth structure, and how she'd been struck by its majesty, its incredible history. Who would've thought she'd have a small part in it?

She saw a rider on horseback gallop toward the castle, and then disappear behind the stone walls. Though she should have been too far away to make out his identity, she knew, by the way her heart began to race, that it was Alec.

That reaction worried her. And it was still worrying her when, twenty minutes later, the horse and rider emerged and did a circular dance, as though scanning the area, then began galloping toward her.

Kendra tensed automatically and forced herself to relax as they came up the hill. Alec's look was appraising as he pulled up on the horse's reins, stopping a few yards from her, and then swung down from the saddle. He left the beast untethered, but the Arabian seemed content to munch on grass where he'd been left.

"You are much improved, Miss Donovan."

"Thank you. You look tired."

He dropped down beside her, stretching out his legs and leaning back on an elbow. "It's been a difficult week," he admitted.

"Gabriel?"

"Buried . . . and hopefully at peace."

Kendra hoped so, too.

Alec was quiet for a moment, then glanced at her. "I spoke with Duke. You told him."

"Yes. I should have told him from the beginning. He was quicker to believe than you—than even myself." She had to smile. "It took me a full day to convince myself that I wasn't in some sort of altered state of consciousness, or hadn't just gone crazy. He had a zillion questions."

Alec laughed. "Yes, and he's quite put out that you haven't answered any of them."

"I'm not sure I can. Or should. Time travel is very much part of the theoretical world. And one theory says that if I gave you or your uncle information about the future and you act on it, it could change the future in unpredictable—possibly destructive—ways." She sighed and shook her head.

"That is one theory. What are the others?"

"That certain milestones are set, unshakeable. No matter what I do, I cannot change them."

"Because it's destiny?"

She frowned. "Maybe. I don't know."

"I was of the belief that we shape our own destinies."

"I was of the belief that there was no such thing as time travel."

"Fair enough." He gave her an unreadable look. "Duke said that you plan to walk into the stairwell again during the next full moon. You believe your wormhole will open, and you will be able to return to your time?"

"It's the only thing I've got. There was a full moon during this time period when I came through the vortex. I'm going to re-create the experience—retrace my steps." She gave a helpless shrug. "I don't know what else to do."

Alec plucked a blade of grass, and twisted it. "You could stay." When she said nothing to that, he asked, "Do you have . . . close friends and family awaiting your return?"

"I'm sure there are people wondering where I am," she said dryly. *The U.S. government, for starters.* Going back meant living her life on the run. For the first time, Kendra realized what that meant. No long-term friends. Always looking over her shoulder.

Then again, there was no guarantee that if the vortex opened and she returned to her time line, she wouldn't be stepping into the assassin's bullet. Time may have stood still on that end of the wormhole.

"People you care for?" he persisted.

She looked at him, and shook her head. "Not really. But I've got to go back."

"Why? The Duke has great affection for you." He paused. "Bloody hell, I refuse to be a coward. *I* have great affection for you, Miss Donovan." He startled her by picking up her hand, linking their fingers. "*I* want you to stay."

Kendra's heart flipped at the expression in the green eyes. She forced herself to shift her gaze away, scanning the rolling hills and forest, the castle below. There were workers in the gardens, with their hoes and clippers. From this angle, she couldn't see the stable yard, but she knew it would be teeming with the workers needed in a world where machines were scarce.

This wasn't her world. But could she make it her world? She couldn't.

Could she?

"I've never met anybody like you," Alec continued, tugging at her hand to bring her attention back to him. "I've never felt what I felt for you. This, I believe, Miss Donovan, is what the poets call love."

For just a second, everything seemed to stop moving. Then Kendra let out her breath. "That's insane."

"Love has always been a form of madness, I suppose." He smiled whimsically, and pulled her closer. "I realized it when I thought you might be dead. I thought I'd lost you. I don't want to lose you to this damn vortex. I want to marry you."

"It's impossible. I don't belong here, and even if I stayed, I can't marry you. You're a marquis. I'm . . ." She lifted her shoulders in a baffled shrug. "Here, I don't know what I am. It won't work."

"Give me time, Kendra. 'Tis all I ask."

She bit her lip, as fear—and something else—churned inside her. "I only have four days."

"Four days." He brought his lips to the inside of her wrist, where her pulse beat rapidly. "That is 96 hours." He moved higher up, to a sensitive spot near the crook of her arm. "Or 5,760 minutes." He nuzzled the side of her neck. "Or 345,600 seconds." He kissed her on the mouth. "That may be plenty of time, I think, to persuade you to stay."

He kissed her again, taking his time. When he finally lifted his head, Kendra was breathless. "Is this your idea of persuasion?"

There was laughter in the green eyes now. "Is it working?"

Kendra smiled. "Well, it's not a bad way to pass the time."

"Good." He lowered his head, his eyes fixed on hers. "Because I plan to make every second count."

EPILOGUE

Present Day

The men were already waiting for him in the conference room. Philip Leeds was careful to mask his exhaustion and worry from their sharp eyes, placing his briefcase on the long table. The dark wood of the table was so polished that it acted as a mirror, reflecting the grim faces of the other three men as well as his own.

"I apologize for my tardiness—"

"You should be apologizing for your goddamn agent!"

That outburst had come from Bradley Thompson, the CIA Associate Deputy Director. His leather chair squeaked as he leaned forward, chin jutting out aggressively. "Do you know how much your agent has cost us in intelligence?"

"You wouldn't even have had Greene without Agent Donovan," Peter Carson, assistant director of the FBI's New York field office, reminded him.

Leeds knew of the animosity between the two men. He suspected Carson wasn't so much defending Kendra as he was as poking Thompson.

Thompson glared at Carson. "Well, we sure as hell don't have him *now*. What's wrong with your agency? The whole mission went south because *your* man was a traitor. And now a valuable asset was eliminated by Special Agent Kendra Donovan!"

"Enough!" The order came from Dean Cooper, the deputy director of national intelligence. Physically, he was the least imposing man in the room, his wiry body reaching a scant five feet, six inches. But he still wielded the most power. "We're not here to point fingers. In fact, we're not here at all." He smiled slightly, but it was a smile that didn't reach the eyes behind his thick, horn-rimmed glasses.

Cooper inclined his head toward Leeds. "Associate Director Leeds, give us your report."

"We know who is responsible," said Thompson. "The production company coordinator, Mrs. Peters, identified the photo of Kendra Donovan—"

"I must not have made myself clear." Cooper cut Thompson off without raising his voice. "I specifically asked Associate Director Leeds to give us his report."

Thompson turned red at the rebuke. Pressing his lips together, he folded his arms in front of his chest and glared at Leeds, as though daring the FBI head to contradict him.

Ignoring him, Leeds clicked open his briefcase. He took a moment to put on his reading glasses, and then opened a manila folder.

"Special Agent Donovan set up a false trail to Mexico, but she actually flew out of New York's JFK under an assumed name. She landed at Heathrow, rented a car, and drove to Aldridge Castle. There, Agent Donovan inserted herself into Stark Productions, posing as an actress. Several of the participating actors identified her as Cassie Brown."

"Do we know if any of them were involved?" asked Cooper.

"We have run thorough background checks. I am of the opinion that Agent Donovan acted alone. While personable, Donovan tends to be a loner. She was estranged from her parents. She was friendly with her colleagues at the Bureau, but had no close ties. She was committed to her job, which is why I believe she took it especially hard when she lost members of her team during the raid to take down Balakirev—a raid in which she nearly died herself, it should be noted. I believe she was in a compromised state of mind."

Cooper raised his brows. "And yet she had the wherewithal to send you on a wild-goose chase to Mexico while she flew to England for her own purpose—a purpose in direct opposition to the United States of America's stated interests."

"You no doubt have read her file, sir. Agent Donovan is a brilliant woman and an exceptional agent."

"And now she is a *rogue* agent."

Leeds frowned. He couldn't argue with that. Still . . .

"We have arrested Mr. Lupe Ruiz. He owns a cantina and has a side business of creating illegal IDs. He confessed to supplying Donovan with several passports, no photos. Donovan has the computer skills to do that on her own. Hell, she has the computer skills to forge her own passports."

"Why didn't she?"

Leeds shrugged. "Maybe she didn't have time. Or she knew we were watching her. We've also discovered that she transferred money to a bank account in the Cayman Islands, which has since disappeared."

"She has no intention of returning," said Thompson.

"Donovan has been clever," Leeds said slowly. "And yet several things puzzle me. Sir Jeremy was found shot in the heart. According to the coroner, he died instantaneously."

"So? She's a good shot." Thompson shrugged.

"Yet three additional bullets were recovered. The fireplace was scored by one bullet and a second shattered a vase. The third was found embedded in the wall. What was Donovan firing at?"

"Maybe she's not such a good shot," Peter Carson said. "It took her three attempts before she managed to kill Greene."

Leeds shook his head. "I personally know that Kendra Donovan is an excellent shot, and there was no indication of a struggle at the crime scene. Sir Jeremy was hardly likely to stand still while Agent Donovan shot at him."

Cooper frowned. "Perhaps someone else came into the room."

"Greene was the only body found. I can assure you, if Agent Donovan was the one pulling the trigger when a second suspect entered, they'd be dead, too. And . . ."

Cooper prodded Leeds when he fell silent. "Yes?"

"Agent Donovan would never shoot at an innocent bystander. She would not murder someone to—forgive me, but to put it crudely, to save her own ass."

"She murdered Greene!"

Leeds looked at Thompson. "Greene was far from innocent."

Cooper steepled his fingers, his expression thoughtful. "You mentioned several things. What are the others?"

"Ricin was discovered mixed into the wine in the room where Greene's body was discovered. It would've been poetic justice, had Greene died of ricin poisoning. But again, we have a puzzle, gentlemen. Why shoot Greene when she had every intention of eliminating him with the ricin-laced drink?"

"Plan A and Plan B," Thompson suggested. "She planned to poison him, but he refused to drink it. She was forced into Plan B—shooting him instead."

"Possibly," murmured Leeds. But he didn't think so. He continued, "The third puzzle, if you will, is that Special Agent Donovan left her bag at the castle. It contained clothes, money, and a passport that identified her as French citizen Marie Boulanger. She also left the rental car. Why?"

"She had other transportation," argued Thompson. "We already know she had other passports."

"But why bother securing other transportation? And who would have brought it to the castle? That would require a partner she trusted. It would also mean questions. And even if she arranged for someone to pick her up, why leave her things behind?" Leeds shook his head. "What we have here is a mystery."

"It's no mystery if she had an accomplice," snapped Thompson. "Maybe she had a lover that you were unaware of."

"In the eight months she was on the task force, Agent Donovan was not involved with anyone," Carson said. "She devoted all her time to her work."

"You can't know that."

Cooper raised his hand to preempt any further argument. A deep frown etched itself on his face. "Despite these inconsistencies, two facts remain irrefutable—Sir Jeremy is dead and Special Agent Donovan was there, but has now vanished. As far as the United States government is concerned, she is a rogue agent and will be treated as such. Her photograph, with several computer variations, has been sent to our embassies and respective agency bureaus, since she will undoubtedly attempt to change her appearance."

"She is not a threat to the United States," Leeds said. He felt the need to protest, though he knew it would make no difference. Kendra was worse than a threat; she was an embarrassment.

Cooper gave him a stern look. "We cannot let our agents determine their own brand of justice."

Whatever had happened in England, Kendra Donovan had most definitely gone rogue. Dammit, Leeds had *liked* her—he *still* liked her.

Wherever you are, Kendra, I hope you stay there, he thought.

Cooper pushed himself to his feet, a signal that the meeting was over. He gave them each a hard look. "Make no mistake, gentlemen: Kendra Donovan will be found. She can't run forever. The United States government *will* find her. It's only a matter of time."

ACKNOWLEDGMENTS

Writing a novel is an interesting adventure, filled with highs and lows. I have to thank my good friends Karre Jacobs, Bonnie McCarthy and Lori McAllister for always pulling me out of those lows (sometimes with a bottle of wine) and pushing me forward with their indefatigable encouragement. What would I have done without you? And I have to give a big shout-out to my agent, Jill Grosjean, whose professionalism is equally balanced with her wonderful sense of humor and decency. I consider myself lucky to have found you. And last, but by no means least, many thanks to the wonderful team at Pegasus, especially my editors, Maia Larson and Katie McGuire. Your deft touch and keen insights were invaluable, and very much appreciated.